EVERYTHING IS YOURS

BOOK 3 IN THE LIFE IS YOURS TRILOGY

ABIGAIL YARDIMCI

Soft Rebel
PUBLISHING

For my Kaynana - the original rose lady

———

"Your heart knows the way.
Run in that direction."
Rumi

CONTENTS

HOW THIS BOOK WORKS

In 2006 I had the most unexpected, tumultuous and life-altering year.

I'll never forget it. And that's why I wrote about it in three parts, of which this book, 'Everything Is Yours', is the last.

I decided to capture the year through the eyes of a fictitious character primarily because when I was a kid I obsessed over the name 'Jess' and couldn't understand why my parents hadn't seen fit to give me it, when it was clearly the most glamorous name ever.

But also, because I needed to create a bit of distance between me and the story. A gap where I could understand more deeply what had happened and allow the juicy stuff to really come to light. It meant I could have a bit of artistic licence with the order of events, I could merge characters where there were too many to keep track of, and change names out of respect for people who might recognise themselves in the pages.

I hope you enjoy the story because a lot of it happened exactly like that, with incredible people showing up and blowing my mind with their timing, their authenticity and their undeniable part in helping my heart to finally wake up. The rest of it is yummy fiction that I hope you relish in your own way. And now, let's see where Jess ends up . . .

PROLOGUE

You might think that returning home to the North East of England after a month in Turkey would be a bit of a slap in the face. The weather *is* bloody awful. There *is* a massive stack of bills waiting for me on my doormat. And my garden fence around my precious little bungalow *has* been defeated by the October winds.

While Gillie is moaning and groaning around the house, muttering profanities into the neck of her winter hoodie and shivering in a fashion that could potentially have her body-popping in the next season of *Strictly* – "Jess, your house is fucking FREEZING!" – I find a different approach.

I hate to say it but I have become one of those people. I loved the way the mist fell onto my cheeks when I stepped off the aeroplane. The threat of ice in the air is refreshing and, if anything, has woken up every single cell of my body to the wonder of being back. It's like I've touched down in an entirely different world. And I guess I have.

Like I say, maybe I'm one of those people now. Annoyingly passive and peaceful. As Gillie heaves open her bulging suit-case, and flings numerous flip flops over her shoulder in a bid to unearth her hairdryer (preferable, apparently, to a radiator not yet warmed), I allow the shivers to travel up and down my spine. I breathe deep and think of him. Coffee. That's what he'd make now. So I put the kettle on.

I look at the living room and am reminded of the total tip Gillie and I left the house in a whole month ago. Thick dust is now settled happily on piles of discarded bikinis and rejected bottles of lotions and potions. It's okay though. In fact, it's better than okay. I've learned recently that the universe has a fondness of flinging signs at us that represent balance. Harmony even. So the total shit-tip my house is in reminds me of the serenity that's settled beneath my bones.

"Are you making a cuppa or what?" Gillie whinges at me from the depths of the spare room.

"Yup. On it." I make the tea. Or tea for Gillie, and black, black coffee for me. A few weeks ago I would have reeled in horror at the thought of consuming anything less than creamy and sweet. But he's changed a few of my ways. Coffee is one of them. There's no milk anyway.

I hand a steaming mug of black tea to Gillie as she uses her other hand to flip on the hairdryer currently stuffed up her hoodie. "Thanks!" She yells. "Ugh. Why's it black?"

"No milk!" I mouth over the drone of her appropriated heater. "Tesco? Later?" She nods and sits back under the bliss of hot air ballooning her top. I take my coffee into my bedroom next door.

In my bedroom, things look kind of different. My books are still stacked on my bedside table. There's a houseplant drooping on a shelf in the corner. My favourite plump cushions still sit at the top of my bed. This is everything I would expect to see in this tiny little room that I decorated myself a few months back, reclaiming my space after a broken heart drove me to do it. But there's something unexpected too. A glimmer? A sheen? I swear there's a slight sparkle to the edges of everything. Either that or I'm overdue a nap.

I sip my coffee and sit on the bed. Yet more shivers shoot through me at the bitterness of it. Still getting used to that.

My bags are waiting to be unpacked but I don't feel a massive rush to do it. I do notice, though, my notebook sticking out the side of my hand luggage. I tug it out and place it on my lap, flicking through the pages. Pages from the last six or seven months. Pages of heartache, pages of discovery, pages of joy and pages of revelation.

Pages of change.

It's all there. The whole of 2006 so far. Photos, sketches, lists, observations, and, more recently, an account of six crazy challenges I completed whilst on my trip. And, even though the book is so, so full, there are yet more pages left. I wonder what I'll do with those.

My phone buzzes from somewhere in my bag and I dig it out. A text:

Gulazer. You home yet? Missing u i am.

My chest lifts and the sparkles on the edges of everything intensify.

Yes, I'm back now. I miss you too. Let's talk soon.

God knows how long it takes for a text to zip across a couple of thousand miles but I send it on its way. Then I tap my phone to find the holiday snaps and click until I find one of him that I caught on our final night. He's leaning against his bar, skinny frame caved forwards in embarrassment, long black hair swinging in front of his shoulders and a smile sneaking out. His deep brown eyes are in there somewhere, gilded by violet-black lashes. It's those I remember the most.

His image pulls away from me in an instant as the phone rings loudly, even over the sound of Gillie's hairdryer next door. "Hello?"

"Eeeeek! You're back! Can you two nutcases get your arses over here and fill me in on your holiday? I'm going to burst if I don't hear everything within the next hour and Jess, that will be no good for little Dinah, who may well eat my remains."

It's Ella. Our gorgeous, vivacious, extravagantly body-pierced friend who looked after my dog, Dinah, whilst I jetted off to Turkey. "Okay Ella, we definitely don't want that. Let me put on a few more layers and grab Gillie. We'll be there quickly, I promise." I snap shut the phone and leap to my feet. "Gillie! We've got somewhere to be. Like, now!"

DIFFERENT ON THE INSIDE

Now this, Lindy thought, *I could get used to.*

She sat with Jess, a woman she hadn't even known existed earlier that night, in a tiny ramshackle café in the darkest, dodgiest corner of this Turkish holiday resort. They'd nabbed a low-to-the-ground table inside a booth that was constructed out of wooden pallets, sumptuous green and orange cushions and ornate Turkish carpets. Tea lights winked and shimmered inside glass jars hanging above their heads and Lindy sat bare-footed and cross-legged on a particularly squashy cushion. Tiny grains of sand had fallen from the folds of her clothes and now surrounded her with an effervescent sense of ceremony – she breathed deep and was rewarded with the burnished scent of charcoal, a reminder of the hours they'd just spent in front of their own open fire. Talking. Reliving. Healing.

Despite the café being in the undeniably dark and dodgy corner, it still had an amber brightness that beamed off the walls. It was the type of brightness that was kind to your eyes and soft on your skin and invited all of your senses to reside there as long as they damn well pleased.

Lindy looked around. Every single customer – and they seemed predominantly Turkish – sat, draped or reclined with such ease, that the cafe may as well have been their home. The loose gesticulation of relaxed conversation moved in soothing waves across the cosy space, so that the buzz of mingled words seemed to follow it.

Okay so the countdown to 2007 was closing in and people would probably be settled here for the New Year celebrations now, but Lindy had a feeling it was probably like this every night.

And the smells. Good lord, the smells.

"What are they cooking?" Lindy asked Jess, who was sitting and smiling opposite her. "It smells incredible."

"I know, right? My mouth is watering." Jess offered the wine list to Lindy but Lindy shrugged and pushed it back towards her. Judging by the delicious bottle they'd drank on the beach earlier that night, Jess would do a better job of choosing than she would. So far, her only experience of Turkish wine had been limited to her mum's method of choosing which was based on the way the name sounded when the waiter suggested it (*"Oooooh, that one sounds exotic, let's give it a whirl!"*).

Not for the first time that night, Lindy wondered what had become of her parents. Would they be at the British Embassy, convincing the authorities to launch a full-on search for her? Unlikely. Especially, Lindy now realised, considering the way she'd spoken to them as she'd stormed off earlier. She could hardly blame her parents for taking notice. Even if it was New Year's Eve.

"You okay?" Jess asked. "You look a bit . . . distant."

Lindy gave her shoulders a little shake, looked right into Jess's wide blue eyes and noticed how her hair glinted with gold under the over-hanging tea lights. What nickname did she say the brooding barman, Mesut, had given her? Gulazer. That was it. Meaning 'yellow rose'. Yellow for warmth, for friendship, for clarity. Rose for love, for affection, for grace. And Jess had somehow displayed all of these things in the short time Lindy had known her. How utterly weird that a connection like this had sprung up from the foul mood she'd been in as she'd abandoned her parents. Did she even deserve it? She didn't know and she didn't care. She just wanted the connection to grow.

"Yup. I'm good. Looking forward to hearing the next part of your story – I want to know exactly what happened when you and Gillie got back home after your epic stay in Turkey. I want to know how much all your friends and family freaked out when you told them about your sexy Turkish barman and your epiphany-thingy on the mountainside. And me? Well I'm just glad to be here to be honest. This holiday was a bit of a last-minute escape for me."

"Escape from?"

Was she ready to talk about this now? After listening to Jess's story and becoming so captivated by it? At least it cleared the way for a bit of honesty and perhaps she didn't need to feel so scared of examining her feelings now that Jess had laid herself bare. "Well, you know, life."

Jess gave a low whistle. "Wow. Life? The whole thing?"

"It's certainly felt like that over the last few months."

Jess nodded and smiled. "Hmm. Well, it is bloody relentless."

"Yeah. Although, things don't seem so relentless right now."

"Cool." Jess said, popping an olive in her mouth. A bowl of them had appeared silently on their table. Along with some fresh floury bread and creamy dips. God, this place was good.

"It is." Lindy said. "I can feel things kind of . . . clearing. I've probably got you to thank for that."

"What are you talking about?" Jess laughed. "You've been listening to me rabbit on all night. I should be thanking you!"

Lindy shook her head and pointed an olive-bedecked cocktail stick at Jess. "Absolutely no fucking way. Jess, you've completely turned this night around for me. Everything you've told me . . . all of your experiences . . . the way you look at life. Honestly, a few hours ago I was to take away and now . . . well, the world seems a lot kinder."

"So, what's changed?" Jess asked as the waiter brought a cool bottle of white to the table. Lindy watched him pour it into their glasses and pondered Jess's question.

"Nothing's changed about my particular shit-storm. I guess that's all still going on. But . . . I just feel different on the inside now. Hearing about all that stuff you went through with Jack leaving you and the business failing and then picking it all up and turning it around. I think you've made me see my own stuff from a different angle. I think it's your energy. Your attitude."

Jess nodded thoughtfully then lifted the waiting wine glass. "Hmmm. Do you think maybe it's less to do with my energy and more to do with yours? I mean, you didn't have to sit with me by the fire on the beach. You didn't have to listen to anything I said. After all, it's not my attitude that will make you see things from a different angle, is it?"

Lindy lifted her wine glass too and mirrored Jess's broad smile back at her. "No." She said, and clinked glasses with Jess. "It's mine."

2

THE TELLING

The first person Gillie and I went to see was Ella. We'd really wanted to take Ella with us on our trip to Turkey – especially when she'd already visited İpeklikum with us earlier in the year – but she'd been too busy and a whole month out of her puppeteering job wasn't realistic for her. And she didn't have a fucked-up business to escape from like we did – lucky for her.

Now she was practically clawing at Gillie and I to get the holiday gossip. "Get yourselves in here," She beamed when we arrived at her little pit cottage to pick up Dinah who was now jumping up at me, every bit as enthusiastic as Ella. "But before you even sit down, for the love of God just tell me everything!"

So we did our best. Ella whooped with joy when we dished the dirt on our completely 'Shit Class' Hotel and its cupboard-like rooms; nodded wide-eyed as we told her about the six insane challenges Gillie's ex, Marcus had set me whilst I'd been away; fell about laughing on her crocheted couch when we described the dance craze that I started and then went on to sweep through all the classiest joints in the resort; and practically choked on her cider and black when Gillie reluctantly told her what had gone on with her spurned suitor, Oliver.

"So hang on, let me get this right," she said leaning towards Gillie, who was looking extremely post-holiday chic in a jet black velour jumpsuit and her ruby red hair tied up in a leopard-print headscarf. "You're newly single because Marcus is a dick." We all nodded in agreement. "Then you meet Oliver on your fancy business course a matter of weeks ago and you know – we all bloody know – that he's well into you?" More nodding. "And thennnnn . . . you ask the lovely man to travel a couple of thousand miles and meet you in a swanky hotel in İstanbul – which, rather shrewdly, you let him pay for – when all the time you've got another dark and mysterious bloke on the go in İpeklikum? Gillie, you totally sly dog!"

Gillie blushed, which was not something you saw very often. "Well I didn't really have Demir 'on the go' at that time. That was after Oliver decided to go off travelling."

"You mean after you sent him packing!" Ella bellowed. "Poor lad! I honestly didn't know you had it in you!"

"Well, I suppose I didn't either. But there was something about being out there . . . the waves and the sunshine and the beautiful light – it was all so freeing, wasn't it Jess?" I smiled at her, remembering. "Oliver's great but, oh, I suppose he was a bit intense in the end. I didn't realise that until I had to share a hotel room with him. Swanky or not."

"Fair enough," Ella shrugged. "His heart will heal, poor bugger." Then she turned to me. "Come on then Jess. What about you? I can't believe you didn't have a bit of action too, in some fabulous form or another. You're not leaving until you dish it."

I stole a glance at Gillie and she smiled reassuringly back, bless her. God, this was it. I was actually going to tell somebody *who mattered* that I'd fallen hopelessly in love with an entirely inappropriate man. And that I was embarking on a long-distance relationship, which may or may not break my heart all over again in a devastating Jack-like fashion.

I looked into Ella's wide, hazel eyes and made a silent wish to the universe that I might suddenly develop the powers of telepathy, just this one teensy, weensy time. Just once? Or maybe two or three times more to give me a chance to let my family know too? Then I'd happily go back to standard mental powers and just let gossip do its work.

"Shit." Ella whispered and dropped back into the couch, as if she'd been pushed. "Something's happened, hasn't it?"

"Erm . . . s-s-something?" I stammered.

"I knew it the minute you walked in here. You're just so bright and well, sparkly! I can't believe it. You've met someone and it's . . ." She trailed off and looked at me expectantly, waiting for me to tell her whatever the hell 'it' was. I searched for the right word, the right way to describe what was going on with me and Mesut. Serious? Magical? Soulful? Unexpected?

"Love." Gillie cut in, matter-of-factly. "It's love, Ella. I've seen it."

Ella nodded and let out a long, low whistle. Then she came to join me cross-legged on the floor and took my hands in hers. "Jess. You fabulous nutcase. Who, pray, is the lucky man?"

"Well, it's erm, do you remember Mesut? From that bar we used to go to? Beerbelly?"

A smile played loosely across her studded lips. "The dark, brooding one with the impossibly long hair who makes the kick-ass cocktails?"

"The very same," I nodded.

"Well, well, well. Who'd've thunk it? Not the spicy-smelling giant from English Rose?"

I laughed out loud at the memory of Ekrem and single red light bulbs, awkward dance moves, wandering hands and, ultimately, his gaggle of hard-as-nails cockney girls who I'd managed to side-step thanks to a spontaneous bout of inner-wisdom. "No. definitely not him. It's Mesut, Ella. Fuck. I've got a lot of explaining to do, haven't I?"

"You certainly have, madam." Ella beamed. "But however it all began, it's certainly got a hell of an ending by the looks of you." She wrapped me up in a massive hug that made my heart beat stronger. "Oooh, that's not everything though, is it? There's a little tremor in your bones there, Jess. Is there something else you need to tell me?" Ella drew back but kept her hands on my shoulders. How the fuck did she know? "I'm not gonna hear wedding bells just yet, am I?"

"Steady on." I laughed. "No, it's just that, well, while I was out there I had a bit of a moment."

"A moment?"

"Yeah. After we left İstanbul, Gillie, Oliver and I went to visit a place called Cappadocia in the central highlands of Turkey. Oh god, Ella, you would have bloody loved it. It was the most insane landscape I've ever seen. Loads of weird-shaped rocks and the colours were ridiculous."

"Is that where you all went up in a hot air balloon?" Ella asked, taking her hands from my shoulder and clasping them together. She really was lapping this up.

"Yep. It was incredible, wasn't it Gillie? But after all that, there was one morning when I was back at the hotel and every-body else was asleep."

"No Mesut?" Ella whined.

"No. He was back in İpkelikum and we were actually miles away from there. Turkey is such a massive country. Anyway, it's kind of hard to explain and there's a load more to it than this, but I'd fallen asleep on the balcony the night before. The balcony was basically just a bit of tiled ground that was sticking out of a mountainside. When you sat on it all you could see was the tops of other mountains all around you. Anyway, I woke up and wrapped myself in a blanket and was kind of pondering on, you know, all that deep, egocentric shit that happens when you're on holiday. And I had a kind of, well, an epiphany."

"Woah." Ella gasped.

"You haven't described it like that to me before." Gillie whispered.

"I know. It's been so hard to put into words. But it was almost like a series of flashbacks to when I was a little girl and just seeing – no not seeing, *feeling* what made me happy back then. The thing that feeds my soul and gives me purpose . . . the thing I have to do more of . . . and also the thing I've always been good at . . .

"Writing." Gillie and Ella said together.

"Really? How did you guess that? It took me the whole fucking trip to figure that out."

"Because, Jessica dearest, we are your cheerleaders, your champions, your absolute best friends in the multiverse." Ella shook cushions from her couch like pom-poms as she spoke. "We have watched you, for years, write stuff for Firebelly – project plans, evaluations, press releases and the most incredible and outrageously creative project reports. And you were the absolute best at helping little kids to write poems and stories and stuff during all of those projects. It's about time you dusted those skills off for yourself instead of for other people."

"Yes, we probably know what makes you tick better than you do. Writing has always been your groove." Gillie shrugged. "Could have told you that before you extended your overdraft and sold off all your jewellery to pay for your trip."

"Well thanks a lot." I laughed. "Oh well, at least I know what I'm doing with the rest of my life now. Should make things easier, what with closing Firebelly down over the next few weeks. Oh god, Gillie, there's so much to do."

"Fuck me. If we're going to start on business-type-stuff I'm going to need fuel. A black tea and a bag of aeroplane dry-roasted can only get a girl so far." Gillie said, as she sprang out of her seat and grabbed Ella's phone off the coffee table. "So, let's settle in for the night ladies. What's it going to be? Chinese? Indian? Italian?"

Ella and I exchanged the kind of glance that years of friend-ship will bring you and shouted out loud in one joyous breath . . . "Turkish kebabs!"

———

The next day I was at my parents' house. Sitting in that same soft, old armchair that had held my sobbing wreck of a body at the beginning of the year when I'd been heartbroken over the end of my seven-year relationship with Jack.

Trying on that memory now, the heavy cloak of it, the thick fabric of it, I found it didn't weigh me down at all. I searched for a tiny tang of sadness relating to it but it just wasn't there. Instead I felt compassion for it. I felt a sense of acknowledge-ment that without it I would not be sitting here again now, feeling the strength and power that was always naturally mine.

"So how was it then?" Mam asked as she settled down on the sofa to hear about my 'wee getaway'. She shoved a plate of shortbread at me, along with some rather generous squares of crumbly Scottish tablet. I was reminded for the bazillionth time in my life that you could take the girl out of Glasgow, but that was as far as it went. "Was it all sun and sangria?"

"In Turkey it's raki, Mam, not sangria."

"Och, right, so it is. And how was it then?"

"Erm, bitter, strong, it's got an aniseed-y kind of taste. You wouldn't like it."

"Not the booze Jessie, for heaven's sake." Mam laughed. "How was your wee getaway? Did you and Gillie get on okay?

What was the weather like? What did you do with yourselves the whole while you were there?"

Telling Mam about Mesut was just the next natural step. How it came out didn't really make a difference, as long as it was from me and as long as it was now.

"Actually, before all of that I've got something else to tell you." She looked at me cautiously, probably with worst-case-scenarios of pregnancy, bankruptcy, or STDs racing through her head. "Well, I want you to know, that I've met a man. A Turkish man. And I love him."

There was a beat of total silence. Then she piped up. "Right. You love him?"

"Yup. I can't think of any other way to describe it, Mam. It is what it is. And I wanted to be honest with you, even if it is a bit of a shock."

"Well it's definitely a bit of a shock," she blinked, "But I know you, and I don't think you'd describe something in this way if it wasn't actually the case."

"Thanks, Mam. But this is anything but practical. I'm in love with a man who lives two thousand miles away and I've only really known him for a month. Plus there's something else. I'm going to be a writer. I am a writer. I mean, oh well, I'm going to be writing. You know, once Firebelly is all closed down." I hugged my mug of coffee. All these things were true, but I was unshakeable. I felt my feet planted firmly on the ground and the support of the ground travel up through my legs. My mam looked carefully at me, her gaze working slowly down from my eyes to my feet and back up again. She smiled.

"Jessie, you look so bloody together right now I don't think I could possibly be worried about you. Writing is a difficult game – I should know after all my years as a journalist. But I guess you could give it a go. You've always had a natural flair. And what about this man? Grab yourself a chunk of shortbread and let's have it out. I might as well have all the details. I'll need them for when your father finds out."

I gulped. Dad was a whole different ball game. "Shit, I know. What do you think he'll say?"

"Och, I don't know, love. But you can leave that to me. What about your brother though? I know he's in fancy London town but it's probably best he knows before anyone else."

I could have kissed her. But Mam just didn't roll that way, so I squeezed her hand. Tight. "Thank you so much. You do Dad, and I'll do Max. Agreed?"

"Agreed. Now come on. Tell me all about this man of yours."

———

Okay, so telling Mam about Mesut and the rapid career change had been a lot easier than I'd expected. Not being the naturally touchy-feely type, she'd wanted the cold hard facts and it was actually quite a relief just to tell the bare bones of the story. She'd looked at Mesut's picture and described him as 'very handsome'. It was then I remembered the old, tattered photo albums upstairs under her bed, full of pictures of dad from the seventies with long, greasy hair and a lean, lanky figure. Had my mam given me such an easy time when she figured out that this was most likely just a matter of history repeating itself?

Telling my brother, however, was not such an easy ride. It was never going to be though. For starters, it had to be done over the phone – never conducive to the revelation of big news that would, most likely, get the protective brother hormones kicking in.

First I told him quite plainly that I'd be trying out a writing career once Firebelly was done and dusted. He'd been strangely apathetic. Absolutely no reaction to my news of having had an epiphany and a very important one at that. "I don't know Jess." He said. "You know how hard I've found being an actor down here. It's the most competitive thing in the world, having a career in the arts. Just be ready for that. Maybe get a day job as well."

Okay, so I couldn't expect everybody to be as high-as-a-kite as I was about finally working out my purpose. It was a very personal thing. So I took this caution as brotherly advice and moved on to the matter of Mesut.

"What do you mean, 'in love?' You've known him, like, five minutes. How can you be in love?"

I sighed inside and wondered how do I tell my gorgeous, funny, wonderful brother that deep down, my soul has known this man for an eternity, that there's a message in the depths of my huge, silly heart telling me that we've never really been apart? So, I just settled for, "Well, that's just how it feels Max."

"Fine. Whatever. But please, Jess, don't think you have to have this man to feel good about yourself. Jack really did a number on you earlier this year, I know, but you can find that confidence again all by yourself – you don't need some slimy Turkish barman."

"I can and I have." I assured him. "Mesut happened after that. I already felt like I could rule the world before anything happened with him. And by the way, he's not even a tiny bit slimy. You'll like him. I just wanted you to know about him and me before I go telling anybody else. I know you're down south but you never know the mysterious workings of the grapevine, do you?"

"Especially a Geordie one." He laughed.

And talk about famous last words. After going back to work at Firebelly, and getting together for catch-ups with various mates, I told just a couple of people that I had this long-distance thing going with a particular Turkish barman, and boom – that was it. Everywhere I went I was getting the Spanish Inquisition. Either that, or the naughtiest, knowing smiles from people who now assumed that they knew something about me that they wouldn't have imagined could be true.

That was mostly the blokes though. Obviously, this new me (or what they assumed was a new me) was something that tickled them pink. I got everything from flirty grins to lewd comments to the worst chat up lines in history. Didn't they understand that although my bloke was absent from their immediate vicinity, it didn't suddenly put me on the open market? Didn't they understand I was now in a RELATIONSHIP? It was as if, by applying the term 'long-distance' as a prefix to that word, it negated it entirely. Now I had not been prepared for this.

So that's why, when I got home one night, after a long day of closing down projects, e-mailing parents of kids who attended our clubs and paying final-demand invoices at work, I was pleased to answer the phone to a crackly line and a low, gravelly voice. "Gulazer? Is you?"

I kicked off my shoes and settled down on the sofa with Dinah's head on my lap. I could just picture his head bent towards the phone, his softly, swishing, dark locks hanging forwards almost hiding an impulsive smile that curved his delicious lips.

"Yes. It's me."

3

THE JEWEL IN THE LAKE

Having moved out of Marcus's house and into mine before we'd had our holiday, the time had finally come for Gillie to find her own home. We'd been up late one night chatting when she brought it up. "I need to do it soon, Jess. It sounds awful but I need to do it before we get Firebelly closed down completely and I'm left with no income. No landlord is going to touch me with a bargepole after that."

"You're welcome here a bit longer though, sweetie." I'd said. "I don't want you under any more stress after Demir being a bit of a fuckwit out in İpeklikum, and shutting down our little business is stressful enough, don't you think?" Demir, as handsome as he was, had somehow got Gillie running metaphorical laps for him whilst we'd been out there. Every drama he had, she was there to pick up the pieces. Every shitty thing he did or said, she put it down to his 'sensitive side'. He'd even failed to tell her that he had a four-year-old daughter with a previous holiday fling and that they were both on the resort at the same time as us. Once he'd found that out he'd tried to send Gillie home on the first flight back to the UK under the guise of a cheap ticket deal. Bloody crafty little Mafioso shit. I wasn't his biggest fan.

But Gillie was adamant about moving out. "It's just something I need to do. I honestly thought, after all the work I've done on Marcus's house over the years, he might offer it to me. I mean, it's all decorated to my taste, and I ploughed shitloads of money into it – remember those turquoise fluffy rugs I spent a fortune on? And that teak root coffee table I took out a loan for? But surprise, surprise, he hasn't texted back. So, it looks like I need to sort myself out."

I knew she was right. I loved that girl fiercely but we had just spent a very intense month together and a little time and space for both of us could well be a wise choice. I could tell Demir's stroppy antics had got her heart all twisted since we got back, and perhaps living in such close proximity to loved-up little old me wasn't really what she needed. Similarly, I needed space for my new-found attitudes to grow and breathe. This was for the best.

So we spent the next day scouring local newspapers and websites for a nice, affordable little dwelling for Gillie. "Somewhere cosy," she'd insisted, "somewhere tasteful, somewhere cheap." Cosy, tasteful and cheap were all available individually, but to expect the holy trinity in just the one house? Well we may as well have been asking for the moon.

Gillie was just about on the brink of tears and I'd brewed one too many sugar-laden cups of tea when we heard a knock at the door.

"Who the fuck is that?" Gillie whined. "If it's not a shit-hot estate agent with a nice little cottage up his sleeve then tell them to do one, will you Jess?"

"Glad to," I scuffed to the door in my slippers, opened it and a blast of cold, misty air hit my face. A pair of bright green eyes smiled up at me and then did their trademark wink.

"Tell me, Jess, did you miss me?"

"Marcus!" I yelped (hopefully loud enough so that Gillie

would hear me and have time to compose herself), "Of course I missed you. Come in!" Marcus strode into the house, bringing a stream of cold air in his wake.

"I'm so chuffed to see you." He said, giving me a quick, cool hug, and then stood back, looking me up and down. "Wowzers. You look amazing. I can't wait to hear all about your trip of a lifetime. But right now, I'm here to see Gillie. Is she here?"

I nodded and gestured through to the living room. "Fancy a cuppa?"

"Yeah, great, thanks." He hung up his coat and swooped into the living room, bold as brass. I ducked in after him to check out Gillie's reaction but it looked pretty stony to me. I made the universal hand signal to Gillie to find out if she wanted a cuppa and she nodded slowly at me. Then something in her eyes just said, *Go*.

I stole back into the kitchen and softly closed the living room door behind me. I did a silent prayer of gratitude to the universe for the amazing miracle that is the action of making tea in times of tension and flicked on the kettle.

––––––

The next day Gillie had a home.

And a rather lovely one too. Apparently, the texts she'd been sending to Marcus had not gone unheard and whilst they hadn't had the desired effect of her getting her old house back (or her teak root coffee table), Marcus had done the next best thing.

Thanks to a mate of a mate of a cousin of a long-lost work colleague (or something), Marcus had found a pretty little terraced cottage to rent slap bang in the middle of the countryside. Despite being a little drafty, it ticked all of the boxes and was available immediately. Marcus even offered to pay the deposit and the first month's rent for Gillie as well as make sure she got the pick of the electrical items they had invested in together over the years. And Gillie being Gillie (i.e. nest-builder extraordinaire), she was already at the top of a rickety ladder and up to her elbows in hot pink kitchen paint. "What do you think, Jess, too much?!" She shouted joyfully from her elevated plane quite clearly not giving the tiniest little shit whether it was too much or not. The girl was on a mission.

I, on the other hand, was on my own kind of mission. I hadn't forgotten the large envelope I'd opened on the second day of my holiday in Turkey. It had been given to me by Marcus, shortly before I'd left. He'd said, "I think – or hope – it will fit perfectly into your holiday. Although it may take a bit of an open mind." So when I sat in a sun-drenched café only days later, a cocktail by my side and a curious Gillie egging me on, I discovered that the large envelope was stuffed with six smaller ones as well as a contract titled, 'Experiments In The Art Of Living', that outlined what I'd be undertaking if I agreed to do this.

Each small envelope contained a simple challenge that Marcus had set. I remembered Gillie reading out the contract whilst we sipped our cocktails together. It had claimed the challenges would give me an 'insight into how life could be, rather than how it has been', and that Marcus could not be held responsible if 'life begins to get a little better.'

I'd initially been totally pissed off at Marcus for assuming my life was that much of a mess that I'd need an intervention such as this. Yes, I'd been dumped by the love of my life only months prior. Yes, I'd been a shadow of my former self. And yes, my business needed to be shut down before any more financial damage could be done. But did it really warrant my best mate's ex-boyfriend wading in with his so-called 'experiments'? What did he know about the art of living anyway? He'd just lost a shit-hot woman due to his wet-rag tendencies towards commitment for Christ's sake.

But, as I recall, after some deep breathing and few more gulps of my cocktail, I'd realised that what he'd actually done was hit the nail right on the head. My life *did* need a shake-up.

And a shake-up was definitely what I got as day by day, I opened the challenge envelopes and rose to the individual tasks. Gillie helped out, of course, but they were primarily mine. Each one setting me off into different directions towards discomfort, excitement, fear, curiosity and radical inner-change. Marcus's genius little envelopes had been, I now needed to admit, absolutely awesome.

So it was time for me to feed back. The contract had said it was my responsibility to '*pay for any and all drinks that may be consumed during the de-brief session*'. That boy didn't miss a trick.

I supposed Marcus had imagined a good few pints down the local for this de-brief of his. But the weather was amazingly mild on the day we agreed to meet up, so I was having none of it. I remembered one of the lovely city walks I'd been on with Oliver earlier in the year. The place by the river where I'd originally practiced that fantastic orangey-yellow happiness meditation. And that's where Marcus and I were sat now. On the river bank, feet dangling, clutching a hot chocolate each and enjoying the weather.

"Come on then. How did the challenges go, my friend?"

"Oh, flipping heck. Where do I start? I know." I punched him hard on the shoulder.

"Ouch! What's that for?"

"For shaking things up, you crafty sod!" Then I kissed him on the cheek. He looked surprised.

"And that? What's that for?"

"For shaking things up also. Your Experiments in the Art of

Living were much appreciated at the same time as being cursed on a regular basis."

"Aha!" he grinned. "Mission accomplished then."

"It would seem that way," I pulled my notebook out of my bag as well as a stash of photos I'd had printed. "Let's see what you think Mr Marcus Lane."

I spent the next hour or so flicking through my notebook and presenting Marcus with doodles, scribbles, diary entries and photos. The first challenge had been to touch thirty people in one day. I still wasn't quite sure how it happened but this had resulted in a ridiculous dance craze sweeping the entire holiday resort, much to mine and Gillie's combined horror and glee.

The second challenge of finding my 'doppelganger' in a sweet little seven-year-old girl at the same time as reading in a book recently gifted to me, The Alchemist, that '*everyone, when they are young, knows what their destiny is*' – and how this cata-pulted me into a passionate mission to 'remember' my destiny.

And oh, the quiet stealth of the third challenge, 'Live In The Now'. How it crept into my consciousness in a way that shook my soul good and proper. How Marcus's 'Moments of God' had revealed to me the magic that is available to us all moment by moment, and the compelling, potent connection that was starting to emerge between a certain dark and mysterious Turkish barman and I. Marcus raised his eyebrows at this one. That was the confirmation he needed that something big had gone down with me in Turkey.

The fourth challenge of 'The Scribbler' when I was encour-aged to make my mark wherever I went. I remembered the creative afternoon I'd spent alone on the beach, writing my name in the sand, adorning it with shells, stones and etchings. Then coming back to it later on in the day, when the rolling tide was greedily claiming it and the cherry-pink sun was sinking over its disappearing grooves as I spoke with Gillie about parts of my history that had sculpted my soul.

'The Great Giveaway' was the fifth challenge, opened quietly on that mountainside in Cappadocia, and met with exasperation at not having anything to give or anyone to give to. And how it had become slowly evident that time was the single most important thing I had to give right then, and I had to give it to Oliver who was reeling from a passionate row with Gillie. Given Marcus and Gillie's history, I didn't give him all the details about Oliver and why he needed my time that night, just that I'd given it to a friend in need. And how that had, the very next morning, steered me gently towards a silent epiphany that grounded me right back to my roots, my purpose.

Stories. People. Words.

"I remember that, Jess." Marcus said, smiling. "You sent me a text saying you'd done it, you knew what your destiny was. And I knew . . . I knew when I got that text, that it had a powerful charge. I've been waiting to hear about it all since that day. And I honestly cannot wait to see what you write."

Finally, there was the sixth challenge, 'Textnology', when I'd been encouraged to reach out to a long-lost contact on my phone. Mesut had randomly picked out an old university friend, Jason Reeves, from my phone and I'd texted him despite the slightly awkward memory of Jack having always been jealous of him in the past. And he'd texted back a few days later too. It had been good to finally hear from him.

"So? Did you reply to his text?" Marcus asked.

"Actually, no, not yet. I completely forgot with how busy I've been since I got back."

"Make sure you do, my friend. Let's make the challenge mean something, shall we?"

"Okay, okay, I will." I laughed. "So, what's the verdict? Do I pass?"

Marcus looked thoughtfully out towards the rushing river and stroked his chin in an exaggerated way. "Hmmm, let me think now. You did all the challenges . . . you certainly look brighter, healthier, less mental than before . . ."

"Oi! Do you want another punch?"

He winked. "Of course you've passed, Jess me old marra! I can't believe you invested in my madness! I don't know what possessed me to put all that shit together. I just had a feeling you would go with it and humour me. But as it happens, you've gone far beyond that. Well done you!"

"Yes, well done me. Now where's my certificate?"

"Certificate?"

"Yes! The contract said I would get one. Come on, give it up." I put my hands out expectantly.

"Well, erm, it's . . . it's in the post."

"In the post? That's lame, Marcus."

"Yes, yes it is." We both laughed and then drained the last of our hot chocolates. It was such a relief being able to share all of this with Marcus. I wondered again how this bizarre friendship with him had actually come about after years of keeping myself so stubbornly separate from him. Strange as it was, somewhere between my release from Jack and his release from Gillie, a space had opened up for a new, inexplicable friendship to form.

Then Marcus asked me what my plans were now that Firebelly was nearly 'a gonner', as he put it. "You know, Jess, it sounds like you and Gillie are nearly all done with winding things up. You've got the closing party in a week or so, haven't you? I know after that you'll want to get on with your writing for one thing. What else is on the cards? In terms of, you know, paying the mortgage and all that?"

Oh, how I'd asked myself that question every night since I'd got back from Turkey. How I'd spent many a long hour staring at the godforsaken ceiling, willing an idea to come to me about how on earth I was going to scrape together a living. I'd been distracting myself with trips to charity shops in search of a dress for the closing party and had almost welcomed the toxic thoughts about never finding anything that would tame my tummy or cinch my waist. They were a familiar distraction, after all, and I'd lived with them most of my life.

But if I really faced it, I had to admit that I was split down the middle between two main schools of thought:

On the one hand, I was so jacked up on the strength and stability that had been unearthed in me I was absolutely convinced that something perfect would appear in the right place and at the right time. Now I'd rediscovered my destiny on a Turkish mountainside, surely the rest would flow effortlessly?

On the other hand, I was new to all this hippy shit and a lifetime of being over cautious gnawed inevitably away at my conscience. Faffing about with my notebook or stressing over party frocks wasn't going to get the cash flowing in now, was it?

And that was how I found myself babbling away to Marcus through a million hyped-up contradictions. "Wowzers, Jess. Steady now. How about you have a little faith in yourself for starters? Where's that confidence I saw you walk through the door with?"

"Erm. In here somewhere?"

"Why are you asking me? You're the one who sat on a Turkish mountainside and allowed your soul to speak. I've got a feeling there's still some shedding to do here. Still some forgiveness."

"Forgiveness?"

"Yeah." Marcus was prodding a very raw nerve here. I could feel it in the lump rising in my throat. The quaking of my ribs. "You're only human. The people around you are only human. And you've been through a seismic shift in your soul. When we go through changes like that, we can't expect everything just to flow and be easy. There will be more challenges ahead, my friend, and they won't be ones that I've written."

"I doubt it. I've had my fair share this year."

Marcus grinned. "Honestly, don't be surprised if the universe throws some shit at you, just to check you're really serious about what you want. And whatever's gone before now, whatever's about to come, my advice is to forgive and accept all the way."

"Forgive and accept?"

"Yup. Forgive it. Shed it. Cast it on the ground like petals falling in the breeze."

"Fuck Marcus. I didn't know we were psycho-analysing today. You might have bloody warned me." I breathed deeply and urged my torso to relax. Marcus had cast a chain around it with those words.

"Shit, sorry Jess. You give me honesty though, you get it back ten-fold. I thought Gillie would have told you that by now." Marcus laughed and his fluffy hair shivered around his head like a cloud bronzed by a setting sun. "Anyway, if you're up for it, I could show you something that helps me feel settled and sorted? It might help as you move into the unknown with your new man and your new-found attitude."

"Okay, I'll bite." I was curious. And Marcus now had his serious face on, which didn't happen very often.

He slowly smiled at me, then beamed that same smile out over the river in front of us, and his eyes kind of sharpened. "Well, close your eyes for starters. Then, if you can, imagine a lake. A huge, deep lake that's stretches right out into the horizon."

"Really?" I asked, opening one of my already closed eyes and peering at his face. What was it with blokes and this river and meditative states?

"Really. There's a deep lake and it's stretched out in front of you, and no matter what colour the lake you're imagining might be, you can see something, some other colours, flashing up from the depths of the lake. That's because at the bottom of the lake is a jewel. A jewel so bright and so vivid that the light and colours of it touch even the surface of the lake from where it rests in the depths of the water.

"But sometimes there are winds and storms that disturb the lake, making waves and deep swells . . . sometimes the waters go dark with churned-up mud and it's impossible to see the jewel. Sometimes, even when the storms have died down, the surface of the lake is troubled and choppy, when the shores and banks of the earth feel they are barely holding the lake together.

"But during all of this, during every storm and every wild night and every restless spell, the jewel is still there in the depths of the lake . . . And when the water is finally still, finally calm, the jewel is visible again, shining up from the deep, letting its colours be seen."

There were a few moments when Marcus didn't speak and I felt the relevance of his words wash over me. Yet again I didn't know whether to kiss him or punch him.

I didn't do either.

Instead, I stood up and took a deep breath, my heart thudding and fingers twitching in a way that they hadn't in a very long time. "Right, that's it," I said, as Marcus stood up next to me, looking puzzled for once in his life, "I'm going home. I can feel a canvas calling."

4

AN INSPIRATION

"So, how long did it take you to paint?"

I heard the man's question push through the groove of a particularly soulful tune. I'd already been through this several times with several people tonight but, I had to admit, the painting was kind of intriguing. And the glass of Merlot I had in my hand was helping to loosen my language as I explained the built-up textures, the rich, subtle colour and how I'd actually used torn-up fabric and copied passages of my new favourite book, The Alchemist, to add depth to the haunting jewel-in-the-lake landscape. "All in all it took about a week I reckon. There's been so much to do with winding the business up, but I couldn't leave it once I'd started."

And that was the truth. I'd rolled my sleeves up every night after work and painted into the early hours of a good few mornings to realise the vision I had in my head. It was the first painting I'd ever done truly for myself. And now it hung on my living room wall, having had its first outing at this party. Something to look at and remind me of the importance of being still sometimes. Allowing that jewel to shine.

"We noticed it as soon as we arrived, didn't we Dee?" My

old uni mate, Vicky, swung into the conversation, brown curls bouncing and her gorgeous fire-orange party dress blooming around her. "I don't know how she had the time to organise this party AND close down the business AND paint something so delectable. The girl's a gem!"

The bloke I'd been talking to, who I think helped us nail our first Firebelly funding bid for some ambitious arts project back in the day, nodded approvingly and wandered off to the buffet which was crammed onto my tiny dining table. Dean, Vicky's other half, leaned in his curly-haired head towards mine and whispered, "Don't fret, Jess, I can't remember his bloody name either!"

I laughed and hugged Dean. God, it was good to have them both here. Gillie and I had agreed, as soon as we'd decided to have a closing party, that Vicky and Dean just had to be invited, even if they did have to travel all the way from London up to the dodgy North. They'd been there when it all started – during the late night, wine-fuelled chats all those years ago when we'd originally had the idea to build a creative business that would engage people in the arts – so it made perfect sense to have them here at the finish.

We had invited Jack too – I mean, he was still technically a director. But, predictably, he hadn't shown up. It was probably just as well. Being invited to his ex-home to mark the end of his ex-business with his ex-fiancée may have been pushing it a little.

But just about everybody else in the history of Firebelly was there. It was hard to believe that they'd all been able to fit into my tiny little bungalow. Dinah was whizzing around like a mad thing, and somebody had opened the back door so she could whiz about some more in the garden. And, as the late October night was actually quite mild, a few of the great and the good were milling about on my decking, swaying gently to the jazz-funk music that floated out to reach them, chinking glasses and speaking up to the stars, clear and bright in the black sky.

Tired as I was from the week's activities, a shiver ran down my spine as I remembered Mesut and his conversations with the stars. He'd told me, one night before anything romantic had even unfolded, *"I am never talking to anyone. I am talking to the moon. I am talking to the stars. But why, now, am I talking to you?"* I hadn't had an answer for him then and I didn't have one now, but the thought of replacing the moon and the stars as his primary confidante had felt like a gift. Would he be talking to them again now that I was gone? Perhaps not, as we'd had a particularly indulgent conversation a few hours before over a crackly phone line, that left me tingling in places other than my heart . . .

"Oi! Canny party pet!" I felt a heavy hand land on my shoulder. As I whirled around a wide smile greeted me and I felt a surge of warmth rush through my wine-charged veins.

"Ikram! Oh I'm so chuffed you could come! Come in . . . have a seat . . . have you got a drink? Gillie? Have we got any wine left?"

"Not to worry, me old marra, I've got me own beverage ta very much." Ikram held up a massive box of red wine, "And a bit of entertainment," in the other hand was his trusty ukulele which traditionally went everywhere with him. "Aye, and me chauffeur n' all . . ." Ikram turned to the kitchen and his partner, Betsy trotted through the doorway, all lipstick, leopard print and high energy. Her face beamed as soon as she set eyes on me and she rushed over to crush me in a heart-felt, perfume-drenched hug.

"Oh Jess!" She said, "This is just magnificent! I mean, it's not magnificent, of course, that you're having to give Firebelly the old heave-ho, but honestly, to see you is magnificent! To be in your little abode is magnificent! And . . ." Here she released me from her hug and stepped back, looking me up and down scrupulously, assessing every inch of me in a way that may have made me flinch but she got away with it anyway, "you look absolutely . . ."

"Magnificent!" Came a chorus of voices that included Gillie, Marcus, Vicky, Dean, Ella and the mystery-named funding man.

"We know, we know," quipped Marcus, "the girl's a walking miracle. Now can we please just get on and get pissed?"

———

The rest of the evening went without a hitch. Ella surprised Gillie and I with a bespoke puppet show of the history of Firebelly, performed around the back of the buffet table with leftover breadsticks and spontaneously accompanied by Ikram on the ukulele, who sat beneath the table, shrouded by a glittery paper tablecloth. Ikram's musical finale somehow transformed into a warbled musical tribute that went as follows:

Gillie and Jess, Gillie and Jess
What are they doing now?
You'll never guess!

Packed it all in, packed it all in
Now Firebelly's gone tits up
Their lives can begin

What will they do? What will they do?
They've got lots of talents
More than any of you . . .

Gille and Jess, Gillie and Jess
Is there life after Firebelly?
I think we all know – fuck yes!

Vicky read a poem which she'd kept since the first ever Firebelly project, detailing her impending sense of doom then ultimate relief that we'd managed to pull off a street theatre performance in the wrong end of town with a gang of teenage rebels.

And then Gillie and I had babbled a few words of thanks to everyone but inevitably got swamped down by our own tears. We ended our speech by clinging to each other, mascara threatening to drip onto our charity-shop party frocks which was not, it turned out, a good look.

"Right! That's enough!" Ella shouted, coming to our rescue with tissues and wine drained from Ikram's generous vat. "Go about your business folks, the formal stuff is done and dusted!" She steered Gillie and I to the sofa and plonked us down. "You two sit here. It's chill-out time." Then she disappeared and Gillie and I sank further into the sofa, glad of its warmth and, to be honest, of her orders.

It had been an all-consuming week and this, ultimately, was an all-consuming night. I mean, amazing, inventive people were in the room, who had supported our creative vision over the years to do amazing, inventive things. I felt so much gratitude for their presence and their support – I know my tears came from all of that. But they also came from my own realisation that this decision to end things was rooted from a place of self-esteem. I was no longer willing to compromise my life for this business, no matter how special it was and that, more than anything, stirred up emotions that were new to me.

Within moments, the sofa that Ella had plonked us onto, became a much more snug place to be as the mood of the party slowed, and people came to join us there. I smiled lazily as I noticed Dean across the room, choosing a more chilled-out playlist on my laptop and the perfectly pitched notes rolled out, supporting deeper, more relaxed conversations and heavy, whispered sighs.

"Right then, pet. Tell us what it's like to be moving on to pastures new?" It was Ikram. He'd snuggled in next to me, from a comfort that was born out of years of chilling together at the back end of late-night parties like this one. I'd known him and Betsy since Jack had formed an improvised comedy troupe with them in Newcastle. Aside from Firebelly, it had been Jack's pride and joy and I'd been to pretty much every one of their gigs except, I guess, for the last ten months.

Betsy and Ikram were a force to be reckoned with. Furiously creative, funny and talented, they loved their work and each other with a wild intensity. Ikram, however, showed his soft underbelly given the chance. And this moment was perfect for it.

"Pastures new?" I said. "Feels like I'm already in the middle of them, Ikram. Have been for some time now."

"Aye." He nodded thoughtfully. "I just haven't been around to see it, pet, I'm sorry." He put his hand over mine and settled it there.

"Well Jack needed you, didn't he? You couldn't be in two places at once." In January, when Jack had announced he might not love me anymore and then deserted me during the Week From Hell, it had been Ikram and Betsy he had turned to. I had known then that Jack needed them more than I did so I'd kept away, even though I'd missed them like crazy.

"Aye, pet, he did. But that's not an excuse like. We should've been there for you as well. Hopefully we'll still see you and chill out on sofas at parties n' all that, eh? You're my favourite person to do that with."

"Too bloody right." I laughed.

"Champion. You just . . . well, pet, you just seem a canny bit different that's all."

"Well I'm not going to lie, a hell of a lot has happened since I last saw you and Betsy. I wouldn't have a clue where to begin telling you about it all. But just be happy for me, can you? I'm doing really, really well. Not a different Jess, just the real one. Finally the real one."

"You're an inspiration pet, that's what you are."

"Well, I wouldn't go that far."

"Seriously," he said, fixing a stern look my way. "Betsy and me've been together since forever but that doesn't mean I don't know what it's like to have me fuckin' heart ripped out. It's like it's fuckin' impossible you'll ever feel better, ever actually feel anything other than a pointless, fuckin' awful pain." At this, he lifted his hand from mine and held it against his chest as if reliving a memory in front of me. "I know that shit pet, I know it."

"Well, yes," I said, remembering all too well the kind of pain he meant. "It is awful."

"Too fucking right it's awful." He smacked his lips together and looked at me, his eyes dark in the shadows of the room. "You. Are. An. Inspiration. Remember it. Cos any hurt, any pain, anyone's feeling, you've shown that there's a way out like, not just to the other side, but to something better. An inspiration. Got it, pet?"

"Got it." I said, and swallowed the last of my wine as well as potentially more tears. "Now whack out a tune on that ukulele you big fool, before my mascara completely ends me."

5

THE PUB

I knew it would have to happen at some point. I would have been a fool to expect to get away with it. But, during the great tidy-up the morning after the Firebelly party, when Vicky told me she and Dean had arranged to go and see Jack, the heavy thud I'd expected in my chest didn't even happen. "We'll just pop and see him in his new surroundings, chicklet. Have a few bevvies with him and, erm, that Katy, and then be on our way. You understand, don't you?"

"Of course I do, Vicks," I said, trailing around the room with a bin liner. "He's one of your best mates, it would be weird if you didn't go to see him. Wait a minute, how are you going to get there and back?" Jack lived in the city now, along with Katy who was landlady at the pub we used to frequent. Actually, at the very pub where he'd announced, last New Year's Eve, that he might want to duck out of our seven-year relationship. Therein followed The Week From Hell before we'd properly split up and the ultimate discovery that he'd shacked up with Katy, but it all felt like a distant memory now.

Dean shuffled into the room shyly in his pyjamas and took

the bin bag from me. "We'll sort something out, Jess. We know roughly where the pub is. There's always the bus."

Vicky's eyes widened. "Yes, and anyway, I miss the cool little shops up here soooo much so Dee has absolutely promised to endure a shopping trip first. Then we'll go see Jack, then get a taxi back or something."

"Hang on a minute . . ." I said, getting my practical head on, "it'll cost you a fortune to get a taxi back from there. I've not got any plans. I'll come and pick you up when you're ready."

They both stared at me with their gobs hung open. "Noooooo." They wailed in unison, shaking their heads and shooing me away with their hands.

I couldn't help but laugh. "Yeeessssss." I insisted. "It's totally fine. I'm fine. Jack's fine. It makes sense. I'd do it if you were going anywhere else." They both took a sharp intake of breath, ready to protest – a beautiful mess of pyjamas, frizzy hair, bare feet and considerate souls. "Children! I'm not taking no for an answer. Let's just get on with this like grown-ups, shall we? Yes? Good. That's sorted then."

———

And that's how I found myself in my little car later that evening, whizzing over the Tyne Bridge, doing this entire journey from muscle-memory, heading towards Jack's pub.

After Vicky and Dean had left, I'd spent the day sprucing up the house, cooking a delicious, warming casserole for their return, and sending out some final emails for Firebelly. The company was pretty much closed now, which felt odd to say the least. Ikram's words about being an inspiration floated through my head from the night before and I shivered inside. Were my finances ever going to be inspired?

I took a deep breath that started and finished in the pit of my belly, loosened my grip on the steering wheel and remembered that jewel shining in the lake.

And weirdly, I did feel pretty calm. You would think, speeding towards your ex fiancé's new life, new woman and new home would be enough to invoke some kind of acute shit-fit. Sweaty hands? Racing pulse? Need to scream like a mad woman out of the car window? Nope. I was good thanks.

And I'd even had a metaphorical bone thrown at me by Jack earlier in the day. I couldn't remember the last time we'd communicated, but today he'd sent me a short text.

Hear u r coming to the pub 2day. Glad u can give V + D a lift. It'll be gud to c them.

I tried not to read into the text too much because it was what it was, but I couldn't help sensing an undercurrent of courage. As much as he wasn't in my life anymore, he certainly had been at the centre of it for a whole seven years and I knew him. I think this text had been difficult, but necessary for him to send. I think he was saying, *I know you're coming. I'm okay with you coming. I know this will be a weird place for you to visit but please don't lose your shit.*

To be fair, I had displayed some pretty full-on emotional anguish in front of Jack earlier this year and there's a chance he may have been petrified I'd break down as soon as I set eyes on him. But what he didn't know was that there was a different story for me now and I was far more concerned with my own story than his. Christ knew I'd worked hard to get to that point, but I was finally there.

So yes, Jack's text was brave but my move to walk into that pub was braver.

And as I pulled up outside the pub, seeing it nestled snugly into the side of a hill and exuding nothing but pure-British-pub-cosiness, I felt a definite pang of fondness. I had, after all, spent many good times at this place.

I got out of the car and felt the gravel crunch beneath my feet. The fresh snap of the city air made a play for my cheeks and I noticed the very picnic table where Jack had informed me he didn't think he loved me anymore. *So what?* I thought. Every table, every pub, every place really, has its own stories. *What about now, Jess? What about the story right now?*

Without breaking stride, I walked into the pub and collided softly with the warm, heavy atmosphere inside. I was caressed by the sudden stream of sounds – laughter, joking, chatting, singing – and moved smoothly around the room until I spotted them. Vicky, Dean and Jack were in a wooden booth at the side of the room, pints in hand. Vicky's face broke into a smile as soon as she saw me and she jumped up, making every pink-cheeked, pot-bellied bloke get out of her way. She engulfed me in a hug of epic proportions and whispered in my ear, "You're amazing, chicklet," and hugged me some more. "I'm getting you a drink" and disappeared off in the direction of the bar.

I turned towards Dean and Jack who were waiting patiently to greet me. Dean swept in first and hugged me as if he hadn't actually seen me that morning, which was sweet. Then Jack. Who just looked, well, like Jack always did except his usually olive skin maybe slightly drained of colour. I noticed that he'd gained a little weight around his middle since the early stages of our break-up which had to be a good thing. I made a quick mental note to give myself the same kind of concession. Then I hugged him quickly and said hello before he had to do or say anything himself, which I thought he looked distantly pleased about, and plonked myself down on a stool opposite them.

I was met by worried expressions and dead stares and a few beats of silence, so I asked Jack about how he was, I asked Dean about his shopping trip with Vicky as it seemed nobody else was capable of starting an actual conversation. What did they expect me to do? Spontaneously combust? Then I saw Jack's eyes flit upwards and behind me and his expression changed from mild worry to downright panic. I knew before I even turned around who was standing there.

Katy.

Right. This was it.

A genuine smile rose up from somewhere deep inside and I turned my head to see her standing there. "Hi Katy!" Her hair was gleaming and golden. Her cheeks as pink and rounded as I remembered them. I stood up to hug her as I would anybody else whose pub I had been to a thousand times.

But when I hugged her, I noticed something I had most definitely not been expecting. Trembling. I mean she was properly shaking like a leaf. I could have never, in a million years, predicted that Katy would be the one to show vulnerability right now. We were on her patch. In her pub. She had her man there and her friends and I think even her dad was sat close by supping a pint. Out of all the scenarios I could have conjured in my head to imagine this moment, this would not have been one of them.

Wasn't I the one who should have been shaking?

Shouldn't I have been the one unable to speak?

I checked in with my body and found a different story there. A story where compassion and acceptance and wisdom took the leads. A story where my body softened and my heart slowed and my willingness to hold another woman in need overwhelmed everything else.

So I held Katy for far longer than I would have done otherwise. I held her long enough to hear the breath rattling in her body and feel the tremor rumbling from inside, and long enough for me to whisper the only words that felt right, "It's okay, Katy. It's okay."

We parted, but I held onto her hands so she could look at my face and see that I really meant what I said. Her hands were still shivering against my steady palms. Her face flushed red and her eyes darting about anywhere but my face. "Katy." I said, firmly. Finally, I had her eyes. "I mean it." Her mouth struggled into the best smile she could manage and she nodded. I released her hands and watched her take a deep breath. She mouthed the words, *thank you*, and went to take her place by Jack's side.

Vicky's timing had always been impeccable, so when a foaming pint of shandy was set down in front of me, it was more than welcome. I took a large gulp of the cool, sweet liquid and delighted in the way it refreshed me through and through. Lord knows I needed that.

Everybody else, too, seemed to be basking in the glory of light alcoholic refreshment and the tried and tested ability it had to break tension and move things on apace. Vicky had hoisted her leg up onto the table to show off the new heels she'd convinced Dean to buy for her and he was miming crying into his now empty wallet. Aha. Some normality.

Except none of this was normal. I'd just comforted Katy? What was that all about? But then, who was I to say how Katy should or shouldn't be feeling about all of this? How did I know what she needed from me? Hell, it suddenly seemed true that both Jack and Katy had *needed* me to do this, not to mention Vicky and Dean.

But none of that mattered. All that mattered was that I had used my instincts to deal with it. Moment by moment. I'd been true to Katy and I'd been true to myself and even if most other women would have gladly scratched her eyes out, that didn't mean I had to.

And because I'd been true in that moment, it meant I could be true in this one too. With my sweet shandy, my sweet friends, and a heart that felt literally full of love.

So full of love, in fact, that when I got home that night, having filled my belly with casserole and my lazy limbs finally sank into a warm bed, I remembered my silent epiphany on that mountainside in Turkey only weeks before. That had come from a true place of love, just like my extended hug for Katy.

Stories. People. Words.

And I didn't need a Turkish mountainside to bring any of that into being. I had all of those things all of the time and it was – it seemed now – just up to me to decide which stories and which people and which words to bring to life.

So I wrote a poem.

The first poem I'd probably written since my university days but I wrote it all the same. I scribbled furiously in my notebook as Dinah, who was curled up at the bottom of my bed, beat her bushy tail furiously up and down with doggy glee.

And for the first time since getting back from Turkey, I wrote without a single care about who would see it, if it was any good, what people would think. I created the same cocoon around me that I had in the depths of Beerbelly Bar so many times, usually with Mesut not too far away silently polishing his glasses in the shadows. I imagined him in the shadows of my bedroom now, a sleek silhouette of heavy, age-old love, and tuned into that creative energy, following my soul's suggestion that I should write. And it should be now.

BRAVE TEXT

You brought me here
Brave text to smoky pub
Bold steps to shaky hugs
Spilled beer then laden shrugs

You need me here
Busy bar with ancient ties

Hasty chat and alert eyes
Tapping feet and polite lies

She needs me here
Tight hug and guilty blush
Forgotten chances and pleading rush
Curious glances into history's lust

I'm okay here
Memories sit and dreams shake
Eyes dance, the heart awake
A moment here for us to take

I'm leaving here
Strong smiles, no stolen tears
Feathered air drawing near
Brimming sighs for precious years

6

TWO MONKS

Lindy shifted her weight on the huge green cushion she was sitting on and pushed her bare feet further into the thick carpet in an effort to fend off pins and needles in her toes. "Well, I'm not sure I could have been as understanding as you were, Jess."

Jess looked up from her wine.

"About what?"

"You know, the whole Katy thing. For all you know – and I hope you don't mind me saying this – Jack could have been going behind your back with Katy for any amount of time before you actually split up. Have you thought about that? Maybe she was trembling because she was shit-scared that you were going to cave her head in for stealing your man."

Jess smiled, the light from the abundance of candles reflected by her blue eyes. "Okay, I'm not going to lie. It did cross my mind that Jack could have been cheating on me and just never had the guts to come out with it."

"So . . . didn't you want to confront him about it in the pub once you saw the way Katy was behaving?"

"Honestly? No."

"Really?" Lindy shook her head.

"I know, but I honestly didn't care about any of that. I felt absolutely invincible when I walked into that pub and the only thing Katy's behaviour did was make me feel for her. Not enough to want to pick out curtains or anything, but enough for me to hug her that little bit closer. Just for a moment."

"For a moment . . ." Lindy repeated and tried to get her head round what level of saintliness, exactly, Jess must have achieved in order to do things this way. She couldn't imagine being able to let go of a seven-year relationship enough in order to let this one slide. Had Jess not just acted like a complete fucking walk-over?

"I tell you what Lindy," Jess said, "Can I tell you a little story slash fable thingy? I came across it in a magazine and I think it explains things better than I can."

"Right, I'm up for that." Lindy said, grabbing her wine glass and taking a swig. "This had better be good."

"Right, well, imagine a couple of monks travelling, by foot, along a road together. After hours of travelling, they come to a river with a strong current. Just as they are preparing to cross the river, they see a beautiful young woman, a little further up, also trying to cross the river. The young woman notices the monks and asks for their help in crossing to the other side."

Lindy raised an eyebrow. "Monks? A beautiful young woman? What kind of magazine is this from?"

Jess laughed. "I know, right? But stay with me. So, the two monks glance at each other for a second because, obviously, they have taken vows never to touch a woman. But then, without saying a word, one of the monks – the older one – picks up the woman and carries her across the river, sets her down on the other side and then gets on with his journey. The other monk catches up but can't believe what has just happened. He is outraged at his elder's behaviour and can't bring himself even to speak to him. They travel for hours in silence, the young monk mentally tortured and reeling in disbelief the whole way.

"Finally, the young monk can't contain himself any longer and bursts out, 'Brother, as monks we are not permitted to touch a woman. How could you even think about carrying that woman up on your shoulders like that?'

"The older monk stops in his tracks and says, 'Brother, I set her down on the riverbank miles back. Why are you still carrying her?'"

At that moment, the food arrived. Lindy watched as everything was set down on the table. Deep dishes of rainbow salad drizzled with pomegranate syrup. Platters of succulent, sliced meat and mounds of sticky white rice sprinkled with parsley. Skewers of barbecued aubergine, courgette and onion. And more of that delicious, warm bread laid out like soft pillows tremored by their own heat.

"Hang on a minute, am I supposed to be the young monk?" Lindy asked.

Jess giggled and tore into the bread. "Never mind, let's just eat!"

7

İŞKENCE

Now that Gillie and I weren't living together, things had changed a bit. Granted, I was no longer tripping over her knock-off Jimmy Choos every time I wanted to move from one room to another, but I was missing the sweet comfort of our lives intertwined. Now she was gone it felt like I had to grow up and face the cold, hard facts that my new boyfriend lived two thousand miles away, my previously precious business was gone, and I had no bloody money coming in.

I also had to face the fact that Gillie needed space. Not just the hot-pink-painted space that was her cute new abode, but also emotional space. And I could get that. I really could. I just couldn't help myself from worrying about her and the way she was playing her cards so close to her chest regarding her recent holiday romance with Demir.

I knew she was having phone contact with him. That was no secret. What did seem secretive was the way she actually felt about him and what, exactly was going on between them. No change there then. It had been exactly the same under the beating sun in Turkey. It seemed totally nuts to me, that Gillie would be so closed about what was going on, because I was the reigning champion in 'Wearing-Her-Heart-On-Her-Sleeve'. But was that grounds to worry about her? Or should I just keep my massive nose out of it?

"Massive nose out of it. Is best, Gulazer. Gillie, she own person. She not your person." Oh how I loved the simple wisdom of Mesut's words, even if I did have to put up with hearing them down the phone rather than seeing them trip off his luscious lips. There's no messing about when you've got a language barrier and a dodgy phone line going on, that's for sure. And he was right. Gillie was not my person. She was her own.

Recently, I'd also started talking to Mesut on video messaging. My ancient laptop didn't particularly like the experience, and tended to cut out halfway through our conversations or make our voices sound like a ropy, experimental pop video. Maybe my laptop was in some kind of weird digital harmony with me though, because I was pretty ropy and experimental with the experience myself.

The first time we decided to 'meet' was nerve-wracking. Mesut had organised to borrow a friend's computer in an office somewhere, and I'd set up a username and Microsoft account for this very purpose. I sat there in my spare room, waiting for the call with my heart pounding and my tummy churning, seriously considering whether I could go through with this or not. It was ridiculous! I'd just walked right into my ex-fiancé's pub and embraced his new bit of fluff with hardly a blink – why couldn't I do a video call with my probable soul mate?

When I first saw him flicker onto the screen, I felt my heart lift out of my chest. For a nanosecond I relinquished all cares about my own potentially dodgy on-screen appearance and focused sharply on the beautiful, dark shadow of a man that now haunted my life.

The image was a little grainy but I saw the hunched, black

outline of his body sat motionless before me. Then a flick of those full, deep brown eyes up and out through the heavy strands of long, black hair. Then a smile, a wide one, revealed itself and the hair was thrown back over his shoulders. "Gulazer, my Gulazer."

That smile. It's not something I'd seen for the first half of my trip to Turkey – but the memory of it clung to the later days we'd spent watching sunrises or sitting on rocks lapped by the ocean.

"Yes, I'm here. How are you, beautiful man? How has your day been?" And, I couldn't help it, the words just tumbled out. "It's so lush to see your smile!"

"Lush?" He looked puzzled. Not a word he knew. He picked up a tattered old book from the desk he was sitting at and started leafing through it.

"Is that an English-Turkish dictionary?" I asked.

A bashful smile flickered across his open mouth and he dipped his head further into the book. "I just needing learn more, Gulazer. For you. For me. Is needed . . ." I waited patiently as Mesut looked for the word 'lush' not having a clue what he'd find in that ancient looking doorstop of a book. He looked up, puzzled. "You is thinking my smile is like drunk man with too much alcohol in his blood? Really?"

I burst out laughing. "Noooo, that's 'a lush'. Somebody who drinks too much. It also means lovely, amazing, fantastic. At least up here in the North East it does."

"So you thinking my smiling is lovely, amazing, fantastic?"

"Yes, of course." Talk about not missing a trick.

"Okay then, I will be smiling all time for you." And he flashed me an absolute corker, just to show he really meant it.

"What are you up to?" I asked. "I don't recognise where you're sitting. It's not Beerbelly Bar, is it?" I think I had every tattered and scruffy square inch of Beerbelly committed to memory and where he was right now looked far more organised and professional.

"Is friend's office." He explained, looking around him. "Is Emlak, erm, I mean, estate agency. Is after hours but he is letting me in because, well, you knows, my smile is lovely and amazing and fantastic he cannot saying no."

"I can imagine." I laughed. "So aren't you working tonight then?"

"Season is finish. No more tourists. I am free man Gulazer."

"Cool! What are you going to do with all your time? What do you usually do over the winter?"

"Oh, I don't know really." He stroked a chin that was dotted in dark stubble. "I am walking . . . and I am sitting . . . and I am eating . . . sometimes I am visiting friends . . . Bar is behind me."

His approach to spare time couldn't be more different than mine. Here I was having just closed my business that I'd sweated over for the best part of ten years and was I having any time off? Was I shite. I'd jumped straight into job-searching and sending emails to work contacts and stressing about what would come next. Maybe I could take some inspiration from Mesut. Walking, sitting, eating, visiting friends. Was that even allowed?

"What do you mean the bar is behind you?"

"I am meaning is finish for me. The bar. I not going back."

"Oh." I said, feeling a thud in the bottom of my chest. "No more Beerbelly?"

"No more Beerbelly, Gulazer."

Okay. I could deal with that. Beerbelly was not the thing I was in love with, was it? I could deal with never sitting at the back of the bar again, on those beautiful big, sequined cushions, pondering my future. It was okay if I was never able to curl up with a book and a wine spritzer on a sun-drenched sofa out on Beerbelly's balcony again, lifting my eyes momentarily to watch Mesut slink around from table to table. I didn't need to sit on the cool, marble steps waiting for him to finish work so we could go walk on the beach and marvel at the world and each other.

Fucking hell, why was I making this about me? "Are you alright? What's happened?"

"Nothing is happen. Sometimes is just right time. You knows Demir not liking me long time now and I not liking him, how you say it? Breathing in my neck all the time. He is cousin with Beerbelly owner, Esad, you knows, and he is telling bad things to Esad. I know it. I not need it. I will find new job in new season. Is no problem."

"Demir's stirring the shit then? Nothing's changed."

Mesut smiled, somehow managed to find my gaze and held it steady. "Everything is change, Gulazer."

Those words, gifted to me with wide, honest eyes and radiantly curving lips flooded me with a warmth that had sweetness in its very current. I devoured it with every inch of my body, sat there in my little spare room. *Everything is change.*

And so began my lesson that Mesut's way with words would constantly turn the conversation back to truth. How he managed to do that with his basic grasp of the English language and a questionably ancient dictionary at his side, I will never know, but I was grateful for it.

He held that smile for a little longer and there was a silence that wasn't altogether unpleasant. I noticed the tiniest microchange in the muscles around his mouth and knew in my bones that he was thinking something else now. He swept his eyes up and down my body slowly and steadily and even from a screen a couple of thousand miles away, made me feel I'd been stripped bare.

I shifted in my chair and the floorboards creaked. It did nothing to put a crack in the mood. I mirrored his smile right back at him and felt my own gaze taking in what I could. His arms rested on the desk in front of him, shirt rolled up to his elbows so I could see his forearms dusted in sun-stolen memories and palms held open so I could remember the invitation of his fingers. The smooth arc of his neck where I imagined his pulse, perfect and slow for kissing. His shoulders, currently covered by grey winter clothes, leaning in towards me, broad and steady, seemingly lacking my own skin pressed against them . . .

"İşkence." Mesut whispered in a weighted sigh.

"Ish-what?" I gasped, suddenly blinking my way out of my trance.

"İşkence. Is mean . . . wait, I am learn." He picked up that heavy old book again and started flicking through the pages. The screen jumped slightly and his image wavered in front of me. *Oh no. Crappy old laptop, please don't fail me now.*

"Ah. Is here." He looked up at me and grinned again, though I could hardly see it through the blippy screen I was getting. "İşkence is mean, in your language, 'Torture'."

Torture indeed.

I nodded and tried to tell him I agreed that this whole video-messaging thing was as torturous as it was brilliant, and that 'İşkence' was a word I would not forget in a hurry. Whether technology was protesting at his end or my end, I didn't know but it wasn't long before we both got cut off. Fuck, maybe the chemistry was all too much for Microsoft and it cut out before there were irreparable reverberations across China or something. Never mind – we still had the phone and our cheap calls deal to be getting on with.

After these video chats with Mesut I was often left with a lingering energy that had been held back due to shitty computer vibes. I got used to jumping up from my laptop screen, swearing a whole lot, then pacing through the house looking for something to do. It wasn't long before the spare room that I was sitting in came under my twitchy gaze and I realised I had a potential project here.

After the mammoth redecorations of the living room and my bedroom earlier this year, this room had been sadly missed out. And I knew exactly what I wanted to do with it. The spare room had to be all about me. It had to reflect and enable the kind of heart-based work I now wanted to do. That meant writing. That meant painting. That meant a creative space.

In my own unique *I-will-do-this-brilliantly-and-I-will-do-it-on-a-budget-of-fuck-all* kind of a way, I smashed down a grotty old wardrobe, sourced a second-hand desk, painted the walls a basic gallery white and dragged my old easel down from the loft. I scrubbed and varnished the floorboards, strung fairy lights every which way I could and stuck old cork floor tiles to the walls to make a giant pin-board. Time to get those musings out of my notebook and into the world.

I started the pin-board off with a vision board that I'd made just a couple of months ago with Gillie and Oliver. Now though, I added quotes, dried flowers and torn pages from my notebook. It was an invigorating sight to see so much of what had been going on inside me now out there, on the wall, in a way that was real evidence of change. A hard copy, if you like.

It wasn't long before I put the easel to good use too, and started painting some abstract pictures inspired by the hot air balloon ride Gillie and I had taken with Oliver in Cappadocia. I built up texture with a mixture of plaster of Paris and glue into whips of creamy mountain tops and licks of fiery earth. I almost forgot about my waning bank balance in the creative flow of it all.

The thing I was most excited about though, was getting started properly on my writing. No matter what Max or anybody else said about how hard it was going to be to make any kind of money out of this, I had to start somewhere, or all of that soul-searching work in Turkey would have been for nothing.

Evolving from notebook to laptop was a bold move, but one I was determined to make. I spent hours at a time, typing up notes from my experience in İpeklikum. The potential plot lines laid out before me like delicate strands all tangled but waiting to be teased out. I had so many ideas I didn't know where to start, but sitting down at my desk in my own little fairy-lit creative space seemed as good a place as any.

After a while, I started to doubt I even had anything to write about. *Aha*, I thought, *this is to be expected. What decent writer has ever written anything without a good dose of emotional toil?* I began looking up bits of advice from famous writers and artists about how to clear creative blocks and how to bring all your ideas together into a cohesive whole. I researched creativity and how to tap into it, artistry, and how to be true to it. I pinned a load of them to my giant pin-board, just to help me whenever I was flailing.

Creativity is intelligence having fun – Albert Einstein

Write what should not be forgotten – Isabel Allende

Creativity is a wild mind and a disciplined eye – Dorothy Parker

You can make anything by writing – CS Lewis

A lot of making art is listening to yourself – Kiki Smith

A writer, I think, is someone who pays attention to the world – Susan Sontag

Art washes away from the soul the dust of everyday life – Pablo Picasso

And the one quote I came back to, time and time again, the one that caught my eye every time I stepped into the spare room was this one from Maya Angelou . . .

There is no greater agony than bearing an untold story inside you

There were definite echoes of the word, 'İşkence' here.

Although I definitely had a much greater sense of peace with myself since I'd arrived back in England, there was a kind of agony, a kind of torture, actually. And I mean aside from the one that stirred up tingles in all the wrong (or right) places when faced with Mesut smoldering on a cheap laptop screen. All these new beliefs, these new ideas about the kind of life I wanted – no, *needed* – to live were kind of blighted by the ongoing torment of 'how'.

How would I continue to stay true to my values?

How would I make people understand what I was trying to do?

How would I find ways to accommodate my new perspectives into my old life?

How would I shed deeply-ingrained confidence issues put there long, long ago?

How would I ever know what to write about?

And how, I wondered, for not the first time this year, would I ensure I didn't disappear up my own arse?

'İşkence' had a lot to answer for.

8

SOMETHING KICKING OFF

"Jessie! You'd better come quick. Something's going on at the old Firebelly offices." My mam's voice was quick and breathless and I could hear the grabbing of car keys and slamming of doors in the background. "A friend of mine just told me – she saw it while she was walking her dogs. We'll meet you there."

The line went dead.

Fucking Firebelly. That was supposed to be all over. Was it really my concern if something was happening at the offices? I'd moved all our stuff out. This was not in the grand plan.

Then, a text.

Jess. Marcus just phoned. There's something kicking off at Firebelly's door. Some woman shouting blue murder. She's demanding to see us. Shall we go?

I sighed and took Dinah's lead off the hook next to the front door.

Yes, Gillie. Let's go.

I figured we'd better go see what was going on. If this woman knew our names and had some kind of problem then we'd better go and sort it out. It was probably just some pissed-off arts and crafts supplier trying to deliver an order we'd have already cancelled ages ago.

"Come on Dinah." I said, mustering all the enthusiasm I could. Dinah got up from her squishy dog bed, pushed her bum in the air and yawned before trotting over to me. We both jumped in the car and headed over to the offices that I thought I'd already said goodbye to.

When I swung the car into the Firebelly yard, there was actually a bit of a crowd gathering under a grey, pendulous sky. It seemed there was somebody at the top of the steps, next to the bright red entrance door. Doors that Gillie, Jack and I had painted years ago, in an attempt to make the place seem more professional.

At least twenty other people were standing on and around the steps, all focused on whoever was at the top, causing a scene. A few people were shouting, a few were hushing and shushing, but most were just watching, waiting and pulling their coat collars up around their faces to keep warm. Some kids I recognised were running around the Firebelly yard – something we'd never allowed them to do when they attended our art clubs on account of the constantly moving cars.

Gillie's car swung into the yard just as I had that thought, narrowly missing two kids spinning round in circles. She parked and jumped out of the car in a strop. "Watch it, you two." She said to the grubby little faces. "I nearly had you then. What have we told you about running about in the yard?"

"Dun't matter no more." Said one, who went by the name of Kaidan if I remembered rightly. "Yur not in charge."

"True." I said, coming to Gillie's rescue and wishing I'd worn a coat as thick and glamorous as hers. "But Kaidan, we still want you to stay safe, don't we?"

"Our mam says yuh don't care if wur safe like." Said the little girl next to Kaidan. She was freckled and rosy. I remembered her too. Kaylee. Good at drawing space rockets. "Yuh don't care about us lot at all."

"Why would you think that?" I said, throwing Kaylee a smile and getting Dinah out of the car. "Of course we care. We've known you long enough, haven't we? Anyway, how's your drawing coming along these days?" I stretched my arm out to ruffle Kaylee's hair but the motion was interrupted by a god-awful scream.

"Divvent ye DARE touch my child ye sly cow! Ye cannit have it both ways ye kna!"

I twirled around and saw a woman practically hanging off the metal railings next to the entrance. She'd pushed past several people to hurl those words at me and now they were standing way back, bodies angled awkwardly to allow her rage to pour out, my poor Mam and Dad among them. She stood with her feet planted wide, a finger jabbing at the space between us. She craned her neck into a rigid line, her dirty blonde hair splaying in spikes across her shoulders. The words exploded out of her spittled lips. "What the fuck do ye think yur doing stopping all these activities like? Without a word to us mams? How are w' supposed to entertain the bairns now? Call yesels professionals! It's a total disgrace. I wan' summat done!"

"Shit, Jess, what do we do now?" Gillie whispered under her breath. "We did tell the parents, didn't we?"

"Of course we did." I hissed, leaning close to Gillie. "I sent emails to everyone weeks before we closed." I looked up and saw that my mam had somehow positioned herself next to Kaidan and Kaylee's mother and I could tell by the lean of her body and the knitting of her brow that she was about to exercise some alarmingly misplaced Scottish sympathy.

"Och, I'm sure we can all sort this out if we just calm down. That's my daughter you're talking to and I just know she'll have an answer for you, won't you, Jessie?"

"Back off, ye ald mare! Who fuckin' asked ye?" My mam backed off indeed and nearly fell down the steps behind her in the process, if it hadn't been for my dad catching her by the elbows. Right. That was my cue to get myself up there. I threw Dinah's lead at Gillie and sprinted.

"Aye, here she comes. Lady of the bloody manor!" The woman went on, staring down at me as I made my way up the steps, the whites of her eyes flashing brightly. "I never did understand why me bairns went on and on about ye lot in here. But now ye've jacked it all in, ye selfish cows. What the hell are me kids meant to do now?"

I didn't particularly like being a step or two down from this woman but there were too many people between us and as much as they'd annoyingly come out here for the drama, I didn't want to shove past them. I could see, however, that our meticulously painted red doors were now blackened with scorch marks. How the hell had she done that? Shit. I grabbed the metal rail next to me and gulped down oxygen into the depths of my rock-hard tummy.

"I'm sorry you feel so disappointed by Firebelly closing. We did talk to all the parents at all our clubs and we sent out emails to everybody so you knew what was happening."

"Emails? Emails?" She roared. "What fuckin' good is an email? I haven' even got internet at me hoose. Neither's half the mams round 'ere." Some of the women around me nodded, and that's when I noticed this woman's nostrils weren't the only ones flaring.

"We sent letters home with the kids too? There were lists of other local services in there for you to access instead?" I could hear my own voice drawing upwards. I was asking questions rather than making statements.

"Other fuckin' services? Where else am ah gonna get three hours' childcare for one pound fifty? I tell ye what this is pet, it's a fuckin' joke. And ye don't give a shit about me little bairns, do ye?! Do ye?!"

I suddenly saw a flash of amber fur down towards my left and a ferocious growl ripped into my ears. Then a cry from behind me. "Sorry, Jess! Dinah! Come back here!" The furry streak blazed ahead and straight into the calves of the woman in front of me, with lips snarled and teeth bared and snapping repeatedly like the bitter beat of a war drum.

"Shitting hell! It's gonna bite! Ye total bitch, ye set yer dog on us!" As quickly as Dinah had flung herself ahead of me, the woman lunged at me with her denim-clad arms and neon pink nails. "I'm fuckin' 'aving ye!" She flew down the steps, knocking back the onlookers as she went and thudded her fist into my temple. It didn't hurt. But falling backwards down the steps did.

Before the gunmetal clouds barrelled into my vision I saw my dad's bearded face rush towards me, but I knew gravity plus momentum would be an equation too quick for him. After that it was a searing sequence of concrete, thudding and pain.

Then, nothing.

9

THE ARTICLE

FURIOUS PROTEST OVER CLUB CLOSURE
Reporter: Danny Pearson

Angry scenes broke out at a local community centre after parents protested at the closure of a children's art club.

A group of sixteen parents gathered outside the building in Budhill and claimed no one had told them the club was shut and their children could not go in.

Onlookers reported an unprovoked dog attack against a local mum and one organiser of the club, Firebelly, was taken to hospital with slight concussion after the incident at the Budhill Community Centre on Morrison Road. This was after she failed to give sufficient evidence that the community was consulted regarding the closure, and in surprised response to her dog's actions.

Around 45 children aged between 5 and 12 had been coming to the club since it opened seven years ago and took part in activities

including drama, art and music. Local parents report that it was
a vital part of their children's welfare and extended education.

Angry mum Treena Wraith, aged 22 of Budhill, said: "It's a total
disgrace that we were not notified that the club was closing. My
two children have been going there for ages and they love it.
There was not one word of warning that the service was being
pulled. There is nothing else round here for them and it's a total
disgrace. No-one cares about our kids."

Firebelly organiser, Jess Parker, aged 28 of Elderside, received
minor cuts and concussion after a row broke out between her and
the parents. She was detained overnight in hospital. She has not
yet commented on the behaviour of her dog or the matter itself.

"You're kidding me? Why would they write it up like that?
That's so one-sided!" I was so mad I had shifted awkwardly
against my starch-white pillows, exactly as I'd been advised
not to.

"Jess, go easy love." Dad said. "You know what the doctor
said." He cupped a hand behind my head and helped me find a
place of comfort again.

Mam folded the newspaper and stuffed it under her arm.
"It's only the local rag. I doubt it'll hold much weight. Wheesht,
Danny bloody Pearson. I'll have his guts for garters. He was just
a wee bit lad when he started at the paper and look at him now,
writing all kinds of rubbish. And there's something about that
woman's name, 'Wraith', I'm sure it rings a bell."

It rang a bell with me too but I guessed that was just because
I was used to seeing Kaylee and Kaidan's name on our youth
club registers. They'd never had anybody dropping them off or

picking them up and they'd had a parental consent form to say that was okay. Euch. I thought this was information I'd have been able to dump out of my brain by now.

I sighed and urged my neck muscles to relax. The shards of pain shooting through the back of my head hadn't got any worse since I'd woken up, but it still bloody hurt. Apparently I'd hit the steps with the full force of my body behind it and was lucky not to have a more severe concussion. The rest was just cuts and bruises, including a particularly impressive slash across my cheek. Gillie, after profusely apologising for letting go of Dinah's lead during the ruckus, had been highly amused that I now looked like a (very) distant cousin of Al Pacino. "Scarface isn't a patch on you." She'd giggled at the end of my hospital bed the day before.

"What do we do now though, Mam? Thank god this Treena didn't get any injuries from Dinah, otherwise I know it would be a whole lot worse. But what are Gillie and I supposed to do to make this go away? We honestly thought we'd closed the business in the most ethical way possible. What if this affects my future job prospects?" My body sank into the creaking plastic mattress with a heaviness I'd not thought possible. Maybe it was the multiple knots in my belly that weighed me down.

"Well firstly," Mam said, "you concentrate on getting better."

"Exactly." My dad piped up. "They're letting you out later this afternoon and we'll help you get settled at home. Gillie's got your killer dog so you won't need to lift a finger for a couple of days."

"Then, I suppose . . ." Mam went on, "well, I'm not sure what you can do really. You and Gillie could decide if you want to speak to this reporter to put your side of things forwards. Or you could go and see this Treena Wraith and tell her again all the ways you tried to make the closure of Firebelly as pain-free as possible."

"Fat lot of good that would do." My dad huffed.

"Your dad's right. I'm not sure she'd listen and I don't really know what else she can do to cause a scene. The damage she did to the Firebelly door is the council's problem now, not yours. Over time she'll probably get over it and find something else for her kids to do. And, well Jessie, I know it didn't say anything in the article about it, but don't you think she was on the drugs or something?"

"On the drugs?" I arched an eyebrow at Mam. I was still good for that.

"Och Jessie, I don't know the proper way to say it. Underneath the influence? Going on a trip? High like a kite? Totally schnockered?"

"Stop! Please stop Mam. It hurts to laugh."

"It's no laughing matter Jessie. Honestly, this makes me wonder if closing Firebelly was worth it after all. At least you had an income then. Maybe this woman is right? And what will you do if she finds out where you live and she's all schnockered again. What then?"

"Wait. Let's get things in perspective." Dad came to my side. He placed a warm hand over mine and flickered a smile at me from beneath his auburn beard. Then he fixed a serious stare at my mam. "There's no question about whether or not Jess should have closed Firebelly. So we're not going back on that now, are we love?"

"No." I whispered.

"Good. So it is what it is. Jess is going to be alright. But only if we get her home and let her rest. None of this talk about visiting this woman or speaking to reporters at the moment. Agreed?"

"Agreed." Mam and I said together.

"Excellent. Right, I don't know about anybody else, but my stomach thinks my throat's been cut. I'm going to the canteen to get us some treats. Flora, You're coming with me. Leave Jess in peace."

As I listened to my parents' animated voices retreat down the corridor away from me, I gulped and stared up at the luminous strip-light above me. The whiteness was startling. The soundscape of the hospital rolled around me – trolleys squeaking, phones ringing, machines bleeping and tubes whirring. How the heck had I managed to end up here?

I could hardly believe I'd been sat in sunny patches of beach, reading books and eating olives only weeks before now. I had known then that things would be different when I got home – of course they would – but not this bloody different. I wiggled my toes out of the blue waffle blanket some nurse had thrown over me earlier and noted that they looked much nicer in flip-flops or dug deeply into golden sand.

I was so angry at Kaylee and Kaidan's mam for putting me here. Granted, she probably didn't mean to chuck me down the steps but the massive fuss she was making was getting in my way. Firebelly was supposed to be finished the minute we'd said goodbye to our last party guest. I needed a clean break, and so did Gillie. Christ, it had taken so much bloody courage to admit that our little business needed to fold and we didn't need this woman stirring up the shit and stopping us from getting on with our lives.

I was angry with the world too, I guess. Why wasn't there better provision for kids like Kaylee and Kaidan? Why should Firebelly have been one of the only good things in their little lives? I'd had talks with the local authority before we closed down, to make sure I was signposting families to other opportunities, but the truth was that there was nothing else that was a patch on what Firebelly had offered. *But that's because you put your heart and soul into it Jess. And that couldn't last forever.*

Fucking hell. Yet again it appeared I had to own up to admitting my part in this. I'd spent nearly a decade building up a business that was ultimately unviable because one day, of course, I was going to realise that I could no longer live and breathe it. I'd been happy to merge myself into it when Jack was around because he'd been just as committed as me at one point. But once he'd gone, all that had changed. Maybe that hadn't actually been fair on all the kids, all the mums and dads. Had it?

Whatever the answers, the closure of Firebelly was now biting me on the arse big-style. And as long as I was incapacitated like this, I couldn't wriggle free.

10

IMAGINATION

I was starting to hate my newly refurbished spare room.

I mean, really hate it.

Since leaving hospital and being given strict instructions to rest for a couple of days, I figured it would be a good distraction to indulge in a bit of leisurely writing time in my newly-decorated creative nest.

But 'leisurely' was hardly the right word. I mean, it was a matter of hours before I decided I hated that room. The way it coaxed me into swear-fests directed at a blank laptop screen, and then to stare up at the unbearably cheerful fairy lights strung above my desk. I hated the weary creak of the floorboards underneath me every time I sighed (which was often) and I hated even more the condescending words of wisdom pinned to that god-forsaken homemade bloody pin-board. How was I supposed to work in these conditions? How was I ever supposed to write *anything*?

I thought I'd had a breakthrough at the hospital. Max had called me, to make sure I was alright after the Firebelly fiasco and once he realised I was, he'd started telling me about a horror movie he'd recently watched. I tried to protest that I'd had enough horror to last me a while (slash across my right cheek a case in point), but Max revelled in telling me about the way the plot had built and ultimately led to the gory demise of some poor fool. And hallelujah for my brother because that's when I suddenly thought, *that's it! That's bloody well it!*

I'd write a horror story set in İpeklikum using all the people I'd met as inspiration. I'd weave a terrible tale of the darkness and deceit that goes on under the polished gloss of a typical beach resort to rival any Midnight Shymalananana-or-whatever-he's-called flick. Actually, the more I thought about it, how could a character like Demir *not* appear in a horror movie? His pointy shoes and shifty eyes were literally made for it. And all the dodgy mafia-type antics that had gone on behind the scenes of seemingly happily-run family businesses? My god, this book would write itself.

This book was not writing itself.

I really tried though. After filling myself up on painkillers, toast and tea, I'd swan into my spare room, prepared to give the idea another chance. I'd hover my hands over the laptop keyboard, ready to create something marvellous. I mean, I'd done the hard bit, right? I'd agonised for months over my purpose on this planet. I'd recognised the omens, I'd followed all the signs, and it had all felt so right. Fucking hell, I'd closed my entire business for this shit AND had my very own *head injury* that could potentially inspire the whole plot. Hadn't I earned the right for creative brilliance to now burst out of me as easily as champagne from a recently shaken bottle?

Apparently not.

I may not have known how to write a novel, but I did know when I needed a break. Minutes later I was on Gillie's doorstep with a bottle of red in my clutches. She opened the door, took one look at me and sighed. "Should you be drinking? Oh, fuck it. You can help me christen the new wine glasses."

It didn't take long before I was clad in one of Gillie's cosiest bathrobes, sprawled in a tipsy heap on her sofa and sporting a clumsily applied avocado face mask.

"So what if you don't know what to write yet? It's bound to come to you eventually." Gillie said, reasonably.

"That's totally unreasonable, Gillie. You know I hate waiting."

"Yes, I do, but you've got to remember this is all quite new to you. Just because you had your eureka moment in Turkey kind of means nothing now that you need to do the hard graft. Maybe patience is just another skill you'll have to learn."

"Fuck that! I'm sick of learning things. I've learned enough in one year to keep me going for several lifetimes. When does this have to come off by the way?" I picked at my chin where the green gunk was itching.

"What did I say? Patience!" Gillie said. "Actually, speaking of which . . ." She checked her watch then gave a little cry. "Oooooh! I'm just nipping upstairs. Won't be long . . . watch the telly or something." And she chucked the remote control at me before disappearing and pounding up the stairs like a mad woman.

"Weird." I said, under my breath before switching on the telly. I guessed a little bit of mild escapism couldn't hurt. If anybody deserved it right now, I did. And I couldn't be soul-searching on a constant basis. It was exhausting.

I was just getting into some kind of celebrity-reality-aerial-acrobatics show, when Gillie ran down the stairs with just as much urgency as she'd ran up them twenty minutes ago. She popped her head around the door. "Jess! I've got a surprise for you – come on!"

"Wha?" I moaned, reluctantly tearing my eyes away from

the bronzed, muscular male torso currently swinging from a glittery hoop. "A surprise?"

"Yes! But it has to be now! Come on!" I sighed and heaved myself out of the luscious depths of the sofa to follow her obediently up the stairs.

Once I was on her landing, Gillie dragged me by a very tightly-gripped hand into the tiny little box-shaped spare room. All I could see was peeling wallpaper, a cushion on the floor and her computer wobbling precariously on a dodgy-looking cardboard box. "Gillie, I really don't think you should put that on there. It doesn't look very stro . . . Oh."

Then I saw him.

Mesut.

He was clear as day and larger than I was used to on my pathetic little laptop at home.

Gillie tutted and pushed me onto the cushion. "I've been talking to Demir and then I saw Mesut passing in the background, so I got Demir to grab him. And he really wants to talk to you and I know you're always saying how you can't manage properly on your crappy laptop so here he is! On my computer! Which shouldn't give you any problems, well, as long as you don't tip the balance on that box. So just try not to touch it. And no time like the present, eh Jess?"

"Gillie!" I half-shrieked, half-whispered, turning away from the screen. "I've got a green fucking face mask on!"

"Oh shitting hell, I forgot!" Gillie cried.

"You forgot? Flipping heck, I look like a ninja turtle. With a facial injury!"

She smirked. "Okay, okay point taken. Let me help you." She came at me, fingers frantically scraping and peeling, rubbing and stripping. "We'll just be a minute, Mesut!" She piped up over my shoulder at the screen. "Don't go anywhere, we're just making Jess beautiful!"

"Ouch!" I shouted as Gillie poked me in the eye for the third time. "That's enough! I'll have to do." I said, huffily, patting my face gingerly. Most of it seemed to be gone. Surely the grainy camera wouldn't pick up tiny bits of it anyway. Of course, I wouldn't know that for sure until I turned around to face the screen. Oh, what I wouldn't give for my ancient laptop and its glitchy software right now.

Gillie was edging back towards the door working desperately hard not to laugh. "Right then, I'll err . . . I'll get you a drink." And she was gone.

There was a silence for a few seconds as I composed myself, my back still to the screen. Then, "Gulazer? You okay? How is your head and your cheek? You feeling better?"

Mesut knew all about the incident at the Firebelly door. He'd called me almost hourly since it had happened and, in the end, I'd had to ask him to stop so I could sleep.

"Gulazer? You talking to me tonight or not?"

I figured it was all or nothing. "Of course I'm talking to you. Here I am!" I whipped round and beamed straight at him, trying really hard not to look at the smaller window with my image in it at the bottom of the screen. It was better if I didn't know.

And wow. Gillie's computer was far better than mine. I could see the grooves in his forehead, the black-metal sheen of his hair, the thick eyelashes, the folds of his jacket as he laid his hands on the desk in front of him. A smirk tripped across his lips.

"You are . . . you are okay, Gulazer?"

"Yes, yes. I'm fine. Feeling much better actually. Why do you ask?"

"You are seeming . . . maybe a little bit . . . different?"

"Really?"

"Yes. Usually you not waving at me like that."

"Oh. Right. I was just excited to see you, that's all. Gillie surprised me."

"Yes. Yes she is doing a surprise. You sure you okay?"

"Absolutely. All good here. Tickety boo."

"Tickety boo?" He leaned forward so I could really see the fine crinkles around his eyes, the soft swell of those lips as they broke into an even wider smile. "Is that your name for strange condition?"

"What strange condition?"

"Forgive me, Gulazer, but the one on your face." And he burst out laughing, his long, black hair sweeping quickly forwards to hide the absolute hilarity of it all. I glanced down at my image hovering at the bottom of the screen and was horrified to see strands of green gloop hanging from my eyebrows, my nose, my chin and from the dressing on my cheek. Streaks of luminous paste spread unashamedly across my forehead, interspersed with bright red, irritated skin peeking out from underneath. I looked like an actual horror show.

"Oh god, oh god, oh god!" I cried and ran out of the room. I grabbed a towel from the bathroom and started rubbing. My skin was burning in protest at having ever put that stuff on in the first place. Why hadn't I done something when I first felt it itching? How was I going to go back into the room and face Mesut with a face that now looked less ninja turtle and more Freddy Kruger? Well, I'd wanted inspiration for a horror story, maybe this was the universe delivering.

A couple of very large glasses of wine later (brought to me each time by a relentlessly giggling Gillie) and I was finally able to disregard how my skin looked and speak with Mesut. "So you knew what was going on the whole time?"

"Of course. I have four sister, remember? I am seeing a lot their idea about booty when I am growing up."

I nearly spat out my wine. "Booty?"

"Yes. They is obsessed with booty. Booty, booty, booty." He tutted and rolled his eyes as if his sisters having an obsession with bottoms or sex or both was a perfectly normal reason for his despair. And there was me thinking that Turkey was generally more reserved than the west.

"Erm . . . Mesut . . . my face mask had nothing to do with booty."

"But aren't you doing it to make you more bootyful? I am understanding it is about the booty or, I ask you, what is point?"

Now it was my turn to burst out laughing. "Oh, you mean 'beautiful'. You mean I was doing it for the 'beauty'."

"Of course, Gulazer. That is what I say. But anyway, you not need face mask. You bootyful anyways, you knows."

"Aw, thank you." I sighed, letting the laughter trail off, my sides aching happily. "Do you know? I do miss you, Mesut."

He nodded slowly and rubbed his temples. "I know. I am miss you so much too."

"It's weird because some days I'm ecstatic that you're even in the world and that knowledge feels like more than enough . . . and then other days . . . particularly since the whole drama at Firebelly and falling down the steps . . . well, I just want you next to me more than anything. Which one is right?"

"I think both is right. Because both is your feeling." He dropped his gaze to the desk and slowly rolled a pencil backwards and forwards in front of him. He picked his next words carefully. "Me, I so glad you in world. But honestly, Gulazer? I not know how I can do this."

My heart began to hammer in my chest. "Do what?"

"This . . ." he said, leaving the pencil to roll off the desk and opening his palms so I could remember exactly how they felt against my own. "Is you and me is problem."

"Problem?"

"Yes. Is big problem. Really."

Oh fuck. Oh holy fuck. He was backing out. He was having second thoughts. He couldn't resist the lure of the holiday-makers and their short skirts and their constant availability. How could I have thought he would? How was I ever a match for that? I could feel the wine I'd drunk that evening plunge heavily into the depths of my tummy and I wanted to be sick.

"Gulazer?"

"Yeah. I'm here." My voice shook. The glare of the screen suddenly became all too bright and I could just about make out his dark form before me. "Erm, well, I need to know, Mesut, if this isn't what you want."

"You thinking I not want you, Gulazer? No. Is problem, I wanting too much." I shifted on the cushion but didn't make a sound. What did he mean? "I am scared now, you understand me? What is happening now . . . you . . . me. Is scaring me."

"Scaring you? Mesut, it's been scaring me shitless since you told my fortune in that fucking stupid coffee cup outside Beer-belly. Being scared is part of the territory." The sickness was being rapidly replaced by anger, and plenty of it.

"My scared is coming out because of what happen to you on Firebelly steps. You fall and I fall. You hurt and I hurt. I not knowing how I doing that from here in Turkey. My feel for you is so strong and I not ever, ever feel this with anyone. I never want to take anyone's hurt like I wanting take yours. But can you forgive me, Gulazer?"

"What do you mean?"

"Can you forgive me I not catch you on steps with crazy woman? Can you forgive me I not there to take you hospital? I feeling so bad and I'm not knowing how we do this. I not even there now to take stupid green stuff off your face. How you going to be happy with that one? You deserving more, Gulazer. And you will realise it. You will."

At this, he hung his head and those glorious, jet-black

strands of hair shrouded him in his own dark moment. This had nothing to do with bloody holidaymakers in short skirts. This was his insecurity, not mine. He was terrified of a broken heart and he had every right to be.

"So, am I right in thinking . . . you're scared I'm going to think this is all too much hard work and eventually just dump you?" I asked, finding my voice again.

"Yes. And I not think I taking that kind of pain, Gulazer. I really not."

I felt the blood rush back to the surface of my skin and the feeling of the cushion beneath me and the cold taint of the draughty room down my neck. Now this was something I could handle. Okay, so we didn't have the luxury of reaching out to each other, but we did have time and words and a screen that wasn't going to freeze.

I recalled then something that Oliver had said to me. It had just been a flippant comment over a morning coffee in İstanbul, but it sprang to life in my mind right now. He'd said, *the imagination can be a powerful thing.*

Maybe Oliver should have said the imagination can be a *dangerous* thing. For just moments ago, having listened to only a few words of what Mesut had to say, I had been ready to jack it all in. Ready to believe that I'd be the one left heartbroken. And for what? For an overactive imagination, that's what.

And so, we spent a good while talking. The hushed tones of our words and the soft murmur of love finally brought us to a goodbye. I think Mesut felt a little better, a little safer. But we both knew, without a shadow of a doubt, that screens and phones would only get us so far.

11

THE VISITOR

"Hello, am I speaking with a Ms Jessica Parker?"

"Yes. You are." Flipping heck, it was just gone seven o'clock and I was truly at one with my sofa and a tube of Pringles when my mobile rang. Pjs on. Dog walked. Dinner demolished. My phone didn't recognise the number so I did a silent wish to the universe that it wasn't a cold call at this hour.

"My name is Danny Pearson and I work for . . ."

"Yes, I know who you are Danny."

"Okay, wonderful." Wonderful? Cheeky sod. "I trust you're feeling better after the recent incident at your previous business's establishment?"

"I'm recovering, thank you." I said, coldly. "How did you get my number, if you don't mind me asking?"

"Well, Ms Parker, it's still on the Firebelly website. Maybe you forgot to take the website down when you terminated the business? An oversight, perhaps?"

Fuck. Had we forgotten to do that? "Yes, well, there was a lot to do once the decision had been made."

"I see. When was the decision made, exactly? To extract a

vital service from this community's already lacking cultural landscape?"

"Look Danny, I don't want to get into this now when it's seven o'clock in the evening and I don't have my business partner with me. I don't actually understand why you're interested anyway. Didn't you get your story when my tiny little dog, apparently 'attacked' Treena Wraith?"

I heard him muffle a sigh at his end. No doubt he wanted to get back to his evening too. He was only human. "The reason I'm calling, actually is that Ms Wraith has gathered together a group of local families who would like answers about why Firebelly is no longer operating. She has invited you and Ms Griffin to her home to talk about it. I'll be there as a neutral observer, of course. She doesn't want any trouble, just a chat over a cup of tea and a plate of biscuits. And no dogs."

I looked down at Dinah, curled up at my feet and her bushy tail twitching in her sleep. "Oh I'm not sure about that. I'd need to speak to Gillie. And really, there's nothing better we can tell her other than what was in the emails we sent out to all of the families before we closed. We even sent the kids home with presents before we closed, Danny – and at our own expense. How many businesses do you know that would have done that?"

"Well, it's points of view like that which will make this an interesting story. Maybe the council will sit up and take notice and sort out new provision. Anyway, she's invited you on Tuesday at four o'clock. Can you make it?"

"I need some time to think about it. I've got your number in my phone now. I'll call you tomorrow." Then I heard a bleep and realised I had a call waiting. Flipping heck, I was popular tonight. "Right, I've got to go. Please don't call me at night again." I jabbed my finger at my phone in an effort to dispel Danny bloody Pearson and find out who else wanted a piece of me. "Erm, hello? Hi?"

"Jess?"

"Er, yeah."

"Cool. It's Jason."

I racked my brains, wanting to get back to my Pringles. Jason? "Okay. Hi."

"Come on Jessica-ca-ca – you can do better than that. It's me, Jason. The arts technician from uni? You texted me a while back, remember? I've got a new number now though."

"Oh shit, of course – Jason!" Bloody hell, it was Jason Reeves, whose name I'd picked at random to send a text to as instructed by the last of Marcus's challenges back in Turkey. Marcus had told me to text him back but I'd never got round to it. It must have been my graduation when we'd last spoken which was bloody yonks ago. "Sorry Jase. You took me by surprise. How the hell are you?"

"Oh I'm fine and dandy my love, fine and dandy. I'm just on a long train journey between jobs – I'm a touring theatre teccie now – and I thought I may as well give you a call while I had some time to spare. How's Jackie boy?"

"Ah well, I'm not sure actually. Okay I think."

"Okay you think?"

I laughed. "It's a long story."

"Well if you've got the time, I've got the time, my love. How's about it?"

If this wasn't a welcome change from a reporter who wanted to hang me and my future out to dry, then I didn't know what was. *Thank you universe. I'll take you up on this one.* "Hang on a minute." I laughed. "If we're going for a proper catch-up then I'm putting the kettle on."

"Tip top," Jason chortled, "let's do it."

———

My cheeks were on fire from laughing so hard, my Scarface wound momentarily forgotten. I'd forgotten what a riot Jason was. I'd always loved being around him back in the day, but back then there had been Jack to think about and he was definitely not Jason's biggest fan. I even had a recollection of once throwing a bag of chips at Jack one cold, rainy night because of the green-eyed monster making itself known out on the street in front of our local pub and all my friends. I mean, Jack *must* have been acting unreasonably if I was willing to part with my chips.

How fantastic then, that I could reclaim this friendship for my own, and to hell with Jack and all the ways I now realised I'd let him hold me back. Life was mine.

And life suddenly felt a load better right now as I coasted out on the open road in my little car. The sky was jet black and the clouds swaddled the stars with generous layers of ruffled violet floss. I had the window slightly open to let in just a gasp of cold November air. While Jason and I had been talking on the phone, he'd realised that the train he was on actually went through the station nearest to my house. "Fuck it, Jessica-ca-ca." He'd said. "What about I just get off the train at Newcastle and we spend a wild night together? I can get on another train in the morning and rock up at work a couple of hours later than planned, no problem."

Well, in the spirit of making my life more in tune with the creative spontaneity I'd got so good at out in Turkey, I thought, *why the hell not?* I was brimming with excitement as I drove to pick Jason up. Yes, I had my scruffy old tartan pyjamas on, and yes, I was driving in my fluffiest-ever slipper boots – but that was all in harmony with doing something unexpected and fun.

Jason whooped with joy when he saw me at the station. "Jessica, my love, I'm liking your new look!" and he lifted me off the ground in a massive bear hug. "But what about your lovely face my dear? What's happened to your cheek?"

"Oh, an occupational hazard. I'll tell you about it later." I said, and waved his hand away. He was exactly as I remembered him. Deliciously on the chunky side of muscular, with wide, smiling lips and sandy-coloured stubble a permanent feature on his ample cheeks. He was as tall as an oak and as strong too. He squeezed the breath right out of me without even realising it.

When we got back to my place, Jason dumped his bags and made a massive fuss of Dinah. "I bloody love dogs," he said, "wish I could get one but I'm on the road so much these days."

"Sounds like a good life though." I said, setting a bottle of lager down in front of him and one for me too. "Seeing so many different places, exploring all those theatres. Don't you enjoy it?"

"Well, kinda. Just been doing it for so long now. You know, there's no point in paying a lot for a flat when I'm hardly ever there, so my place in Manchester is a bit of a dive. Not nice to come home to. Nothing like the set-up you've got here." Jason scanned my living room, taking in the cosy lighting, stripey rugs and plump sofa. "This is just so . . . you. Well," he looked at me with a fondness that flowed into the space between us, "what I remember about you, anyway."

"Yup, same old Jess I think. Just minus Jack and therefore plus a whole lot of other things." I hastily found somewhere else to look. I still felt guilty about how I'd treated Jason back then, as a result of Jack's jealousy. Not exactly gold-star friendship material. "You hungry?"

"Nah, I'm alright actually. Are you?"

"No. Well, I had started these Pringles before I got a random phone call from a random bloke I hardly know."

"Really?" He smirked, treating me to the dimples embedded in his stubbled cheeks. "You wanna watch out for these random blokes, Jessica. You never know what trouble they might get you into . . ." Jason sat down and patted the sofa next to him. I felt a thrill shoot up my spine that lingered and vibrated pleasantly at the very top of my scalp, and then I sat down next to him.

"Don't worry," I said, "I can handle a random bloke."

———

Jason's visit had been a whole lot of fun. He had been nothing but the gentleman I remembered him to be. We'd chatted about our lives and where we were geographically, emotionally, mentally. We talked about what we wanted for the future and what we could do to make those things happen. I told him about my dreams of becoming a writer, and he mused about a life off the road with a wife and kids in a cottage somewhere. He was so easy to talk to and the conversation had flowed as freely as the lager – a welcome change from Turkish-English dictionaries and unreliable phone lines or internet connections.

And yes, I'd told him about my recent trip to Turkey and about Mesut too. He'd been a little bit wobbly on the whole Mesut thing. *"You do know you're gorgeous with or without a fancy Turkish boyfriend, don't you Jess?"* and *"Please make sure you're not just outrunning your past with Jack. You need to run towards yourself, not away from yourself."* In fact, he'd revealed quite a bit about his opinion of Jack which was, as it turned out, as low as low could be. *"You're certainly in a better world without him, my love. He was a controlling little shit. Everything is yours now."*

I couldn't stall him with rubbish answers about the wound on my cheek for much longer either, so I told him all about the trouble Gillie and I had experienced over the closure of Firebelly. "Shit, Jess. What's that woman's problem? It was a private business. You can close it whenever and however you like."

"I know." I agreed. "But that's what happens when your

business is so engaged with the community. You have to give a shit about people. You have to have a social conscience."

"And now she wants to see you and Gillie again? With a reporter in tow? Is this really a drama you need in your life?"

"Probably not. But it's already in my life." I said, rubbing the back of my head where I could still feel a nasty bump. "I wanted a clean break so much but that's just not what I'm getting. I really don't know what to do."

As a distraction from shredding my nerves any further, Jason suggested a movie. We settled for an awful nineties comedy, but one that had been at the height of popularity back when we'd last seen each other so it had a nostalgic feel to it. We giggled our way through it, snuggled on the sofa, with Dinah resting between us, all warm furry limbs and heavy, contented sighs.

When the end credits to the movie started to roll, and just when I thought Jason might be sleeping, I felt him stir softly and whisper ever so quietly, "I think you should go and see that Treena woman and just dazzle her with your loveliness."

"Hah. That didn't seem to work the first time."

"Ah, Jess. How could you fail?" His words trailed sleepily like honey dripping off a spoon. "If it was me, I reckon I'd fall so deep into those ocean eyes there'd be no coming back. And if you smiled? Well, I'd be beaten."

Not knowing quite how to answer this, I just closed my eyes and enjoyed the steadily rising and falling warmth of his chest beneath my head. There was quiet for a while, merely laced with Dinah's pretty little snore and the slight buzz of the TV on standby. I got the feeling that neither of us wanted to say goodnight, worried that the charm of the evening would be shattered upon that very word. So instead I melted into his broad chest and allowed his arm to curl around my waist, his fingertips idly brushing the bare skin of my hip. I could feel his breath on top of my head and knew, without a doubt, that if I lifted my chin, that would be all he needed to kiss me.

I didn't lift my head.

Of course I didn't. After all, it wasn't really Jason's breath I wanted dangerously close to mine. But I have to admit, for a few moments there – maybe even a whole night – it did seem deliciously easy to go that way.

12

THIS MOMENT

"Flipping Heck, I think you might have missed a trick there, Jess." Lindy laughed, whilst tearing up bread to dip into the sauce on her plate. "The possibility of two tasty fellas on the go?"

"God, Lindy, it was so tempting. I mean, I don't know for sure whether Jason was into me or not . . ."

"Into you. Obviously."

"Well, let's say he was, then it would have been delicious, I'm sure. And much easier than trying to forge a relationship with someone so very, very far away in terms of distance, culture, language, religion – everything really. But that's just convenience. Not love." Jess scooped up a final chunk of roasted aubergine and pushed it into her mouth. She sat back and chewed it with all the satisfaction of a toddler downing a jaffa cake, whilst rubbing her hands over her belly. "Woah. I'm stuffed. In the words of Ella, 'give me a push and I'll roll home.'"

Lindy glanced down at her own belly and agreed wholeheartedly. "I'll second that. Although I'm not ready for home yet. This place is far too comfy."

"Isn't it?" Jess yawned. "I could just curl up and have a snooze about now." She fluffed up some cushions behind her and sank slowly into them. They really did have the best spot in the restaurant. The low table, the tea-lights wavering overhead. It was like a little den built just for them. Perfect for bringing the rush of the outside to a slow, sensitive hush.

"Not exactly in the party spirit though, is it?" Lindy commented. "2007 is closing in." She checked the time on her phone. Just over a couple of hours to go. Still no message from her parents.

"I guess not." Jess agreed. "But I'd rather go into 2007 like this than necking some random bloke with lager-breath and singing a song I am actually only miming to."

Lindy giggled. "I know, right? I mean, does anybody actually know the words to 'Auld Lang Syne'? My sister used to make up her own version, something about 'old egg signs' and Quakers being forgotten. We always ripped the piss out of her but she swore blind those were the lyrics."

"How come your sister isn't on holiday with you?" Jess asked.

"She's busy with her family. She's got two kids and another one on the way. Brilliant job. Brilliant fella. You know, all the stuff that keeps you from the desperate act of holidaying with your parents."

"Oh, I wouldn't say it was desperate." Jess commented. "I mean, some people wouldn't even be wise enough to know that's what they needed."

"I'm not entirely convinced it's what I need." Lindy sighed heavily. "Honestly, I don't have a clue what I need. That's the whole problem." She downed her wine and stared at the floor. The patterns on the carpet beneath her feet swirled into a mess of burgundy, blue and green as her eyes started to fill with tears that rose up from nowhere. Jesus. Couldn't she refrain from crying for one sodding night?

Then she felt a gentle warmth against the top of her hand and looked up to see that Jess had taken it. "Hey, you're here now. Be here."

"How?" Lindy sobbed. "How can I be here when all I can do is think about what waits for me back home?"

"That's even better reason to be here now. All these thoughts you're having, even though you haven't told me what they're about, my guess is that they're rooted in your past or they're pushing you into some unknown, scary future." Jess paused and Lindy nodded. "Okay. So all we've ever got, Lindy, all we ever need to be invested in, really, is now. This moment. Take a deep breath. Go on."

Lindy had heard enough this evening to know Jess was for real, and that helped her put her self-consciousness to one side. She did her best to take a deep breath in, shuddering and shaking all the way, and then slowly, gently, out.

"Good. And a few more. Until you feel like you can just allow your breath to be as it is." Lindy breathed steadily and quietly as Jess spoke. "You know, it always comforts me to think that every breath we take is new. Just like every moment is new. The past is shed instantly and we're always moving into newness. Freshness."

"That is, annoyingly, quite a lovely thought." Lindy agreed.

"It is. And it can be a lovely feeling too, the more you practice it."

"Practice it?"

"Yeah." Jess smiled. "I just mean practicing noticing your breath. Sometimes deep breaths in and out help – there's a load of science to prove how nourishing deep breaths are for the body and the mood – but sometimes you don't have to do anything at all. Just watching your breath, getting to know it, in that moment. A moment of stillness in all the chaos, that's just for you."

"Oh, there's chaos, alright."

"Of course there is. That's life. But the chaos we create inside us is often far worse than what's actually going on. Look at me falling down those bloody steps – what an absolute horror story I made out of it. If only I'd remembered that the breath is always there. Constant. Supporting me in all that I do."

"What happened to you *was* a bit of a horror story though, to be fair. You only wanted to get on with your life and somebody chucked you down some concrete steps! Not sure what the breath could have done in those circumstances." Lindy dabbed at her eyes with a paper napkin and sat up straight. She was feeling better already.

"It could have done a lot. Anyway, it wasn't long before I got my chance to try and be all zen about life. I needed an attitude like that if I was going to face the infamous Treena Wraith."

Lindy clapped her hands together and tilted her head to one side. "Oooh, nice one. I was hoping you'd take her and her cronies up on their offer. Come on then, spill it."

"Honestly? You really still give a shit? Haven't you got better things to do on New Year's Eve?" Jess had a lively smile tugging at her lips, freckles highlighting the joy behind them. She was as happy to have found a new friend as Lindy was.

"Jess." Lindy said. "Look at me. Sitting here. Giving all the shits. Now please, for the love of Turkish beaches and camp fires and starry nights and excellent restaurants and warm, white bread that is truly sent from the angels above, just bloody well get on with it."

13

THE WRAITH HOUSEHOLD

Gillie shivered in her swooping, floor-length velveteen coat then buried her chin and cheeks into the sumptuous purple depths of the cashmere scarf wrapped around her neck. "I can't believe you talked me into this." She mumbled. "Why can't we just leave things alone?"

I unbolted the garden gate and there was an ominous creak as I pushed it open. I motioned for Gillie to go first and she stepped into the weed-ridden yard with a sigh. "Because we need to sort this so we can bloody well get on with our lives, okay? I'm sick of being held back. Watch your step, sweets. It's like dog-poo roulette in here."

We picked out a clean path to the front door and Gillie pushed the doorbell. "Fine." She huffed. "But you're doing the talking."

As soon as the doorbell shrilled out, a commotion could be heard on the other side of the battered door. Judging by the loud, overlapping voices we could hear, the Wraith household was currently hosting quite a lot of people who had quite a lot of opinions about what to do next.

"Answer it!"

"Tell them to fuck off!"

"We've got no milk!"

"They can let themselves in."

"I'm not getting it, you bloody get it!"

"Cheek of it, actually turning up on the doorstep."

Gillie and I glanced at each other and gulped. "Ah, so you're getting the inaugural Wraith welcome, I hear. Usually lasts at least three minutes before anybody comes to the door." We spun round to see a short, squat man in a coat almost as impressive as Gillie's, a camera round his neck and a folder under his arm. He was grinning wildly, and seemed completely at ease with his surroundings, even though his upmarket attire would have suggested otherwise. "Good afternoon ladies, I'm . . ."

"Danny bloody Pearson." Gillie and I both finished for him.

He chuckled and dipped his sandy, balding head. "My reputation precedes me. Let's get this done then, shall we?" He leaned past us both and rapped a very particular rhythm on the door, even though the great debate about whether to let us in was still going on.

"I kna that knock!" A woman shrieked. "Pearson! Get yer arse in 'ere!"

At that, Danny turned the handle, opened the door, and stepped into the immediate vicinity of a cold, dark kitchen and strode over to the kettle. "Come on, Treena!" He hollered. "Let's get the kettle on for your guests. I've got a five thirty over at the rugby club so I've got to wrap this up."

"Wrap it up?" Treena appeared in the doorway with a sleepy-looking baby on her hip. The flickering light of the TV from the room behind lit her edges so that she glowed like an apparition. A sliver of something ran down my spine. "I'm not rushin' this Pearson. S'important." She chucked her chin at Gillie and I as we stood, awkwardly by the kitchen sink, which was about as good a welcome as we were going to get. "You two can 'ave a cuppa s'pose. Pearson, ye kna where everything's at. Mine's strong wi' loadsa sugars." She snapped back round and headed into her living room then hollered back at him over her shoulder, "And ye can make cuppas for ev'ryone in 'ere 'n' all, Pearson."

Danny's hands flew over all the tea-making paraphernalia and he had several cups of tea and coffee brewed up in no time. "You come here often then, Danny?" Gillie asked, taking a cracked mug of coffee from him.

"Well, let's just say that Ms Wraith is a local resident actively invested in the best for her community. And I'm the community reporter so . . ."

"So she gets whatever she bloody well likes in the papers?" Gillie asked as she turned to make her way through to the living room, dragged by the hand by Kaylee who had appeared about the time the custard creams were opened. Kaidan was now dragging me too, two biscuits hanging out of his mouth like a naughty puppy. I felt strangely reassured by the presence of the children. Like they were somehow going to take our side and recognise the years of hard graft we'd put into working with them. Maybe a few words of commendation from these kids and I could glide on out of this house with a clear record and the Wraith family blessing.

"So, yous two. I'm on me best be'aviour cos, well, the bairns 'n' all that." Treena was sitting on the edge of her grey leather couch, jiggling her baby on her knee whilst slurping the tea Danny had made. There were six other mums sitting next to and around her as if she was a queen on a throne and they were her ladies-in-waiting. Except there were fags hanging out of mouths, tuts uttered incessantly and whispered swear words cutting through the smoke that swirled across the room. Gillie and I sat on plastic garden chairs in the corner and held our drinks tightly. Danny stood in the kitchen doorway, still decked out in his ridiculous coat, pen poised over notepad. There were also kids everywhere – crouched, kneeling, sitting, slack-jawed and wide-eyed, waiting to see what kind of a show the adults were going to put on. A shaggy haired dog was licking its arse in the corner with more enthusiasm than I would have thought possible in this heavy, expectant atmosphere.

"Well? Ye ganna tell us what's what or do I 'ave to take me hair straighteners to yer front door again?" Treena drawled and all the other mums laughed. "Come on man, this is yer chance like."

Must not point out she's a mad woman. Must not point out she's a mad woman. I repeated to myself before beginning. "Firstly, Gillie and I are really sorry to hear how upset you are about Firebelly closing. We knew it would be a bit of a let down to a few people so we did the best we could to soften the blow and give as much notice as possible."

"Bit of a let down?" One woman sneered over her mug of tea. "My bairns were in tears when they couldn't get in to do their colouring-in."

"It was a bit more than colouring in . . ." Gillie protested.

"What we mean to say is," I cut in, "we know your children loved coming to visit the centre. And we loved having them there. But unfortunately certain circumstances in our lives mean that it's not feasible for us to continue with the business as it is. And Firebelly wasn't financially sustainable so we couldn't carry on I'm afraid."

"I bloody knew it would be down to the money." Treena wailed. "It's always about fuckin' money. Couldn't ye just get a grant or summat? We'd've been behind ye, wouldn't we lasses?" Treena turned to her cronies and there were nodding heads all round. I could suddenly see what a powerful weapon it might have been if I'd met Treena Wraith several years earlier and gotten her on side.

"That's so kind," I continued, "but we've spent the last seven years accessing all the grants we were eligible for and it just came to a point where there was no more funding for arts-based projects. Plus, as I said, Gillie and I have other commitments. So those two things combined just meant that we couldn't keep going."

"Got a fancy new job, 'ave ye?" One of the mums catapulted these words at me as she comforted the baby she was holding with a dummy and a kiss on the forehead. "Nobody stays roond 'ere for very long in the end."

"I'm born and bred here as it happens." I smiled. "And no, there's no fancy new job for either of us, is there Gillie?" Gillie shook her head and looked down at the floor.

"So what's these 'other commitments' then?" Treena asked. "What can be more importan' than the bairns in this village and keeping 'em safe? Yer really telling us that yer 'appy to see 'em out on the streets wi' nowt to do like? Yer sittin' there eating *my* custard creams 'n' tellin' me that yer 'other commitments' are more importan' than me own kids? What am I meant to do with 'em now? Born and bred my arse. I'll give ye fuckin' born and bred . . ."

Treena shifted forwards and practically chucked her baby into another mum's waiting arms. She clattered down her mug of tea and rolled up her sleeves, eyeballing me the entire time. Gillie gripped my arm, digging her nails in so that I winced.

"Now, now, Treena. We don't want any repeats of the other day, do we?" Danny droned and she stopped in her tracks. "My headlines have been kind to you in the past and we don't want to change that, do we? I suggest you settle back down and listen to what the ladies have to say."

I rode the waves of Danny's quite brilliant interruption. "Treena. I'm telling the truth. Gillie and I loved working with your kids – we did it for years, and if I'm totally honest, it was at a financial cost to ourselves and the company. We never made any money from the arts clubs at the centre. We did it because we love this community and I grew up here myself and would have loved something like Firebelly when I was Kaidan and Kaylee's age. It was our other projects in schools and across the region that helped keep the business going. At least for a while. What school did you go to?"

Treena blinked. "Wha?"

"What school did you go to, Treena? Just tell me."

"Budhill High."

"Okay. I went to Ashton Comp. Just down the road. We had a German teacher who used to teach at both schools. Mrs Rennett. Do you remember her?" All the women on the couch started nodding, lips snarling at the memory.

"Ginger witch." Treena laughed. "She once said summat so awful abou' me da they 'ad to drag us off 'er. Nearly 'ad 'er eyes oot."

I nodded, trying to build some kind of rapport whilst not condoning violence against teachers. "Yeah. She was a piece of work, wasn't she? And we had joint sports days, didn't we? I even went on a residential with kids from your school once. And your school fairs were the best. Didn't you have a fancy food technology department or something? I remember buying some amazing doughnuts with white chocolate bits on them."

"What's yer point?" Treena drawled, although licking her lips at the mention of the doughnuts.

"My point is that I'm a local lass like you and all I ever wanted was to build something good in the community. But I'm human, Treena, also like you, and I didn't understand that one day I'd have to decide between my life and the business. You know what I chose. I know you don't like it. But Gillie and I aren't going back on it and we really think we did the best we could to inform parents and children."

"Okay. I s'pose I get it. But we 'eard nowt. And now we're stuck wi' the bairns ev'ry night climbin' the walls wi' nowt to do."

"I understand." I smiled. "Gillie?" Gillie reached into her impressive shoulder bag, dug out a few tissue-wrapped parcels and put them in a pile in the middle of the floor. "We brought these art packs for Kaidan and Kaylee and all their friends to get out when they're bored. Should keep them entertained for a while. And we know that, for whatever reason, you missed out on the original emails and letters home about the close of Firebelly. So, we've also made up info packs for all of you and any other parents you feel might need more explanation. Can I leave them with you, Treena? You could hand them out if people ask."

"S'pose." She grumbled, but there was a twitch of a smile on her mouth. She enjoyed being put in charge.

Gillie rose and started handing out the packs to the mums whilst the kids pounced like tigers on the art parcels on the floor. Suddenly there was torn tissue and crafty bits everywhere. The creative chaos started to calm my nerves. "In the info packs you'll find a whole list of other local clubs and services for young people. We know they're not exactly like Firebelly – and probably not as cheap either, but we have had words with the council to see if they can drop some of the costs. They're totally on board with it and trying to do that. It was the best we could get from them."

Treena allowed her baby to chew on the plastic folder holding her info pack as she tried to find the right words. "Okay, well, I'm startin' to think I needn't 'av took me hair straighteners to yer door."

"It's okay. It's not our door anymore."

"And maybes, well, maybes yer dog was just lookin' out for ye. Maybes I needn't 'av spivved out so much. Soz, like, that ye were in 'ospital like."

"It's okay. No harm done." I smiled and mentally brushed my injuries under the carpet. The Scarface thing would be a good story for my future grandkids. "Now. Shall I go and put the kettle on again whilst you look through the packs? Then Gillie and I can answer any questions that you might have before we leave." I stood and dashed into the kitchen before anybody could stop me. I needed a breather and it was Gillie's turn to hold fort.

I was filling the kettle and staring through the greasy metal blinds out of the kitchen window as I reflected on what had just happened. I really hoped I'd managed to diffuse the situation. If I could just look, for a second, beyond the flailing fists and psycho-eyes, I could see a mum that genuinely wanted the best for her kids. I remembered Kaidan and Kaylee as being sweet little things, really, so she can't have been that bad. I just hoped now that she could move past this and leave Gillie and I to get on with the next chapter in our lives.

After setting the kettle down and flicking it on to boil, I heard that ugly shriek of the gate opening in the yard. I peered through the blinds again and saw a woman, hunched against the cold, hurrying towards the house. Hopefully not another angry mum to deal with.

Rather than hearing a knock, I saw the door fling open and the woman swept in bringing the unwanted threat of ice with her. She chatted as she twirled into the doorway, already taking off her coat and shaking it out like a red flag to a bull. "Jesus, Treena, it's brass monkeys out there. Right, I've been to see your dad and . . ."

Then she looked up and her eyes locked with mine. The realisation that I wasn't Treena clouded, then cleared her wide grey eyes and she brought her hand to her mouth with a little gasp. I hadn't seen this woman for over a decade but I knew instantly who it was. We both stood stock still and the air in the kitchen lay thick and flat against our inert bodies. "Well, hello Jessica. Fancy meeting you here."

My gut sifted through a thousand memories like wet sand turned to sludge. *Come on Jess, compose yourself.* I found the words and summoned a smile. "Hello Sandra."

"Little Jessica Parker." Sandra said, clasping her hands at her chest. "Eee haddaway and shite. I can't believe you're standing in front of me. What on earth are you doing here? In our Treena's kitchen like?"

Sandra was slightly shorter than the last time I'd seen her, or maybe it was just that she was stooped a little. The tight pencil skirt and flouncy blouse I used to admire so much in the eighties were absent and instead she wore a grey jersey dress with thick black tights over a figure sporting jolly curves and soft lines. No high heels either. She wore chunky brown boots with patterned woollen socks folded over the top. She still had awesome skin, streaked as it was now with lines and wrinkles.

"Erm, well, she kind of attacked me a few days ago Sandra. Then she invited me here to sort it all out. Which I think we've done now."

"Eee, you're not the lass who fell down them community centre steps are you?"

"I am." I said. "But like I said, all sorted now. Anyway, how are you? I haven't seen you in ages. Wait til I tell my mam that

I've seen you." I busied myself with cups and spoons and tea bags as Sandra spoke.

"Well pet, I'm totally canny thanks. It has been a long time, hasn't it? And how's your Max? He was such a canny little lad what with all his freckles and red hair and cheekiness. Eee, it's funny, isn't it? Because you know the bairns you look after are gonna grow up eventually and all that but when you've got one in front of you. Well, it's all just a bit of a shock like."

"Yes, I'm all grown up now." I chuckled, wondering why the chuckle didn't sound more convincing. Sandra had never been anything but nice to me when she used to be our childminder. To me, she was the epitome of glamour and I was always totally in awe of her diets and her clothes and her perfumes and her magazines. "Do you still childmind then, Sandra?" I asked.

"Not likely, pet. Once you and Max grew up I decided to pack it in like and start a family of my own. It never quite happened unfortunately, but me and my husband, Luke, we did alright just the two of us in the end. Here, you'll never guess what I do now Jessica." Sandra looked over her shoulder as if she was about to share a secret with me. There were voices coming from the living room starting to shout for the next round of cuppas but we both ignored them. She set down her coat on the kitchen table and took a few steps closer. Her cheeks were high and smiling, her shoulders drawn up in excitement. It was really quite cute. "These days, pet, I'm a hypnotherapist."

"Woah. I did not expect you to say that."

"You wouldn't!" She laughed, clapping her hands together. "When you knew me I was chip-frying extraordinaire! Champion of trimming fingernails! Hair de-tangling genius! But well love, there comes a time when a woman needs a change in direction and that was mine."

"Well you look good for it." I said, meaning it totally. "I

knew it was you straight away but Sandra, you do look different."

"And you too pet, you too."

I suddenly remembered where I was. In a dank, cold kitchen I'd never been in before, making tea for people I didn't even know. "But Sandra, how come you're here? I'm hoping Treena didn't chuck you down the community centre steps as well?"

Sandra laughed but shifted nervously in her boots. The enthusiasm of telling me about her new vocation slipped silently away with the question I'd just asked. "Well, love, do you remember Trev?"

That slither down my spine I'd felt earlier when I'd seen Treena, suddenly came back again. And this time it held tighter.

So that was his name. That bloody awful, mean and horrible man who Sandra used to bring home sometimes. He was her boyfriend for a while and somebody I had to put up with whether I liked it or not. Even at such a young age, I'd never understood what she saw in him with his yellow teeth and his crooked face and his jabbing, bony fingers.

"I'd forgotten his name but yes, Sandra, I really do remember him."

"Aye pet. I remember he used to give you a hard time. But you just being a bairn at the time you won't understand, love. The man had problems. Far deeper problems than even I knew, only being a twenty-something year old myself, and being lured in by a bit of charm and fancy talking. Anyway, the drink got hold of him. He was – is – an alcoholic."

"You still know him?" I asked, praying she'd given him the boot by now. Didn't she just mention a husband?

"Yes, pet. We split up years ago, when I was still looking after you bairns, in fact, but I couldn't walk away completely. That's hard to do with someone in the pits like him." Sandra stared downwards at the cracked lino for a few seconds, her eyebrows drew together in a peak and her lips pinched together. Then she gave herself a little shake and looked right at me. "Anyway, I made him a promise a lot of years ago – when he was at his darkest – that I'd always help look after his family when he wasn't able to. So here I am."

Just then Treena sauntered into the kitchen and spotted Sandra. "Mammy Sandy! Aw, ta for comin' over. Ye getting a brew?" She'd delivered a huge smack of a kiss on Sandra's cheek and gestured to me like I was kitchen staff. "Ye bringin' them teas in or wot?"

"Oi, cheeky!" Sandra said, swatting Treena on the backside. "You don't speak to your guests like that. I knew Jessica a long time ago. I used to look after you and your brother, didn't I, love?"

I nodded and was also vaguely aware that I might look like I was trying to work out an incredibly complex maths problem. "Yes. You did."

"And this here," Sandra continued, popping an arm around Treena's waist and hugging her close, "is Trev's daughter. Treena. But you already know her."

"Trev's daughter?"

"Ye kna me Da?" Treena asked, gawping slightly. "How do ye kna me Da?"

How on earth did I answer that question? *Oh well, Treena, he used to stab me in the belly with his car keys and call me 'Fattie'. He used to force me to run around the garden and he laughed out loud when I got too breathless to carry on. He used to pin me down with his knees and slap his hands all over my tummy, saying he was playing the bongos and that it was just a game when all the time there were tears in my eyes and my arms hurt under his weight.*

But I didn't fancy enduring the wrath of Treena Wraith

again so I just said, "Sandra used to bring him to our house sometimes."

"Oh. Right." Treena seemed relieved. She turned to Sandra. "Have ye seen our Da today then, Mammy Sandy? Is 'e alreet?" The two women looked at me, did their best to smile, then huddled their heads together so that I couldn't hear what was said next. I turned back to the teas and the coffees and found that it was hard to see what I was doing on account of new, hot tears brimming in my eyes. I felt a presence at my shoulder and noticed a ripple of purple cashmere at my side. Gillie.

"Hey beaut. What's going on in here?"

"Gillie, can we make our excuses? I need to leave."

"Of course we can. I'm more than ready to go. You okay?"

I sniffed back the tears and stared down at my hands which were making mechanical movements over the cups and mugs. "Put it this way, I think Treena Wraith chucking me down those steps was the least of my worries."

15

CHOICES QUEEN

Hey Jessica-ca-ca. Top night the other night. Can't thank u enough for putting me up. When do I get to see those ocean eyes again then? J. x

Flipping heck. Was it really okay for friends to reference each other's eyes like that? And a kiss? What did that mean?

"Let me see that!" Ella snatched my phone off me, a massive grin shining from her lips. "You're not pulling that *'what-the-fuck'* face for nothing, I presume?" She leaned back onto the weathered steel ridge and the gigantic curves of red copper arced behind her, making the amethyst-silver streaks in her hair appear even more vibrant.

We'd nipped off the A1 after a long, woodland dog walk in the rain and had settled at one of my favourite places to enjoy the winter sunshine that was now breaking through the clouds. We sat on the metallic dome of the feet of the Angel of the North – a twenty-metre high sculpture of a huge human form with outstretched arms that morphed unquestionably into aeroplane wings. It was designed by artist, Antony Gormley and was built while I'd been away at uni in 1998, supposedly symbolising human hopes and fears as well as the transition from the industrial to the information age. I just loved it. It had been the cause of massive controversy when it had first been commissioned, but now I loved that it had established its place as a cultural icon for the North East. A disarming, gargantuan emblem that embraced newcomers with its solid, weighty presence. Gillie and Ella could never understand why I wanted to spend time here. "Once you've seen a colossal rusty bloke with a pert bum and an aeronautical mutation, you don't need to see it again." Ella had quipped as we'd swung off the motorway. But she smiled anyway, in a way that told me Gormley's Angel was finally winning her over.

Our walk in the woods had been glorious despite – or maybe because of – the stubborn drizzle that eventually turned into a downpour. With the company of sodden, drooping branches and squelching footsteps on the spongy, leaf-ridden ground, I'd updated Ella on the things that had happened since I'd left hospital. She had a tendency to disappear for days at a time into her garden shed / puppet-making workshop – especially when she had ideas for new puppet characters. Then she'd emerge into the world again, blinking and smiling and asking what she'd missed. Well, at least there was something to tell her.

After getting drenched, we'd figured it was our god-given right to now enjoy the sunshine so we'd grabbed creamy coffees at a scran van in the car park and now lolled on the Angel's feet whilst the dogs ran off yet more energy in the fields below. Tourists milled around us, oohing and aahing and – quite frankly – also scratching their heads in confusion as they stared up at the Angel, whose head skimmed the drifting clouds. There were always tourists around the Angel. It was something I'd come to expect whenever I visited here. And now I was used to being featured in their holiday snaps so Ella and I kept chatting as if we had all the privacy in the world. And she wasn't letting me escape that text from Jason.

"Ooooh, ocean eyes, eh? Jess, did you tell me everything that happened the other night or what? How did he get close enough for you to bewitch him with those lamps of yours?"

"It was only a cuddle." I huffed. "Like I said, we caught up, we reminisced about uni days and watched a movie. It's been so many years, Ella."

"Blah, blah, blah Jess Parker. You know perfectly well what I'm fishing for." She winked at me and her eyebrow piercings glinted with just as much exuberance.

"I do, and I'm afraid you'll be sorely disappointed Ella, because NOTHING happened."

Ella leaned forward and inspected my face. "Hmmm. Okay, I believe you. But he obviously wanted it to. And there's something else going on in there, isn't there, lovely lady?" She prodded in the direction of my heart with her little balsa wood coffee spoon. "Care to share?"

I sighed heavily as the frivolity of the story of me and Jason started to fade. After seeing Sandra recently, and discovering Treena's connection with Trev who was, basically, a seven-year-old girl's living nemesis, I'd been feeling extremely uneasy. Memories that had stayed buried for so many years were stubbornly resurfacing and bringing with them an icy blanket of self-doubt. I suddenly wondered if every relationship I'd ever had with a man had been built on some rocky dynamic of the push of male ego against the pull of my insecurities.

"I don't know what it is, Ella. My heart has been through so much this year. Just when I thought things were clearing, all this crap with Trev gets dragged up. I knew that Treena was familiar – my mam knew it too – but I didn't expect to basically have a childhood trauma thrown at me in her shitty little kitchen. I can't believe that a whole twenty-one years later and his bloody daughter is carrying on his efforts to destroy my character."

"Nobody could destroy your character, sweet pea – it's far

too strong for that. And anyway, from what I hear, and from the write-up in today's paper, you totally bossed the meeting with Treena. But yes, I can imagine that suddenly seeing Sandra again must have been a bit of a shock."

"It was." I felt a tremor in my voice and grabbed the steel ridges either side of me, letting them hold me steady. "What if every man who's ever paid attention to me, I've just snapped them up because I'm so scared no-one else will show any interest? Is that why I stayed with Jack for a whole seven years when deep down I probably knew it was all a bit toxic? These things start when you're young, don't they? Trev was such a dick to me. I can see that now. But what if there's a complex little piece of my soul that doesn't know any better and just makes all the wrong choices?"

"Are you kidding me?" Ella stared, swatting me on the arm and letting out a weird bark of laughter. "You've been the Choices Queen so far this year. Number one, you did not take Jack up on his crappy offer of moving into the city and into a loveless relationship. Number two, you decided not to compromise your life for a business that was doomed."

"Okay, okay. I get it."

"Nope. Not done." Ella stuck her coffee spoon against my now-closed lips and held it there with her index finger, instantly making all the milling tourists' holiday snaps even more bizarre. "Number three, you chose to go to the mystical land of Turkey so you could figure out your life's purpose rather than rot away in your own self-pity. Number four, you gave up a lot of sexy action with a proper tasty giant Turkish waiter in order to give your soul the space to speak. Number five, you chose to listen to your heart and follow your dream of being a writer and number six, you got it on with a bloke who scared you half to death on account of the mystifying likelihood you might have known him in a past life. Now," She finally took her finger off the spoon and I rubbed my lips into a smile, "does that sound like somebody who makes all the wrong choices to you?"

"Possibly not."

"Don't let the memory of that total pig stop you from being you, Jess. You've come way too far." She motioned towards my coffee cup. "Get that down your neck. There's nothing coffee can't solve. And anyway, if that were the case, you'd have jumped into bed with 'Ocean-Eyes-Boy'. At least, I'm assuming he didn't manage to drag you into the shower for a steamy sex sesh the next morning to make up for all the vanilla hugging on the couch the night before?"

"No he bloody didn't! In the morning I just took him to the station and that was that."

"Disappointing." Ella whined.

Truth be known, before leaving me to get on his train, Jason had gently cupped my face in his hands and fixed me with a fierce stare that I'd never seen on him before. Then he'd ducked in for a kiss but I'd swerved at the last minute so he hit my cheek instead. After that he'd rewarded me with nothing but honest-to-god friendliness in his eyes and his next hug had flooded me with a sense of real tenderness. "It does feel a bit weird though, Ella. I mean, Jason is somebody who I would have totally considered if Jack hadn't been in the picture. I realise that now. But I was far too busy tip-toeing around Jack to even notice there might have been other options. Oh god, what have I been missing out on all these years because of a lack of confidence derived from my verbally-abused seven-year-old self?"

"Now, now." Ella wagged a finger at me. "Let's not dwell on the past. Because what I really want to know is . . . is Jason fit or what?"

"Ella! I absolutely refuse to sink to your entirely shallow and morally-deprived motivations in this conversation." She pouted dramatically and yet more of her facial piercings dazzled me into submission. "Okay, yes, yes, he's totally lush."

"I knew it!" She declared, fist-pumping to her heart's content. "So why didn't you just bloody well snog him?"

"I don't know. Something stopped me. He's so warm and cheery and just bloody lovely. And he's at a point in his life where he wants to settle down. That's kind of appealing, you know? God, sometimes I do wish I'd known him better at uni but it was much less stress just to keep him at a distance. Jack's wrath was too much."

"Sounds like Jack had a reason to be wary."

"Wary doesn't even cover it." I said, remembering the bag-of-chips episode and the police stopping me in the middle of a damp, blackened street to make sure I was alright. If only I'd said no and let the policeman tell Jack to do one, I might not have had to go through seven more years of handling his insecurities.

"Okay, darling," Ella said, fixing me with one of her serious looks. Rare as they were, I knew what this meant. Honesty time. "Who do you really see in your life? Jason or Mesut?"

It took less than a heartbeat. "Mesut."

Ella grinned and rocked back and tipped her head to laugh up towards the Angel. "There you go, you nutcase. No need to fret."

"I so know it's Mesut, Ella. Even if he's thousands of miles away, I can feel him in everything I do."

"Lucky bitch." She quipped. "Seriously though, that's why Jason didn't get any action."

"Exactly. So why am I feeling like this? Agitated? Uncertain? Maybe even scared?"

"Fucked if I know. There's probably a few things going on. You're totally freaked by remembering this Trev bloke and his voice might still be strong somewhere in your psyche."

"Tick."

"And it sounds like you're worried that the way he made you feel as a little girl then went on to inform all your other relationships."

"Tick again."

"And, sweet pea, you're regretting the way your love for Jack made you behave and, perhaps, opportunities you might have missed out on. Jason was one of those opportunities."

"Tick and tick and tick."

"All this stuff though Jess – and by the way, it's YOU who's taught me this over the last eleven months – it's in the past. Leave it there. You're here now, breathing. Being. Sitting on an angel's feet for god's sake! You're kicking total ass. And Mesut – bearing in mind I don't even know the bloke aside from his exceptional pinacoladas – Mesut is in your future. I can feel it in my bones."

"I can feel it in mine too. Fucking hell, you're an exceptional friend, did you know that?"

"Naturellement." She winked. "Now, next item on the agenda is Gillie and what the hell she thinks she's doing with that fuckwit Demir. Agreed?"

"Agreed." I said. "But for that, I believe we will need another latté."

16

OYALAMA

"How much?" Gillie shrieked down the phone at me.

"The normal daily rate plus travel expenses." I said, firmly.

"Each?" She further shrieked.

"Each." I said, satisfied I had her hooked before I dropped the real bombshell.

"Woah, Jess. This has suddenly made things a whole lot easier."

"You're telling me." I smiled into the phone. "It's not set in stone yet though. We have to write a proposal and go for an induction meeting."

"Brilliant. Absolutely, arse-tinglingly brilliant. Jess Parker, you have made my day."

"Okay, but, well, it's not so much me that's tingled your arse. It's actually, well . . . really . . . in fact . . ."

Gillie sighed, knowingly. "Come on then. Spit it out. What's the catch?"

"The catch? Well, it's Oliver."

Silence.

And then, "What the fuck?"

"Yes, I know. Apparently he recommended us to a friend of

his who is a big boss lady at this youth organisation – he knows them in his capacity as a photographer – and they were looking for someone to deliver an arts project. And Oliver thought, who better than us? Next thing you know I'm getting an email and then a phone call and next week a meeting and it all looks like it's going to happen and we're not going to be skint, Gillie, we're not going to be skint!"

That really was the key message here. And I needed Gillie to focus on that rather than the fact that Oliver was involved. Neither of us had seen him since she dumped him in the rustic mountains of Cappadocia and I had been starting to wonder if we would, in fact, ever see his lovely face again. Even as a result of this work opportunity, I still hadn't actually seen him, just noticed his presence on the back-end of an email.

Bless him, wherever he was, he knew that we'd be looking for work about now and he had done his best to make sure we got this project. A project that lasted six months and a hint more beyond that. That man, I thought for the umpteenth time this year, was an angel in disguise.

By the time I got off the phone to Gillie I had managed to convince her that Oliver had no ulterior motive (which I had absolutely no idea about), and that he wouldn't just appear out of nowhere and try to win her back (which I also had absolutely no idea about). But, there were higher things at stake here, like a mortgage and food shopping and electricity bills. And why was she so bothered anyway? It's not like she couldn't handle herself, she'd certainly proved that in Turkey. I had a suspicion it might have something to do with a certain devilishly handsome someone with gleaming, pointy shoes, gelled back hair and a sharp Turkish tongue. But she wasn't going to actually tell me that now, was she?

———

It was seven o'clock on a Friday night and I was sitting at the desk in my spare room, staring at the splintery, scratchy patterns of ice forming across the window. The jet black sky outside allowed the tiny, shimmering crystals to glow whiter than they probably were. The North East winter was here and it wasn't messing about.

It was so quiet. Dinah was curled happily at my feet, shrinking and expanding her furry mass with each breath. I'd been sitting here for quite some time now, drinking a practical vat of hot chocolate under the warm white glow of the fairy lights I had so hoped would inspire my writing. But sadly, they weren't working. This horror story idea was well and truly beating me into submission and writer's block was now taking the absolute piss.

I wanted to burn off some of this energy that had been building over the last week or so. I wasn't in the mood for painting, and besides, I already had several canvases of my Turkish hot air balloon ride scattered all over the room. What, exactly, I was going to do with them remained to be seen.

Shit, it was hard being creative sometimes. I needed to do something normal like watch a box-set or walk the dog or eat an actual meal. Fuck all that though. I just didn't feel like it.

I'd already spoken to Mesut that day – only on the phone which made it easy to evoke the rich vibration of his voice. *"You not yourself, Gulazer. I knowing that."* Yes, he did know that. I had to remember that he knew me better than I could even comprehend. *"I think you needing 'oyalama', I think you say, 'distraction'? Do something different. Is good for you."*

Right. A distraction. I looked again at the ice on the window and shuddered at the thought of going outside. But then I looked down at the flimsy little top I was wearing, riding up over my waistline and realised it was nowhere near the proper attire for a winter in the north east of England. "I need new clothes." I whispered to myself.

I'd been putting this off for a while on account of the potential shit-fit I might get myself into, but basically, I needed bigger clothes. When Jack had dicked off earlier in the year, I'd lost weight at an alarming rate because I hadn't been able to entertain the notion of food. Nobody had really said anything, because, well, that's the typical thing, isn't it? Girl loses boy, girl finally achieves the figure she's always wanted despite being desperately sad and chucks out all her old massive clothes to buy new, tiny ones. I think most people assumed / hoped I'd be back to my old, solid self once I'd moved through the heartbreak.

And they were right. I knew really that it wasn't worth trying to maintain the flatter, leaner version of me at the cost of actually being happy. But that didn't mean that gaining some weight hadn't hurt me in its own way. I'd never quite made it into a bikini whilst I'd been in Turkey but I had made it into the most incredible man's bed, and, if anything, I think he'd have been happy with even more to grab onto.

So with that in mind I decided to go shopping. Yes, it was a Friday evening and high streets shops were shut now. But the lord didn't create the twenty-four hour supermarket for nothing now, did he? Plus I'd just found out I was going to be working and have a bit of an income – so a few quid on a couple of Tesco's bargain jumpers couldn't hurt.

When I got to the shop I was alarmed at how busy it was. Didn't people have a better place to be on a Friday night? As I looked around me and clocked everyone chucking multi-packs of lager, boxes of tasteless wine, massive sharing bags of Doritos and sacks of chocolate treats into their trolleys, I mused that staying in was most definitely the new going out.

I made my way to the frostily-lit ladieswear section and gazed at the rows of ribbed, fluffy, padded and fleecy garments predominantly in shades of brick brown and navy blue. Jeez. Where were the rainbow colours when you needed them?

I trailed my hands over the hangers of a selection of cute little blue sweaters with stars on them. They were playful but also kind of moody – a perfect embodiment of my current state. I had to have one. I trailed my fingertips across the size eights, the size tens, the size twelves and knew that if I was being honest with myself, I needed to keep going. *Fuck Jess, it's just a number. What's the big deal?*

I picked up one I thought might fit and found a full-length mirror that hung next to the handbags. I held it up against my body and checked that the colour would suit me. Yep. The deepness of the blue brought out the creaminess of my skin and the little stars just made me smile. Nice.

Just then a gang of lads pushed past me, hugging packs of lager with huge packets of crisps piled high on top. They were typical Geordie lads in that they were making far more of a scene than was anywhere near necessary, booming their voices out over the spaces between them, bumping into racks of clothes, swearing profusely and punching each other hard for no apparent reason. But when they pushed past me, a couple of them stopped and looked me up and down.

They were right in the way of the mirror I'd just been looking into so I hastily moved and pretended to look at the handbags. But not before I'd seen the look in their eyes. Judgement. Scorn. Amusement.

They moved off, laughing, before I could even begin to blush. They disappeared into their world of lager and snacks and swearing and the constant threat of emasculation and I was left clutching a top that would never do, holding a handbag I didn't even like and fighting back tears that really belonged to a seven year old.

Ye'll never get that t-shirt over that belly ye stupid little thing.

It's like a beer keg, that is. Oi! Sandra! Come 'n' see this little shite thinkin' she's Cindy fucking Crawford. We'll 'ave to get ye a bin bag luv!

How could his voice be so strong in my mind? The memory so vivid like a movie? I'd not thought about this man in years and now he was back in full force which was something I had not signed up for.

I dumped the starry jumper, grabbed a couple of black polo necks and packs of comfy knickers and practically sprinted to the checkout. I had memories to outrun.

17

PERFECT

I just couldn't figure my mother out.

Like, ever.

As long as I could remember she had flitted between the roles of stony-faced, Glaswegian legend who wielded her crossword skills like a weapon and whose microwave meal obsession was alarming. But then, on another day, she'd be singing love songs whilst pruning the roses and rolling out her soft, gentle wisdom as effortlessly as waves break on the shore.

Tonight she was the former. And there I was, stood in her kitchen watching her hunched at the microwave and listening to the sound of my youth: the startling and repetitive stab of a metal fork in the taut plastic wrap of a tray of seaside pie. Stab, stab, stab. It was almost comforting.

"So let's see what you bought at Tesco's then?" She asked, twirling around to face me after slamming shut the microwave door and pressing a button to begin its monotonous thrum. "Och Jessie, you look like you've seen a ghost. Did you spend a wee bit too much on your credit card or something? I know they've got a two-for-one on those big winter knickers at the minute."

I sighed and dumped my Tesco bag on her table. I did buy

some of those knickers. How did she *know*? Dad was watching some car review drivel on the telly next door so I had Mam to myself for a minute. Or at least until the seaside pie pinged.

"Yes, I got some. And a couple of black tops. But Mam, do you remember you said you thought you recognised the name 'Wraith'?"

"I do. Still haven't figured that one out."

"Well I think I have. When I went to Treena's house on Tuesday, to sort out the total mayhem over Firebelly, I ran into somebody I haven't seen in ages."

"Did you, love? Who was it?" She got a giant jar of Hellman's out of the fridge – standard issue for all of my mother's meals.

"Sandra. Who used to look after us when you and Dad were at work."

"Och, I don't think her second name was Wraith, Jessie. Anyway, how is she? It's a wonder you recognised her."

"Yeah. Well. She's fine, I think. She did look massively different but really, really good. No, it's not her with the Wraith surname. I couldn't figure out what her connection was with Treena, and when Treena walked in the kitchen she almost acted like Sandra was her mam. I think she even called her 'Mammy Sandy'."

"You're losing me, love."

"Well, I was confused too. But anyway, Sandra asked me if I remembered a bloke she used to bring to the house. He was her boyfriend for a while. I remembered him instantly but I'd forgotten his name. Anyway, apparently it was Trev – Wraith – and he's Treena's dad."

The spoon my mam was about to use to scoop out a shit-load of Hellman's clattered to the worktop and she stumbled over to sit next to me. She was almost as white as the mayonnaise. "Surely she's not still with that, that ... man?"

"Nope. Sandra's married to somebody else now. But, well, I don't know if you remember but he wasn't very nice. At least, that's how I remember him and Sandra told me that he was an addict all along. Still is an addict. So she's somehow still involved and feels a duty of care or something, I don't know. It looked to me like she helps Treena out with the kids as some kind of obligation to Trev? I didn't ask for the details. Anyway, that's why she was there and I just thought I'd join the dots for you. Make the connection."

"Well thank you, Jessie." Mam's voice trailed off and she sat looking at her hands. The microwave pinged loudly but she didn't move an inch.

"Mam? You okay?"

She slowly brought her gaze to mine and on our eyes locking, something changed. Her chin jutted out, her lips flattened into a straight line and she drew in a deep breath through her nose. "Right. Yes. I remember that god-awful man. I asked Sandra to get rid of him if I remember rightly."

"Did you?"

"I did. Your Dad was on nights at the newspaper and didn't do a blinking thing about it. But I knew that man was underneath the influence the few times I met him. I couldn't have that around you and your brother, no matter how good a childminder Sandra was."

"Wow. So that's why he suddenly disappeared one day. I didn't know."

"A mother does what she has to Jessie." My mam stood up to her full height and ruffled my head. Most unlike her. Then she waltzed over to the microwave to save her dinner. "Sandra needed the job so when I told her either he went or they both went, she made the right decision."

This was news to me. I thought back to all the times I'd run out of the house to get away from Trev. All of the times my brother had to come and find me and tell me he was gone. I was so young. Why hadn't I just told my mam or dad what he was saying, what he was doing?

Mam sat down next to me again, a steaming dollop of her microwave pie on a plate and almost as much Hellman's piled on top. She pushed a small glass of Chardonnay towards me. "Go on, Jessie. You can have a little bit even if you're driving. Do you want some pie?"

"Definitely not." I smiled.

She tucked in and stared at the wall in front of her, as if summoning a memory to burst out of it. "Do you remember when I brought that old typewriter home for you from work once?"

Oh god, I totally did. That typewriter had been my absolute pride and joy and the night she brought it home I'd probably loved her more than I ever thought possible.

"That was the night I told Sandra he had to go."

"It was? Why didn't you say anything?"

"Och, you were so wee at the time. You were maybe seven, that would make Max around five. And you were so caught up in your excitement about the typewriter – you got going on your stories straight away, do you remember? Anyway, it was all a good distraction because just before that, when I sent wee Max out to find you, that's when I insisted that man had to get out of my house and not come back. I'd heard him blethering you see, as I came home that night."

"Blethering?"

"Aye. He was sitting with Sandra in our front room, acting for all the world like he owned the place. I could hear him lording it up over Sandra and, well, what really did it was the way he was talking about you."

"Me?"

"Yes, Jessie. I know he was three sheets to the wind and that people act out of character and say things they don't mean but honestly? There's no way I could have let that kind of thing carry on under my roof. I'd already asked your dad a thousand times to do something but he never believed it was that bad. That night though, as I lugged that bloody great typewriter through the door for my little girl, there he was shouting and bellowing and howling all kinds of horrible things about you. I'd never known the like. Who talks about a wee lassie like that?"

"What did he say?" I asked, in a whisper.

"No, Jessie, I'm not getting into that now. Nothing that makes a difference now. Point is, he was gone as soon as I knew his noxious ways were directed at you and that was that."

I swallowed. "Weren't you mad at Sandra?"

"I was. Very mad. We had words and I don't know if you remember but I took a month off work after that to look after you two whilst she got her act together. Apparently it wasn't all that easy breaking up with somebody addicted to alcohol. Anyway, she did it and she came back and we never had any problems after that."

"Wow." I breathed, sitting back in my chair as if I'd suffered a blow. "I had no idea about any of that."

"Why would you? A mother doesn't need to bring her kids into such things."

"I guess not." This retelling of a story I could barely remember settled over my body like a wave of warm water. The extra information seeped slowly into my skin, my flesh, my bones as if it needed to be absorbed by the workings of my body. So my mam had come to my rescue without me even realising it. I'd been distracted, that day, by everything the typewriter meant to my creative little soul. Wow. No wonder my recent calling back to writing packed such a powerful punch.

Instead of feeling sad for the little girl who'd endured a nightmare from this desperate, damaging man, I actually felt happy for her. For me. The confirmation of my mother's rescue – no matter how late it might have been – meant that I'd been right to think Trev's behaviour towards me was wrong. That it was him who fell on the immoral side of this story and there was actually – and never had been – anything at all wrong with me.

Nothing wrong with my belly. Nothing wrong with my body. Nothing wrong with me.

And as if to confirm exactly that, my mam scooped the last mouthful of seaside pie into her gob, smiled at me with eyes that sparkled more than I'd ever noticed before and said, "Because you're perfect, Jessie. You always have been."

18

WORTH WRITING ABOUT

It had been a good day's work.

Not only had I managed to construct a giant butterfly made entirely of recycled materials, but I'd managed to do it with an energetic bunch of ten-year-olds with an apparent death wish. Never in my life had I had to keep scissors, cable ties and wire cutters so close to my person but in my doing so, everybody had left the library with all fingers and toes intact. Spirits had been high all day and now I was ready to go home and properly chill.

As I packed up my things, I wondered what kind of day Gillie would have had. She was working with an older group across town also with the aim of making a giant butterfly. We were getting these sculptural pieces ready for the project photographer who would turn up at some point to document what we were up to.

Being photographed wasn't my natural comfort zone but it was a small price to pay for being in work at a time when I really needed it. With any luck, the photographer would be able to use some kind of miraculous Hollywood filter and I might actually bear to look at the photos. Perhaps I'd even email some to Mesut.

And now, a huge, warm smile brushed my lips. How did he do that with just the thought of his name? It was ridiculous. I packed up my final box of sculpture stuff and rested my hands on top of it for a few seconds. I closed my eyes, felt the cool, hard plastic of the lid against my palms and gifted myself a deep breath in, then out. *You're in this moment now, Jess. This one.*

"Didn't anybody ever tell you to keep your eyes open when you're at work?" I whirled round to see a tall, lanky figure striding across the room towards me, a huge camera around his neck. "It's part of the risk assessment."

"Oliver!" I shrieked so his name echoed off the bookshelved walls. "Oh my god, what are you doing here?" I flung myself at him and squeezed hard, him managing to swing his camera out of the way before I crushed it. "I'm so happy to see you! Where on earth have you been? What have you been up to?"

"Woah, matey – one question at a time! I'm here to photograph the project, it's so good to see you too, and, well, I've been all over the place actually, doing all sorts of things. Loads to tell you."

I looked him up and down. Was it possible he was even lankier than before? He certainly had a healthy glow to his skin, his hair hadn't lost its trademark spikiness and his smile beamed down at me with a genuine edge of excitement. "Well, you're late," I said. "My horde of ten-year-olds have deserted me and I'm packed up for the day. There's nothing to see here."

"Well, I'll tell you what. I'll snap that gorgeous beast of yours," he pointed up at the butterfly hanging from the ceiling, "and then maybe we can have a bit of a catch-up. What do you reckon?"

"Will it be the kind of catch-up that involves coffee and cake?" I asked, hopefully.

"Come on now Jess. What kind of maniac do you take me for?"

———

How good it was to have the marvellous Oliver Chen back in my life. And the double chocolate muffins. It was good to have them back too.

We'd picked one of our favourite cafés. The café, in fact, situated near the river where we'd had our first coffee together and our first heart-to-heart all those months ago, aptly named 'Epic'.

Oliver caught me up on his disappearing act. Since Gillie and I had left him in Cappadocia, he'd spent time travelling around central Turkey. "I just needed some time to wander, you know, matey?" He'd dossed, camped, trekked and stumbled around until he knew enough was enough. "The travelling bit was honestly great. But the running away bit didn't really do it for me. I had to go home sooner or later and get over my stamped-on ego, didn't I?"

I hated to admit it, but Gillie had done rather a lot of that stamping. She'd kept him hanging with texts and phone calls during our first two weeks in Turkey, then practically lured him to İstanbul on promises of romance. Once they'd finally got it on, he'd been alarmingly loved-up. But I knew all along that Gillie's heart wasn't in it, that she'd had it distracted by a certain someone back in İpeklikum.

Anyway, once Oliver really put his heart on the line and tried to show Gillie how he felt with a truly stunning piece of Anatolian jewellery, she'd completely flipped. The glint of love hinted at by that ring sent her running, literally, for the hills and Oliver was left broken and confused on the balcony of the tiny village hotel where we were staying. The rest, as they say, is history.

"I have to ask," he said, denting the froth of his cappuccino with a spoon, "how is she?"

"Oh you know, Gillie is Gillie." I said in a voice that was just a little too high-pitched for comfort. Oliver looked at me, doubtfully.

"Yep. Right there. You're doing a high squeaky voice thing. Matey, you always do that when you're keeping something back. What is it? What's up with Gillie?"

My shoulders slumped down in defeat. "Fine, Sherlock. Nothing's up, exactly. Well, I don't know what's up because she won't bloody talk to me. As usual."

"It can't be totally nothing to get you doing your squeaky voice thing. Come on, Jess, just tell it like it is. I'd much rather hear it from you."

Fuck. Being a grown-up was hard. "It's just . . . well . . . you see, the thing is . . ." To tell him about Demir or not to tell him about Demir? That was the question.

"There's someone else." Oliver said.

"Kind of."

"What, do you think scratting around rural Turkey for a few weeks didn't prepare me for this?" he said, chuckling. "Matey, you're not the only one who did some soul-searching out there."

"I suppose not." I said. And then I went on to tell him about Demir. No gory details, just that Gillie had met someone when we returned to İpeklikum (slight twisting of truth), and was still in contact with him. "Don't get me wrong, Oliver, I have no idea why she's bothering with him. He is practically a member of the Turkish mafia and I really don't think there's any way he can be serious about her."

"Maybe she's not serious about him." He offered.

"Aw, I'm so sorry Oliver. But I really don't think you should be pinning your hopes on her."

"No, it's okay. I don't mean that. Gillie is firmly in my past now, honestly. But I still mean what I say. Maybe she's not serious about him. Maybe she's just having a bit of fun. Maybe you should let her have it."

Oliver was right. I'd found it so hard to see Gillie in distress at the end of our trip away, and I really hoped she'd come home and find peace in familiar surroundings. But what was familiar about anything since we'd come home? She'd closed down her business, was getting over the breakdown of a long-term relationship, had moved into a new home, and witnessed the local mad woman chuck her best mate down some concrete steps. Who was I to deny her a bit of fun? If that's what this was.

"Seriously, matey, just give her a bit of space. She knows you're there for her if she needs you. You two are like that." And her held up his hands, interlinking two skinny fingers and pressing them together.

I sighed. "You're right as per usual. Jesus, what have I done without you while you've been away?"

Oliver did a little bow. "It's all part of the service. Anyway, I want to hear about you, not Gillie. How are things with Mesut? How are things now you've given your business the boot?"

Now it was my turn to give Oliver an update. I realised he didn't know that Mesut and I were together now. When I'd last seen him, I'd known that Mesut was significant in my life in a big way, but I just hadn't known how. So, I told him about how we'd got together. It was almost impossible to put what had happened into words that carried the right amount of value, but Oliver valued it all in a way that many others just couldn't. After all, he'd been there at my side, when my heart had been ripped open at the possibility of what Mesut could mean to me. And, true to form, Oliver listened patiently, without showing any signs of judgement. He just nodded and smiled and seemed happy for me.

"And you're Firebelly free now, aren't you? It must feel good, right?"

Flipping heck, there was a lot to get through. I gave him the whistle-stop tour of my life over the last month and a half, including the hair-straightener-wielding wrath of Treena Wraith, the unexpected reunion with Sandra and the sad resurrection of some deeply buried psychological shit stowed there by the infamous Trev.

"Lordy, matey. That's a lot. No wonder you're in need of coffee and cake. And a friend."

"I am. But, I don't know, Oliver. I just honestly thought I'd done all the hard work in Turkey, right? I mean that's where all the big decisions got made, where all the realisations happened. I felt invincible when I got back. I really did. Why can't the universe just bloody well follow my vibes?"

"Well, I remember those vibes and I agree that they are awesome and well worth following. Wasn't it your mate, Kadafi in İpeklikum, whose catchphrase was 'Follow the Goodness'? So tell me Jess, what *are* you doing to follow the goodness?"

I should have remembered that Oliver had a total knack of just cutting through the crap. *And* that he tended to remember pretty much everything I'd ever told him. Kadafi, the seventeen-year-old ball of insanely handsome energy had, indeed, made an impression on Gillie and I with his perpetually effervescent character. Pity I couldn't have put him in my suitcase and brought him back to England with me.

"Hmm. Let me see. I am eating cake with you, that's a start."

"Agreed."

"What else? Well, I've decorated my spare room and I've been painting a lot." I told him about the jewel in the lake metaphor Marcus had described to me and how my interpretation of it now hung on my living room wall in all its textured, abstract glory. I remembered all the attention it had received at the Firebelly closing party and that wonderful conversation I'd had with Ikram beneath that very painting when he'd called me 'an inspiration'. "And I've been painting pictures inspired by our balloon ride in Cappadocia. Do you remember all those creamy mountain-tops and fiery rock that looked like it had been clawed out of the earth by somebody in a rage?" Oliver nodded and grinned broadly at the memory.

"I'd love to see those." He said.

"Of course. Any time you want. So basically, my spare room is kind of like my creative headquarters now. I've got my easel up, a huge pin-board with loads of inspiring stuff on it, and a new desk with my laptop all set up. I've even got the cutest little fairy lights . . ."

"What's your laptop set up for?"

"Well, for writing I guess. I thought it was time I graduated from my notebook. You know, maybe take some ideas from it and get them down digitally. See what happens."

Oliver rubbed his hands together and stamped his feet in a light, rapid rhythm on the floor. "Come on then. What have you written so far?" he pinched another chocolate muffin from the sharing platter we'd ordered.

"Not much if I'm honest." I said, cramming the last of my own muffin into my mouth, washed down with my latté. Maybe if I was busy eating and drinking, he'd stop asking me about it.

"Nothing at all?"

"Well not *absolutely* nothing." I said. "I did have an idea for a horror story. I think it could be really good."

Oliver raised an eyebrow and smirked over his coffee cup. "A horror? Any particular reason why?"

That was it. I was defeated. "No particular reason other than I am stuck, Oliver. So fucking stuck. I have got so many ideas but well, life has got well and truly in the way over the last few weeks and every time I sit down in front of that god-forsaken laptop everything just goes blank. Everything. It's not fair! I'm so close to giving up because it doesn't feel like I'm ever going to be able to write anything that anybody would want to read."

"Does it have to be something that other people would want to read?" Oliver's calm tone annoyingly quelled my frustrated one.

"Well yes, of course. Oh, I don't know."

"Can't you just write for you, just like you did in your notebook?"

"I could." I looked at him through my fingers, which were now covering my face. "Yes, okay I suppose I could if I didn't think anybody was going to read it. But what do I write about?"

"Yes, yes, I see your point Jess." Oliver nodded and smiled again. A cheeky one this time. "Because nothing interesting ever happens to you, does it?"

"Well, I don't know if I would go that far . . ."

"Because you're never making unusual choices or making interesting things happen or doing things out of the ordinary, are you? I mean, there's nothing worth writing about at all. Maybe that Trev was right."

"What? Now hang on . . ."

"It's not like people are even interested in anything you've got to say. It's not like you have a story of your very own. It's not like people at parties blatantly tell you that you're an inspiration, or anything like that." He was laughing out loud now. "Come on matey, it's obvious what you can write about, isn't it?"

"Is it?"

"Jess, with everything that has happened to you this year, with all the challenges you've faced and with all the adventures you've been on, surely, *surely* you can see that the thing you need to write about, the inspiration you're looking for . . ."

"Oh my god." I whispered, warmth spreading like sunshine inside my chest.

"The story you have absolutely, irrefutably have to write about is . . ."

"Mine." I breathed.

19

AFTER THE SUNSET

It took real courage to sit down and face that blank screen once I'd made my realisation. But I did it. And the screen wasn't blank for very long.

Of course, I'd known straight away that Oliver was right. But sometimes we need a friend to harness our own voice, to tell us what our heart is actually longing to say. And once it was said there was a note that struck so deep that I physically felt the thump resound through my body. This was the song of my soul. This was the rhythm of my heart.

The north eastern winter was having a total joke and catapulting high winds and hard, unrelenting hailstones at my window one day, when I found myself a few chapters into a story I wasn't sure I would ever show anybody. I took a break to make a cup of tea and wondered, as the kettle boiled, what had stopped me from realising that writing about my own experiences, was absolutely the way forward.

I smiled to myself as I remembered all the times this year when I'd had an epic moment of self-discovery. There seemed too many to wrap my head around. And none of them, I now knew, were the end point. They were all just part of a mad ride I was on to get to know myself.

How arrogant had I been, to assume that just because I'd had an epiphany on a mountainside, and a couple of dramatic episodes with an equally dramatic Mediterranean man, that I now had unlocked some sort of secret to life?

This kind of authentic living took hard graft.

But I wasn't going to waste time berating myself about it. Now was the time to rescue myself the same way my mam had done when she'd told Sandra that Trev had to go. If I could have gathered myself up in a massive, reassuring hug, I would have done it right there and then, standing in my little kitchen, as I watched the water in the kettle bubble and boil.

Last night, I'd taken The Alchemist down off the book shelf. I'd turned the tattered paperback over in my hands and tried to remember how it had felt before I'd even read it, before my trip to Turkey. I remembered feeling anticipation. Looking forward to getting stuck into a good read on a quiet beach somewhere. I'd had no idea how it would make me feel, how it would wake me up.

I read, for the first time, the author's note at the beginning of the book. Paulo Coelho described his joy at the success of the book, the fact that it had been translated into sixty-one different languages and had sold over thirty million copies worldwide. He said he didn't know the secret behind it, other than the message that we all, like Santiago the shepherd boy, need to be aware of our personal calling.

He went on to talk about the kinds of obstacles we face, if we are lucky enough to know what our personal calling is. How we can lack the courage to confront our own dream and the reasons why. I grabbed my notebook and a pen and had a go at summarising it:

1. *Sometimes, in childhood, we are told everything is impossible – we grow up with this idea and so our personal calling becomes buried so deep it's invisible. But it's still there!*

2. *Love. We can be afraid of hurting those we love by abandoning everything else to pursue our dream (but those who really love us will go with us on that journey)*

3. *Fear of defeat. We will meet defeats on our path so the suffering can be great. But we have to keep getting back up.*

4. *Fear of realising the dream. Just when it's in our grasp, we reject it. We have to believe ourselves to be worthy.*

All of these points were now making so much sense to me.

It wasn't like in the movies. Once the principal character fell in love / got the job / finally stood up for themselves, that didn't mean everything ended happily and they jetted off into the proverbial sunset. After the sunset, there was a whole load of other happenings and learnings that would take place. Now I'd had my fair share of sunsets this year, and sunrises too, so I knew what I was talking about.

Yes, there had been a shit-load of stuff that had knocked me sideways since I'd returned from my holiday. And yes, I'd perhaps been a little naïve in thinking that never again would I encounter any internal difficulties. But I was on my path now and I wasn't veering off it. I knew there would be potholes, craters, earthquakes even, but while I was spending time doing the things that had me in my absolute element, I knew I could find the strength inside to keep doing it.

So do you know what I did? I made that cup of tea and I carried on writing.

―――――

If I'd had any doubts about taking on this arts project that Oliver had recommended us for, they had now disappeared.

I had to admit, at first I had been hesitant about whether to take it or not. Aside from the obvious Gillie / Oliver conflict, I had also just promised myself no more compromises in terms of my own creativity. No more spending the majority of my time showing other people how to tap into their innate creativity and then not have the time to do it for myself.

But, as it turned out, things were going great. Without the crushing pressure of Firebelly's overheads to meet, the fee that I was being paid was mine, all mine. I could afford to work two to three days a week with lovely people who were reaping the benefits of a collaborative, creative process, and still have time to do my own thing for the rest of the week. I wasn't flush, by any means, but if the mortgage people were happy, then so was I.

And it just so happened that the director of our project, Terri, was also the owner of the café, 'Epic', that Oliver and I liked to frequent in town. Apparently, the café was some kind of community-led initiative with a social impact objective which accounted for its relaxed and inclusive vibes.

I was at Epic one day, having just finished a planning meeting with Gillie. She'd dashed off to scour the pre-Christmas sales whilst I sat a little longer under one of the patio heaters they had on the street outside, and ate lunch looking out over the silvery cobblestones of the old marketplace. Terri was serving that day and we got chatting about the fact that she was looking for some new artwork to refresh the walls. "It just needs an artistic revamp, darling. Do you know what I mean? It needs a fabulous revamp that is distinctly 'Un-Ikea'." She mock spat on the ground, narrowly missing her silver dreadlocks that swung low past her shoulders. "I want something, that when you're ready to swan in for your double-skinny-mocha-chocca latte it just stops you in your beautiful tracks and makes you all breathless and spellbound. Something that makes you go wow. Something, well, epic, darling."

I saw my opportunity and took it. "Well, Terri, I have some paintings I've been working on at home if you'd like to take a look. I don't know if they'll be your style but I think they'd suit the space."

Luckily, when I brought them to show her at Epic a couple of days later, she was hooked. "Oh, how could I not love those?" She crooned when I carefully unwrapped the first one that showed the blazing rock of Cappadocia from the great heights of a hot air balloon. "So expressive, so dramatic, so atmospheric . . . errr, what are they lovely girl?"

"They're inspired by a balloon ride in Turkey." I said. "I doubt anybody would know that but that doesn't really matter. Do you think they'd fit in here?"

Terri looked up from the painting she was grasping in hands adorned in knuckle-duster gems and assessed the maroon-coloured wall space with a quick roll of her head. "I think they're absolutely perfect, darling. How many did you say you have altogether?"

"Seven."

"Okay. Can you do me three more, lovely girl? Bigger this time. Then we can get them up as quick as a flash. I know a man." She winked. "Now, let's talk money."

And it was as easy as that. We made an arrangement whereby the paintings would hang in Epic for a while and after that they would be available for customers to buy, with a small percentage going to the philanthropic aims of the café. I honestly didn't care, at this point, if none of them sold. I was just chuffed to bits that my actual work was going to be looked at by actual people.

And although I would be spending the next couple of weeks creating three more paintings for Terri's walls, I suddenly had a fresh rush of confidence in my writing. These paintings, after all, represented part of my story and they were going to be on a wall for all to see. How they'd materialised, how they'd got here, were exactly the same way my words would emerge. All I had to do now was channel the same amount of energy into my laptop.

20

THE NINTH STEP

To: jessp@firebelly.co.uk
From: wraitht@shotmail.co.uk
Re: Ninth Step

Hello Jessica.

My name is Trevor and I don't know if you will
remember me. I knew you a long time ago, when
you were just little. I'm betting it might be
a bad memory for you.

My Sandra told me that she saw you again just
the other week. Well, she's not my Sandra
anymore but I still see her sometimes. She
comes to see me in my little flat where I live
now, after rehab. I've been in rehab four
times but that's my last time I reckon. They
must be getting sick of the sight of me.

Anyway, now you know I am an alcoholic. Recov-

ering. You don't need all the details. I'm
working hard to get better.

I was with Sandra when I knew you. You and
your little brother — she used to look after
you both. I was with her there, at your house
sometimes, and I can't remember much about it,
but I do know I wasn't good to you. No little
girl deserves that.

I'm doing really well with my recovery this
time. I don't know if you know (I hope you
don't) but if an addict wants to get better
they have to follow 12 steps. I've now made
it to step 9. It's the furthest I've
ever got.

Now it's my job to apologise to all the people
I've done or said bad things to because of my
addiction. The list is long. But I'm doing
alright with it.

When Sandra said she'd seen you I was pleased
because you were on the list and I didn't know
how else to find you. Now I've found you I'm
hoping you will say yes and meet me and let me
apologise.

I'm clean and presentable and not drinking at
all. So the experience for you will be okay I
hope. I really hope.

Anyway, if you want to do it you can reply to

this email. Or my Sandra always knows how to
get me if that's not good.

I hope everything in your life is going well.

Trevor Wraith

I squeezed my eyes shut and rubbed them until blue sparks
appeared beneath my eyelids. Then I snapped them open again
for fear of falling off my chair. The whole surface of my skin
prickled with a million exploding shards of shock and I tried to
understand what I had just read on my laptop screen. No time
to think about it. I had to rush to the loo.

"Jess?" Gillie beat on the toilet door a few minutes later.
"You okay in there? I didn't know where you'd disappeared to.
This wine won't drink itself you know."

"I'll be out in a minute, Gillie. Go and look at my laptop."

"Ooh, I hope it's Mesut warming himself up for a steamy
online sesh." She giggled and I heard her footsteps pad into my
spare room. She'd come over for the night so we could chill
together outside of work. I'd been so busy 'following the goodness' with all the writing and painting, that we hadn't really had
much time just the two of us. Ella was due over soon too. But
now this email had stopped me in my tracks.

I emerged from the bathroom emptied and deflated in more
ways than one. My skin still prickled and I noticed my hands
were shaking. But those two things were almost blasted away
when Gillie ran out of the spare room and threw herself into my
arms. "Oh my god, Jess, are you okay? I can't believe the bastard
made contact! The absolute nerve of the man. And why didn't
you delete your bloody Firebelly account? That's what I did
with mine."

"Actually, that's what I was going on to do." I whimpered

into her shoulder. "It was my last job of the week. Typical. Isn't it?"

Gillie stepped back and rubbed my wet cheeks with her thumbs. "You don't have to answer it, you know that, don't you? He can take his ninth step and stick it up his arse. You don't have to do anything about it. At all."

I flumped down on the sofa just as there was a loud knock at the door followed by a cheery whoop blared straight into the kitchen, "Whoop! It's the weekend, bitches!" Ella.

Gillie ran to greet her and no doubt give her a ten-second whispered summary of what the hell she was walking into. God, my friends were getting good at dealing with spontaneous onslaughts of drama.

Ella appeared at the doorway in her rainbow dungarees and holographic Doctor Marten Boots that laced up to her shins. Never had I ever seen such a serious face on such a jubilantly dressed person. "Shit Jess. Are you alright my beautiful friend? What can I do to make it better?"

"Drop me into another time and place?"

"Done. Gillie. Get the DeLorean. Now, before we leave for 1955, what did the shithead say in his email?"

"You can read it if you want. Basically just that he wants forgiveness. Something to do with it being part of his recovery as an addict."

"Oh yeah, I've heard about that. The twelve steps, isn't it? They're supposed to be really effective. Still, no reason why you have to get involved sweet pea, if you don't want to."

"I've got no idea what I want. It's just so out of the blue. I thought after meeting Sandra that was it. That was my dance with the past and I was over it now. I didn't expect him to ever actually contact me. This means he's real. I didn't want him to be real. Can we drink some wine now please?"

Gillie was already on it and handed me a frosty glass of

white. We all sat and took our sips in silence, eyes cast down-wards, breathing in sighs, party atmosphere sadly absent. I half-lay, half-sat on the sofa, the very definition of a couch potato. I poked my stomach as it bellowed out in front of me. All round and soft and sitting on my torso like a jelly trying to force some frivolity into the scene. "He used to poke it." I said, swallowing hard. "With a fork or his car keys or a pencil – whatever he could find really. He'd poke it and laugh at it and tell me it was too full of chips. It really hurt. And I can still remember his laugh. It was more of a cackle really. I remember as soon as I knew he was in the house I used to try and suck it all in so it wouldn't occur to him to make fun of me. I grew up thinking a fat belly was one of the worst things in the world."

"Well it's not." Gillie stated, bending forwards to give my tummy a kiss. "You could be a dickhead. Like him."

"True." I said, pulling my tummy in and attempting to pull my jeans up and over it anyway.

Then Ella star-jumped out of her chair, making Dinah start chasing her tail on the other side of the room. "Eeek! I know what we're doing tonight!"

"We're staying in." Gillie said. "We're eating Minstrels and watching shit on the telly and feeling sorry for ourselves, aren't we, Jess?"

Ella was having none of it. "No, no, no! We're not doing any of that." She grabbed us by the arms and hauled us up to our feet. She was freakishly strong. "We're getting back in my van right now and we're going down the road to that pub in Budhill. The one on the corner? I heard about it weeks ago and totally forgot that I was going to ask you both to come. It was Jess jabbing her beautiful belly like that, that reminded me." She checked her Minnie Mouse watch and yelped. "Shit! It will have been going for a while but if we go now we'll defo catch the end of it. Come on! This is so going to be worth it!"

So magnetic was Ella's enthusiasm that Gillie and I were somehow already pulling on jackets and finding our shoes. "But what is it, Ella? What on earth are you dragging us out to?" Gillie whined.

"Ah, ah, ah!" Ella wagged her finger at us and shone out a thrilling smile. "We won't be dragged anywhere my sweet peas, we will strut and we will flounce and we will *sashay* our way there. Who's with me?"

"But what is it?!" Gillie and I shouted, now out of the door, under the cold, black skies and maneuvering ourselves into Ella's flower power van. Once we were all in, she slammed the driver door shut, started up the engine and blasted hot air onto the icy windscreen, she shouted with pure glee and torment, "Do you know what? I think I'm going to leave it as a surprise."

———

"What do we want?" came the voice, booming over the tannoy.

"Freedom from diets." Replied the feverish masses.

"When do we want it?"

"Now!"

Then there was a deafening cheer, which was really quite impressive for a load of middle-aged women in a small-town pub, and much chinking of glasses ensued. Then somebody turned the jukebox on and virtually everyone inside 'The Miner's Arms' pub jumped up to dance to 'I am The One And Only' by Chesney Hawkes. You really could not have written it.

"Well it's different, Ella, I'll give you that." Gillie smiled.

"It's bloody fantastic, is what it is." Ella shrieked above Chesney's melodic appeal, swaying herself and her spectacular dungaree-clad booty around so that her cider and black was in immediate danger of being worn by somebody. "I love all this body positivity stuff. Sorry though, Jess. I honestly didn't know that Sandra would be here."

"She's not just here, Ella. She's running the whole bloody show!" I said, hardly able to believe it myself. I mean, I'd gone almost two decades without ever bumping into the woman and that was twice now, she'd rocked up in my life unexpectedly. We all looked over at the little makeshift stage and there she was, dressed in a silver, sparkly jumpsuit that left nothing to the imagination, and abandoning her microphone to be with a crowd of 'fans' vying for her attention.

"She's like a local celebrity." Gillie breathed, in some kind of awe. "How cool is it that she was your babysitter, Jess?" Sandra was now kissing every one of the women in front of her on the forehead and gesticulating towards their bodies with blatant adoration. "And look at the flyer." Gillie said, holding up the one we'd found on the bar which showed Sandra wearing a bathing suit and holding up her middle finger to a massive set of scales. "'Body Positivity For All – be the rebel your body needs you to be'. Was she always this awesome?"

"Erm, actually, I remember Sandra *constantly* being on a diet. And especially when Trev was around. He monitored everything she ate and used to poke at her as much as he poked at me, to be honest. I did used to love reading her diet magazines though, and was always amazed when she could go several hours without eating anything. Then there were other days, when she'd send me and Max to the shop for a shit-load of chocolate. It was kind of confusing but I just thought that's what adults did."

"That *is* what adults do." Ella agreed, slurping from her pint and slurring adorably. "That is why I refuse to be one." Suddenly the bar wasn't where Ella needed it to be and Gillie and I caught her before she did herself an injury.

"Okay, my little diet rebel." Gillie laughed. "Hand over your van keys. There's no way you're driving tonight." Ella did it and whooped that she was free.

"Freeeeedoommmmm!" She yelled and every other female in the place took this as a sign she was being all body positive and echoed back at her with all the more ferocity:

"FREEEEDOOMMMMM!" and then Ella shoved her cider and black at me so she could dive into the crowd and disappear among the bodies who had started proudly bopping their curves and ripples and angles and grooves to 'Independent Women' by Destiny's Child. To be honest, it really was a beautiful sight and not one I ever thought I'd see in a North Eastern pub. There wasn't a flat cap or a politically questionable tattoo to be seen.

"Jess! I didn't know you were coming, pet."

I twirled around on my bar stool to find Sandra standing in front of me. She really was dazzling. "Sandra! I – I feel like I know a popstar."

"Aw, haddaway and shite, love. It's just my little sideline, that's all. Well? Did you enjoy the session, you two?" Sandra leaned on the bar and a sprite of a barmaid slid a vodka and tonic into her waiting hands.

Gillie opened and closed her mouth like a fish, clearly a little bit star-struck simply because Sandra had been wielding a microphone five minutes ago. "Yes, it's great, isn't it?" I said, not really knowing where to start. "We got here a bit late but we got the general gist of it."

"Really?" Sandra smiled at us both. "You don't look convinced, our Jessica. Don't you want to feel positive about your body and love it is for all that it is and all that it does?"

"Well, yes, of course. Doesn't everyone?"

"You'd be surprised." Sandra said. "The toxicity in society is strong and you have to reeeeaally pull your mind out of the diet mindset. No easy task, poppet. Most people get there in the end though, with a bit of help from me."

"Wow. I thought most hypnotherapists trained people to go on diets. I mean, like, to lose weight and never eat chocolate again or something."

"Well I'm not most hypnotherapists, love. I'm going against the grain." Then she leaned forwards and stuck her face right next to my ear so that her breath tickled me. "And I bloody love it!"

Gillie nudged me, still apparently speechless, but I knew she wanted me to get more from Sandra. "But Sandra, when you used to look after me and Max, I remember you were always on some new diet. I thought you were amazing the way you had so much self-control. I wanted to *be* like you."

Suddenly her face clouded and some pointed lines appeared across her shimmering brow. "Aw, pet. I can't even begin to say how sorry I am about that. I didn't know then what I know now and, well, I shouldn't have let you see me like that. It's not good for a little lass, like. I was on diets for years and that's how I know – that's how I really know – that they just don't work. They only make you feel like absolute shit and as if there's something wrong with you as opposed to the world you're living in. And, there's been a shit load of research done on how diets actually make you gain back more weight than you had on you beforehand, like. I'm living proof of that. And I've had enough of it. Absolutely enough."

"So you're telling us that you love your body now? Unconditionally?" Gillie found her words.

"Most days, I absolutely do. I've been practicing for a very long time – since I left Trev and found my Luke – he's over there by the way, packing up my stuff. Isn't he a doll?" We looked over to the stage and there was a man with one arm lugging around speakers and cables into huge metal boxes. He was hardly breaking a sweat. "He's a living legend, that man and he made me see that our bodies are absolute gifts from God. Took a while like, cos of the scars Trev had left and all that. There isn't anything else in the world like being in love with an addict to do one over on your self-esteem. Stay away from them lasses, that would be my advice." She downed her drink and the impish barmaid slid another one her way without even a word uttered.

Gillie nudged me again. And I knew what she meant. "Speaking of Trev, Sandra. You'll never guess what."

"You got an email?" Sandra asked, raising an eyebrow.

"Well, yeah."

"A ninth step email?" She raised the eyebrow further still.

"Yes. How did you know?"

Sandra sighed and leaned her back to the bar, both elbows resting behind her and looking me square in the eyes. "Firstly, I told him I'd seen you. Sorry, pet. Maybes I shouldn't have. But, as I said, I still see him from time to time. Oh fuck-a-doo I'll just tell you."

I braced myself for another bombshell as Gillie wrapped her arm around my waist and pulled me close. 'Respect' by Aretha Franklin tempted yet more people onto the dance floor, giving us enough time and space to have this conversation.

"I don't know if you know this, pet, but all them years ago, when he used to come to the house like, there was one day when your mam told me he wasn't to come back. Looking back, I totally get it, like. He was terrible. And she caught him saying awful things about you and your gorgeous chubby little body so she drew the line. As a mother would." Sandra took a deep breath, tossed her curly head back, and carried on. "So anyways, what your mam said that night was hard for me cos I was falling for him hard – an alcoholic can be, by the way, almost bewitching, like. Certain drinks and they're hell on earth to be with, but honestly, sometimes? He was the nicest man I knew."

Gillie tutted and squeezed me even closer.

"Hard to believe, but there it is. Anyways, what your mam said was a bit of a wake-up call for me, so I thought it best if we split up. I needed that job and I loved you and Max like yous were my own. Long story short, he was having none of it and it took me several weeks to make him see I really meant it. Those weeks weren't pretty and I've got scars in both senses of the word to prove it."

"But why are you still involved with him? How can you have forgiven him for the way he treated you? And me? The man's a total shit!"

"Is he though?" Sandra asked, earnestly. "I don't know. Or is he a victim? He's got a disease, he's not had an easy life. When we split up he hit absolute rock bottom and he almost drank himself to death. You can imagine that I blamed myself, even if I know now I didn't actually put the bottle in his hand. He was such a mess and he had little Treena and I couldn't just leave him like that even if we weren't ever going to be a couple again."

"So you promised him you'd help out? For Treena's sake?"

"Yes. And my own. I suppose I felt I owed it to him, pet. When you've seen an alcoholic literally at death's door, it's hard not to just do something – anything – to help. And that was my thing. To help."

"And twenty years later you're still doing it?" Gillie asked, getting well and truly drawn in.

"Yes, pet. I am. For my sins. And these days I just watch the kids for Treena sometimes. Help her make appointments for her dad and stuff like that. Some years I hardly see them. Other years it's all hands on deck to get Trev through a rough patch. And to be honest, that's one of the reasons I went and bit the bullet and did my hypnotherapy training. It's got to be one of the most joyful jobs in the world and it balances out all the darkness, if you know what I mean."

"So how did you know about Jess's email then?" Gillie asked, folding her arms in front of her chest, her star-struck attitude clearly wearing off as Sandra revealed more and more of her humanity.

"Eee, I was just so beside myself that I'd seen you, Jessica, that I did let it slip to him that you'd been in his Treena's house. And, because he's doing really good at the minute, he was appalled that Treena had done what she did to you outside the community centre. He said he'd had you on his apologies list for a canny while now and did I know a way he could message you. I always try not to get too involved in his twelve steps stuff – cos I know it's got to come from him, like. But I did tell him you might still have your Firebelly website up and he might find a link there. Looks like I was right, eh pet?"

"Yup." I said, feeling that swirling in my tummy again. "It was a bit of a shock, Sandra."

"Are you going to see him?" She asked, the wrinkles around her eyes clearing as she stared up at me. I couldn't stand the hope I saw there.

"I – I really d-don't know."

"Jess doesn't know if she wants to go there again." Gillie explained. "And who can blame her? He was a bully and she's past all that now. She's more or less body positive now. A body positive, grown-up woman – just like you. And you'd be amazed at what she's come through so far this year. You don't know the half of it, Sandra."

"I'm sure I don't, love. But I do know that our Jessica was always such a resilient little soul. I used to find her run off somewhere having these little moments to herself. Blowing the heads off dandelions, weaving daisy chains or typing on her little typewriter or something. Your strength wouldn't surprise me, pet. It really wouldn't."

"Thanks." I mumbled into my drink.

"Right – enough ladies, enough!" Sandra slammed down her empty glass onto the bar and took both mine and Gillie's hands. "We have given men the arena far too much in this blessed conversation. Now let's get our canny little arses on the dance-floor and give your mate a run for her money. Look at her! She's like a pilled-up Andy Pandy!"

Gillie and I tried our best to bounce after Sandra just as 'I'm Every Woman' by Whitney Houston burst out of the pub's speakers. Ella was laughing up towards the giant glitterball that threw gleaming shapes at her holographic boots and she danced in a shimmering jumble of cider-fuelled beauty. God, we loved her so much and – if we were going to believe the infamous words of Ms Houston – that meant we had to love ourselves too.

21

BEAUTY BEGINS

"A Body Positivity event in a Geordie pub?" Lindy laughed. "I've only ever been that far north once and the pubs I went in wouldn't have known what had hit them!"

"Totally." Jess giggled. "But that's Sandra for you. She knows how to make an impression and, more importantly, she knows *where* to make it."

"I wonder how that kind of thing would go down here, in İpeklikum. Do you think it's a cultural thing? I've never even heard of Body Positivity."

"I thought exactly the same thing." Jess said, picking up a dessert menu that had been brought to the table. "So, I asked Mesut the next day when I was telling him all about it. He said something along the lines of, 'I am positive I am having a body, Gulazer, so why I need someone telling me I like it?' Bloody typical! He's got the self-esteem of a cockroach in a nuclear war, that man."

Lindy glanced at the back of the dessert menu Jess was holding up. A bit more of that Turkish baklava they'd had earlier in the evening wouldn't go amiss. "Do you really think what Sandra said about diets is right, Jess? Do you really think they're a load of rubbish?"

"I do." Jess said, firmly, passing the dessert menu to Lindy, as if reading her mind. "We – particularly women – spend far too much time trying to make ourselves smaller. Why do that? I mean, why stop ourselves from taking up space?" She outstretched her arms and touched everything she could reach her fingers to: the edges of cushions, the corners of the table, the smooth underside of the glass jars above them and the overlapping carpets below. "Sandra was right – it's rebellious of us to go against the grain and refuse to be small. I, for one, want to make my mark on this world and I won't be able to do that shrivelling away in a corner somewhere, weighing out lettuce. I need sustenance for my soul as well as my body."

"Right, that's decided then. Two helpings of baklava?"

"Absolutely. On it." Jess's winning smile caught the eye of the nearest waiter and she pointed to the menu to indicate what they wanted. "It's absolutely so much more than that though, Lindy. I've learned quite a bit from Sandra since then, and it's more than being able to eat cake or feel comfortable buying a bigger pair of jeans."

"Meaning?"

"Meaning so many people are judged by their bodies depending on things like size, race, gender, sexuality or disability. It's about challenging the views of society and promoting the acceptance of all different types of bodies. It's a whole political movement and Sandra's little sesh in the pub was just the tip of the iceberg."

Lindy nodded. "God, you're right. Fuck, society really needs an overhaul, doesn't it?"

"Too right." Jess yawned and stretched again. "But believing in your own beauty is a start I guess. At least Sandra is trying to make people realise that. If it wasn't for her I'd still be prodding my rolly tummy with the same disgust as Trev all those years ago."

"Well, I'm glad for you. You deserve not to feel disgust at your own body parts."

"Don't we all?" Jess mused.

"And I guess it must have helped you get on with the things you wanted to do like the writing and all that. I can't believe you started writing your own story. That was genius of Oliver to point that idea out."

"Yeah. He's an angel, he really is. Once I cleared that particular hurdle, the writing came so much easier. I've been loving writing about what's happened this year so far."

Lindy shifted in her seat and swallowed as she realised what this meant. "Shit. And the part of the story you're now telling me is almost here and now. Not much longer to go before we're sitting here in this restaurant on New Year's Eve. Hey, here's a thought. Now you've met me, you should write me into it. I mean, if you're going to do things properly."

Jess nodded. "Yes! You will be in it now because I'm writing about the entire year. From last New Year's Eve to this one. So you'll have to be in it."

"Woah. Doesn't that mean I'll be in the closing scene then? Jesus, Jess. Now I'm going to be watching my words. And can you please glam me up a bit? At least some kind of improvement on the emotional wreck you see before you?"

"Come on now." Jess moved closer, creating a small expanse of shadow that was somehow protected from the rest of the restaurant, the rest of the world. "I don't see an emotional wreck."

"Really?"

"Really. You know what I see? Beauty."

"Hah. Fucking hilarious."

"I'm not joking, Lindy."

Lindy squirmed on her cushion. "Well I just can't understand that. I'm a total scruff. I've probably got a blotchy face and mascara all down my cheeks and god, we spent so long on the beach earlier my hair is likely the consistency of straw. I fail to see where the beauty is, body positivity or not. But you're the author and if you see it then who am I to stop you writing me in as a total babe?"

"I will." Jess said, softer now. "Lindy, when you sat down by the fire on the beach earlier tonight, I think there was something in you, something important, that told you to do it. I think that for a split second, you listened to the wisdom of your soul. You took a decision for your real self. Not the one your family expects to see. Not the one society expects to see. Your *real* self. And it didn't matter if you didn't know what the consequences would be."

Lindy sniffed. How did Jess suddenly turn the conversation like this? "Okay. You may have a point. But so?"

"So . . . in the words of one of my very favourite wise ladies who was, incidentally, a total babe too, Coco Chanel – and I pinched this from my giant pinboard back at home in my spare room . . . '*Beauty begins the moment you decide to be yourself'*. And it has definitely begun in you, my new and brilliant friend. It has definitely begun in you."

22

OUT OF SEASON

"Have you found any bargains yet?" Gillie hollered from the kitchen.

"Not yet!" I called back. "Hurry up with that coffee, will you? I'm dying in here." It was the morning after Sandra had gatecrashed The Miner's Arms with her Body Positivity event and I was back at my house with Gillie and Ella.

Gillie was fresh as a daisy, having taken the wheel for a drunken Ella last night, and was now flouncing around the kitchen looking like a flipping supermodel with her soft, tumbling curls framing all of her movements in a fragrant, fiery vision. It never failed to move me how stunning she could look in jeans and a t-shirt and I made a mental note to myself to never allow her to be this gorgeous in my house again.

Ella was hanging half-in and half-out of my bed, with Dinah literally on top of her head yet somehow still sleeping as if the future of the universe depended on it. There was an interesting odour of cider, blackcurrant, dog farts and pub toilets emanating from the room so I'd closed the door on them both, telling myself I'd get a full can of air freshener out later on.

I was in the spare room, barely holding it together, visions of glittery jumpsuits, bopping bodies and spilled drinks crashing unbidden into my pounding head. Gillie had cracked open the window to let in a thin sheet of crisp, cool air that wasn't entirely unpleasant, and I was staring at my ancient laptop's glitchy screen. I was on a mission.

I was looking for a flight to Turkey.

"Aw," Gillie appeared at the door, "is somebody feeling a little fragile?"

"Yes. Somebody is. Now give me my coffee." I grabbed the mug she offered me and took a huge slurp. "Ah. The elixir of life. Maybe I will join the land of the living today."

I squinted at the screen and Gillie plonked herself next to me to have a look too. We'd decided last night, whilst walking Dinah around the fields at approximately three in the morning, that a trip to Turkey was on the cards. It was almost like I was holding my hands up in surrender.

Since I'd arrived back in England, I'd had verbal abuse hurled at me in public, I'd been chucked down some steps resulting in a stay in hospital, I'd encountered blasts from the past that had shook my soul, I'd realised writing was HARD and I was missing my Turkish man more than I'd thought possible. Plus, after Trev's nightmarish email yesterday, I'd also had a lovely one from Terri at Epic to say a few of my paintings had sold already, meaning my bank account was unusually flush.

Alas though, my internet search was proving fruitless, which was, let's face it, fucking typical of my life right now. "I can't find anything leaving from Newcastle that gets me anywhere near İpeklikum." I whinged at Gillie. "And we're talking mega bucks too. Shit, how am I ever going to make this happen?"

"The problem is," Gillie started, authoritatively, "that you're looking completely out of season. Flights in December are not going to be easy to come by. Your best bet is to drive down to Gatwick then fly to İstanbul. Then you should be able to get a connecting flight to İzmir, which is about an hour or two's transfer to İpeklikum. I reckon you could sort the lot for in the region of three hundred quid. Here, let me have a go." She nudged me along and started tapping away on the keyboard in an alarmingly expert fashion.

"Sorry, but I didn't realise you'd suddenly become a travel agent. Bit of a departure from painting banners with radgie kids, isn't it?"

"Ha bloody ha. I just found it on a website the other night, that's all. I was asking questions."

"Asking who questions? The god of cheap flights?"

"I was talking to some girls who know their stuff. Some girls who have been in a similar situation to you. To us."

"I'm sorry Gillie, you know my head is mush this morning."

"I was on one of those chat room thingies. It's full of English women who are going out with Turkish men. I was asking them about how they managed to keep things going when they lived so far apart and they gave me a few tips. I thought it might help you. Us."

Wow. The girl had done her research. "Oh. Okay. Us?"

"Well, yes. I've been flirting with the idea of going over there with you. What do you think?" she said, not really asking a question at all, more like stating the obvious.

"Clearly that's not all you've been flirting with."

"I've been having my fun," she said, smiling to herself. "Unlike yours, my computer tends to behave itself so I usually manage to get more than just words out of Demir . . ."

"Fucking hell, Gillie. Please tell me you're not saying what I think you're saying. Have you been partaking in phone sex? I mean, oh god, this is even worse, *screen sex*?"

Gillie just smiled secretively and went to back to her work of finding us some cheap flights. "My lips are sealed. Anyway, you should be glad of any shenanigans I might be getting up to with Demir, when I can find you deals like this . . ."

I looked at the screen she'd brought up. Gatwick to İstanbul. İstanbul to İzmir. Full baggage allowance. All taxes included. Return flights. Two hundred and ninety-eight pounds each. "Oh good lord above, I can afford that Gillie! I can afford it! Wait, when is that for?"

"Boxing Day." She said, proudly. "Coming back a few days after New Year. So you'll be able to start 2007 as you mean to go on. With your Mesut."

"And you, my dear friend, will be able to have sex that doesn't involve a web cam!" We clashed our coffee mugs together in glee. This was good news. This was very good news. Finally I could escape the shit-show that was going on here in crappy old England and I could embark on an easy, simple and SEXY life in Turkey! No need to reply to Trev's email. No need to admit he existed at all. Everything was going to get easier now. Everything was mine. "Let's find our credit cards." I shouted, potentially waking up the human / dog assemblage in the next room but not caring one tiny little jot. "We're going back to Turkey!"

23

LUCKIER

Later that day, when Gillie and Ella had gone home and my house was less of a hangover den, I picked up the phone and dialed my special code to get cheap calls to Turkey. I couldn't wait to tell Mesut that I would be with him in a matter of weeks.

It had gone completely silent on the other end of the phone when I'd announced it, and this time I didn't let my imagination run away to the land of *oh-fuck-he's-having-second-thoughts-and-is-dumping-me-imminently.* Actually, the silence evolved gradually into a deep, ecstatic, joyful breath and the words, "Really? End of December? Gulazer. You not messing with me, isn't it?"

"No. Not messing with you. I'm really coming out there."

"You not knows what this meaning."

"I think I do." I sighed, dreamily. "No more işkence."

"No more işkence is good. You sure you want it Gulazer? You sure you wanting me? Is not hot and sunny, and beaches very cold right now."

"Well you'll just have to keep me warm then, won't you?" I laughed. Idiot. Thinking that would put me off. I was a Geordie for God's sake. "I can't wait to see you and get away from all the shit that's happening here. I just want to run away from it all."

"You knows you can running to me any time you wanting, Gulazer. But you knows, I think, that you not run from yourself. Is not possible. You need to running towards you, not away from you."

Shit. I remembered Jason saying something very similar when he found out about Mesut the night he'd come to stay. I hadn't replied to his last couple of texts, slightly embarrassed that they were just a tad over-familiar, but I really should have at least acknowledged them or something. "You're not the first one to say that to me. I don't know. It feels like running to you is the right thing to do."

"Who is saying to you as well?" Mesut asked.

"Erm, Jason."

"Jason? You not saying his name before."

"Ah, do you remember when I got that challenge from Marcus about texting someone random on my phone? You chose somebody for me that afternoon we were sat outside Beerbelly in the sun? And it was Jason. An old friend from university."

"Yes of course. Is same day we kissing for first time." God, this man was good.

"That's right. Well, he texted me back when I got home and then came to visit me one night. It was nice to see him again."

"He visit you one night?"

"Yes he did. He was passing through town on his train so got off and stayed with me for the night before getting back on the train the next day. It was exciting! God knows if I'll ever see him again but it was good to catch up and tell him all my news. Marcus was clever giving me that challenge."

"Yes. Clever Marcus."

Oh fuckety-fuck. What was that change in tone? Please, please, please don't let it be jealousy – I just couldn't handle that from a two thousand mile distance, if at all. After everything I'd been through with Jack's insecurities, I really could not deal with this now, from Mesut. Why should I have to defend myself for seeing an old friend? I could have a man in the house without jumping into bed with him, couldn't I? I'd proven that. Hadn't I?

"And you okay, Gulazer? After Jason's visit?"

Wow. I had not expected that.

"Yes. I'm okay. Why?"

"I just checking. Is sometimes hard seeing old friends. Is sometimes, bringing things to our minds is not easy to forgetting."

"How the hell did you . . . ? Oh, never mind. You're good, did you know that? You should be a psychologist, not a barman. Or maybe a psychologist who also serves his clients cocktails. Nothing like a nice dose of cognitive restructuring with a creamy pinacolada on the side. I honestly thought you were jealous." He smiled and I just glowed. That's what his smiles did to me.

"Jealous? Oh, please waiting, Gulazer I think I knows this one but need to look in book to be sures." I could hear him fumble with the phone whilst he leafed through the pages of what must have been that ancient English-Turkish dictionary. Bless his full, gorgeous, beating heart – he always had that thing with him when he spoke to me these days. "How you spell? Is starting with 'J', yes?"

I spelled out the word for him, something I probably should have done to Jack right at the beginning of things. "Jealous. Kıskanç. Ah. Tabi. Of course I am Kıskanç. Jealous."

"You are? Then why aren't you saying something? Why aren't you shouting or swearing or making me explain in minute detail what happened that night?"

I heard Mesut take several slow, deep breaths at the other

end of the phone and could only picture what he was doing. Rubbing his temples? Closing his hands into fists? Standing up to pace the room? "I not need it Gulazer. You not need it. Am I jealous this Jason is staying with you and talking with you and being in your house and can touching you if he wants?" I heard a short, sharp exhale and I imagined him standing. Definitely standing. "Yes. I am jealous. He very lucky man. But me? I thinking I more lucky."

"You are?" I breathed deep too and decided to say that again. "You are."

"I am. I am Mesut. And you are Gulazer. My yellow rose. And you choosing me. And you are phoning me. And you are coming İpeklikum visiting me. I tell my jealous part that, and I knows I okay. That is why I ask, are you okay too?"

"You're amazing, do you know that?"

"I am."

"You are."

"I am."

I burst out laughing. "Okay, okay, we all know how amazing you are. And yes, thank you for asking, I am okay. It was nice to see Jason but all it did, really, is make me think how much I want you. So you're right. As per usual. You are luckier."

"I am."

"You are." And I knew now, what that meant for both of us.

24

GILLIE'S BIRTHDAY

"Bloody hell, Gillie! I'll never manage another one!" I shouted over the Afro-Caribbean jazz music as Gillie pushed yet another Black Russian towards me on the sticky, puddled table-top.

"Rubbish." Gillie insisted. "I know they're not as good as Mesut's but it's the best we're gonna get in Newcastle. Anyway, it's my birthday so I'm in charge."

"Fair enough." I smiled and took a sip of the rich, dark drink. She was right. Mesut's version was far superior. Blacker, stronger, with ice crushed by his own hands. Oh god, his hands. I missed them so much. I shook off the thought of how they always knew where to touch first. A basement club in Newcastle was not the time or the place. I turned to Gillie, grinning. "So, have you enjoyed your birthday?"

"Yes! I bloody love this place. Thanks for bringing me here. Remember when we came for Jack's birthday years ago? That was a proper laugh, wasn't it?"

I did remember. This jazz café had been one of Jack's absolute favourite haunts and that night, in particular, had been pretty good. Up until a point though. Basically, up until he had downed one too many tequilas and decided I was the Whore of Babylon because I'd put lip gloss and a skirt on and was in the vicinity of male human beings other than himself. As I recall, things had gotten very ugly very quickly and Gillie, as well as everybody else we were with, had deserted us in the assumption that we would 'work it out'. Which we did not, unless you call a screaming match in the rain and getting separate taxis home, 'working it out'.

But sitting here now with Gillie, I could afford a whole new perspective. Lip gloss and skirt included. "God, it's so good be here again. And lush to be just with you – no green-eyed monsters in sight."

"I'll drink to that." Gillie gave a dazzling smile and slurped her incredibly elaborate drink. "It's a shame Ella couldn't join us though. She'd have been working that dance floor like nobody's business."

"She would." I agreed and smirked at the memory of Ella throwing her shapes at the Body Positivity night. She was away at a puppeteering convention, probably rubbing shoulders with the likes of Emu and Basil Brush. "Still, she's spending a few days in her natural habitat so she'll be happy."

"She totally will. Do you know what she got me for my birthday? One of those dancing flowers. From the nineties. Do you remember them?"

"Yes! The plastic ones in little pots with sunglasses on?"

"The very same. I honestly don't know where she goes to find these things."

"It's a special talent." I laughed. "Remember when she got me that purple, sparkly vibrator? If you consider that, you got off lightly really."

"I didn't get off at all – that's the problem."

We fell about laughing, slamming our drinks into glossy puddles and clutching our sides. "Why does everything always seem completely hilarious when we're out on the town?" I breathed, helplessly. "I can't feel my cheeks!"

"It's a good feeling, though, right? And nothing whatsoever to do with the Black Russians you're throwing back." Gillie's laughter subsided and she looked aimlessly around the room at the rhythmical mass of bodies on the dance floor. The flashes of brightly-coloured outfits, the gleam of drunken smiles and the madness of shouted conversations into awaiting earholes. The edges of her mouth twitched and she suddenly seemed to shudder from head to toe. "Honestly, Jess? I'd prefer the vibrator right now."

"Right now?"

"I'd consider it. Demir's got me demented."

"Serves you right for doing dodgy sex stuff on the computer together."

Gillie tipped her head back and laughed again. "It's not that dodgy. He's just so bloody hot. And randy. The Turkish are such a randy race, don't you think? I mean, you must know it as well as I do."

"I'm not sure about that, actually."

Gillie downed the last of her drink, expertly managing not to take an eyeball out with the adorning paraphernalia. "Jess! Of course you do! You've bedded two of them, for fuck's sake. You are definitely qualified to comment."

"Bedded? Ugh. That sounds awful."

"'Tis true though. Anyway, you must be desperate to see your man now. It feels like forever since we were in İpeklikum and it's not long until we jet off. I know the first thing I'm doing when I get there and I can tell you what, it isn't taking in the local scenery."

Poor Gillie. She was properly gagging for it. And it's not like I could say I wasn't. She was right. I was desperate to see Mesut. The memory of his touch – it was as if my body remembered it before my brain did. Was that normal? To have body-memories? God, those hands, those fingers. The smooth hardness of his skin, the kink of muscles that moved and surged and worked their way all over me until the combination of dark and light skin was no longer identifiable as one person or the other. My skin prickled. Again, this was not the time or the place.

"Can we talk about something else, please?"

Gillie gave a knowing grin, her brown eyes sparking through her inexplicably exquisite eye make-up, smoky and glimmering. Her curved lips a perfect shade to match her deep, crimson top. She grabbed my hand and squeezed it tight. "I've got a better idea. Let's dance."

―――――

I had no idea what had gone wrong between the dance floor and the taxi rank, but I did know that it was time to stop talking. No matter what words I uttered now, it was winding Gillie up even more and fraying the remaining threads of our friendship.

"So now you've gone silent." Gillie spat out as we got to the end of the taxi queue. "You had plenty to say back there though, didn't you?"

God knows what I'd done to make her this angry, but it definitely had something to do with Demir. For fuck's sake, he could even cause trouble from two thousand miles away. The man was toxic. My comments were something along those lines when Gillie blew up and stormed out of the club, leaving me to grab our belongings and go on a wild goose chase for her across the moonlit streets of Newcastle.

I thought hard. We'd been dancing. Some strikingly handsome bloke had sidled up to her on the dance floor and tried to chat her up, which certainly wasn't unusual for her. I'd winked and turned to go and sit down but she'd grabbed my arm to get me to stay put. All cool. Never leave your mate with a bloke she's not sure about and all that.

So I'd kept dancing and we both turned our backs on the striking but nevertheless rejected bloke in question. Gillie had said thanks and something about her and Demir being faithful to each other no matter what. I'd laughed. I mean, really laughed, and said, "What, even if he dances like that?" pointing at the bloke who was now body-popping to his heart's content in a bid to get Gillie's attention. He certainly had everybody else's.

Gillie had thrown me a scowl and her tone suddenly changed. "What, am I not allowed to be serious about Demir?" And, fuelled by inferior Black Russians and the music and the free-flowing atmosphere or what, I don't know, but I started giggling.

"Yeah, right, Demir. Like *he's* going to be faithful." I kept saying things like that, tumbling around and clutching my belly with genuine laughter, being occasionally bumped into by our body-popping friend.

When I'd finally found her striding up and down the main shopping street, her face an absolute storm and her posture forbidding, all of that warm merriment I'd felt in the club drained out of my bones and was quickly replaced by the cold. I knew I'd overstepped the mark. The previous smoky softness of her eyes had turned severe and I wanted to creep away from her glare. "Who do you think you are anyway?" She said, in a voice as quiet as a whisper. "You're supposed to be my friend. No hang on, you're supposed to be my *best* friend. My sister."

"Gillie, I didn't mean anything by it. Honestly? I thought you'd be laughing too. This is Demir we're talking about!"

"Yes it fucking is." She said, raising the volume now. "And how I feel about him is up to me. Do you understand? It's up to me and nobody else. I want you to remember that."

"Of course." I tried to link her arm but she flinched away

from me. "Sweetheart, let's be realistic. This is the Demir with the daughter he never told you about. This is the Demir who tried to get you to go home days early with a pilfered flight ticket. This is the Demir you said you were just having a bit of fun with. I honestly have no idea why you'd want to waste three hundred pounds going to see him again. You could do a million times better than him."

"Waste? Why am I 'wasting' three hundred quid but you're not. What's the fucking difference? And anyway, what crystal ball have you got that makes you so sure Mesut is going to be faithful to you?"

Point. Made.

"I don't have a crystal ball." I said, quietly.

"Fucking exactly. You're such a hypocrite, Jess." She screamed the word 'hypocrite' into the bitter, black air, where snowflakes were starting to drift down.

"But I trust him, Gillie. I have to after everything we've been through. You were there. You saw it. So you can understand it, can't you?"

Gillie snatched her coat off me and threw it on, pulling the collar up around her neck, which was now straining with frustration. "To be quite honest, I am done with trying to understand everything you've been through. I don't see why I should keep making the effort. What makes your experience in Turkey so much more valuable than mine? Nothing, that's what. I'm going to Turkey. To be with Demir. And I don't care if I don't see you at all. You can keep your precious Mesut and I don't want to hear another bloody, arsing thing about it." She spun on her heel, and marched off into the night, her loose hair streaming out like flames behind her.

So it was silence that got us to the front of the taxi queue. Because it just seemed safer. I was standing there, breathing in cold blasts of December air, shivering from the throbbing shocks to my lungs and hoping we'd be able to claw our friendship back together in the days to come. To give it the best possible chance I kept my mouth firmly shut. Too many Black Russians and whatever the hell Gillie had been drinking had gone before to ensure a happy ending to this night out.

When an empty taxi finally edged towards us, I handed Gillie her handbag which I'd been clutching since I'd run out of the club to find her. She gave me a cold look and snatched it before jumping into the taxi and slamming the door behind her.

She'd had her final word. And it looked like I'd be travelling home alone that night.

25

THE PAST LIFE PARTY

Ella stretched the pink woolly blanket over my legs as well as her own, taking care to tuck our toes in too. "We can share, can't we, Jess? This blanket is big enough for both of us."

Sandra passed by and dimmed a frilly lamp that stood on a small round table right next to the reclining chairs we were sprawled out on. "Champion, lasses. Get yourselves comfy, we'll start in a minute."

Ella's smile beamed out at me in the soft, golden light. Even though I was wondering how on earth I'd ended up here, in Sandra's house of all places, on a cold, December night, I had to admit it was all very cosy. Sandra did always know how to calm things right down.

Ella shuffled a little under the blanket, digging herself deeper into the soft, chintzy chair, and did a squeal not quite loud enough to disturb Sandra's other guests. "I'm soooo glad I was with you when Sandra called yesterday. Face it, Jess. You'd never had said yes if I hadn't been listening in, would you?"

"Too bloody right I wouldn't have. After what happened with Gillie on her birthday, I'm having enough trouble dealing with this life, thank you very much, without opening up a whole load of past ones as well."

"Well, I happen to think, my darling girl, that a Past Life Party is exactly what you need. And don't worry about Gillie. Emotions are high at the moment. She'll be fine in a few days."

"God, I hope so." I swallowed, feeling a little bit sick at the thought of my best friend not speaking to me for the second time this year. The way I'd handled Firebelly's demise in the summer had left a lot to be desired and Gillie had made it plainly known that she was pissed off with me then. The trip to Turkey had sorted that out in the end. Would a couple of cheap flight tickets be able to do that again?

"How cool is it that Sandra had a couple of people drop out last minute?" Ella pulled the edges of the blanket up towards her chin. "And how further cool is it that she thought of you and me to come and take their place?"

"The absent guests are probably out doing late-night Christmas shopping which, incidentally, is what I should be doing. And I'm still trying to work out how the hell Sandra is back in my life. It's all very weird."

"There's not enough weird in the world, if you ask me sweet pea. And as for Christmas shopping, just give everyone a goat from Oxfam. That's what I'm doing. Oooh, look! I think it's starting."

Sandra had lit about a thousand candles on shelves around the room so that copper shadows now bulged and bellowed on the beige anaglypta walls, clashing softly with the multi-coloured glow of the Christmas tree lights by the bay window. There were three other women lolling on various bits of furniture that Sandra had dragged into her living room for the purpose of this evening – a couple of garden recliners and a camp bed that looked like it had seen better days. "Okeydokey, everyone. It's important you all feel relaxed and comfortable now that we've been through our emotion trawl." Sandra finally set down her matches and took a seat on a high stool in the corner of the room. She looked like one of Santa's elves sat up there with the lights from the tree right behind her and her red fluffy jumper on. "Please let me know if there's anything that's bothering anyone. Temperature, noise, discomfort. I can sort it before we start."

Bearing in mind the set-up had taken the best part of half an hour, I wasn't surprised when there was a resounding silence to this. Bless Sandra though – this hypnotherapy stuff obviously meant the world to her.

The 'emotion trawl' had taken even longer than the blanket and candle action. Painstakingly, Sandra had asked each one of us to decide on an emotion we felt was holding us back in our lives. "Flipping heck!" I'd blurted out. "Shall I just do a lucky dip?" Sandra hadn't been amused. Neither had anyone else.

"There will be one emotion, our Jessica, that trips you up more than any other. Have a think pet. What is it?" I immediately converted my jovial, witty self into a solemn, nodding person who couldn't possibly be accused of using pointless banter to divert from her deeply ingrained emotional pain. Because I had a feeling that was going to happen next if I didn't buck up my attitude.

"Just do sadness or something." Ella had said. "Keep it simple."

"What are you doing?" I whispered.

"I'm doing impatience. You know me – always trying to rush into the next project and the next project. I need to learn to back off a bit. I know I do."

Right, okay. If Ella could have that much personal insight then so could I. Sadness it was. Even though this year had been awesome on so many levels, I guessed the sadness I'd felt at Jack leaving last New Year's Eve had been pretty all-consuming.

Maybe there would be a way to ward it off in the future? Time to find out.

Once we'd all chosen our life-limiting emotion, Sandra had gone round the room and asked each person individually a particular series of questions:

"For what purpose do you want to deal with anger / sadness / impatience?"

"Will the outcome increase your choices?"

"What will happen if you resolve this emotion?"

"What won't happen if you resolve this emotion?"

"What will you gain?"

"What will you lose?"

"How much do you want to change?"

"How much do you not want to change?"

"What colour are your pubes?"

Okay. Maybe not the last one. But it might as well have been. Perhaps this was part of the hypnosis, I'd mused, where she confuses us so much with ridiculous questions and then shoots a curveball at us just to see if we're in the correct 'state' to proceed. God, I was cynical.

Anyway, we were finally here, blanketed up to the eyeballs and our limiting emotions waiting on the periphery of our psyches, ready to be blasted to kingdom come. Sandra had informed us (sadly) that these emotions wouldn't completely disappear from our lives, but they would most likely stop holding us back. That would do for now, I supposed. And if, in the meantime I got to visit my past self lording it up as an Egyptian Queen or an Indian Goddess, then I was on board.

"Okay, yous lot. Now remember what I said about hypnosis not being a scary, embarrassing thing? There will be no clucking chickens here tonight. All I'll be doing is speaking directly to your unconscious mind whilst you are in a state of deep relaxation. So there is nothing you will do or say that you don't want to do or say. The hypnosis part of it simply relaxes your critical ego so that we can find past-life memories to do with your limiting emotion. All yous have to do is focus on the sound of my voice and trust the first impressions you get. Just go with them. Even if you feel like you're making them up. That's just your conscious mind creeping in and, quite honestly, taking the piss. Be curious, open-minded, and go with whatever your unconscious mind brings out. It'll be right."

Wow. Sandra had come a long way since making stinky egg sandwiches for tea.

"Right. Everyone close your eyes and allow your body to just sink into the couch or chair. Relax as best you can and let your body be heavy and full."

Not difficult, considering Ella and I had practically inhaled curry sauce and chips for dinner on the way over to Sandra's house. Come to think of it, I hoped my relaxation levels didn't reach the mortifying stage of stinking the house out. That would potentially impinge on my decadent, Cleopatra-like fantasies.

Sandra continued, her voice taking on a smoother tone. "In a moment, but not yet, I am going to speak directly to your unconscious mind. If you're comfortable with me doing so, please say yes."

"Yes." Came the reply from the three other women and Ella, steady and firm and right on time.

"Yes." I added, a millisecond later, keeping my eyes closed whilst urging the tension in my jaw to disappear.

Sandra didn't miss a beat. "Jessica, in a moment, but not yet, I am going to speak directly to your unconscious mind. Are you comfortable with me doing so?"

"Yes." I said again.

"Are you perfectly willing to present the limiting emotion of: 'Anger', Bethany; 'Guilt', Linda; 'Greed', Doris; 'Impatience',

Ella; and 'Sadness' Jessica? . . . for resolution and for healing to take place to resolve it . . . now?"

"Yes." We all breathed, as one.

"Thank you. That's just perfect. So, I'm inviting you now to just relax and keep those eyes softly closed. Now find a way that allows you to be aware of your memories, past, present and future . . . now . . . turn and become aware of your memories from the past."

Sandra paused. I had no idea what everyone else was doing but in my mind's eye, I was turning to my left and looking back over a long, silky ribbon of time. The ribbon was thick and shiny and purple. I had no idea where that image had come from but, as Sandra said, I tried not to freak out at the weirdness of it and just allowed it to be. So I looked all the way down the ribbon into some kind of swirling, misty landscape.

"As you do that now . . . begin to identify the earliest event where you felt your limiting emotion. Go to the scene where you first ever felt it and raise your hand for me when you're done."

It was the strangest thing. I could sense Sandra moving around the room and whispering questions to each lady individually. At the same time I was absorbed in travelling along my ribbon to look for events in my life with sadness attached to them. Was this what hypnosis was like then? A parting of the mind into the usual awareness of moment-by-moment happenings but at the same time a section devoted to an enticing fusion of imagination, memory and curiosity?

There was my sadness right now, at having offended Gillie on her birthday night out, but I had to go much further back than that. I swept backwards to Jack leaving and was kind of amazed at how I didn't actually feel the emotion of sadness, it was more like I was looking for it, in a trembling lip, a rolling tear, a listless body.

Further back I remembered my brother leaving for drama school, my nana dying just as I was about to go visit her in the Highlands of Scotland, a best friend deserting me at secondary school for the cool crowd, having the family dog put down when I was nine. And then there it was, bobbing gently on the shiny ribbon as a little module of memory.

A seven-year-old me, sitting on a tarmac path right at the bottom of my village, hanging my head down and hugging my knees in tight to my chest, quaking with every tear that spills into the cracks of the pavement. The stunning views of the valley that would be there if I just lifted my head, wait quietly as I cry. The sunny heads of dandelions grow nearby, proud and pretty, offering comfort I don't yet understand. I know why I'm crying. It's that man. The one who won't leave me alone when Sandra's not looking. Or sometimes even when she is. My whole body is lost in sadness because nobody has ever treated me like this before. Why now? Why me? What is wrong with me?

"Jessica, love. You've raised your hand. Have you found your earliest memory of sadness?" Sandra is suddenly beside me. I can feel her fluffy jumper brush against my arms. I keep my eyes closed. I hadn't even realised I'd raised my hand.

"Yes."

"Okay, love. Is it before you were born or after you were born?"

What a strange question. "After I was born."

"Right. What age are you?"

"Seven."

"Perfect. Now you've got a timeline there, haven't you?"

"Yes. It's a lovely purple ribbon."

"Oooh. How nice. Now I want you to step off your ribbon and imagine that all around you there is a transparent, plastic shield. Like a bubble. It's thick and protective and nothing can get through it unless you allow it to, okay? Tell me when you've done this."

It wasn't hard. I could imagine the plastic bubble straight away. It was quite good fun being inside it, actually. Like a fairground ride that I had control over. "Got it, Sandra."

"Perfect. Now, look again at the sad memory you found from when you were seven years old. Stay inside the protective shield . . . that's right . . . now . . . turn and place your back to that event and now I'm inviting you to look even further back down your ribbon for any other event that has the emotion of sadness attached to it. Tell me when you've done that."

I did what she asked and peered back down the path of the ribbon. It led to a darkness that wasn't foreboding, just unclear. "I don't think I see anything else, Sandra. It's such a long way back to remember."

"I know, love. Just get in touch with that emotion of sadness again . . . feel it? . . . And see if there's anything that pulls you further back. Search for an earlier event. However you do this is absolutely right and perfect."

On Sandra saying this, I remembered that I could do whatever I liked in my protective, plastic bubble so I floated, quite pleasantly further down the ribbon / timeline, looking for signs of sadness along the way. Just when I thought there was nothing else, I thought I saw a glimmer of something peeling its way out of the dark mist ahead. Was that a shimmer of ocean?

"I think I can see something, Sandra, but I'm not sure."

"Go with it, Jessica. Go and have a look."

This time I'm standing on a beach. I'm a young woman with dark hair swept back in a low bun and I'm wearing a heavy, grey skirt, white blouse and fitted coat. I'm standing in one sorry spot on a massive expanse of silver sand and I'm not alone. There are other women here. We are all waiting. I am looking out to the horizon, shivering and waiting. There's a sadness so strong I don't know how I'm still standing. It's hard not to let it into my plastic bubble.

"I've got it." I say, knowing Sandra is still there.

"Is it before you were born or after you were born?"

"Before." I say, not even pausing to dissect such a ridiculous answer.

"Was it in the womb or before the womb?"

"Before the womb."

"Okay, love. Whose lifetime is it? An ancestor's or a past life of yours?"

"A past life of mine. I can feel it. The sadness." I was vaguely aware of my pulse quickening at the strangeness of my answer but a large portion of my brain was telling me to wait it out.

"Remember your protective shield. How many lifetimes ago is it, Jessica?"

"One or two . . . I'm not sure."

"Yes you are." Sandra confirmed. "How many lifetimes ago is it?"

"It's two. Two lifetimes."

"Okay. Thank you. Now please turn in your protective shield and look back down your ribbon. Check further back again. Is there an earlier memory you could go to?"

I knew what I was doing now. Nothing shimmering or glimmering this time. Absolutely nothing. "Nope. Just this one."

"Fine. Now turn in your protective shield towards the memory you've found. And, if you want to, tell me what is happening . . . you don't have to and it can be very helpful if you do."

"I'm a young woman but I look nothing like me. I've got dark hair and pale, freckled skin and I'm maybe a little bit younger. I'm standing on a horrible, depressing beach and looking out at the ocean in front of me. There are other women all around me and they're all waiting too. They're all crying – some with hope and happiness but some with sadness like me. There are ships appearing on the horizon but I know who I'm waiting for isn't on any of them. There is an older woman with wiry grey hair at my side and she's sighing, like she knows what will happen next is inevitable. I know it is too . . . and I'm sad because the man I'm waiting for is never coming back . . . my life is doomed now. The sadness is unbearable. I think I'll be crushed by it. I hope I'll be crushed by it."

"Perfect. Well done, Jessica. Now . . . what is there for you to learn so that by gaining the learnings, the emotion relating to the event can leave . . . now?"

There was a part of my mind screaming, *'That question doesn't make any bloody sense!'* but I somehow answered it anyway. "I'm not sure. I'm so sad here. I want to give myself a cuddle."

"Is there anybody there who could give you a cuddle?" Sandra asked, reminding me that I had some autonomy here.

"Yes. There is a woman standing next to me. But I'm not sure if she will or not."

"She will."

As if on cue, the older woman turned and took me in her arms, patting my back and shushing me even though no sound at all came out of my devastated body. "Okay. We're hugging."

"What else is there to learn?"

"Acceptance. That's just the way things are now."

"What do you mean by that, Jessica? What can you see from your shield?"

"I can see that I just have to get on with things. I can see that's the way things are now and there's nothing I can do about it. I'm alone and that's how it's always going to be. I'm sad and that's how it's always going to be."

"Listen carefully, our Jessica. What resources do you have as an adult that would benefit that other you in the memory and allow healing to take place . . . now?"

I straightened up inside my plastic bubble and let the Jess from this life think this one through. "Patience. Faith. Remembering that things can change." I thought about my challenges from Marcus and writing in my journal and going to Turkey. "This other me could benefit from having some belief in herself. In her capacity to change."

"Okay." Sandra's voice sounded a little lighter. A little quicker. She guided me through a few more questions and then encouraged me to reflect on the learnings I'd mentioned. She guided me away from the sad scene on the beach so that I glided along my purple ribbon, inside my plastic bubble-shield until I passed all of the memories I'd found on the way earlier. I was able to use the ideas of patience and faith and belief in myself to tinge each of my previously sad memories with a little bit of comfort. The sadness wasn't gone completely, but it was slightly more bearable. By the time I was back in the present moment, I realised my cheeks were wet with tears and Sandra was giving me a short pep talk about being safe and grounded. There was no dodgy counting from ten to one or being told to come 'back to the room', just a simple, "Open your eyes, our Jessica. You did really well."

I blinked and looked around me. All of the other ladies, including Ella, were up and out of their makeshift therapist couches and helping themselves to sausage rolls and pickled onions at Sandra's dining table. "Ooops. Did I take longer than everybody else to sort myself out?"

"Divn't fret, pet." Sandra said, rubbing my arm and giving me a smile. "It takes as long as it takes. How are you feeling?" She squinted at me and I got the sense she was assessing all of me from my skin tone to my posture to my pupil dilation.

"I'm okay. I feel a bit sad to be honest. That I couldn't help that lady. Or, I guess, I couldn't help me. Is that normal?"

"Eee, divn't be worried by what's normal, pet. Go and get yourself some scran. You'll need it after all that."

So I unfurled myself from the pink blanket and stretched my crumpled body up and out of the chair. I made a beeline for the pickled onions, but not before encountering an exultant Ella. "Jess! How was it? Did you remember anything weird? I found myself inside a rock! Yes! Inside a bloody rock and not being able to chisel my way out of it. I don't even think I was human and it was possibly at the dawn of time! No wonder I'm impatient to get things done – I couldn't get out into the world! Anyway, here are some pickled onions for you. I saved you some because now that Doris has obliterated her limiting emotion of 'Greed' it was nearly game over by the time I got to the dining table."

"Aw, thanks, Ella. A rock, eh? Trust you!"

Ella chattered on about her rock experience and how much better she was feeling having gone through the hypnosis process. She certainly looked more carefree with her movements and her expressions were more alive. In fact, looking around me now, everybody seemed to be an upgraded version of the self that had walked through the door earlier that evening. I checked in with myself as I chewed on Sandra's party food to see what differences I could notice. I felt okay. But if there was anything out of the ordinary, then it was a slightly unpleasant buzz circling my heart. What was that?

After we'd all eaten our own body weight in buffet food off paper plates with dancing Santas on them, Sandra called us back into the living room. "Right, yous lot. You've all done so brilliantly tonight, and I hope yous all feel a canny bit more empowered, a canny bit more like who you're meant to be. If you've got any questions over the next few days about how you're feeling, or if you notice anything at all about different ways that you do things now that you've had your limiting emotions released, just give me a bell. Before I send yous all home though, you can pick a card from my affirmation deck. These are dead canny. Each card's got a mantra or a quote or something on it to go away with. Doris. Do you want to go first?"

Each of the ladies took a random card from Sandra. They all seemed delighted with what they were given and started suiting and booting up at Sandra's front door as Ella and I went to take our cards too. Ella got a card printed with *'The world is making space for progress.'*

"Hell yeah it is." Ella whooped. "*My* progress bitches!"

Sandra laughed along with her – how could you not? This girl was going to take the world by storm, we all knew it. When I reached out to take my card, Sandra immediately stopped laughing, as if she was profoundly interested in what I was going to get. Her wide, grey eyes landed on me as I turned the card over. *'The best is yet to come'*.

"Perfect." Sandra said, with a gravity that didn't seem fitting for the back end of a party. "Jessica? Ella? Can you stay for a bit longer?"

We looked at each other and shrugged. What the hell. "Yes." We both said.

"Canny. Let me kick this lot out and I'm coming back to yous. Jessica, your card is right and that means there's a bit more work to do, love. That's if you're up for it?"

Ella linked her arm through mine and snuggled in close. I had no idea what Sandra wanted to do with me, but tonight had been too weird and wonderful to stop now. Plus there was that odd buzzing gripping my heart and I wanted it gone. "Of course," I smiled, meeting Sandra's gaze with my own. "I'm more than up for it."

26

GOING DEEPER

Before I knew it I was in two places at once.

1. At Sandra's house, laid out on the reclining chair, that pink woolly blanket settled over the top of me again. My eyes were closed but I could still enjoy the roll of soft shadows on my eyelids caused by the flickering candles and I knew Ella was right next to me because I could smell her pickled onion breath and feel her palm in mine.

2. Stood on that wretched beach again. This time I knew I was in France. And this time I knew that the person I was waiting for as I looked hopelessly out to sea, was my fiancé. Unlike the other women stood on the beach I knew in my bones that I'd never see him again. Something had happened to him and I'd known for days. I was just standing on the beach because that's what was expected. And I knew, with every strand of my soul, that my life was now doomed to this. Greyness. Sadness. Nothingness.

"It's all so sad." I breathed, my voice held a tremor even though I was inside my plastic bubble. "I just know I've got years of nothingness to come. There's no hope at all."

"It's okay, Jessica. Remember your plastic shield. You're just watching. You don't have to feel it twice-over. Take a deep breath, pet." I did what Sandra suggested and the plastic bubble steamed up a little, offering a slight detachment from the scene. "Now, look again at the sad memory from two lifetimes ago. Stay inside the protective shield . . . that's right . . . now . . . turn and place your back to that event and now I'm inviting you to look even further back down your purple ribbon for any other event that has the emotion of sadness attached to it. Tell me when you've done that."

I was pretty sure there was nothing there because my conscious mind was telling me I'd already tried this and there had been nothing there the first time. May as well get back to eating the dregs of the buffet so Sandra didn't have to chuck any food out. But just as I was about to tell her there was nothing, I saw – or felt, I'm not sure – a flash of blonde sunshine on wood. And then I smelled the wood. Freshly cut and cloying, a sweetness in my nose that I recognised. "I think there's something weird down there, Sandra. But I don't know. I might just be making it up."

"It doesn't matter, pet. Even if you're making it up it's for good reason. Let's go and have a look, shall we?"

So I floated further down the purple ribbon – quite sorry to leave the woman on the beach – and found myself in a barn surrounded by the rustle of tall trees with millions of bright green leaves. I looked up, way up, and saw that the barn wasn't finished. There were great strips of open air above me where the roof needed fixing, the afternoon sunlight shining through the leaves on the branches and creating spots of emerald and gold across the wood chip floor. I was kneeling on the ground, panting because I'd been running. I was only around four years old, a younger version of the sad woman on the beach. This was the same lifetime.

"I'm in the same lifetime but I'm just a little girl. Four years old and wearing a white dress."

"Okay, love. Before we look more closely at that memory, can you just have another look down your timeline? Is there anything else back there with sadness attached to it?"

"No."

"Okay. Let's have a look at this one then, shall we?"

I told Sandra what I could see as it was happening. There was something wrong with that poor little girl with the incredibly long, dark hair and the dirty, scratched feet. She crouched, as still as she could on the ground, hoping that the commotion of the crashing trees above would mask the sound of her tears. Her white dress covered her bent knees and she bowed her head forwards, crying softly. A sadness infused her little body. She was overwhelmed.

"Is there another emotion behind the sadness, Jessica?" Sandra asked, her full attention on me. "If you moved the sadness to one side, what would you find?"

"Fear." I said, as I observed (and felt) the shaking of the little girl's bones. "I'm scared. There's somebody coming and it's going to happen again." Almost as soon as I said these words to Sandra in her living room, a huge, black shadow threw itself across the barn. The light changed from gold and green to black, and I felt that same, hopeless acceptance I'd felt as a grown woman on the beach. This was how it was. Nothing could change it.

The source of the shadow, a great big hulk of a man, held a belt in his hand which swung low at his side, the buckle trailing in the wood chip and making a long, snaking groove towards me. It was always me he went for. Never any of the others. I was past trying to understand it or even pretending to care. I just knew it would always be me and there was nothing I could do about it.

"He's going to hit me." I sniffed. "I can smell his breath and his sweat – it smells awful like it always does. Like burnt sugar. I think I'm going to be sick."

"Breathe, Jessica. You're not going to be sick. You're just watching from your shield, remember? Now, what's happening? If the little girl is in danger, what can she do to help herself?"

I knew there was nothing I could do because this was the way things were. I stayed in that crouched position, and felt the air blast in a shock over my bare back as he clumsily reached down to lift my white dress, almost falling over me in the process. The belt buckle thudded on the ground before me as he struggled to regain his balance. It glinted in front of my eyes. Then he hooked the hem of my dress over my head and hot drool splashed over my neck.

Ma fille. Pourquoi tu m'obliges à faire ça? Tu sais que tu devrais bien te comporter.

His words were slurring and rough so I knew there was nothing I could say to stop him now. He said I should behave but I hardly ever made a move or said a word when he was around. I'd learned that by now. I didn't even brace myself for the strokes anymore. I'd learned that by keeping my flesh soft and sad, there was less of a burn afterwards.

Putain de gamine, que t'es bête. C'est trop facile. T'es trop mole. Tu le mérites.

I didn't understand how I deserved this but he said I did so it must be true. And yes, I knew I was stupid otherwise how would I always be found? Every time?

I didn't even feel the first blow because the buckle missed me by a mile. He really was out of it. But the second and third were more on target. I wrapped my hands around my head because I knew that if he hit me there I wouldn't be any good to anyone. Better my hands get battered than my head.

"Jessica!" Sandra urged. "You said the little girl was feeling fear. Now that her father is beating her, what's the emotion behind the fear?"

"I don't know. It hurts!"

"You do know! What is she feeling right now?"

Somehow I felt Ella's hand squeeze mine really hard as I also felt the blows hard and thrashing to my back. "I think, I think she's confused. About why he always picks her."

"Okay. Confusion. And what's behind the confusion love? There will be something there."

I could feel my breath hot and quick against my knees with my head tucked in towards them and my dress pulled up and over. A tiny white tent, a tiny white space I could stay in while he continued to hit me. No sense of rhythm or flair. Just awkward, ridiculous lashes that sometimes struck the ground harder than they did me.

"She's frustrated. This always happens – no matter what she does to try and stop it. It's frustration, Sandra."

"Of course!" Sandra clapped her hands together, I think. "Of course she's frustrated. This shouldn't be happening to a four year old. He's a grown man, our Jessica. Now, look carefully. Feel carefully. What's behind the frustration?"

I felt it before I could even say the word. This time, with two versions of myself present for the beating, the emotion had extra power. It tore at my heart and twisted my veins and gave a heartrending clarity to my grubby knees in front of my face, my breath pyretic and shooting out in screaming hot shards. It was like a bullet charging out of a gun. Black. Hard. Inescapable.

"Anger."

"Anger. Good. Now, look around you, Jessica. Make that little girl see something, anything she can do to change the situation. She's going to grab something or use something or create something that gets her out of this as quickly as possible. Do you understand? And you're going to help her . . . now."

I knew Sandra was right. I could do this. I let the beatings rain down as I poked my head quickly out of my white tent. I noticed he was slowing down. Lagging. Even at four years old I might be stronger than him right now, with all the poison flowing through his body. The next time the silver belt buckle dropped among the wood chips, I knew that was my second to act. I grabbed it and pulled it and owned it before he even knew what had happened.

I sprung to my feet and whirled to face him. My dress floated down over my blood-ripped body like a ghost landing on a grave and his face turned a nauseous shade of green.

"Say something, Jessica. She's going to say something to put an end to this right now."

His eyes were wide and drooping. His mouth too. The drool that landed on my neck before now plummeted to his boots and he stared downwards, as if wondering where it had come from. I wrapped the belt around my tiny little hand and summoned all the strength god gave me as I arced my arm backwards, ready for the sweet momentum of the buckle to swing high.

Tu ne me traiterais plus jamais comme ça.

You will never treat me like that again.

There was just enough time to watch his face distort into a sagging mess of shock before metal struck flesh and bone and eyeball. The potency of the strike was otherworldly and I managed to do it again three more times before he fell to the floor, clutching his ruined eyes behind huge quaking hands that would never touch me again. The might of my words had slashed the air with such ferocity that they still remained, scorching and tight.

You will never treat me like that again.

These weren't the actions or the words of a four-year-old girl. I knew that as I stood in my plastic bubble, watching her walk out of the barn and into the woods, her white, blood-streaked body gradually swaddled by the dappled green light, held safely by the whisper of the trees. But because I'd also been there as this self, in this life, I'd been able to help her. We both knew, in the same heart, that she was safe now.

"She's okay now, our Jessica?"

"Yes." I smiled, feeling Ella's hand loosen slightly. "She's okay."

"Wonderful. Now . . . what is there for you to learn so that by gaining the learnings, the emotion relating to the event can leave . . . now?"

I didn't care if the question made sense this time. I just interpreted it in my own way. "Strength. I am so much stronger than I realise. Physically and emotionally."

"What else is there to learn?"

"And I'm deserving. Deserving of love and peace and respect. And I won't let anybody threaten those things again. I won't."

"What else is there to learn?"

"That's it. Strength and deserving of love and peace and respect. So I can be all the things I'm meant to be."

"And how do you feel, Jessica? How do you feel and how does the little girl feel?"

"The little girl. Me. I've gone. Off into the woods probably to find my brothers and sisters or something. I'm happy and breathless because I know I've ended it. And lying here now in your living room Sandra, I'm so calm." And I meant it. A refreshing wash of positivity arced over me like a rainbow sweeps through a town after a storm – I felt cleansed and still and perfect. Yes. Perfect.

"Okay, love. This is very important now. I want you to

take the learnings of strength and being deserving of love and peace and respect and store them where you store your learnings."

I didn't know what Sandra meant at first. Where do you store your learnings? In your head I supposed? But I was in such a deep state of relaxation that I waited until my body caught up with my brain and suddenly the answer was there. My learnings didn't go in my head. Of course they didn't. At least not the big, powerful ones like this. They went in my heart, for certain. So I imagined my heart opening up like a big old creaky treasure chest, and I gently placed them inside. Strength. Deserving of love and peace and respect.

"Raise your hand so I know when you've done it love." I did so as soon as I could see those learnings all nestled snugly next to each other inside the chest. "Now . . . I want you to install the new learnings of strength and being deserving, in the space that was previously occupied by the limiting emotion you chose earlier. Tell me when you've done that."

I peered slightly deeper into the treasure chest of my heart and could see a dark, softly pulsing object a bit like a teardrop made of inky, metallic water. I watched it swell until it eventually burst softly and silently under the weight of the strength and the deserving. The sadness was gone.

"Okay, Sandra. I've done it."

"Wonderful. In a moment and not yet, I want you to travel back along your ribbon timeline, all the way back to the present and use your learnings and your resources to reframe all events to which the limiting emotion was previously attached. Tell me when you are back in the present. If you get stuck, let me know. Are you ready? Go . . ."

I'm back on the beach and I'm still looking out to the ocean with tears in my eyes. I'm sad and I know he's not coming back. But even now, with this knowledge that I won't see him again, there's a tiny flame inside that I know, with time, will burn and grow. Maybe he will even show up again. One day.

I'm seven years old and sitting on the tarmac pavement. I'm looking up and out towards the valley below and the lump in my throat is quelled with every second that I notice the green curve of the hillsides, the white velvet of the clouds bumping dreamily into the yellow sun. What that man said was bad. He doesn't get to treat me like that. When my parents return from work, I will tell them all about him . . .

I'm sad about my dog not coming back from the vets. But she was wonderful and I can still smell her on the sofa cushions. It will be alright . . .

In class, she's gone to sit with those other girls, who think they're better than everybody else. That's okay. I turn and start a conversation with the new girl which will be far more interesting anyway . . .

My nana's gone. She was amazing. She wrote poems and made sculptures and taught me how to play all the best card games. I can't wait to tell my own children about her one day . . .

My brother left an hour ago and there's a silence in the house. He's going to love drama school so much – he's following his purpose, I just know it . . .

Jack has left me standing here, outside a pub in the pitch black on New Year's Eve with the possibility that love has gone. I love him. But I love myself more and whatever happens I'll get through it . . .

Gillie got in the taxi without me. She's so angry. I don't know how we managed to get to this point but I know we'll sort it out. The best is yet to come . . .

"I've done it, Sandra. I'm back here now."

"Perfect, love. Now I want you to travel out to a time in the future when you would have previously felt the way you used to. What new feelings and beliefs do you have instead?"

This was trippy. I floated along my purple ribbon to the right, a direction I hadn't explored yet, and I found it pretty quickly. I was a few years older and I was standing on a pavement in a busy street watching a toddler have a tantrum on the ground. My toddler. I'd tried everything to calm him down but his face had grown redder and his screams louder and his movements more violent. People were passing and tutting and staring. I felt sad that I couldn't take away his frustration and that I didn't seem to have the resources a mother is supposed to have. But because I knew I was simply learning (and so was he), I sat on the ground next to him and waited. "It's okay. We'll figure it out." I said, and made a show of breathing deeply and slowly. That respect and that deserving? I was going to lavish it upon him as much as I was on myself.

"Jessica, you're nearly done. Now take those learnings and store them where you store such learnings and when you've done that, come back to the present, letting all these new learnings inform all you will be and all you will do in the future." Sandra had an edge of excitement to her voice. I had a feeling I'd be getting a cuddle in a minute.

I did what she said without much effort at all. That beautiful, creaky old treasure chest, right in the centre of my heart, opened up and welcomed curiosity and self-belief and present-moment awareness in its soft, satin folds deep inside. I locked the chest to keep them safe, knowing that I'd be getting them out again soon.

"Done, Sandra."

"Lovely, pet. Now give good old Ella's hand a squeeze and wiggle your fingers and toes. Feel your body in the chair and notice the sensations of your clothes against your skin, the blanket on top of you. And when you're ready you can open your eyes."

I followed each of Sandra's instructions. When I opened my

eyes, I looked at Ella, who had been holding my hand the entire time and saw that she was fighting back the tears. "Jess you absolute beauty – you did amazing!" Her bottom lip was a quivering wreck and the tears now flowed fast and free, splashing onto our joined hands. "I can't believe everything you've just been through!"

"Hey, I'm alright you nutter. Was it really that awful? I feel incredible." I shuffled myself further up into a sitting position and crossed my legs beneath me. "That was some weird woo-woo shit though Sandra. You might have warned us."

Sandra shoved an ice-cold glass of water in my hands. "Here. Drink. You never know what's going to come out of these things, pet. And, well, there's no way I could have sent you home with that sadness still hanging over you. We had to go deeper. And I'm so glad we did. Are you feeling alright?"

After knocking back the entire glass of water, I stood up and stretched my hands above me, almost knocking off a plastic Santa hanging on the wall. That buzzing round my heart had gone. "I honestly feel great. A little bit exhausted, that was some harrowing stuff, but I feel lighter. Freer."

"Job done then, love." As expected, Sandra flung herself at me for the softest, fluffiest cuddle I'd had in ages. Then I realised she was crying too. "Oh our Jessica. I'm so, so sorry for letting Trev treat you like that all them years ago. I was proper snared up in his love and I was completely blinded by him. I'm not surprised you had a memory like that one in the barn in your past life, pet." We drew apart and Sandra continued to hold me by the arms, her rapidly dripping tears taming the previously outrageous fluff on her jumper. "At the risk of getting even more woo-woo," she sniffed, "we do sometimes have recurring themes in different lifetimes. You know, like always being dominated, or always being poorly or lost or persecuted. That's why hypnotherapy is so bloody amazing – you get to go back and investigate. I hope you feel better, pet I really do."

"Sandra, you've worked so hard with me tonight. I can't believe all the attention you've given me when you were supposed to be entertaining all those other ladies too."

"Never mind that. That lot have been to loads of these sessions and I'm sure they'll be back again. I'm just so proud of you. You really took every triggered nerve, every tremble in your spirit, every butterfly in your belly and you said, '*No. I'm not doing this anymore.*' I can bet you now that your ancestors are rejoicing. Properly partying for you, they are."

"Cool thought." Ella gasped. "A multi-generational rave-up!" And she started giving it big-fish-little-fish in the centre of the living room, in an alarmingly proficient fashion.

I turned back to Sandra, laughing. "I don't know how to thank you, I really don't." Ella paused her rigorous mash-up of dance styles to chuck us a box of tissues. Sandra and I ripped the contents out of it eagerly.

"Now listen carefully . . ." Sandra sniffed. "I want you to consider that you've stirred up a hell of a lot of energy here tonight, both within you and around you. Don't be surprised if the universe gives you some challenges next. All too often I hear from my clients that not long after one of these sessions, they are confronted with something difficult with similar themes. You know, summat that'll test you to them boundaries again. So be ready for it, okay?"

"Oh god, really? Okay. I'll try to remember."

"Eee, divn't stress, pet. Because now we know you can handle it. Just tune back into that amazing strength you've gone and cultivated and that lovely knowledge that you are deserving of love and peace and respect, just like you said. Then nothing can touch you, love. Nothing."

"Agreed." I said, dabbing at my eyes. "And Sandra? There's

something I know I can do now. Something I never would have been able to do before."

"What's that, love?"

I drew myself up to my full height and remembered all those scrumptious learnings I'd locked in that treasure chest only moments ago. I felt their power and their worth and their pounding, precious pulse working along with the very blood flow of my heart. I knew I could do this. So I said out loud, looking Sandra right in her beautiful grey eyes, "I'll meet with Trev."

27

OBSESSED

"There's only one question I've got after listening to all of that." Lindy said, with a sideways smile.

"Yep?" Jess asked.

"How does it feel to be a time-traveller?"

Jess released a peal of glittering laughter and a few heads in the restaurant turned towards the two women sitting in their little alcove. Lindy didn't care. Let them stare.

"Honestly." Lindy continued. "It was amazing. You didn't even need a DeLorean or anything!"

"Right? Sandra would give Doc Brown a run for his money, that's for sure."

"True." Lindy agreed. "You were honestly okay though? It sounds like the whole thing was fucking exhausting, not to mention ridiculously dramatic. Do you really think those were past lives?"

"Fucked if I know. Maybe I'll never answer that question. Maybe they were just incredibly elaborate metaphors that my unconscious mind came up with because it knew I had to learn a thing or two."

"Ugh. Metaphors? Makes me think of boring poetry lessons. Wouldn't that just be a massive let-down if that's what they were?"

"Not really." Jess sighed and held Lindy's gaze. "It doesn't really matter that much what they were or whether I was really hypnotized or whatever. The point was that I was in safe hands and I worked through some crap I needed to work through. Men with huge, formidable personalities like that, they've always daunted me. Always got the better out of me. And that horribly violent scenario in the barn with that little girl was horrific, but helping her finally take control of things was such an incredible moment. It changed everything."

"And what about the scene on the beach with the sad lady. Did she really feel less sad after the four-year-old you was such a badass with that belt?"

"Oh my god, absolutely. The whole scene felt different. The situation was the same – she'd still lost someone she loved, but because that moment in the barn changed it all, she wasn't so conditioned into being a victim. She knew her worth was more than that. She knew things could change."

"Lucky for her. Or you. Lucky for you." Lindy licked her fingers with relish. The baklava had been even more delicious than the portions they'd shared on the beach earlier, and she'd taken Jess's cue in eating it slowly, deliberately, savouring the nutty density, the sweet honey and cinnamon twang. Jess had said at the time, as Lindy had observed the pace at which she ate the stuff, *'If you're going to have a treat, you may as well be present for it'*. She'd been right. And now there were only a few forkfuls left.

"I don't think it's luck at all." Jess continued. "I think it's just part of the shifting story."

"The shifting story? Come on. You'll have to give me more than that."

"Well, what I'm thinking is, that energy is a powerful thing, right?"

"Right."

"Good. So, when we're feeling good we put out an energy that is what, joyful? Helpful? Easy? Relaxed?"

"Yep. Depending on the circumstances, it could be dynamic? Confident? Catching even?" Lindy thought about how much better she felt since she'd met Jess earlier that evening. Yes, good energy could definitely be catching.

"Totally!" Jess said. "And we know, from the genius science people, that energy is changeable, yes? It never disappears into nothing, but it does change and morph and grow and vibrate. It's always doing something."

"Agreed."

"And energy affects the things around it. Like the way a flower blooms in the sun or a baby feels happy when his mother smiles. And there's a load of research that shows that thoughts hold their own kind of energy. That what we think about somehow resonates further out than our own little minds and the universe takes it on, does something with it."

"You've been spending too much time with that Sandra." Lindy laughed, but still nodding for Jess to carry on.

"I know, right? But it's true. We've probably all noticed it. The minute you decide you are worthy of something, an opportunity comes along. Or, at the other end of the scale, the longer you feel you aren't worthy, the more likely you'll stay stuck. Anyway, what I'm learning is, that it takes enormous shifts in your mindset and your beliefs, if you want these energies to work for you. And, without even realising it, that's what I've been doing this whole year!"

"Oh my god, you totally have." Lindy agreed. From starting to journal about her beliefs and values after breaking up with Jack, to meeting Mesut and doing Marcus's challenges and sitting here now, having indulged in past life therapy, Jess was certainly shifting the energies. And her story, like she'd said.

"Anyway, I think something weird happened when I walked out of Sandra's house that night. I'd made the decision to see Trev. And that was such a big change in my mind –"

"– and your heart."

"Yes. And my heart. It was such a big change that like a pebble being dropped into a pond, that energy rippled outwards and the universe served up even more stuff to see if I was really serious. To see if I really meant it."

"More stuff? There's more?"

"Come on Lindy, we've talked about enough woo-woo shit tonight for us both to know that I couldn't have visited a past life, whacked my then alcoholic dad in the eyes with a belt buckle and get off scot-free. The things that happened next were off the charts and pretty damn hard to get through if I'm honest. The universe really knows its stuff."

"Well the universe is mean."

"No, no, no." Jess smiled and her blonde curls tumbled forward to frame her lips. Was there no end to this woman's positivity? "The universe loves me. Like, really loves me. Is obsessed with me, in fact. It's embarrassing."

Lindy giggled and stamped her feet out on the cushions in front of her. She was starting to get pins and needles but it was actually mildly pleasant. A reminder that she was alive. "Yeah, that would be embarrassing."

"You get used to it." Jess shrugged. "And I hope you get used to it too, Lindy, because I can tell you something . . ." Jess leaned forwards and lowered her voice to a kind, caressing whisper, "The universe is obsessed with you too."

28

CHRISTMAS DAY

"Happy Christmas!" My mam bellowed as she swished open the curtains in the spare room so that winter sunlight poured over me in the bed and my brother on the air mattress on the floor.

"Mother!" Max moaned from the ample depths of his duvet. "It didn't work when I was ten and it won't work now. Close the bloody curtains please."

"Resistance is futile." I laughed, sitting up and stretching my creaky arms towards the ceiling. "You should know that by now, brother."

"Hmph." He retorted, sinking as far into the air mattress as he could. Which was quite far given how much it had deflated overnight. I stepped over him to grab my dressing gown and go downstairs to my parents' living room. And there I found a scene I knew all too well. My dad knelt over the fireplace venomously swearing, twisting bits of newspaper and striking matches in an attempt to get the Christmas Day fire on the go; little bowls all set out on the coffee table brimming with Quality Streets and fruit jelly slices; overly-buttered brown bread draped heavily in Tesco's bargain smoked salmon; and four empty champagne glasses waiting next to a giant bottle of cheap fizz.

I shouted up the stairs. "Come on, Max! Get your arse in gear. I think Dad needs your help with the fire."

"I bloody don't," puffed my dad, giving me a withering look. "I could do this in my sleep, you know. But get that fizz open, will you, love? Then it'll feel like Christmas."

I crouched down to wrap him up in a tight hug. "Merry Christmas to you, Dad."

"And you, love," he said, hugging me back just as tight. "But come on, get on with the fizz. Your mother will be having kittens if it's not opened by the time she brings the vol-au-vents out."

———

That night, as I settled into the sofa in front of the fire that had finally got going after all, my feet resting in my brother's lap, and feeling deeply comforted by all the festive crap we were watching on the telly, I contemplated how this was yet another significant milestone in my new life without Jack.

The last seven Christmases had been spent alternating between our parents' houses either up north or down south. And last Christmas had been hard, even though I hadn't realised why at the time.

It had been my family's turn to have us for Christmas and I remembered feeling there was a subtle sense of spite about that. It was nothing Jack had mentioned, as such, just a tone to his speech, a nasty turn in his words that made me feel unsettled and small. Max had even mentioned it at the time. It had been a white Christmas and we'd gone out for an afternoon trudge over the snowy hills at the back of my mam and dad's house.

"Why's he speaking to you like that, Jess?" Max had asked. "Why does he feel the need to belittle you for absolutely no reason?" I think I'd brushed it off and said that I hadn't noticed. But I had. I'd just been too scared to do anything about it at the time, a deep, central kernel of my heart knowing that something wasn't right.

It was easy, now, to look back and see some of the warning signs that Jack hadn't been happy. I wasn't cross with him about that now. How could I be? Having had the year I'd had, I understood that Jack had been acting in the only way he possibly could. The snide comments and deprecating remarks that tainted my festive celebrations? That was just his guilt channeled into energy that was never going to be sustained. It would have to transform into something else at the end, and it did – it transformed into the end of our relationship.

Having said that, I wouldn't take that kind of treatment again. I knew I was worth more than that now. Sandra's house party had seen to that.

And that's why I had my laptop with me, as everyone else was sinking deeply into the telly's festive offerings. I couldn't put it off any longer because tomorrow I would be jetting off to Turkey. I was going to reply to Trev's email.

What I wrote didn't need to be too long. It didn't need to be complicated. He'd asked a very simple question and I was going to give him a very simple answer:

To: wraitht@shotmail.co.uk
From: jessp@firebelly.co.uk
Re: Re: Ninth Step

Trev,

Thank you for your email. I'm glad you are getting better from your addiction.

```
Yes, I have been reunited with Sandra again
recently and it has been lovely.

If you think meeting me will help you get
better and complete your ninth step then yes,
I would be willing to do that. I'm going on
holiday tomorrow but when I get back I will
contact you, or speak to Sandra about organ-
ising a time and place. I'll be back in the
New Year.

Regards,
Jess.
```

There. Job done. Now I just had to make sure I didn't obsess over it too much and remember that forgiving him wasn't guaranteed. I snapped shut my laptop and snuggled in closer to my brother, ready to indulge in the Morecambe and Wise Christmas Special (NEVER fails to entertain).

After a hilarious rendition of *Bring Me Sunshine*, and an obscene number of Quality Streets, I checked my watch. Flipping heck. Time to pack. Today had been the most wonderfully lazy Christmas day but it was now time to acknowledge what was really happening in the morning. I stole a few Quality Streets to take with me ("Oi! Not the green triangles!" Max protested) and went upstairs to sort out my stuff.

Once I'd managed to separate my stuff from Max's, I could see that I was pretty organised really. I'd brought everything from home I thought I'd need and all I had to do was squish it into the suitcase I was borrowing from my mam. I smiled to myself as I packed my pink tartan pyjamas. They were the oldest, scruffiest things imaginable and if Mesut was expecting sexy, slinky nightwear then he was in for quite a shock. I'd even packed my big Tesco knickers, after intensive deliberation the day before. I'd stood there, in my bedroom at home, a stack of silky French knickers in one hand and massive, stretchy cotton briefs in the other, weighing up which ones I should take.

Logic, and an adult lifetime of experience with men in bed, said that I should take the sexy French ones. Obviously.

But, logic wasn't something I went much by these days.

The way I saw it, this trip to Turkey was going to be massively telling. Mesut and I were either going to want to rip each other's clothes off at first sight . . . or we were not. We were going to take a big sexy spoon and stir up the magic from the previous summer . . . or we were not. And whichever way it went, I wanted it to be me. Jess. With my big, comfy knickers and my eternally scruffy pyjamas. Why give false advertising? I had to give him the real deal. It was only fair.

So I swallowed my pride and I packed the big knickers. Bridget Jones would be proud.

———

After a long, hot shower, shaving in all the important places and smothering myself in a body butter that smelt like actual roses (Mesut was getting big knickers, yes, but I wanted him to like what he found inside them), I cosied into bed with my notebook and those last Quality Street chocolates.

I didn't need a pen. I just wanted to flick through the pages and take a little journey through the experiences I'd had that year. So much of it had been with Gillie at my side, it felt really strange that I hadn't had the usual Christmas day phone call from her.

Since her birthday night out, we hadn't spoken at all, so she knew nothing about my past life escapades or my decision to meet with Trev. Ella might have told her, of course, but I'd had my occasional text met with one word answers only ever dealing with our imminent trip away. I didn't want to push my luck so I left it at that. On reflection, I think I had been a bit bitchy about my attitude towards her and Demir. As Mesut had warned me before, she was not my person, she was her own.

And in actual fact, I was glad she'd shouted at me. At least it gave both of us a bit of a clue about where she stood. I didn't particularly enjoy being dressed down in the middle of the city on a Saturday night, or being deserted at the taxi rank (Jack had done enough of that during the last seven years). But honestly? It was preferable to tip-toeing around her and trying to guess how she might be feeling.

And, flicking through my notebook, I could see that Gillie wasn't the only one who had pushed me to limits of some sort over the last twelve months . . .

Ella had made me explore my deepest, darkest feelings when I broke up with Jack, with stern but loving questions that can't always have been easy to ask.

Max had challenged me over my new-found connection with Mesut, encouraging me to explore what I was really in the relationship for.

Jason had turned up in my life perhaps hoping for something more, but by doing that he'd helped me work out that my preferences didn't lie in convenience and ease, but in instinct and truth.

Oliver had shown me how to discover my own personal values and beliefs – helping me underpin all of my actions with real authenticity AND he'd made me realise I needed to write my own story.

Marcus had gifted me a little bit of heaven and hell wrapped up in those godforsaken challenges. Only he could have come up with a scheme that challenged me as much as it excited me.

My dad had helped me wade through the seemingly impossible decision to end my much-loved business, a decision that I could see, now, was going to open up the future for me.

My mam had helped me reframe the past by telling me about how she'd once rescued me from the clutches of an addict – with a clunky old typewriter to help things along.

Sandra had turned my world upside down and put it back again with her euphoric advocation of body positivity and her skillful commitment to help me scour a past that was much longer and more dramatic than I could have dreamed.

There were so many people – close and not so close – who had shaped my experiences and helped me this year not just to survive, but to really thrive. There was only one thing for it. I grabbed my phone, which was charging by my bedside, and tapped out a text message:

Hello lovely one.
Before I embark on my journey back to Turkey, I just want to wish you a massive Happy Christmas and let you know something too. It has been a hell of a year for me and I'm happy to say I'm at the other end of it with nothing but a deep eagerness to keep moving forward. Having your support and your wisdom has meant the world to me so thank you!
Love, Jess.

I sent it out to everybody. Gillie included. It was up to them to do what they wanted with those words now. For me, it was time to get some beauty sleep. I had a plane to catch.

29

SIX HOURS

The road trip down to Gatwick was as smooth as I could have wished for. It was obvious that most of the British public preferred to stay indoors on Boxing Day, probably downing the last dregs of Baileys and lounging around in flannel pyjamas, which is most certainly what I would have been doing if I'd been at home. As it happened, though, I was speeding away from home as fast as my little car would carry me. My heart pounding just as fast.

Shush now, I thought to myself. I'd learned a lot this year but I was a way off knowing how to slow down my actual heart rate like those enlightened Buddhist monks I'd once read about. Deep breathing just wasn't cutting it.

And I had so much to be nervous about. How would I feel when I saw Mesut? How would he feel when he saw me? Would I be able to hold it together at the airport? What would he think of my big knickers? Oh god, oh god, why hadn't I packed the sexy French ones?

And before I even got anywhere near that moment, I had to get there first. Would the plane be on time? Would I know enough basic Turkish to get me through the transfer at İstanbul?

Would my luggage be okay? Did I have enough Turkish Lira? Would they sell sexy underwear at the airport?

All of those questions were doing a merry dance in my head at top speed, to the point where I slowed down the car for the last few miles in an attempt to get my thoughts to slow down too. And as I followed the constant, reassuring signage for Gatwick Airport, I knew there was one question that needed to be answered before any of the others.

Were Gillie and I going to be alright?

We'd arranged to meet at our check-in point. Her brother was giving her a lift from her mum's in Sussex, and I'd park in the long-stay car park so we could both drive back up north together after our trip. That was it. There had been no embellishments about the cocktails we would drink or the beach walks we would go on or the old haunts we might visit.

So, having finally found a parking space, and having dragged my luggage through eternal space-aged tunnel-type things, I'd found our check-in point and was waiting for her right next to it. I could feel the same icy swell I'd felt that night we'd argued outside the club, creeping up from my toes and into my belly. The noise and clatter of people all around me did nothing to soothe my nerves. In fact, they felt more strangled, more torn, with every luggage trolley that crashed, every child that whined, every muffled announcement over the tannoy. *Just breathe, Jess. Just breathe like you know how.*

"Shall we check in then?" I whirled round to find Gillie behind me, her face angled slightly away from me and towards the check-in desk. For somebody who was clearly in a massive huff with me, she looked pretty damn fabulous. *Why,* I wondered to myself, *do I look like I wear all of my emotions on the surface, physically embodying the nervous wreck I am, yet Gillie looks like a fucking model?*

She wore a coral and turquoise handkerchief top, draped

with a white pashmina and finished with a pair of perfectly distressed light denim jeans that clung to her curves beautifully. Her hair was swept back into an elegant, twisted knot with spiraled wisps escaping in a maddeningly nonchalant fashion. Her skin glowed with some kind of glittery body lotion and a perfect amount of lip gloss and eye shadow finished off the beach babe vibe that I would have thought impossible in the UK on Boxing Day. Still, if anybody could do it, Gillie could.

"Wow! You look incredible, Gillie. Erm, happy Christmas!" I blurted out and threw my arms around her. She returned the hug with one hand barely patting my back and the other hand flying up to her hair in an effort to protect it from my affections.

"Yep. Yep. You too. Come on, let's go and queue." Okay, so she was talking to me at least. We had to start somewhere.

When we got to the queue it wasn't long before I knew something else was wrong. The people in front of us were huffing and puffing in that spectacular way that seems unique to us Brits. "Shit." Gillie sighed. "What's going on?"

An elderly lady in front of us turned and faced us with a most excellent Christmas jumper which read, *I'm Sexy and I Snow It.* "The flight is delayed, dearies. They're saying it's going to be another six hours."

"Six hours?" Gillie and I gasped, our mouths unashamedly hanging open.

When we got to the front of the queue, it turned out the old lady was right. Six hours we'd have to wait for another flight. Six more hours of heart-wrenching nerves and rampant butterflies in my belly. Six more hours of Gillie giving me the cold shoulder in this god-forsaken place. What were we going to do for six whole hours? Consume extortionately priced sandwiches and bleak, bitter coffee until a.) our bank balances imploded or b.) our digestive systems did similar?

So I called Mesut. He was going to flip.

"Oh really?" He said down the phone, amusement toying with his tone. "Is funny Gulazer." And then there was a chuckle. A bloody chuckle!

"Erm, excuse me. What the hell are you laughing at?"

"Is a little joke on us I think. Really. We so desperate to being together. We need to know. Six hours not making any difference."

"No difference? Well that's easy for you to say. You're not the one stuck in the airport where it's cold and miserable and the only refreshments available come at a cost comparable to re-mortgaging my house!"

"You be okay." He laughed, yet again. "Gillie is with you?"

"Yes. But, well, you know. Things still aren't great between us." I lowered my voice as Gillie was just a few paces away, madly gesticulating down the phone, presumably to Demir.

"Still? Aha."

"What do you mean, 'aha'?"

He chuckled again and instead of pissing me off, I found it had the effect of automatically softening all the muscles in my body. "I am thinking the six hours is gift to you. And Gillie."

"What? A gift?"

"Come on, Gulazer. You are knowing your omens. You are knowing your signs. Now, what can you be doing with this six hours?"

"Honestly Mesut? I have no idea. Just wait I suppose."

"Well . . . maybe waiting is what you both needing."

"Yes, but come on . . . for six hours?"

"For six hours."

————

Gillie and I had walked the departure lounge's floor several hundred times. We'd tried out every single perfume in the duty-free shop until we both smelled like a stripper's dressing room. We'd read the back of every holiday novel going and still didn't fancy buying any of them. We'd shared several bags of wine gums which were the only things on special offer and therefore under a tenner. And now we'd had enough.

It was also late at night by this point and our plane didn't depart until very early the next morning. It would make sense to get some sleep if we could find somewhere to lay our heads. We knew the airport pretty damn well by now and neither of us had seen anywhere that even remotely resembled a potential resting place.

Eventually though, we did find a quiet corner where the floor looked kind of clean and with our rucksacks as pillows, we could probably fashion some kind of bed situation. Gillie had a blanket she'd saved from a previous flight and, after pausing and appearing to think this one through, she threw it over both of us, so we had to nestle in closely to both benefit from its warmth.

"Six. Fucking. Hours." Gillie muttered into her rucksack.

"Actually, it's only three and a half now." I said, checking my watch. "We're nearing the halfway mark."

"Mmm."

"What did Demir say when you told him about the delay?"

There was a short, stony silence. Then another sigh. "Do you really want to know?"

"Of course."

"He said that it actually worked out better for him because he had some business to take care of."

"Business? Isn't the holiday season finished now?"

"My thoughts exactly."

I propped myself up on my elbow and looked at Gillie. Depsite her indisputable gorgeousness, she had those tell-tale worry lines across her forehead and her jaw was set like stone.

"Gillie. Just tell me what you're thinking. And you don't need to shout at me this time. You've had your shouting quota."

The lines softened slightly. "I'm sorry I shouted at you, Jess. But to be fair, you really pissed me off."

"I know I did. It wasn't with that intention though. I think you know by now, I just don't like Demir. And I can't hide it. Not since, you know, all the stuff I've been through and where I'm at now. I'm not keeping my feelings under wraps anymore, Gillie, it doesn't lead me to good places. But I'm sorry if I was insensitive. That was shitty."

"It was. But I do get it. I just need to get used to this new, upgraded version of Jess. And I don't know. Most of the time I see this thing with Demir as fun. He's fun." I raised an eyebrow and she nudged me. "He really is. Honestly, when it's just me and him we have such a good time and it's been like that since we've been connecting on the phone and video chat too. And I think, hey, why not? Why shouldn't I go to Turkey and have another fling with him? I bloody well deserve a good time."

"I know." I chanced a go at placing my palm over her hand. She let me keep it there. "So what's the problem?"

"Well, it's as if he's a Jekyll and Hyde kind of character. One minute everything's great and I'm thinking this is all totally cool, that me and him and the fling could perhaps go further. The next minute . . . he shuts down. Acts like a shit. I feel let down. But then I feel like a fool because why should I feel let down if it's only a fling? Why can't I be cool about all this and just take it in my stride?"

"Because you're human?"

Gillie laughed, exhausted with it all. "Well, being human is shit sometimes."

"Indeed it is. You know, even if it is a fling, there's no reason why you can't have expectations. But you have to make them known."

She screwed up her nose. "Noooo. I don't want to be a clingy girlfriend type."

"Right, for starters, you're not his girlfriend. And, you're spending a lot of money going to see him, taking time away from your family and friends at Christmas. Did you check to make sure he'd be free for a fortnight whilst you're here?"

"I just kind of expected he would clear the decks for me."

"Well I suggest that you get him to sort that out as soon as you get there. You have to spell things out for him if you don't want to be disappointed. Tell him what you want and how you want it."

Gillie arched an eyebrow. "He already knows that."

"Ugh! Gillie! The sex is one thing but I'm talking about the rest of the time you're there – assuming you come up for air at some point. You know I'll be there if you need me, but I do plan to share as much time with Mesut as I can. So you need to make Demir understand what it is you want. Then, if he's still a massive bastard at the end of it all then at least you can deal with that then, can't you?"

"Such an optimistic outlook, my friend."

"So I'm your friend again, am I?" I gave her my best, most winning smile.

"For fuck's sake, of course you are!" Gillie grabbed me and pressed me close to her. "Sometimes it's just hard to deal with the change in you, okay? I'm not used to the Jess that speaks her mind quite so freely. It's good though. It's a good change. So don't change back."

"Not a chance," I smiled, as she released me. "Now, let's try and get some beauty sleep. We're going to need it."

30

THERE HE WAS

It was the dead of night again before we finally arrived at İzmir Airport, the original delay having knocked off our connecting flight. But it wasn't just the exhaustion that made me shake, and I could barely apply the lip gloss I held in my trembling fingers.

I looked into the mirror. My skin had gone far beyond the realms of English rose and I looked more like an infinitely less attractive Morticia Addams. Not helped by the stark glare of the overhead strip lighting of the airport toilets, but still. I let out a long, slow, shuddery breath and leaned close to the mirror so I could see the wide spread of my pupils, the silvery glint of blue that surrounded them. The words came out, barely a whisper, an echo of a memory somehow tethered to the present moment. "He's just a man, Jess. He's just a man."

"Jess, you look bloody gorgeous!" Gillie hollered from the toilet cubicle. "Chill your boots. It's all gonna be fine."

"Yup. Absolutely." I tried out my voice. Weird as it sounded, it would have to do. I smoothed down my top, fluffed up my hair and stepped back from the mirror. From a distance, I guessed that I would pass as somebody normal, having a perfectly normal trip away, perhaps to see a normal family member or visit a normal friend. Inside, of course, I knew there was nothing normal about any of this.

Gillie emerged from the toilet cubicle and splashed some water on her hands in a mad rush. "Shit, bloody shit." She grabbed me by the arm and dragged me out. "I forgot you're not supposed to flush the paper down the loo in this bloody country. Let's get out before the place floods!"

For once in the history of man, our luggage emerged on the conveyor belt before anybody else's. *Great,* I thought, *just when I need to buy a bit of time to get myself in order.* As we walked towards the exit, knowing that Mesut would be waiting on the other side of the doors, I felt my heart protest loudly and the beating got heavier and louder with every step I took. I glanced around at the other passengers making their way alongside us, to check if they might actually be able to hear it. I wouldn't have been surprised. And the last thing I needed right now was for somebody to attack me with a defibrillator.

My heart felt all at once too big for my chest and I wasn't sure my frame would be able to withstand its insane pounding a moment longer. I had visions of Gillie kneeling down beside my collapsed, lifeless body, the over-sized heart bouncing gleefully off through the automatic doors, never to be seen again. The headlines would read: *British girl dead as rogue heart deserts her at Turkish airport.* All of this seemed more likely right now than me actually reaching Mesut in one piece.

And then, there he was.

Before I could even take in the sight of him, I was pressed against him so hard that if my heart had decided to burst out of my body, it would have found itself deep inside his. I had the fleeting thought that his nerves must have been as tattered as mine judging by the manic pace of his heartbeat, but then, after a few moments where we both forgot to breathe, they slowed at once, together, and there was just enough room for the breath to slip back in.

"My Gulazer." I felt, rather than heard his words against the nape of my neck. The warm pressure of his broad hands spread out across my back, sending waves of rapture throughout my body. "Is alright. Is alright."

I couldn't say anything. I just nodded into the crease of his neck, tears and snot likely drenching his beautiful, jet black hair that splayed across his shoulders. This was months of tension and wanting and waiting purged in one single, glorious embrace. I didn't care how long it took.

We peeled back our heads from each other's shoulders, not willing to unlock the rest of our bodies just yet, and found each other's eyes. There he was. That deep, dark soul and an ancient core of connection spun in its own space and time. I don't know what he saw in me but whatever it was made him smile broadly and kiss me hard enough on the lips that all the time that had passed since we'd been together, just melted into the space around us.

"Ayıp, Mesut. Çok ayıp." A voice said next to us, gruffly. Mesut pulled reluctantly away from my lips to address it. It was Demir.

"Tamam Baba." He said, calmly.

Demir had an arm slung protectively around Gillie and a look on his face like thunder. He still had the same impossibly rock hard hair styled into a quiff, shifty eyes, gleaming shoes and pressed chinos – but none of that seemed quite as amusing as I had found it before. Gillie was grinning from ear to ear and apparently oblivious to whatever it was that had put Demir in a bad mood. She said with a little giggle, "Come on you two love-birds. Let's get going."

We reluctantly let go of each other and allowed the rest of the world to come into focus. Airport. Luggage. Night time.

People. Cold air blasting through the doors. Hang on a minute, cold air? "Why's it so bloody cold?" I asked Mesut, shivering close to him as we walked out into the car park. "Last time I was here it was so hot on a night I couldn't breathe."

Mesut pulled the neck of his woolly jumper up high and chuckled. It occurred to me that I'd never seen him in a jumper, let alone a woolly one. "And this time, Gulazer, you not breathing because of cold, not heat."

"But I brought my swimsuit!" Visions of lounging by a pool slowly escaped me. Everybody stopped and turned to gape. Mesut. Gillie. Demir. And perhaps even a couple of, quite frankly very nosy, strangers. I felt the grip of cold against my cheek and down my collar. "Okay," I shrugged, mournfully, "no swimsuit."

Mesut laughed and wrapped a lanky arm around me, pulling me into the warmth of him and his woolly jumper. "You not worry, Gulazer. I keeping you cosy whole time."

———

Cosy was the word.

The last time I'd been to the house Mesut stayed in, it had seemed stark, yes, but light and airy too. It had been full of sunshine streaming through the windows and cool, tiled floors sweeping through the entire place. This time was different. This time, the house was in winter mode.

Right now though, the pearl-white of my soft curves were equally as hot and clammy as the dark, hard body they were pressed against. My naked skin was stirred by the scratchy fibres of the criss-crossed carpets that now lay across the tiled floor. My breath, and his breath, rose and fell in an easy rhythm, having finally calmed from the rapid clawing of passion, and cushions fell around us like scattered jewels. The constant glow of the electric fire had become a protective shelter from the cold, encasing us in the safety of a smooth, orange light and a spiced heat that infused the bones. This was what cosy was all about.

"Is cosy enough for you, Gulazer?" Mesut's voice vibrated against my breasts, where his head finally lay.

"Yes." I sighed, pulling him closer so that his lips pressed pleasantly against my nipple, where they'd already spent quite a lot of time. "I love the house like this. It's so different."

"Really?" He looked up at me, comical wrinkles appearing across his forehead. "You not even seeing rest of house yet. You only come through door then jump on me."

"Jump on you? It didn't go quite like that . . ."

"Okay, okay, you give me enough time to switch on fire. But that is all. Then, you jump."

I couldn't argue. "Fine. I jumped on you. But you can't blame me. It's been nearly three months. And there was that old woman hanging around outside with all those flowers. What was that all about?"

"If you not jump on me I would have had time to tell you." He teased.

"Okay, okay! But tell me now. Why did you take all those flowers from her?" I pointed over to the kitchenette, which we could see from our spot on the living room floor, and at the sorry-looking bunch of roses that had been dumped in the kitchen sink. They could hardly have been for me because he'd dropped them with such a casual sense of routine. Was he in the habit of buying himself roses?

"Is old lady, Fatma Hanım. She rose-seller in İpeklikum. The best one, really. I know her such long time, since I first coming here – she very kind to me and help me with finding somewhere to live. Anyways, sometimes she not sell all her roses to holidaymakers and I always tell her, 'Come to me. I buying them.' And now, is not lots of tourists here for her to do her selling. So, if she at my house I knows she needs selling them. And I buy them. Is not much money, Gulazer."

"Ah. That's nice of you. I suppose in the summer, she has lots of people buying them for their partners."

"Yes. And Turkish boys is doing it all the times to impress English girls."

"You never did it for me!" I swatted him on his bare thigh.

"You are yellow rose yourself, Gulazer – you not needing roses."

"Nice answer." I smiled.

Mesut slowly peeled himself away from me and sat up to light a cigarette. "She is old, old woman Gulazer. If she in work like that, walking all night in lots of heat or, at this time of year, lots of cold, I'm sure she really need the money. More than me, anyways."

"Why don't you just give her some money then?"

"I tried. She never will take it. But she letting me buy her roses so I do that instead. Is our arrangement."

I nodded from my spot on the floor, from my tangle of cushions and blankets and carpets, and watched as the smoke from his cigarette trailed upwards to the ceiling, curling and twisting like ink in water. I shuffled over and lay my head on his naked lap, noticing the pulse of blood in his thigh that lay reassuringly beneath the flex of muscle, the stretch of dark olive skin.

He rested one hand on the crown of my head and used his thumb to rub my forehead. It must have been the only bit of tension left in my body and his thumb found it naturally. It was then I realised just how tired I was. The journey here, the delays, the build-up, hell the whole of the last three months of waiting, wanting, wondering, planning, it was no wonder that now I was here, finally in the lap of him, that I was allowing myself to be tired.

Then I felt something stir and stiffen in my resting place

and raised my head in surprise. I looked up and Mesut was smiling. "What is this?" he asked, his voice dangerously close to the edge of hilarity. He'd finished his cigarette and was now holding something up from our discarded pile of clothes on the floor.

Oh God, I'd hoped he hadn't noticed earlier with the speed that we'd ripped off each other's clothes. Why hadn't I thrown a cushion over them or something? And why, for the love of god, hadn't I had the good sense to bring the sexy French ones?

He smoothed the massive expanse of them out on the floor and nodded thoughtfully, that ever-present smirk playing on his lips and, inexplicably, I felt him harden even more. "Hmmm. Very nice. I am thinking you buy these especially for me, yes?"

I made a grab for the overstretched, beige monstrosities but he was too quick and snatched them back. "No, no. no. I need to see these in proper place. Just looking like this, is so sexy, yes. But I am thinking on you they really special."

I yelped as he jumped up and flipped me round so that my legs were in the air. He was laughing out loud and I was too, but I was also screaming and kicking to stop him from putting those bloody things back on me. His strength outweighed my protests though, and I was laughing too hard to properly defend myself anyway. Before I knew it he'd already got them around my ankles and was sliding them back up my legs with total relish. I figured I may as well stop writhing and enjoy the kisses and nibbles he was offering on the way up. As I looked down, I could see that this was not just for a quick laugh. He was ready for more than that.

He skimmed the knickers over my bottom and let go of the elastic so that it snapped high up over my ample belly, leaving a pleasantly stinging sensation across my waist. He knelt back and growled deeply, looking at me. "Is better than I expecting, Gulazer. So . . . how you say it? Stretchy?" He bit back the fabric and then hooked his finger round so that it exposed the soft, blossoming part of me he was really looking for. Then he flicked his tongue out so that it disappeared for a second, making me gasp.

"You think these are good?" I managed to whisper. "You should see my pink pyjamas."

"Pink Pyjamas too? Ah, you treating me too much." When he laughed it vibrated deeply throughout all the right places. "But first, these . . ." he dipped his head down so all I could see were the roots of that mass of black hair and the god-awful knickers that stretched obligingly to one side. My whole body shivered with the immediate promise of pleasure and a tiny thought darted through my mind: *maybe I did bring the right underwear after all.*

31

INFINITELY

It was the dead of night and the rose lady had just been. I couldn't understand why I couldn't just go back inside and put these half-rotten roses in the sink with the others.

"Why do we have to be out here?" I whined as I stood shivering from head to foot, wrapped in a fleece blanket I'd grabbed on the way out of the door. I was watching Mesut dig into the hard, black earth just at the boundaries of the house, under a silvery flare of moonlight.

"You say you want wine?" His voice cracked slightly under the exertion. His hair was hanging annoyingly in front of his face so I couldn't get any clues there. Just a playful twinge to his words was all I had to suggest he was enjoying my confusion perhaps a little too much.

"Well, yeah, I did want wine. But I don't see how this is going to help. What on earth are you digging for? Is your emergency wine money down there or something?" This was the first time we'd ventured outside in twenty-four hours as we'd been shamelessly shacked up since I'd arrived. We'd so far gorged on an unabashed stretch of lolling around, talking, laughing, sleeping, eating and basically indulging in each other in every way we could possibly find. With and without the big knickers.

"Well, Gulazer." He said, throwing his spade to the side and finally looking at me, his mouth in a roguish curl. "Is my little experiment. I think you will like." Then he forced his hand into the hole he'd dug and grabbed something. He gave a good, solid yank and fell suddenly backwards with a dirty round object in his grasp.

"What the hell is that? Buried treasure?"

Mesut stood up and shrugged, brushing the dirt off himself and the object which I could now see was wrapped in a bit of fabric. "Is not buried anymore."

Back in the kitchen and next to the welcome warmth of the ever-present electric heater, Mesut set to work at the sink, where I'd hastily removed the sagging roses. He unwrapped the filthy cloth to reveal a bulbous, glass carafe, sealed with wax and then rinsed it under the hot tap, until the glass was clean enough that I could see it was filled with a dark, ruby red liquid. Then he stabbed the wax seal with a kitchen knife and poured the liquid carefully through a strainer and into a bowl. All at once I was hit by the deep scent of caramel and berries and I realised what was going on here.

"You've made your own wine?"

"Yes." He said, not even flinching at my tone of surprise.

"You've made your own wine?" I repeated. "By burying it in the garden?"

"Tabi. Of course."

I don't know why I was so amazed. I mean, it's not that unusual to make your own wine, I suppose. But there was something about the surrealism of this whole experience. Watching Mesut dig in the splayed moonlight, his confident silence, the grubby glass, the splash of warm water, the wax seal giving way under the sudden stab of sharp metal and the rich, cloying scent stabbing the air just as forcefully. It was such a world away from nipping to Tesco's for a bottle of Merlot I almost wanted to cry.

"Can you find bardak? I mean, err, culps?" Mesut held up the bowl and sniffed the smooth liquid, his nostrils flaring and his eyes closing in mindful analysis.

"It's ready?" I didn't have a bloody clue about how long the wine-fermenting process must take. It looked and smelled ready, but I was hardly the expert here. I looked around the kitchen for whatever it was he was asking for. "Culps? What's a culp, Mesut? Is that something you need to complete the fermenting process? Is it a special piece of equipment to siphon it or air it or whatever you do to make it drinkable? Oooh, I can't wait to see this. I've never seen wine made before. Is it complicated?"

"Gulazer, is too many questions. I just needing culps now. Can you find? Is in one of guardrobes."

"Guardrobes?" I got flashbacks to GCSE lessons on Shakespeare. Didn't that mean wardrobe? Why were these culps in the wardrobe? I turned and drifted off to walk up the stairs. I'm sure the culps would make themselves known in amongst all his clothes and things. I was envisaging something metallic and sieve-like. Perhaps with shiny handles.

"Gulazer?" Mesut continued to stand with the bowl in both hands, looking just as perplexed as I felt. As his hands were full he motioned with his eyes. "The culps. In the guardrobe." I followed to where his eyes were going, trying to figure this out. He was motioning towards the kitchen cupboards. Okay, I supposed that he might have meant cupboards when he said 'guardrobes'. Weird as it was.

"You mean the culps are in the kitchen cupboards? Ah, okay. Let me see . . ."

"Cupboards." Mesut whispered just beneath his breath, probably mentally noting that word for future conversations.

"Now . . . there must be a culp in here somewhere . . ." I

spoke to myself, opening and closing cupboard doors, looking at plates and bowls and cups and chopping boards.

"There. You go past them. Culps."

"What? I opened the previous cupboard and stared into it for complex-looking, metallic, sieve-like things. "Mesut there are only glasses in here and a few plastic cups."

"You looking at them! Culps! We need them for the drinking."

I whizzed around and stared at him, smiling. "Flipping heck. You mean cups, don't you?"

"Cups. Cilps. Calps. Culps. I not knowing, Gulazer. I just really wanting drink now!"

I chose a couple of glasses with little handles on them. Tulip shaped and jolly. I placed them down on the counter top in front of him and he sighed with relief that we'd finally understood each other. We traded bashful smiles that morphed quickly into easy laughter, flowing as freely as the wine from the bowl. "From now on they shall be called 'culps' in my world. It's much better than the word, 'cups' anyway. Infinitely better."

"Infinitely?" Mesut asked, as he placed the half-empty bowl back on the counter top. He picked up both glasses and handed one to me.

"Let's not even go there." I chuckled. "So, you reckon it's ready to drink?"

"I thinking so. I been making for nearly three months. Since you leaving really. I am thinking you might like when you come back. It is in and out of soil too many times. Really, it should, erm, be getting older?"

"Age."

"Yes. Age. But you wanting wine now, isn't it? And there it is in soil so . . . let's we try it." He raised his 'culp' towards mine and we gently clashed them together. I took a tentative sip. Oh, I was right about the caramel. The wine had a rich, buttery taste that smoothed happily over the sharp tang of red berries. I felt it work its way down my throat and into my belly so that a kindly, glowing ember remained there. Just what I needed after the chill of watching him dig outside.

"Mesut. It's really good."

"Is okay." He shrugged. "I hope you like."

"I like, Mesut." I whispered now, curling into him and resting my head on his chest so I could detect that beautiful heart that had threatened to leap into mine yesterday at the airport. "I like very much."

"Infinitely?"

"Infinitely."

32

THE OUTSIDE WORLD

R u going to this dinner thing? Let me know! We're walking there now.

"Right, I've texted Gillie again." I told Mesut, quickening my step to catch him up as he strolled along the beach. "That is absolutely the last time. If she doesn't answer me soon I'm calling the embassy or something. God knows what that Mafioso shithead has done to her. She could be buried under somebody's timeshare patio for all we know."

Mesut chuckled and wrapped his long fingers around mine. He ignored the silvery pull of the damp, glistening beach and found my eyes. "Demir not that bad, Gulazer."

"Really?" I half-chuckled. "It's not like you to stick up for him. He's hardly your favourite person."

"I knows. But he not criminal. Not that kind anyways. And I hoping you relax tonight. Demir not spoiling that. You having shock today and you needing good times and relaxing times." We stopped walking for a moment, the sound of our footsteps being sucked each time into the hungry sand now silenced. Instead we stood facing each other, and he cupped his hands around my chilly cheeks. I did the same to him and felt the scratch of stubble against my palms. I loved that all the lines, all the nooks and all the ridges of each other's faces were now intimately familiar to the other. Maybe it had always been that way. "You okay, Gulazer? After the email?"

I nodded. The email. It had only arrived a few hours before. I'd had my laptop out, trying and failing to work on my writing whilst Mesut was showering. At the cheerful chime of the notification, a burst of excitement had swept through me. Maybe it was Gillie, ready to update me on her antics with Demir – as much as I was loving being shacked up with Mesut at the house, a little taste of the outside world could be refreshing.

But instead, I'd read something completely different:

```
To: jessp@firebelly.co.uk
From: wraitht@shotmail.co.uk
Re: Re: Re: Ninth Step


Litttle Jessie$ . . . yoU was never that Baad,
just a fat little thinG. Only me That was bad.
Am glad you'll meet me maybes sandra CAan come
+ it'll be a fattie reunion or sumthinG.
H4pp*y Christmas*? I duNno. Forgiving isn't
easy is it. T.
```

I don't know why, but I hadn't expected to hear from Trev yet – at least not like this. As soon as I'd finished reading the words, I'd felt a twist of glassy ice drive like a thousand needles deep into my core. It was not unlike the way he used to make me feel as a little girl.

After showing the email to Mesut, I realised it was likely that Trev could have been drunk when he wrote it. How could he? He'd obviously not changed at all. How could he do this to himself? To the people around him? Did he not care at all about Treena or Sandra or his little grandkids? How could I meet him now and do the whole ninth step thing if he was drinking again? Surely he couldn't ask for forgiveness when he was out of his head? Oh fuck it, I didn't know – this was all new to me.

It was probably a good thing then, that Mesut and I had been invited to a friend's house for dinner, as well as Gillie and Demir. I needed the distraction. And now that we were out, walking along İpeklikum's beach, which had an entirely different feel during the winter months, I did notice that I felt slightly calmer.

The sand was more silvery now, than the golden sheen cast upon it by summer skies. It appeared grey in the harsh light of the December sunshine and merged seamlessly with a tide that had turned from sapphire blue to the colour of dark slate. The lack of parasols, sun beds and sun-drenched people made it seem vaster, more sweeping, and gave it a stirring romanticism that completely outstripped the heat of a summer's lust. I looked at Mesut as we started walking again, and my heart ran as wild as the lengths of his hair whipping recklessly in the wind.

"So tell me again how you know these people? Kaz and Ömer, right?" Mesut had been reluctant to share me at first, but I wanted to meet his friends and I *really* wanted to see Gillie so I'd said we should take up the invitation.

"Ohhh, I know Ömer long time now. He come to İpeklikum same time as me and we both not know any English. We learn together. And Kaz come to Beerbelly every year and I am thinking they is, erm, I think you say, 'good match'?"

"Yeah. You thought they'd like each other?"

"Yes. I am certain. So one day I make plans for boat trip. All of us. I tell Ömer I taking friend. I tell Kaz I taking friend. They not thinking anything. Then I being little bit cheeky and at last minute I say, 'Ohhh, I not well, I can't go'. And they goes anyway. Guess what?" he threw me a wicked grin. "I am right. They good match."

"Really? You totally set them up? So how long have they been together now?"

Mesut looked out at the horizon and narrowed his eyes. "Is, must be, is four years now I think. Yes. Four years."

"Wow. So they're pretty serious then. And Kaz lives here in İpeklikum?"

"She does. She not interested staying in England. She old lady and had enough working."

"Old lady? How old is she?"

"Ohh, I am thinking, about . . . forty-two."

"Forty-two? That's not old at all you loon!"

Mesut laughed in a low, knowing way. "Okay, is not so very old. But Ömer only twenty-two so she is seeming old to me."

That shut me up. A nineteen year age gap. And if they'd been together for four years, that meant they got together when he was only eighteen. I was pushing thirty and not sure I could manage a twenty-two year old. Thank goodness I had a wisened old man trapped in the body of a twenty-six year old walking next to me. Honestly, sometimes when I looked at him I could actually see the long, black hair morph into silvery-white, and a thin, wispy beard reach down from his chin. It was the most strange sensation, to be completely turned on by someone yet quite clearly see a vision of them in their elderly years.

I'd had the most acute sense of it the day before, when I'd been watching Mesut in a corner shop, picking out his groceries and cigarettes. I mean, I could actually *see* him as an old man. Clear as day. I knew the way he was going to reach for something, the exact angle and speed with which he'd nod his head in the direction of whatever he wanted. I knew with exquisite detail the tone in which he'd bid goodbye to the shopkeeper. It was as if I'd travelled to the right along my purple satin ribbon from Sandra's hypnosis session.

"I thought Demir really didn't like Ömer? Wasn't there a fight at Beerbelly last summer or something?" I remembered the story Mesut had told me. That whilst Gillie and I had been in İstanbul there had been altercations at the bar because Demir had wanted Ömer, who had a reputation as a bit of a party boy, out. Mesut had been put in charge by the bar's owner, Esad, that night and was having none of it. It had ended in flying fists and a bar closure enforced by the local police. It had been yet another reason for Mesut and Demir to dislike each other and to be honest, I was glad I'd missed the whole thing.

"You right." Mesut agreed but started grinning. "But I knows Kaz and she not care about these things. She wants friends for dinner, she gets friends for dinner. Ömer not have a chance. And Demir will come. I knows it."

"How do you know it?"

"Because Kaz not poor lady. She rich. She white. She British. Demir will forget Ömer for one night if it meaning he maybe get investors for his business next year. He always needing investors."

"Shallow bastard." I said, through gritted teeth.

"We not needing nasty names, Gulazer. And you not worry about Kaz. She handling herself all time. She İpeklikum expert now."

"Okay. If you say so. And what about Ömer? He's clean now? Not taking stupid pills anymore? Because that kind of party is definitely not what I'm looking for." Trev's email slithered into my mind, blinking and vying for my attention. I took a deep breath and pushed it firmly into the peripheries of my mind.

"You not getting that kind of party Gulazer. You really thinking I do this to you? No. Ömer's party days over. He not dare. Why you think I put him with Kaz?"

"Clever sod. Well, I'm bloody glad of that because my body is crying out for actual nutrients here. We can't live on those little chocolate-filled biscuits forever you know." The biscuits were called *Tutku* (Which translated as 'passion', appropriately enough) and we'd devoured several packets of them since my arrival. That wasn't all we'd devoured and I was really starting to realise that an empty belly does not a sex goddess make.

"Your body is crying?" Mesut's lips hung open, paused halfway between a delinquent smile and an expression of disappointment. "Your body not happy Gulazer? After everything?"

I stopped in my tracks at the top of a small flight of wooden steps we'd been climbing, that led from the beach to the red brick slickness of the main promenade. I turned and blocked his way so he couldn't get to the top to join me and looked down at him. The infinite, salted dewdrops clung to his hair so that it shone straight and flat with tar-black beauty. His large, brown eyes watched me silently and wetness settled on his nose, his chin, his lips like tiny pearls. I wished for a lengthy second that I wasn't wearing my winter clothes so that I could know what it would feel like to crush my soft, white body against his mouth right here, right now, in the curling, pearlescent mist. "My body is not crying, Mesut. My body is very, very happy."

He raised his hands and spanned his fingers across my torso at the waist. Even through my coat I could feel the warmth that was unique to him radiating through my skin, finding millions of miniscule opportunities to blast joy into my soul. "Is good." He murmured, tightening his grip and telling stories of what he wanted to do next with his eyes that almost made me pant. "Is very good."

"Flipping heck, have you two not had enough of each other yet?"

I twirled round, Mesut's hands still firmly planted on my waist, to find Gillie standing right behind me. Her hair curled around her head like a flaming bush of berries and her stance was the confident pose of a warrior. "Can't true love wait until we've at least had a bread roll? I'm starving!"

Mesut dropped his hands with a smile and I let out a little whoop. I bounded over to Gillie and squeezed her close. "Gillie! I'm chuffed to bits to see you! Didn't know if you were coming. Where's Demir?"

Gillie rolled her eyes with all the panache of a Hollywood starlet and tightened the belt on her shiny maroon raincoat. There were boots to match. "He's gone to pick something up. A special bottle of wine or something, I don't know. He'll join us in a few minutes. It's all good though. More bread rolls for us and apparently the apartment is around here somewhere. Demir chucked me out of the car when he saw you two. He said Mesut would know?"

"I knows." Mesut nodded, the lust we'd both just experienced still toying with the corners of his mouth. "Is that one there. Blue door."

Gillie and I gave a little gasp as we realised that Kaz and Ömer's apartment was pretty much in *the* prime location of İpeklikum. The posh end of the promenade. Glass-fronted balconies that wrapped around the whole building. Spot-lit sunbeds and flamboyant potted flowers. Views of Bodrum and beyond. "Well I hope their cooking lives up to the standard of their living." Gillie said. "Because if that's the case, then we are in for a treat."

My tummy growled and Mesut heard it, cupping it with his hands and then fondling it gently as he came to stand behind me and look up at the apartment we were about to visit. "Come on then ladies. We going in or not?"

"We're going in." Gillie and I said together. And off we went to ring the doorbell, taking our growling tummies with us.

33

THE PHOTO CUPBOARD

We weren't waiting on the doorstep for long, before, Kaz, in a blaze of peroxide and stringy, overly-tanned limbs, whooped with joy to finally see "Jessy and Messy all loved up!" and crushed me in an unyielding hug. Then we spent the next five minutes untangling me from her many golden, jangly bracelets so she could repeat the process with Gillie.

Ömer rounded the corner into the plush hallway and flashed us all a gold-toothed smile. He appeared to be the ultimate raver with trainers the pure brilliance of snow and wildly curly black hair with frosted highlights gelled back in a zig-zag plastic hairband á la David Beckham circa 2002. Put it this way – he did not seem the type to be home after dark.

"Oh me and Messy, we having some fun tonight, eh, old friend?" He grinned and slapped Mesut on the back hard with a grin that was just as startling. "It will be like old days, yes?"

Mesut smiled with that ridiculous inner wisdom he had, waved Ömer's words away and said, "I am hungry is all I know. What is for dinner?"

"Oh Messy, you and your belly!" Kaz crooned. "Come through to the kitchen and have a look-see. Jessy, I had a slight freak-out when I heard you were a vegetarian because me and Ömmy, well, we're meat eaters, for sure. So basically, I made a few bits and pieces for you to choose from. Ömmy thinks I've gone overboard but . . . well I guess that's just me!" Kaz outstretched her slim, tanned arm and swept it across the space she'd just led us into. I nearly had to shield my eyes with the pure, gloss-white brilliance of the kitchen-diner and blinking several times meant it took me a few seconds to register the banquet laid out on the huge kitchen island in the centre of the room.

There were five or six mountains of salad in psychedelic colours, dotted with pomegranate seeds that fell like rubies among the leaves. Rounded heaps of bright white rice topped with dark green, shredded dill, steamed and shimmered under the diamond glow of the kitchen spotlights above. There was a huge roast chicken, as golden and glistening as Kaz's jangly bracelets, placed regally on an elevated dish in the centre of everything. Then there were stuffed peppers the colours of traffic lights; potato and carrot wedges arranged in a complex spiral; rolled-up vine leaves all glossy like wet shells; aubergine, courgette and tomatoes bursting with spiced bulghur and caramelised onion; little dishes of dips all creamy and whipped and dusted with flame-red paprika; and the bread – good lord, the bread. "I'm going for that big, warm puffy one first." Gillie whispered to me, eyeing up the traditional Turkish lavaş which lay in soft pillows, adorning the top-left corner of the island.

"Nice choice." I whispered back. "I'll meet you at the simit in twenty minutes." I was eyeing up the bagel-like rings of bread which were sprinkled with toasted sesame seeds. Mesut had told me it was traditionally eaten for breakfast but hey, who was I to care?

"So!" Kaz clapped her hands together and looked at us all, the sun-kissed wrinkles around her green eyes creasing up with apparent satisfaction. "I think there's something here for every-one. As soon as Demir arrives, we'll dig in. I'm sure you're all well hungry." Each and every one of us nodded with mouths hung open in anticipation, and made noises of gratitude and amazement towards Kaz. She was in her absolute element, as Ömer slung his arm around her shoulder and she batted him away with a cotton-rich tea towel. "Oh you lot. It's nothing. Just a bit of dinner. Now, let's get you all sorted with some wine."

Just then the doorbell chimed (the Eastenders theme tune which made Kaz my new hero, obviously) and Ömer went off to answer the door to Demir. Gillie shifted playfully on the spot and the edges of her mouth curled upwards, which gave me my first clue that things were going well between them. Demir strode into the bright white space of the kitchen, smudging it with his hulking, dark presence. He wore a heavy overcoat that reached almost down to his black, patent-leather toes and a phone was glued to his ear. He spoke sharply and loudly into the phone, not giving whoever was on the other end of it any kind of break and click-clacked across the glossy floor to Kaz. He dumped a heavy bottle of wine on the marble counter-top and kissed her with a puckered stab on the cheek. She gracefully placed a glass of red wine into his spare, leather-gloved hand and he sat down on a tall chrome stool at the kitchen island, continuing his harangue down the phone whilst also presenting his sharp, angular cheek for Gillie to kiss. Which she did. Of course.

I felt Mesut's presence at my side and that was enough to snap me out of my voyeuristic trance. "Is fine, Gulazer. You not letting him bother you. Relaxing times tonight, remember?" He whispered it into my ear so that shivers of the nicest kind trav-elled in tiny, pleasurable pinches across the skin of my neck.

"I remember." I whispered back. "I'll try my best, I promise."

By the time Demir had finished his phone call, we were all seated around the massive expanse of the kitchen island, smooth jazz-funk music was now streaming from invisible speakers somewhere and drinks had been poured. I noticed that Mesut had opted for water rather than wine and marveled inwardly at how wonderful it was to be with somebody who didn't need alternative substances to bolster his confidence.

"Right, you lot – dive in and try it all. And for god's sake, don't tell me if it's awful!" Kaz squealed as she stuck large serving spoons into every dish.

"Really." Ömer said. "Don't tell her. She go crazy-cuckoo if you not like her food."

"Oi you!" Kaz batted him yet again with the posh tea towel. "It's because you're so bloody fussy I go 'crazycuckoo'. Cheeky beggar." Kaz had a delightfully broad Brummy accent which was such a contrast to that of Ömer's, so they did make a bit of a double-act. I could see why Mesut had thought them a good match. Kaz was sleek, well-groomed and feminine, but there was a hard-edged toughness to her that was kind of compelling. Ömer was a joker and full of frenetic, charged-up energy, and he quite clearly enjoyed – in a certain measure – to be tamed by Kaz. I really enjoyed watching them over dinner, even if I did have to fend off my Demir-induced frustrations on more than one occasion.

Not that I'm the centre of the world or anything, but on this particular night, it did feel as though Demir went on a mission to piss me right off. I tried to remember what Mesut had said about relaxing, but honestly? This was ridiculous. I began to wonder if Demir had never, in his life, seen a romantic movie. Because if he had, he would know that the unwritten rule is to get the best friend on side. Instead, he did the following:

1. Demanded to know why the food was mainly

vegetarian and initiated a fifteen-minute long tirade spoken in irate, spiky Turkish, Kaz blissfully oblivious as she piled yet more stuffed peppers onto his plate.

2. Poured, not sprinkled mind you, but *poured* great streamers of salt on every single one of the salad bowls.

3. Played some ancient, bawling-type Kurdish music on his phone, tinny and tacky, volume up to the max, over the top of the very pleasant music Kaz *already had playing*.

4. Coughed on ALL of the bread.

5. Grunted at Gillie every time he wanted something, be it napkin, salt, ashtray, the flipping moon on a stick.

6. Tried vehemently to get Mesut to drink the wine he'd brought, implying he was rude if he didn't at least sample it. Mesut buckled in the end which was, I think, in an effort to stop Demir from stressing me out.

7. Started smoking a cigarette before anybody else had finished eating and blew the smoke *all over the remaining food*.

Despite the delectable flavours of every mouthful I devoured, it was a relief when finally, Kaz accepted help from Gillie and I in clearing away all of the plates. The lads retired to the balcony so Demir could finally blow his smoke outdoors, where it belonged, and I could quiz Gillie about how things actually were behind closed doors.

"Are you okay, gorgeous? How's it all going?" I asked, as Kaz took the recycling rubbish outside and we were left alone in the kitchen.

"Pretty good actually." She grinned. "As soon as I arrived I did exactly what you said and told Demir what I expected while I'm here." She licked her lips and got rid of a rogue smear of garlic dip. "I made the point that this is an important time of year for us back in England, and he's bloody lucky I'm here. I'm giving up mince pies and Baileys for this!"

"Agreed. And?"

"Well, he went a bit speechless for a while and opened and closed his gob like a goldfish at first but . . . he's over it now and all in all he's been quite sweet."

"Sweet? Fucking hell I'm sorry Gillie but I wanted to pour those bowls of salty salad over his tiny coiffed head."

She laughed and gave me a nudge. "Now, now Miss Patience and Understanding. He's not that bad. I'm feeling much more easy-going about it so maybe you should too."

"Yeah . . . I'll get back to you on that one."

"What about you anyway?" She half-whispered as she glanced over her shoulder. "How's it going with the long-haired lover? Fuck me Jess, he looks hot tonight. I never thought I'd see Mesut out of those torn t-shirts and ripped jeans but Jesus, can he rock the dinner party look."

"I know, right? I'm practically salivating most of the time, and I've basically lived on a diet of him, which is why that meal was sent from heaven."

Gillie nodded in agreement and we both said "God bless Kaz" at exactly the same time.

"Honestly though, it's all been good. I did have a weird email from Trev earlier, but Mesut has been fab and calmed me right down. In fact, aside from that? It's going amazingly well." I had to speak from behind the broadest smile. "We haven't really been out apart from to get a few packets of biscuits . . . we've had a couple of walks on the beach. It's like we're just making up for lost time and there's a bit of a sense of 'seeing if it works'. Do you know what I mean?"

It was only dawning on me now as I was talking to Gillie, that without even discussing it, Mesut and I were conducting an intense, important experiment. "We've chatted about all the topics under the sun. We've agreed. We've disagreed. We've had several language barriers. We've laughed. And yes, we've had a bit of a cry too. It's like we're baring our souls in a way that we perhaps couldn't last September because there were so many distractions around us." Gillie grinned and went all misty-eyed at the memories. "But now Gillie. Now it's just me and him and those four walls. If it's going to go wrong, it's going to happen there and it's going to happen soon."

Gillie pulled me into a soft hug. "Well, I hope for your sake that it doesn't. But if it does, I will drop Demir like a bad habit and come find you. Understood?"

"Understood."

"Right, now let's get these dishes dried because here comes Kaz and I'm hoping she's going to pour us a bit more of that Cappadocian wine. It's flipping delicious, isn't it?"

"God it really is. It's a shame Mesut can't enjoy it but Demir keeps pushing that other stuff on him. Don't you find him a bit controlling?"

"Nah, he's not like that with me. He insisted on going off and finding that wine earlier, said it was special and from Mesut's hometown or something. It was quite thoughtful really. He's just being nice Jess."

"Ugh. I suppose so." And as if on cue, the men came trooping back into the kitchen, looking for top-ups on their drinks. Kaz swept in, riding on a wave of Dior, at exactly the same moment and shooed them away with her perfectly mani-cured hands.

"Nope. Boys out there." She pointed rigidly to the impressive balcony that we'd been admiring earlier from outside. "And girls in the living room. I'll bring out some coffee so you can play your weird Turkish backgammon and smoke and chat or whatever it is that you do. Go on, men. Be told."

Ömer sighed, hunched his shoulders and turned back towards the balcony. Demir made a fuss of helping Kaz with the coffee and disappeared into the kitchen with her, but Mesut was left standing in front of the balcony door, apparently unable to make a decision. His eyes darted about the room, flitting over me as if I wasn't even there and he was gripping the edges of his trouser pockets so that white rings appeared around his knuckles. I thought I saw a slight sheen of sweat on his forehead and some strands of jet-black hair sticking into the ridges of some worry lines. I was just about to move instinctively towards him when Gillie grabbed my hand and dragged me over to a plump, golden (yes, golden) sofa.

"Come on, Jess. Let's chill and let the boys do their thing."

And before I could protest, Ömer had already stuck his head round the balcony door and snapped his fingers at Mesut. "Mesut abi. Gel." And that's it. They were both gone.

As my body plummeted into the depths of the ridiculously sumptuous sofa, I asked Gillie. "Did you notice anything strange about Mesut just then?"

She just shoved another glass of wine into my hand and said, "Honestly, Jess, chill the fuck out. You're on holiday, remember? He's fine. They're all fine. Let's just sit back, relax and enjoy the very rich and very abundant vibes. You could fit five of your little bungalows in here. Easy."

"That you could." I agreed. We both stared around the room. It was almost comical to make a comparison to my own home. "I think my kitchen would fit in that cupboard over there." I said, nodding towards a glossy white door in the corner of the room, with the inexplicable feature of no handles or hinges. "How do they even get that open?"

"I've absolutely no idea." Gillie laughed. "And my toes are far too enraptured with the pile of this carpet to ever move again. Go on – have a go. Quick. Before Kaz gets back." She urged as she dug her bare feet yet further into the excessively thick, sea-glass blue carpet.

I hauled myself up and joyfully ploughed my feet through the swanky carpet until I got to the other side of the room. "Good lord, every step is a triumph, isn't it? Have I left track marks?" I twisted round to look over my shoulder. "Shit. I have. Gillie, can you follow me with a broom or something?"

"Don't be ridiculous. Rich people walk across carpets too." She giggled.

"S'pose so." I shrugged. "Right. Opening this thing. It can't be that hard, can it? I mean, as well as walking across carpets, rich people need simple cupboard-opening mechanisms as much as the rest of us, surely?" I pressed the massive expanse of white gloss with my elbows, not wanting to leave any finger-prints on this impressively polished façade. It didn't give at all "Nope. Not like that."

"Try kicking it." Gillie said, smiling behind her wine glass.

"Behave. I'm not kicking anything in this house." Instead I tried moving backwards and forwards, waving my hands around the general vicinity of the cupboard door, thinking there might be some kind of motion sensor mechanism.

"Oh yeah. I forgot about your magical kinetic powers."

"Very funny. I don't know. Maybe Kaz has a microchip in one of those golden bangles that synchs with the door and opens it only on a particular flick of her wrist. Maybe this cupboard has all her secrets inside. Maybe she's got another Turkish toy boy in here for when she gets sick of Ömer. Maybe this door leads to his underground lair where he lies in wait for the arrival of that day, silently doing crunches and planks and push-ups and drinking protein shakes and injecting himself with vitamin D until he's required to satisfy Kaz's every bodily need. Oooh – just think, Gillie. What a story that would make, right?"

"You really need to start writing that shit down, is what I think." Gillie smiled. "What's the verdict then? Un-openable?"

"Possibly." I said, now sliding my back up and down the door pressed against its impressive sheen, whilst simultaneously arcing my arms all over the place like an air-traffic control person in training. "But I don't want to give up . . . there's got to be a way . . ."

"Ah, so you found my photo cupboard." Kaz merged into the room on the (quite literally) magic carpet and stood just a few feet off, next to her offensively large flat-screen TV. She caught my outlandish maneuvers with an irretrievable smile breaking on her lips but I stopped dead, suddenly inspecting my finger-nails before she could ask me what I was doing. "Well, girls, seeing as we're all cut from the same kind of cloth, let's have a look-see what's inside, shall we? Ömmy bloody hates it when I get the photos out but he's busy doing blokey things on the balcony so why not, eh?"

I joined Gillie back on the sofa that was possibly from the original set of Dynasty and watched in awe as Kaz casually said the word, "Open" and the white door, that had previously seemed so sturdy and unmovable, began to peel back into the wall above it like an extremely posh roller garage door. "Note to self," I whispered to Gillie, "I have not made it as a writer until my book royalties pay for a cupboard with voice recognition."

"Agreed." Gillie whispered back. "Definitely what life is all about." And we clinked our glasses together.

"Right." Kaz stepped into the cavernous expanse and grabbed not a spare Turkish toy boy but a bright pink, plastic basket stuffed with papers and packets that looked sadly at odds with the mechanism that housed it. "We're all with Turkish men. We've all totally fallen for someone we didn't mean to. I mean, am I right?"

"Urm, yes?" Gillie said and I nodded.

"Exactly." Kaz turned back to the gap in the wall after stepping out of it. "Close." The white gloss door slid back into place as silently as an evening cloud slips past a star. "So, basically, we three know that it all starts with that holiday romance, doesn't it? It all starts with a bit of sun, a bit of sand and a bit of . . .well, pretty damn hot sex, am I right?

"You're right!" Gillie exclaimed gleefully, whilst I was still in nodding mode. "How did you and Ömer meet, Kaz? I'd love to hear the story."

"Oh luvvie, I can hardly remember it was so long ago. But that's why I've got these photos out." She placed her slight but lengthy frame between us on the sofa and I suddenly realised that these outrageously plump sofas were far better suited to somebody of Kaz's size. She wasn't going to have to fight her way out of it each time she wanted to move. I, on the other hand, had already given up any hope of moving my arse until Mesut could come and haul me out.

Kaz balanced the plastic basket on her lap and started rifling through the stuff inside. "I've got a whole stack of them from back then, round about when me and Ömmy met. Here we go, luvvies. It's all in there." She presented a bulging brown packet to me with a look of eagerness I couldn't stand to disappoint.

"Okay. Erm, thanks." As soon as I pulled out the first photos I saw a line of faces I knew all too well. There they were, with their arms draped around each other, each with the bright, glowing faces of boys who had just spent the entire night dancing.

"Oh look!" Gillie squealed. "There's Bad Boy and Esad. And that's lovely Kadafi – how I miss him! He's back in his hometown now, Demir said. And look! Demir and Ömer appear to actually like each other in that one!"

As Gillie named all those familiar faces, my heart absolutely lifted at the sight of them. The photo I was holding in my hands right now could have honestly been one of my own, except the faces were so much brighter and younger.

"Gorgeous young things, weren't they?" Kaz piped up, beaming from ear to ear.

"They were. They are." I started browsing through some of the other photos, passing them to Gillie as I went. There were lots of Kaz looking stunning with a tan I would have quite happily traded a limb for, hanging off Ömer in various locations like the beach, the promenade, on a boat or at the market. Most of the photos were taken in Beerbelly though, and so time and time again I was seeing familiar faces, familiar scenes.

It was all quite bizarre, actually, as I sat and half-listened to Kaz explain to me who everybody was and how this all fit in with the story of her and Ömer. "Of course Demir and Ömer have had their problems over the years. But hopefully that's all behind them now. I was a bit sneaky tonight, inviting you and Demir, Gillie. I really wanted him and Ömmy to patch things up. Ömmy doesn't do any of them party drugs no more. That's all behind him. He prefers his slippers and a few ciggies now and it would make İpeklikum life so much easier if they'd just bloody well speak to each other."

"Well I think you've done what you set out to do, Kaz, if the laughter coming from the balcony is anything to go by." Gillie was right. There were jovial sounds coming from outside, even if Mesut's low, rumbling laugh seemed to be absent from it all. I reminded myself he wasn't the type to squawk with laughter in front of anyone, let alone Demir.

After a bit more wine, a *lot* of reminiscence from Kaz and at least a hundred and fifty photos later, I could confidently say I did not give a shit who any of the people in the pictures were anymore. Only that the familiarity of the faces, the mood, the scenes and the places were scaring me half to death.

I increasingly realised that these really could have been *my* photos. It didn't matter one bit that some of the people in them were different. What mattered was that I saw the same carefree smiles, the same relaxed arms slung around bare shoulders, the same light of romance flaring in people's eyes, and the same unspoken agenda of indulgence, sex and abandon. I looked at Gillie who continued, rosy-cheeked and smiling, to show interest and enthusiasm for Kaz's photo collection and wondered how the same nausea wasn't rising in her. Whether it was the earlier abundance of food, the wine drunk too hastily or the sense that my own unique experience was slowly being stolen piece by piece by Kaz's basket of photos, I didn't know.

And there were pictures of Mesut. Mostly caught in the middle of pouring somebody a drink, wiping a table or polishing his glasses. Polishing his fucking glasses! I could remember now, with heart-stopping clarity the moment in the summer when I'd looked up from my book, The Alchemist, to find Mesut getting rid of his 'negative thoughts' by polishing in the exact same way the main character in my story was in the chapter I was reading. That memory was *mine*. And it was *special*. How could it possibly be in somebody else's photo stash?

And there were photos of him with other women too. Fucking hordes of them. Okay, so he didn't exactly look happy in any of them, and it seemed the women were clawing at him to stay put for the briefest snap of a camera, but it was still him. With other women.

There was a creeping doubt slithering up and down my spine like a snake looking for the right place to pounce. I could feel its devious glide, its inexorable search for the weakest point, the coldest part of my heart that might finally crack. What made my experience any more special than any of these girls'? Why should I find a man whose soul I felt fused to, whose heart I had known forever? It was far more likely I was having an experience that had been had time and time again in İpeklikum, or in any bloody holiday resort for that matter. An experience that a trashy magazine would pay fifty quid for as long as they got some shitty photos that looked exactly like the ones now balancing on my lap and spilling onto the stupidly furry carpet beneath my feet.

I stood up and all the photos fell to the floor like playing cards in a losing game. "I have to go." I said quietly, turning to Kaz. "Please tell Mesut I have to go."

"Messy!" Kaz yelled. "I think you'd better come and take care of your lady."

Mesut's head snapped round the curtain of the balcony. He took one look at me and dashed past Gillie and Kaz to grab my hand and tilt my chin so he could see into my eyes. I couldn't even look at him but I could feel his hands were slick with icy sweat. "Gulazer? What is wrong? You feeling unwell?"

I nodded and turned away from him, gave Kaz and Gillie the briefest of hugs and whispered my goodbyes. Then I left the apartment.

Mesut would have to follow.

34

TAKEN SOMETHING

Mesut at least had the decency to give me a head-start.

I knew he was some way behind me as I charged down to the shoreline, kicked off my shoes and stomped through the tiny rapid waves now trickling under the relentless moonlight. The sudden splash and the cool shock of the water against my bare skin was deliciously immediate and helped my breath to unstick from my throat. I needed to be here, under this misty moon and not up in that apartment looking at those fucking photos.

"Gulazer. You. Alright?" He was a few feet behind me. I could tell by the distance of his voice.

"No. I'm not."

"You not." He confirmed. I heard the shush of wet sand giving way beneath his feet. "You. Want. Talk? I. Here."

"What on earth has happened to your words?" I demanded as I turned around to face him. His English was usually better than that.

He stood crumpled under the shifting greys and blues of the night sky. Despite the inward collapse of his shoulders and his torso, a static energy had ridden his fingers, elbows and knees with an eerie stiffness. He moved towards me awkwardly and for the first time ever, I backed away.

"What's wrong with you? Are you ill? Did the food not agree with you or something?"

"No. Is not. Food." I chanced a step towards him and willed the moonlight to streak itself onto the face that I knew and loved. If we could just find each other right now, under the glistening will of the moon then everything might be alright. The photos wouldn't matter and my doubts wouldn't matter and his weird words and body language wouldn't matter.

I tilted my head upwards to look at him and what I saw turned me sick to my stomach. White spittle was gathered in the edges of his mouth, his jaw was as square as a brick but his teeth were clashing together like a crazed animatronic. And his eyes were actually vibrating. Those deep pools of brown were tremoring rapidly from side to side as if they'd been injected with an electric current.

He stepped towards me again and his lips tried to break free from their rigid, gnashing trap into something resembling a smile. It was chilling. The combination of those electric eyes and awkwardly curved lips prevented me from recognising my Mesut. Where had he gone?

"Fucking hell, you've taken something. Haven't you?"

"I . . . I take something?"

"You've bloody taken something at a fucking dinner party! How could you?"

"Gula . . . Gulazer. No. I not. I can't. What?" He crashed his spiked fingers into his sweating brow and then pulled them back in front of his eyes, dragging lengths of damp, black hair with them. "Is not. Fault. Not my fault. Is just happen."

"You and Ömer." I breathed, barely able to get the words out. "I was inside with Gillie and Kaz, having a complete shit-fit over a stack of photos that basically means anything we've ever had together is a load of cheap rubbish."

"Cheap rubbish?" He gnashed, finally letting his hands drop and his hair too.

"And the whole time you and Ömer and even Demir are laughing your backs off, popping pills like there's no bloody tomorrow! There's no fucking need for it! You know how I feel about that kind of thing. Yet you still thought it was okay to do this. How could you?"

"Demir didn't. I not. I really not . . ." he looked down at his feet as if they had miraculously just appeared there. Fucking idiot.

"This is a total joke! Not only has Kaz got virtually every photo of mine back there in her apartment, but now you've gone and done this. Jack did this time and time again when we were together. He never listened to me. I wasn't enough for him on a night out – it had to be more of a party, more of a release. What is it, Mesut? I'm not enough for you either?"

He was grinning like a maniac but the lines on his face clashed madly against it. A scorched twist of uninvited amuse-ment "You. Always enough." He forced the words out of his gritted teeth.

By now I was crying, furious tears sliding into every word with salty rigour. "It's not right! You're supposed to understand. You're supposed to know not to ever do anything like this. For fuck's sake, it all started with Trev!" Now I was shaking, trem-bling, my feet sunk into a sludgy spot on the shore, jerks of cold claiming my legs and surging upwards. I felt I was back on that beach in France two lifetimes ago, the sadness seeping through me like poison. "Am I always going to have drugged-up men stopping me from living my life? What have I done to deserve that? And why do YOU have to be one of them, Mesut? Why?"

"Gulazer, is okay . . ." He chanced a step towards me but I'd already started moving. I hauled my feet out of the heavy grey sand and strode over to him, whipping up livid foam and sprays of barbed seashells as I went. I stuck my index finger into his chest and jabbed repeatedly to make my point.

"Why the fuck do you have to call me that? My name is Jess for god's sake. J.E.S.S."

"Gulazer . . . I . . ."

"Can't you hear me? Don't you understand? How many times do I have to tell you? It's Jess!" I screamed my name. With all the hurt and sorrow that was barrelling through my soul, I screamed it into his warped, beautiful, gurning face.

Then, I made a run for it.

35

BACK TO VILLAGE CORNER

I'd never have guessed the walls of Beerbelly could feel so suffocating. I was sitting in Village Corner, the secret little dwelling at the back of the bar that I'd spent so many nights in during our previous trip to İpeklikum. It had been a kind of haven for me then, just three short months ago. But now, when I sat on the embroidered cushions I felt nothing but irritation at their twisted, iridescent threads and sickeningly jaunty sequins.

I tried to feel soothed by the flickering glow of the tealight Gillie had lit on the low-to-the-ground table, but with every carefree lick of the flame I felt bile forming in the deepest corners of my mouth. My breathing ran as ragged as the edges of the ancient Turkish carpets that had once welcomed me into their soft and restful lair. I didn't know how I could be here.

"Right. Here's a drink. Actually two drinks." Gillie said as she wriggled past the drapes that kept this space separate from the rest of the bar. She placed down a mug of something hot and black and a frosted glass of amber liquid. "A coffee and an apple juice. I know how much you liked your black coffee on our holiday and, well maybe the strength of it will do you good. Or, the fruit juice is there to give you a bit of energy because Jess sweetie, you look all washed out."

"Hmph." I managed.

Gillie sighed. "And I remember how much you enjoyed sitting here with your little notebook, so I've brought you a pad from behind the bar and a pencil was all I could find. Oh and look! I found a paperback too. It's not exactly The Alchemist, but maybe you can get lost in it for a while. *'The Tears of His Sword – will he take her to the sharp edge of love?'* Oops. Maybe not." She giggled and chucked the book over her shoulder so it disappeared with a soft thud into the curtains. "Oh come on Jess, I'm sure Mesut was just having a laugh. Demir says it's quite typical of him and Ömer to get wasted like that."

"Point made." I whispered into my hands as my head fell heavily into them. I couldn't even bear the smell of the coffee Gillie had brought. It smelled like grey, mouldy cardboard. Stiff and rancid.

"Is it really such a bad thing if he pops a few pills from time to time? I'm sure that if you explain to him how it makes you feel, he'll stop doing it. Just give him some time to come down. Anybody can see he's as loved up with you as you are with him."

"He's not. He can't be. He knows how I feel about that kind of thing – abusing substances or whatever you want to call it. He knows about Trev. And about how Jack used to be. I can't believe he's done this to me. And after looking at all of those photos as well. I really needed him tonight and now he's just fucked everything up." A sob jumped out of my throat, as unwelcome as the foul stench of the coffee. "What am I even doing here Gillie?"

"Oh, come here, gorgeous." Gillie moved over to me and threw her arms around my quaking body. I wanted to curl up into a ball so small she could just swallow me up into herself. I couldn't feel any clear sense of me. Of what it was to be Jess in this moment. I just wanted anonymity and greyness and the consolation of oblivion. This place used to do that for me. These cushions and these carpets and these drapes that hid me from the rest of the bar. But now, even though there was nobody on the other side of the curtains because the bar had been closed for weeks, I just felt too much the sharp stab of deceit. It overwhelmed everything.

It was hard to name anything else I might be feeling. The words, 'sadness', 'anger', 'fear' and 'disappointment' just didn't seem to cut it. I felt cheated that all the crap I'd been through in Sandra's Christmassy living room didn't seem to be useful here. The treasure chest in my heart where all of my learnings were kept was clamped tight shut and all I could identify was that things felt wrong. "It's wrong, Gillie. This is all wrong." I heard myself wail as she rocked me gently and made soft shushing sounds.

Just then Demir bolted through the drapes as quick as death and looking just as ominous in his heavy black coat. But there was nothing different about him. He was his normal self. Sober and serious. Gillie released me as if her arms had uncoiled springs in them and I catapulted back onto the cushions, looking up at Demir through a tear-ridden gaze.

"Is okay. I sort it." He announced. "Kaz not upset now and knows none of this her fault. I tell her nothing wrong with her photos or her food. She going to meet me in next few days for coffee and we will talk business."

"Who is she meeting for coffee?" Gillie had a lilt in her voice that suggested Demir needed to improve on his original statement.

"Okay. Us. She meet us for coffee."

"That's better." Gillie smiled and blew him a kiss that was barely perceptible, presumably on my account.

"Thank you Demir." I whispered. "I didn't mean to cause any trouble."

He didn't smile, but his eyes sparked momentarily with something. "Is okay, Jess. I sort it for you. You upset person. You cannot doing for yourself, so I do it."

"And what's happened to the boys?" Gillie asked. "Where are Mesut and Ömer?"

"I send them out." Demir lit up a cigar, the smell of which hit the back of my throat like a fist. "They a complete mess and Kaz not want them in house. I says to them they must getting sober and grow up into men. Is silly boys I think. Silly, silly boys. They not happy with me and I think Mesut want to maybe kill me but I not let him near me. He not bother me."

The image of Mesut's strange, square jaw and the juddering irises of his eyes flickered back through my mind. I couldn't even imagine how he'd be able to see straight to do any harm whatsoever to Demir. And, for once, it wasn't Demir who deserved any harm to come to him. Demir was the only one who hadn't taken any pills and had actually tried his best to fix this, even though there was nothing anyone could do to stop the chaos unravelling in my soul. I suddenly felt awful that Gillie and Demir had had their night out at a dinner party ruined because of me and my fucking idiotic boyfriend.

"Shit. I'm so sorry, guys. You were supposed to have a nice night out. I've ruined it for you. So has he."

"No, no, no." Gillie said. "You can't think like that. We're always here for you, aren't we Demir?" She turned her head up towards him and her hand followed, grasping the edges of his coat and pulling him closer towards us. He stumbled slightly but he did move closer and then crouched down, looking me right in the eyes. No smiles, but at least he held my gaze steadily.

"Of course, Jess. We here for you. You want us to go get your stuff? Is at Mesut's house, yes?"

"Well, yes, but . . ."

"Is okay. We get it. I can get key to house because you knows my cousin's fiancée, Beryl, it is her house really. I get key and I go in and get your stuff."

"Yep." Gillie added. "I'll recognise all your things and gather them up for you. You don't need to go back there tonight. Or at all if you don't want to. You can come and stay with us if that helps, can't she Demir?"

"She can." He rose up, took a final suck on his cigar and then snuffed it out on the tiny tealight in front of me, so that the only remaining light was a ruffled stripe of moonlight, smearing the carpets with silver. "Why you not try sleep here Jess? I get you blanket." And he strode over to the darkness of the bar, looking for something to cover me with.

"Are you sure Gillie? Is this a good idea?" I whispered. "Should you really just walk into Mesut's home without asking?"

"He's in no fit state to give us permission, Jess. And anyway, if we wait until tomorrow we'll have to reason with him when he's sober and it'll be a whole lot harder. Demir's right. We'll be in and out and get your stuff then at least you have a choice about where you want to be. Okay, sweetie?"

"Okay. If you think it's best. I'm just so sorry this night has been ruined for everyone."

"Not. Your. Fault." Gillie said in clean, isolated syllables, pushing me ever so gently with each one backwards onto the cushions on the floor so that I was now laid out flat, my trembling limbs at last still. "Here's Demir with your blanket."

"Flipping heck, he's turned into a hero tonight, hasn't he?"

"Told you he wasn't all bad." She smiled. Then I felt a soft and heavy waft of fabric settle over me and I snuggled under its inevitable warmth. "We'll be back in a few hours." Gillie whispered, now close enough to kiss me on the cheek. Which she did. "You try to get some sleep, sweetheart. I know this is one of your favourite places."

"It is." I nodded dreamily, vaguely noticing that the patch of moonlight fell right across my face so I could see the whole of Village Corner cast under a strange, metallic glow. Gillie stood up to go and grasped Demir's hand in hers. I could see her incredible maroon, knee high boots and his pointy, black patents tracking away from me. "Gillie?" I called. "There's just one last thing."

"Yeah?"

"Can you find 'The Tears of His Sword'? I might give it a go after all."

36

RELUCTANT MORNING

Daphne touched the very tip of his sword and drew a sharp, rapturous breath at the thought of what it had performed so far. All in the name of love. "Don't you get scared carrying it around all the time?" She asked, breathlessly. "Don't you worry you'll . . . hurt somebody?"

"I only hurt the people who deserve it." He said, drenching her in his icy blue stare that she had tried, until now, so hard to resist. "Only the people who get between you and I." He prised her fingers from the sword and took it back with his own tough, calloused hands. He slid it once more inside the hard, leather sheath that he usually wore so comfortably against his ample thigh, but that was now discarded on the rocks where they sat, the drip-drip of cave water puddling sumptuously around them.

She knew this moment had been coming. She'd known from the first moment he'd saved her from those thunderous horse's hooves back at the mansion. There was something else clattering towards them now, and it wasn't big and shaggy like her prize stallion, Eleazar. Or maybe it was . . .

I slapped the pages of the book shut and sighed.

Despite its generous invite into escapism, 'The Tears of His Sword' just wasn't cutting it. Daphne was annoying. The hero was annoying. Even Eleazar the horse was bloody annoying. Where was The Alchemist when I needed it? The literary offerings behind the bar in Beerbelly were sadly deficient and my poor, shredded heart was yearning for distraction.

I put the book down on the table in front of me and drove my body further into the blanket Demir had given me, ignoring the subtle scratch of the ornamental cushions beneath. The moonlight was slowly waning and the items I was looking at were now less struck by silver and more bathed in the sickly glow of a washed-out, reluctant morning.

There was the still-full cup of black coffee, with stubborn drips of black clinging to its white, porcelain sides, frozen in their inevitable slide downwards. The apple juice was untouched too and a dusty film now settled on the sallow surface of it. Gillie and Demir must have been back to check on me whilst I'd been sleeping, as there was a page torn from the notebook Gillie had found, and a note hastily scribbled with the pencil that now lay against the snuffed-out tealight. *We've got your stuff back at Demir's. Call me when you wake up.*

But I hadn't called her. I knew that if I did, it would begin the unavoidable descent into a day of facing up to what had happened. I didn't want that yet. I wanted to find the consolation and calm that Beerbelly had become famous for in my mind. I wanted the drapes of Village Corner to cocoon me, the soft carpets to carry me, the breeze blowing gently in from the sea to dry my eyes until I was ready to spill back out into reality. Was that really so much to ask?

I checked my phone. Nothing from Mesut. Yet. I assumed he would come crawling to me at some stage, begging forgiveness, pledging innocence. Isn't that what addicts did? Was he an addict? Fucked if I knew. I wasn't sure that taking pills was an act of addiction, but I did know, for certain, that it was a world I never wanted to be a part of and my mind was still spinning from the fact that he didn't seem to know that.

Weren't we supposed to have a connection? An inexorable link that defied shit like this? Hadn't we made that connection *here* of all places. For fuck's sake, I was just a few metres away from the spot where he'd told my fortune from a Turkish coffee cup and blasted my inner world into a million, glorious fragments. I shifted on the cushions and sat up wearily to look at that exact spot now. But it was sadly lacking the glittering sunlight of my memories, and seemed obscured now, by the perverse grin of morning shadows, the stubborn cling of the night.

Then my phone did buzz. I tapped to read the text message:

Jess darling. Sorry to bother you during the festive hols but knew you'd want to know. I've only gone + sold ALL of your paintings. They were a hit darling + we need to talk more. But for now, I've made the bank transfer + you're a richer lady for 2007. Congrats doll. Terri at Epic Café.

Wow. I had not been expecting that. Those swirling, textured representations of that balloon ride in Cappadocia had obviously been appealing to somebody somewhere. How weird that my artwork would now hang on the walls of strangers' homes. I wondered if those strangers would know what those paintings had meant – the breath-taking ascent of the balloon, the silent sailing through clouds, the blushing radiance of the dawn sunshine on ancient rock. At least that was a memory Mesut couldn't taint because he hadn't been there for it, even he might have slipped in on the ghostly will of my unmet passion at the time.

Okay, that means I've got some money, I thought. If I really wanted to, I'd now be able to afford an early flight ticket home and get out of this utter shambles.

Home though. What was I supposed to say to everybody back there? *"Oh yeah, remember that guy who I thought was my soulmate? Turns out he's a total tosser who'd rather get jacked up on Ecstasy than spend an evening with me."* That would go down well. Ella would go ballistic and Mesut may face an untimely death by puppet. At least that would be something to write about.

Another sigh escaped my lips and I lifted the notebook and pencil off the table. Maybe I should write some of this shit down. After all, hadn't my notebook helped me figure out torrential towers of turmoil before now? I'd written in it after the coffee-cup fortune-telling incident and things had suddenly opened up. I'd written in it when I thought I might die from heartbreak after Jack left and here I was, still breathing. And hadn't Oliver urged me to write my own story? He hadn't said anything about it being a happy story now, had he? Had I learned nothing from 'The Tears of His Sword'? What I wrote didn't even have to be any good, so what was I waiting for?

Pencil hovered over paper and I held my breath. Pencil pressed down on paper and I exhaled long and slow. Where to start? The carafe of ruby wine dug up from the cold, dark earth? My big knickers caught captivatingly in his salivating mouth? The rose lady's flowers softly wilting in his kitchen sink? The way my beating heart almost climbed into his at the airport?

Or the shivering shock of his eyes last night? The pointed limbs, the gritted teeth?

The pencil was scoring ragged lines through the paper before I realised it was even happening. Furious tracks of leaden-grey tore through the yellowing grain as if words were an impossibility.

My phone rang and I jumped, the pencil falling to the

ground and clunking on a rogue square of floor tile between patches of threadbare carpet. I left it where it was, not caring about the inevitable crack of the lead inside, and answered the phone. "Hello?"

"He – hello. Our Jessica?"

"Yeah. Sandra? Is that you?"

"Aye, pet. It's me." A labored sigh. A shaking breath.

"Sandra. What's wrong. Are you okay?"

"I'm sorry, pet. I know you're on holiday and all that. I know you're with your lad."

"I'm not. Never mind. What's happened? What's wrong?" Why was Sandra calling me now? Did this woman's psychic powers know no bounds?

"I just thought you'd want to know. It's not long since happened and, well, I felt compelled to call you if I'm honest."

"What is it Sandra? Just tell me."

"It's Trev." She gave a small sob, barely noticeable.

"What about him? He emailed me yesterday and he sounded weird. What's he done now? Has he hurt you?"

A louder sob. A moan, really. "No, pet. Nowt like that. He – well, last night you see. I hate to tell you this, Jessica, but well, last night our Treena called round to see him and bless her heart, it was awful."

"What did he do to her, Sandra? Is she alright?" My chest tightened and my fists closed and an inescapable heat tore through my body. I waited for Sandra to find the words.

"It's not our Treena, love. The thing is, Jessica . . . It's Trev. He's dead."

37

APOLLO'S TEMPLE

"I'm so glad we're doing this." Gillie whispered as Demir pulled the car into a parking space. "It'll help get your mind off things." She leaned right over me and pulled the handle so I could get out of the car with minimal effort. "Go on. I'll meet you on your side." And she was gone with a slam of the car door that rattled my bones.

I'd stayed with Gillie and Demir the previous day and night. I really hadn't known what else to do. The news about Trev was still seeping into me, bit by bit. And each moment brought a new wave of feeling that I didn't know what to do with. He was gone. Just when he'd hauled himself out of the misty realms of fiction in my childhood mind and was beginning to stand there, in the gradually clearing fog as a flawed and tangible being . . . he was gone.

I'd cried an ocean since I'd found out. I couldn't confidently say they were tears of sadness but they were tears of something and there were plenty of them. I'd cried as Gillie and Demir had scooped me up from Beerbelly and driven me home. I'd cried as Demir dragged all my bags up to his apartment and piled them up in his spare room. I'd cried as Gillie had dumped me naked and shivering into a hot shower, my tears indiscernible from the driving water. I was a wreck. And flashbacks of January flashed through my mind with alarming clarity. I did not want to be back in this place. Especially not here. Not in Turkey.

I didn't know why I was having such an extreme reaction. Of course, I was sad for Sandra. Desperately sad for her. And Treena too, to be honest. But there were huge flames of feeling that were hotter and keener than sadness. I'd only known Trev for a split second really. He'd lived as a spectral fragment of a memory in the back of my mind for years, but more recently expanded into something more alive, something more treacherous. And now that he'd allowed alcohol to claim him with its viscid, clinging fingers, all that emotional energy I'd spent on the terrifying edges of forgiveness was wasted.

Gillie and Demir were giving me all the time and space I needed. Demir in particular, actually. He'd been the one to find fresh linen and make up a bed for me yesterday. He'd been the one to make a hot, wholesome soup which we'd eaten in the soft, dark silence of his balcony, as the moonlight slid like a silver chain across the solar panels on the rooftops of İpeklikum. Gillie responded to his kind acts with beaming smiles and frequent kisses kept small and bursting with gratitude. And for once I didn't care. He'd come through for the both of us, he really had.

I'd woken last night, in a twisted snarl of bedsheets and sweat, to hear voices hacking at each other from the steps outside Demir's apartment. I think I knew before I even woke up that it was Mesut because when my eyes opened, my body was already tilting inevitably towards the deep, lolling ribbon of his voice. A voice that had finally transformed back into a sound I knew so well, a sound that had lavished me with comfort and love these past few months, even if it had been over the phone.

It was obvious Mesut was looking for me, and he'd probably found all of my stuff gone from his house by now. He would be livid. But by the sounds of things, Demir was standing strong and not letting Mesut anywhere near me. Good. The last thing I needed was to face him when he might still be coming down from whatever shit he'd put into his body. I was so angry with him and those scratchy, swatches of anger were stubbornly mangled into the news of Trev's death, so I could hardly think straight. The jewel in the lake that I remembered from my painting back home was well and truly obscured by turbulent, tar-black waters. I wondered how long it would take to see its shine again.

After Mesut and Demir's confrontation on the steps, I'd closed my eyes, willing sleep to come. I'd listened to Demir's confident stride back through his own doorway, the definitive slam of the metal door and Gillie's soft murmur, welcoming him back to bed. Things had been completely quiet for a while. Almost eerily so. And I thought I'd been left alone with the torturous hush of my emotions careering through me at their continually nauseous pace. But suddenly I heard the gentle scuff of pebbles grinding underfoot. A sigh brimming with stifled defeat. The warm crackle of a just-lit cigarette. For a brief moment my body billowed with curiosity and I moved over to the open window, pulling the embroidered curtain back ever so slightly. But I was too late. All I saw was the indelible flick of long, black hair and he disappeared around a shadowed corner.

"Come on then. You getting out or what?" Gillie snapped me out of my trance by reaching into the car and offering me her hand. I took it and she hauled me out into the bright, unforgiving sunshine. "This is going to be so cool." She said, linking her arm through mine and leading the way. "Demir can catch up. He's seen it loads of times. I can't believe it's been just up the road all this time and we've never been here!"

We were visiting Apollo's Temple which was located at the very edges of İpeklikum. I'd seen it briefly before, as we'd driven through the town after arriving from the airport – ruined columns stretching up towards the sky with an understated sense of resplendence. Gillie thought it would be a good idea to get outside and experience a bit of history. "We loved all our visits out and about last time, didn't we, sweetie?" She'd said over a sesame-adorned simit bread this morning. "I'm sure we can conjure up the magic of Dalyan or the awesomeness of Ephesus by visiting somewhere new." Demir, being a busy man, had suggested Apollo's Temple because it was literally only five minutes' drive away. So here we were. About to take on an ancient wonder of the world when I'd hardly even been able to get dressed that morning.

"Well, it's certainly something, isn't it?" I said to Gillie as she bought our entry tickets at the little booth. And it was. The entrance was on a hill that led down towards the ruins and was quite possibly already the best view we were going to get. The swelling mass of white cloud broke only for brief patches of blue-grey sky and beams of winter sun and it framed the soaring stone columns as if by design. It kind of reminded me of the Angel of the North, where I'd sat with Ella only weeks ago. But the temple lacked the contemporary arrogance of Gormley's Angel, as you had to squint your eyes to imagine what this incredible place might have looked like if it hadn't been stolen by some powerful, destructive force.

"We not really know what destroyed it." Demir appeared behind us and motioned for us to start walking down the steps that led to the ruins. "It was about 500BC and some people think it was earthquake, some people think it was Persians come and ruin it. It used to be sanctuary and they trying to rebuild after that, but then Christianity is spreading and that stop it from getting finished. No more need for mythical gods like Apollo after that." I'd forgotten for a minute that Demir would obviously know all about this place. He did run a tour company, after all.

"Did you say sanctuary?" I asked, feeling like that was exactly what I needed right now.

"Yes. Is place people come to feel better and relax and also to speak to high priestess, to Oracle. They getting wisdom from her here. Is very famous place. You not hear of it before?"

"The only Apollo's Temple I know is on Newcastle Quay-side and does an extended happy hour on a Thursday night." Gillie said, grinning mischievously. She jumped down the steps with a buoyancy that turned my stomach. "Come on then Jess – let's explore!"

And exploring was happily encouraged here. Having come from England, where you have to write a risk assessment in order to write a risk assessment, I was stunned that us mere mortals were allowed to actually walk right up to these ruins and touch them. We could walk around them, sit on them, climb on them if we liked. It was all very immersive. I couldn't understand why the Turkish historians weren't worried about the natural oils in people's fingers slowly eroding these sculpted rocks, or the grip of their very modern trainers treading concaved dips on the antiquated steps. But as soon as I trailed my palms over the cool and bulky circumference of an upturned column base, I understood. Here, history was solid.

Demir spoke loudly into his phone for the majority of the time, so it was no wonder I slipped away from him to find my own quieter experience. Because Gillie followed him, I set about putting one foot in front of the other, attempting to rip my mind away from the thrashing confusion that seemed to live there now. Instead I breathed deep and focused on the bare, black branches of trees surrounding the site, the dappled grey steps beckoning me to magnificence and sloping stone tunnels that offered a moment of dark and dewy silence.

I eventually found the sacred spring where the Oracle herself was rumoured to have drunk, before giving prophecies to her visitors. Sadly, the water in there today didn't look particularly sacred, otherwise I might have scooped some up for myself, in an effort to rise above all this earthly shit and transcend my way out of it. Although, I reflected, that might have made me just as bad as Mesut and Ömer and their dodgy pills.

After wandering around for a little bit longer, skirting the edge of the massive rectangular site, and tip-toeing my way along the edges of ornate column bases and long-ago tumbled rocks, I found Medusa. I knew she'd be here somewhere. Unlike the stone relief of her head that I'd found in an underground cistern in İstanbul, this one was the right way up and startlingly elaborate. Her brow was deep and furrowed, presumably caught in concentration as she stared somebody down into a petrified state, and the locks of her famous head of hair squirmed and thrashed just as you'd imagine snakes would. There was an almighty, horizontal crack in the stone that severed the deep crevice of the cupid's bow above her lips, just shy of either silencing her forever or blinding that deadly glare. Luckily, the stones had been forced back together and instead she kept her powers. *Good for her,* I thought. *Maybe I'll get to keep mine too.*

Just then a great gust of wind practically slapped me in the face and I heard a sharp voice exclaim, "Hayır! Geri gel!" I looked up and saw a bulbous mass of fluttering white adorn a nearby tree and a flash of a dark figure dart out from behind it. Fuck. It was Mesut.

I instinctively shot down behind Medusa's head. My breath tripped in my throat and a cry nearly burst out of my mouth but I caught it in my hands just in time. I peered around Medusa's full head of snakes and watched him quietly. What the hell was he doing here?

The tree he'd appeared next to was bald and knotted like all of the others except for thousands of white pieces of fabric, ribbon and string tied to every one of its branches. I'd seen something like that before. A 'Wishing Tree', I think it was called. You were supposed to tie something onto it at the same time as making a wish or imagining your hopes and dreams would come to fruition. And this was one was full of the frayed and ragged yearnings of so many people. If I listened closely enough, I could hear that the sudden change in the wind had gathered up the edges of every tiny scrap and teased them into making pleasantly burbling noises, a bit like a rushing brook in the middle of a forest.

Mesut was moving quickly and chasing after something that had escaped his grasp. He was bent awkwardly whilst trying to run over the uneven ground, avoiding knotted roots and jutting rocks. Finally he knelt down and scooped the rogue item up. It was white and small. A piece of ribbon for the tree.

He straightened up and I noticed his chest swell then collapse again before he moved back towards the tree. He stood stock-still as he looked up at the oscillating branches, the lengths of black hair flowing down his back like a mass of dark ribbon to offset the white above. He then seemed to decide on something, and I was sure I detected a tiny nod before he pushed up the sleeves of his jacket and flexed his fingers. He brought the scrap of ribbon to his lips and I felt my muscles loosen as he kissed it firmly and with resolution. God. I knew what it felt like to be kissed like that.

He reached up and tied his ribbon to the tree. He knotted it once, twice, three times, before standing back and watching it join the others in their quivering dance. There was a sudden and slack expression on his face, and any tension he'd had in his arms instantly dropped as his fingers dangled down towards the ground. He let his head flop forwards and I thought the whole of him shrank with sadness in that moment. From my crouched position behind the stone, I felt a strong impulse to run over there, gather him up and whisper all the ways it would be alright into his ear. But I couldn't. I was as still and rooted as if Medusa herself had struck me down.

I blinked back tears much hotter than the wind and settled my eyes again on the wishing tree. But he was gone. Not even a broken branch or a patch of flattened grass to suggest he'd been there at all and I did wonder for a second if I'd imagined the whole thing. If it had been real, and he had been making any kind of wish to do with me, then surely that was as far as the wish should get. I couldn't let it get any closer.

Could I?

I was sure he was gone so I stood up and allowed my knees to stretch out again. I looked down to brush the grey skeletons of leaves and black skins of twigs off my jeans and willed myself not to cry anymore. Enough with the tears. Whilst my gaze was cast downwards, I noticed a uniform row of stones that lined the path away from Medusa. I hadn't seen them before. They were a slightly more burnished colour than any of the other remnants of Apollo's Temple, which suggested to me they might be of another time. It wouldn't be that unusual. Turkey was the very embodiment of cultural, religious and historical diversity, I was coming to learn.

I needed to pick out a path back to find Gillie and Demir and these stones seemed as good as any. I dragged my hands along their ridges as I walked and allowed the rough contours to prickle my fingertips into the present moment. It was a strange, meditative thing, walking like that. I needed my breathing to even out and my tears to dry. I simply couldn't be crushed by what I'd just seen. Mesut had made a wish – so what? It might not have even had anything to do with me. The wish he'd tied onto that tree probably had as little to do with me as his decision a couple of nights ago to pop pills with Ömer.

After everything I'd been through this year, I knew I needed to forget other people's wishes and concentrate on my own. If 2006 had taught me anything at all, it had to be that.

I suddenly stopped in my tracks as one particular stone felt different from all the others beneath my fingertips. It was smoother under my hands, but carved with more detail, more care. I crouched down to check it out and could see there were words chiselled onto its surface. There were huge daisies sprouting from the point where the stone met the earth, not dissuaded by the winter winds or the exposed location. It reminded me vividly of the dandelion clocks I used to pull from the pavement at the edge of my village as a kid. The very place I used to escape to, and make wishes when Trev visited our house with Sandra.

I pulled the daisies gently back so I could read what was written, being careful not to crush their feathery petals against the harsh surface of the stone. They bowed to the side and I could see that whatever was written on the stone had been said by a man named Ali İbn Abi Talib. The words were incredibly clear, given that they were probably carved some time ago, although I did have to push out a bit of grit from the grooves with my thumbs. It didn't take much though, and I read the words as hungrily as a child devours a juicy piece of fruit.

'Be the flower that gives its fragrance to even the hand that crushes it.'

I didn't have any cohesive thought after I read these words – more like an uninvited montage of images streaking through my mind:

The swing of a belt buckle, high and rapid. An ocean horizon, grey and fluid. Dandelion clocks soft and fluttering. Trev's fingers, jabbing and pointing. My adolescent belly rounded and quivering. The keys of a typewriter jumping and jolting. Mesut's hands wide and open. A shock of yellow roses, full and blooming.

I took a breath that was as deep and cavernous as the hole in my heart from which it came and exhaled everything back at the words on the stone. Then I turned my back on them.

For now.

38

ABOUT TO BLOOM

I found Gillie waiting for me in a generous wedge of shadow at the exit of the temple.

"What kept you?" She asked. "You've been in there for ages."

"I was okay. Just . . . looking around." There was a pounding inside me that I didn't know how to share with her just yet. I didn't even know if it was coming from my head, my heart or my gut.

"Well, Demir's got a business meeting at the tea garden just up the road now, but we can get coffee there and wait for him to finish?"

"Perfect." I said. "Let's go." We started walking up the hill and the words I'd read on the stone streaked through my head again, like a fork of lightning.

'Be the flower that gives its fragrance to even the hand that crushes it.'

In an abstract and unimaginable way, these words asked me two questions:

1. Do you want to remain crushed?
2. Do you want to share your fragrance?

And I knew the answers. Even if it meant these relationships could no longer be what I had assumed then to be, I still knew the answers.

"Gillie! Jessy! Isn't it a beautiful day? Get yourselves over here and park your bums." Kaz saw us before we'd even made it through the rose-woven arch of the tea garden. She was sitting at a table that looked directly out over Apollo's Temple, Demir at her side, hovering over a leather portfolio of files, papers and graphs.

"Demir's meeting is with Kaz?" I whispered to Gillie as we both approached, smiling.

"Yup. Remember he said they'd be meeting up? She might be investing in Mega Tour so he's really excited. Don't worry. She won't mention the other night."

"What happened to you the other night?" Kaz asked as she air-kissed us both. I felt Gillie squeeze my hand in silent apology. "I thought my cooking had finished you off."

"No, no, nothing like that." I said, as Kaz removed her enormous designer handbag from a nearby chair so that I had somewhere to sit. "I just needed a breather really. It was a lovely night, Kaz, other than that."

She nodded and pursed her lips together. "It was that couple of fools, wasn't it? Bloody idiots, they were. Thank god for Demir, here, who chucked them out of the house. It made a change from me doing it! I can't be doing with them party drugs under my roof, thank you very much, and Ömmy should bloody well know that by now. I had no idea, Jessy, that they were taking anything other than what I'd put on the bloody table. It'll be a while before Ömmy comes pithering back to me, I can tell you. At least, if he knows what's good for him."

"Yeah, I should think so." I agreed and eyed the strong, black coffees the waiter was now placing down on the table in front of us. I was going to need the energy. "Anyway, Kaz, I'm glad we've bumped into you. When you and Demir are finished, I've got a couple of favours to ask you, if that's okay?"

"Of course. We're nearly done here, aren't we, luvvie?" Kaz cast her eyes up to Demir who was still standing in presentation mode, waiting with tapping feet for us to finish our conversation.

"Well, Kaz, I really wanting show you plans for new coaches and signage. Then last year's turnover. Then new staffing ideas. Then . . ."

"Yes, yes, yes – we'll get to that eventually." Demir pouted like a toddler being refused another go on the swings and I chuckled inwardly at Kaz's spectacular capability to put him in his place. "Let's spend five more minutes then I want to hear what Jessy's got up her sleeve. She's practically gleaming and that can't be for nothing. So, what's this about new coaches?"

Demir plunged back into trying to impress Kaz with all the effort (but none of the grace) of an Olympic diver and I raised a coffee cup to my lips. It was startlingly hot. But it was good.

"Erm, excuse me. What in the actual fuckery is going on?" Gillie whispered, making sure Demir was glued to Kaz's side before questioning me. "She's right – you are kind of 'gleaming'. What's happened? Did the Oracle at Apollo's Temple resurrect herself just for you or something?"

"Quite possibly. In a way. I saw some words inscribed on a stone before I left the place and, well, they just spoke to me Gillie."

"What words? Weren't they in Turkish?"

"Nope. English. But attributed to some important prophet or something. Let me see if I can remember them." I took the notebook Gillie had given me at Beerbelly out of my pocket and flipped past the pages that I'd scored through with a pencil earlier. Then I grabbed a pen off Demir's pile of stuff on the table and wrote them down for Gillie to see.

"Be the flower? Ah, I see. This is about forgiveness?"

I nodded and my heart slowed. "I think so. And the fact that I want to keep being the flower. Uncrushed."

"So you're forgiving Mesut? You're taking him back? Oh please say you're taking him back!" She started shifting in her chair, knees jiggling and head tilting to the side with a fidgety smile.

"I don't think it's as simple as that. And anyway, he comes later. It all starts with Trev."

Gillie's eyes widened and her jiggling suddenly stopped. "You're forgiving Trev? How? He's dead."

"I know." I said, tears of a different kind stinging the edges of my eyes, tears that had every right to be there. "But I have to forgive him somehow. For him. For his family. For Sandra. For me."

"So what do you need Kaz for then? What's the favour you've got to ask her?"

"Well, first I need to use the internet and she's bound to have it at her apartment, what with all the technology she's got going on over there."

Gillie giggled. "Yes, considering the cupboards that open at the sound of her voice, I would guess that internet access is a given."

"Exactly. And then, we'll see. She's lived in İpeklikum a good while and I have a feeling I'm going to need her to find Mesut. I'd ask Demir but he's already done so much and I don't fancy getting him and Mesut in the same room anyway."

"Probably wise."

"In fact, can you go back home with him please Gillie? I need to do this by myself but I also need to know where you are for when I'm done. Because it will be you I'll come running to when it's all over. As always."

"Of course, sweetie. We'll go home and wait for you. But are you sure there's nothing at all I can do to help? Find Mesut? Cover him in baby oil? Tie him to a bed for you? Something like that?"

"Generous offer, but no." I laughed and hugged Gillie tight, lingering in the warmth she gave me. As I looked past her copper-coloured curls and over her shoulder, I spotted the ornate archway that marked the entrance to the tea garden, the one that was woven with roses. "Although, there might be one little thing . . ."

"Oooh – anything, anything! I want to be part of the grand plan!" She sprang back from me and waited for instruction, her eyebrows raised in excitement.

"Right, well when you get back to Demir's, ask him about local florists. I want some yellow roses. Big ones. Extravagant ones. Lots of them. And don't worry about the cost because I've got the money. Okay?"

"Got it." Gillie sprang to her feet and pretended to tick things off on her open palm. "Roses. Yellow. Big ones. Lots. All the money. What about ribbons? Cellophane? Balloons?"

"Nope. Just the roses. Plain as can be."

"Not even a nice ribbon?"

"Oh okay. One ribbon. You can pick the colour. Happy?"

"Ecstatic. I'm so proud of you, Jess – you always figure out what you need to do in the end. And because you're an upgraded version now, I don't need to worry that you're bending arse over tit for only other people. You'll be doing it for yourself too. You're so bloody clever."

"No, I'm just lucky, Gillie. Lucky that the universe eventually beats me in the face with all the signs that I need. And lucky to have you. Obviously."

"Obviously."

We had another long and lingering hug and I just knew the next time I saw her I would be an even further upgraded version of myself. Those crushed petals? They were about to bloom.

39

YELLOW ROSE

"Right luvvie. I find the signal is strongest if you sit out on the balcony. So you go out there and I'll fetch my laptop for you. Even if it rains I've got those cover thingies that roll out automatically so you'll be fine out there."

"Thanks, Kaz." I took the tall glass of orange juice that she'd given me, out onto the balcony. I sat down on a high metal stool that was almost as golden and sparkly as the sofa I remembered from her living room, put the drink down on the table in front of me and looked out at the impressive view. Bodrum was just about visible across the rolling waves as a rugged mass of dark green dotted with tiny white specks that must have been hotels and apartment blocks. Low, grey clouds bumped carelessly into the hills and mountains that rose up further back from the shore and created a shimmering mist that was as haunting as it was beautiful. Funny how nature could create such contradictions.

"Here you go, luvvie. Now you just tell me if you need another drink." Kaz set the laptop down in front of me, all hooked up to Google and ready to go. "And, erm, can I just be nosey for a minute Jessy? Before you get started?"

"Okay." I said, bracing myself.

"It's just that I wanted to let you know, in private, that Messy doesn't usually do stuff like what he did the other night. You know – popping them pills." She started flapping her impressively painted nails in front of her face and it took me several seconds to realise she was trying to stop herself from crying. "It was him what got Ömmy off stuff like that in the first place, you know. And, well, all I can think is that Ömmy somehow convinced him to do it. He can be awfully persuasive, else how would somebody like me, an old cronie – end up living with a twenty-two year old?"

"Kaz! You're not an old cronie!"

"It's okay, luvvie. I know I am, in comparison to him. But before you do whatever you're going to do about you and Messy, well, I want you to know that I've never seen him with anyone the way he is with you. Actually, strike that – I've never seen him with *anyone*. You're the first girl he's ever introduced to us. And whilst I know he won't be an angel or anything, I reckon that he's been waiting for someone like you. Or, strike that again . . . he's been waiting for you."

I was determined not to flap my hands like Kaz but I did have to swallow back something in my throat. "Well that's all very nice, but if drugs are a part of his life then I'm afraid I can't be. But . . ." Kaz sniffed back some tears and flapped her hands some more. I breathed deep and reminded myself that I needed to get on with my plan. "I can understand that he's only human and, well, for that I can forgive him. None of us are perfect. He's been an incredible part of my life and there's only him to thank for that."

"So, so what are you going to tell him? I'm sorry. I told you I was a right nosey cow – and I really do care about that boy."

"I have no idea what words are going to get me through this. But I do know that they'll come to me somehow. I'll be kind, so don't worry. If Mesut and I really do have the connection I've always suspected we have, then the two of us will figure out how to say it all." And I meant it. Mesut had made the past six months of my life completely unforgettable and I couldn't let one stupid decision on one stupid night cancel out all of that. If we were going to part, it needed to be on good terms, or it would have all been for nothing.

But there was something else to attend to first.

Kaz slipped off into her apartment, whispering to herself about missed chances and sad endings, whilst I set to work at the laptop. I checked my bank balance online and, as Terri had mentioned in her text the day before, I was now a considerably richer woman. Thank god for those crazy paintings – they were going to make everything possible.

Throwing money at anything was not my usual style. But, then again, I didn't usually have the money to throw. After seeing the words on that stone at Apollo's Temple, I knew, without a doubt, that I wanted to do something good for Trev's family. He had crushed me as a little girl, there was no escaping that fact. And his cruel treatment had been responsible for many of my later insecurities and for holding me back in so many ways. But now, after putting in place all of my adult learnings, and having been privilege to a state of hypnosis on Sandra's chintzy reclining armchair just before Christmas, I knew there was so much more to it than that.

I did a quick Google search on the cost of funerals. Luckily, it was not something I'd had to endure before, so I had no idea what kind of amount was involved. I took a sharp breath after I used an online calculator. It was a lot more than I'd expected. That kind of sum would just about wipe me out.

But that was okay. Being wiped out means you get to start afresh.

I had Sandra's bank details after paying her back for a load of drinks at the Body Positivity event at the pub. God, that seemed like an age ago now. She'd said at the time, "Don't you dare give me money for those drinks, our Jessica . . . I'm good for shouting you a few bevvies for you and your marras." What would she say when she saw this money land in her account?

Well I'd soon find out. I picked up my phone and used my cheap calls code to dial her number in the UK. It took a while to connect, but she picked up in the end.

"Hello?"

"Hi Sandra. It's me. Jess."

"Ah, hia love. You alright?"

"Yeah, I'm fine. How are you doing? How's Treena and the kids?"

Sandra took a huge breath and her words fell out on the inevitable exhale. "As well as can be expected, love. It's all been a bit ugly, as you can imagine." Sandra paused and I heard a child fussing in the background and then a dog bark. She must have been looking after Kaylee and Kaidan. "Trev's been moved to the hospital morgue and we're just waiting on funeral arrangements. The post-mortem's taking forever even though we all know what took him."

"God. That sounds awful."

"Yeah. It is. But it was a given it would happen one day. Trev was a bit of a ticking time bomb really."

"And what about you? Are you holding up okay?"

"You know me pet, trooping on, as usual. And I've got my Luke so I'll be fine."

"Good. Make sure he looks after you."

"He will. What about you, pet? It must be expensive you ringing me. And shouldn't you be off having a nice time with your lad? Have you got anything nice planned for New Year's Eve?"

"Never mind that right now, Sandra. I called because I need your help with something."

"Okay . . . what's going on, our Jessica?" I could just picture Sandra's nose wrinkling, her whole body shifting as if she wanted to climb into the phone.

"I know it's not much. And I don't want you to flip out, okay? But, well, I've put a little bit of money in your bank account."

"You've done what? . . ."

"Hold on! Let me explain. It's meant specifically for Trev's funeral, okay? I thought it might help. I know Treena doesn't have a lot, and, well, it's the least I can do." I checked over my shoulder to make sure Kaz wasn't listening in. The last thing I needed was to justify this to her too.

"The least you can do? Jessica, you don't need to do anything at all, pet. He was a monster to you and I wish I could go back in time and stop him, I really do. You don't owe him a single thing."

"But I do." I pleaded, knowing that I was pleading with my own heart too. "I owe him forgiveness . . . I really wanted to meet him, Sandra, and try to show him it was okay. That I'm a grown-up now and I'm confident and strong and not a sorry little lass pulling her belly in anymore. I didn't know how I was going to do it but I was hoping that when I met him in the new year, I'd be able to forgive him somehow so he could get on with his twelve steps and I could get on with my life."

"But you didn't get the chance . . ."

"No, I didn't get the chance. And that's because he was so, so ill, wasn't it? Not because he was a monster." I felt a flutter in my chest that wanted to break free, the muscles in my torso tightening in response.

"You're so right, our Jessica. But still . . . this?"

"Yes. Absolutely this. And you don't need to tell Treena or anyone else where the money came from, okay? Just let it take the pressure off. Organise whatever Trev would have wanted and whatever makes Treena and the kids happy. Even if it's a rave-up in the working men's club. And if there's any money left over, just donate it to an addiction charity or something. Are there any that have helped Trev in the past?"

"Yes, love. There's a local rehab centre that he went to a few times – they always tried their best with him."

"Perfect. Donate to them."

"Well, if you're absolutely sure. Oh petal, this really is a beautiful thing to do. And will you be here for the funeral? You know you're more than welcome, don't you? I promise I'll keep Treena away from you and any concrete steps."

That made me laugh. And I felt some sparks of tension leave my body, the flutters in my chest starting to expand and ease. "I don't know if I'll be back in time. It could go either way at the moment. Mesut and I . . . things have happened. Well, actually, can I ask you something, Sandra?"

"Of course, pet. Anything."

"How did you do it? I mean, things didn't work out between you and Trev because, well, because of the addiction and everything. But how did you keep being a part of his life? How did you forgive him but not block him out after all the hurt he caused you?"

I sensed a smile on Sandra's lips, I could hear it in her voice. "Well, it's really hard to explain to other people – so much so that I rarely even bother putting it into words, pet. Of course, there were the worries about little Treena and who would look after her. I felt an obligation to him, obviously, because he was such a poorly man. But, well, aside from his enigmatic little soul, Trev and I were kind of magnetized . . . attracted to each other on a level that went well beyond any levels of romance. Remember all that past life stuff you did at mine before Christmas? Well I think we knew each other on that kind of level, if that doesn't sound too weird."

I thought about me two lifetimes ago, standing on that beach in France, looking desperately out to the horizon for the man I knew was really just another part of me. "It doesn't. Not anymore" I said.

"Aye. You understand, don't you, pet?" Then she sighed softly and asked me in almost a whisper. "What's happened?"

"I don't really know."

"You don't know?"

"Well, I do know, but it all feels a bit wrong. He did something . . . he took something . . . he made a choice that really changed the dynamic between us and I haven't spoken to him since. I'm going to though. I'm doing it today."

"You'll be okay, love."

"I know. I do know that basically because of everything I learned at your past life party. I'm deserving of all the good things in life and I won't let him get in the way of that. I'll be strong and I'll stand up for myself and if I can wield a belt buckle in a French barn then I can bloody well wield a few strong words here in Turkey . . . but . . ."

"But?"

I tried to ignore the prickling of my scalp, the chilled wind greeting me at my spot on Kaz's balcony, rushing all the way over from the misty shores of Bodrum. "But what if the connection is stronger? What if I compromise my values for a connection that's ultimately going to be destructive? After the year I've had, I can't afford to make the wrong decision about him."

"Jessica, let me tell you something. The head and the heart can be pesky sometimes. It's all 'listen to me!' and 'check me out!'. But what can be far more useful, and what I have asked myself time and time again when my head and my heart are competing for my attention is, 'what is my gut telling me?'"

"It's telling me that something is wrong."

"Then something is wrong."

"Really? It's as simple as that?"

"In my experience, yes. Follow that feeling. The rest will work itself out, pet."

"My gut told me to buy yellow roses."

Sandra let out a little yelp of joy. "I love it! So buy yellow roses. What will you do with them?"

"Fuck knows! But I'm buying them."

"Marvellous. Well, you let me know what happens with them. And you're a yellow rose yourself you know, love. You really are. All bright and glowing and graceful and sunny. You do know that, don't you?"

"I do. At least, I know I can be. Sometimes."

"Any time you want, our Jessica. Any time you want."

40

THE ŞAHIN

I put down the phone to Sandra, feeling resolute about what needed to happen next. It was time to find Mesut.

Before I shifted from my stool out on Kaz's vast balcony, I flipped open my phone once more to text Gillie. I wanted to know how she was getting on with the little mission I'd given her.

How goes it with the flowers sweetie? Did you get hold of some yellow roses?

Her answer came back so fast, it was almost as if she'd been waiting for my text.

No luck I'm afraid. It's not the right season. Where's a Tesco's when you need one? Don't worry – will keep trying. Have you seen Mesut yet?

Nope. He's next on the list. x

I checked in with my body to see how I felt before I embarked on finding him. There was a sense of lightness that hadn't been there before, now that I'd transferred that money to Sandra. I knew full well that chucking money at Trev's family wasn't going to obliterate the heavy grief they must be feeling now, but it felt good to do something small. My hands fell instinctively to my tummy and I pondered on what Sandra had said about following your gut. The smooth ripples of flesh under my t-shirt didn't make me feel ashamed anymore. My stomach was so much more than an aesthetic property. And who didn't like ripples, anyway? If they could be beautiful on the surface of a glassy lake, in the folds of a silk scarf or upon swathes of golden sand, then they could be beautiful on bellies too.

I closed Kaz's laptop and tucked it under my arm. I took the glass back through to the kitchen and set it down on the gleaming, marble worktop as Kaz came swooping in, wearing the most outrageous pair of pink, fluffy slippers I've ever seen.

"You've finished, then? Did you manage to do what you wanted?"

"I did, Kaz, thanks so much." I handed her back her laptop and she clicked her fingernails on it whilst fixing me with an expectant stare. "So?" she said, letting the 'o' hang in the air like the chime of a bell.

"So . . . ?" I smiled, knowing full well what kind of question was on her lips.

"Oh Jessy come on, you must be going to see Messy now, yeah? I tell you what, that shit will be well out of his system by now and I happen to know he's absolutely chomping at the bit to see you."

"Oh, you just happen to know that, do you?"

"I do. Because, well . . ." Kaz shuffled to the side and a hunched figure edged out from behind her and straightened up into full view. Ömer.

I stared, open-mouthed, at Kaz and Ömer. They didn't appear to have just emerged from a confrontation of any sort. Their bodies leaned in towards each other, their expressions soft and smiling, their fingers twitching to hold hands. Had they already had this out before now? Was Kaz okay with the whole

Ecstasy-at-her-dinner-party thing? I thought she'd been really angry with him.

"Jess, I so sorry about what happened. We not know . . . well, Mesut and me we not realise what we doing. Just stupid decision. Stupid." Ömer's gelled curls bobbed around his face as he shook his head and looked down at the floor.

Kaz jumped in with the same flapping hands and blinking eyes from before. "Right. You two. Never mind all that. We know it was stupid and it's done now. Ömmy? You can take Jessy to Messy's place, can't you? Go and get your car keys. She's ready to see him now, aren't you luvvie?"

I gave a small but sure nod and straightened out my shoulders. "I am." I said, because quite frankly, how Kaz and Ömer conducted their relationship was none of my business and this wasn't about them. At least, that's what my gut was telling me.

———

Ömer and I climbed into his impressive little sports car and he started driving along İpeklikum's narrow, cluttered roads. There was hardly anybody out on the streets. It was, I realised, around siesta time, so that was probably why, but the mist was also closing in like shrouds of damp cotton, leaving anybody in its wake sticky and smothered. The winter sun that had played across the columns of Apollo's Temple that morning was now hopelessly lost.

"Jess, I am thinking we need talk." Ömer said, as he swung around a roundabout with more care than I ever would have thought he was capable of.

"No, it's okay, Ömer. You don't need to justify yourself. It's Mesut I need to have things out with, not you."

"No, Jess, I think you not understand. There is something you not know. You not know yet." He twisted a coil of his hair briefly and flashed me a pained look, his eyebrows fused together.

"Listen, Ömer. I'm really grateful that you're driving me to see Mesut. But I've had a tough couple of days . . . I've had some, well, some bad news and I just need to see Mesut before I go home so we can settle things. I don't need to know about your reasons or whether you'll be doing it again, or how sorry either of you are . . . it's just not important now."

"This thing is important, Jess. This thing I needing tell you . . . even Kaz. She not know."

"Well I definitely don't need to know whatever it is before you tell Kaz – your own girlfriend! For fuck's sake, Ömer, please don't draw me into whatever . . ."

"It was Demir."

"Excuse me, what?"

"It was Demir. He putting pills in our drinks. I think you say, 'spiked'?" Ömer kept his eyes on the road ahead. A long, grey stretch that I knew would lead us, in a minute, to Mesut's front door.

"Spiked?" The word thrummed off the walls of the car's interior. My body felt exposed to its impact, like the bruises were imminent. But I said it again. "Spiked?"

"Yes. He spiked us. We not wanting it. We not planning it. He did it with the wine he bringing. You remember? He bringing special wine to dinner from Mesut's hometown? He was late because he getting it. Well now I know where he getting it from and who is giving him pills to put in. He not good person Jess. I think Mesut telling you this before."

"Yes, but . . ." This information had floored me. My body felt like it was merging, ever so slowly and heavily with the fabric of the car seat beneath me, whilst the thoughts in my head took flight and whirled into a delirium of memories from that night . . .

Finding Gillie alone on the beach outside Kaz's apartment because Demir was busy picking up a 'special bottle of wine'. How adamant Demir had been that Mesut try the wine and Mesut finally buckling in an effort to shut him up. The time the lads had spent out on the balcony laughing and how Mesut's laugh had been noticeably absent. How quickly Demir had been to help Kaz in the kitchen with the coffees. That sneaky little bastard. He'd orchestrated everything perfectly so that it looked like he was on the outside of Mesut and Ömer's 'stupidity'. What had he called them that night as I'd sat devastated in Beer-belly? Silly, silly boys? *I says to them they must getting sober and grow up into men. Is silly boys I think.'*

God, he was good. He'd come across as the perfect hero. Chucking the lads out on Kaz's behalf; picking my stuff up from Mesut's house and giving me a place to stay; making me soup and fluffing my fucking pillows. I'd been sucked in good and proper.

"But why would he do that, Ömer?" I asked, my voice barely a gasp. "Why go to all that effort and lie to all of us? What's he getting out of it?"

"Jess, you need understanding Demir very strange little man. He have big, long history with me and he very upset the way I behaving in past times. For this, I not blame him but he not know how to forgive."

"Forgiving can be hard."

"Yes. Very hard. But he had lots time and lots apologies and still he not doing it. He also not like Mesut working at Beerbelly. I think you knows this. He want it only family working there and Mesut not family so . . ."

"I get it."

"And then two more things. Firstly, he want Gillie to like him. I not know how much he actually liking Gillie but he knows she gorgeous and he not like it if she not think he amazing like big man. So he make himself look better than other men around her. He needing it for his ego, I think. I see before with lots other girls."

"You have?"

"I have. And it never ending well."

"You said two more things. What's the other thing?"

"Is most important one for Demir I think." Ömer paused for a few seconds as he pulled the car up on the flash of wasteland outside Mesut's house. The gravel crunching under the tyres stopped abruptly and we were left with the obdurate drone of the car engine. İpeklikum's mist slithered across the windows so the house was partly obscured. I couldn't see if anyone was home. "Is money Jess. He waiting few years now I think, for Kaz to invest in Mega Tour. He watch her like a, how you say, he watch her like şahin, erm . . . wild bird with this," he made his fingers all crooked like claws, "and mouth like this," he mimed the shape of a curved beak coming from his mouth.

"Hawk! You mean he watched her like a hawk."

"Yes. Hawk. Şahin. Demir watching Kaz like hawk for so very long now and I knows it. Another reason I not liking him. And another reason for him not liking me because he not want me take all her money. He thinks I wasting it." He gestured towards the very car we were sitting in which, I was betting, he didn't pay for himself. "He want her money for Mega Tour. He sly. He nasty. He not right man."

I arched my back and breathed the fullest, deepest breath I had done all week. Maybe all year. As the breath filled my body, the solid feeling in my gut that something was wrong started to dissolve and a warmth settled there instead. A soft, earthy, sun-kissed warmth, perfect for planting flowers.

"But why haven't you told Kaz, Ömer? I don't understand. Surely if you told her Demir was behind the pills then she would have forgiven you more quickly. She would have thrown him out the other night and not you and Mesut."

Ömer hung his head and beat his fists off the steering wheel in front of him. "I am in very hard place Jess. I really not liking Demir and not wanting him near my Kaz but she so very, very excited about Mega Tour. She knows Demir watching her like şahin all this time and she waiting to invest at right time. She wanting spend her money on something, how you say, worthy? She thinking him worthy. And everyone thinking I take her money and I waste it anyway. She need this for her. I can't telling her what Demir really like."

"But you can. You have to! What he did with spiking your drinks, that was really dangerous. You and Mesut could have had any kind of awful reaction. If he's willing to do that to you, then what might he do in the future with her money or even her? You say it yourself, he's not a 'right man'. Kaz needs to know."

"Maybe you right."

"I'm right. I'm so right." Just then, even though all of the car windows were shut, all the hairs on the back of my neck stood up and my breath caught in my throat so I could hardly even speak the next words. "Gillie. We have to go tell Gillie."

"What about Mesut? We here now Jess."

I leaned forwards and wiped the condensation off the windscreen so that it clung, mightily, to my fingers. The house looked empty. No lights on. No flicker of movement. Was Mesut even inside? Should I run to him now and tell him that I knew everything? Fold back into his arms like a seed sown into warm soil. Oh god, I wanted to do that so much. I wanted to tell him that I was sorry I had assumed he'd done something so stupid; that Kaz's photos were nothing like ours; that he could call me Gulazer anytime he liked; that he was nothing at all like Trev or Jack and that I should have seen him for who he really was. The inevitable shadow to my tireless, love-filled light. That it hadn't been his hand that had crushed my flower at all . . . it had been Demir's.

"No." I said to Ömer, clicking my seatbelt back in, even the muscles in my toes and fingertips tightening in readiness. "We need to go and find Gillie. Now."

41

AN INVESTMENT

Still can't find any yellow roses sweetie. It might be too late anyway if they were for Mesut. Coz he's here. Weirdly. Are you coming over? I'll keep him here as long as I can. xxxxx

I snapped up my head from reading Gillie's text and looked at Ömer, who was frowning at a complicated display of road closure signs that we were approaching. "Mesut's there. At Demir's. What the hell is he doing there?"

Ömer wrung the steering wheel so that his knuckles turned bright white. "I not know. I just hope he not making more trouble with Demir. That man not worth it."

"Shall I call Gillie and find out?"

Ömer nodded. "Yes. We be there in five minutes."

Gillie answered the phone after about seven rings. I breathed deep and just hoped she wasn't breaking up a scrap. "Hello? Jess?"

"Hey. Everything okay?"

"Yeah. Are you coming? Mesut is here. Demir won't let him into the apartment but he says he doesn't care and he needs to speak to me. I'm just going out there now."

"Out where?"

"Out to the steps where Mesut is waiting. Demir's just done my head in for the last twenty minutes, trying to 'forbid' me to go out there to see him. He must really care for you, Jess, if he doesn't even want *me* speaking with Mesut."

If it really was possible for blood to boil then that's what mine was doing just then. I was worried it might spill out of my ears and ruin Ömer's pristine upholstery. "I don't think that's his motivation Gillie. Why does Mesut want to see you?"

"I don't know. I'm guessing it's to talk about you. Why else would it be?"

"I don't have a clue but right now I honestly think you're safer with Mesut, Gillie, not Demir. So go out there and wait for me. I'm on my way."

"Safer? What the hell are you talking about? Demir's not the one pumping chemicals into his body. Never mind – I'll . . . – then you . . . – Mesut will be . . . – When? . . . – Wha?"

"Shit. The signal's breaking up. Gillie? . . . Can you hear me? Fuck it. She's gone."

"Is okay." Ömer said. "We nearly there."

"Thank you so much for this, Ömer. I needed somebody to be honest with me and it was you. What Demir did . . . it changes everything. I can't wait to get Gillie out of his clutches."

"I help you Jess. I try. You helping my friend, after all. Mesut is good man."

I nodded and let those words seep into my soul. I knew he was a good man. I'd always known it. And that's why my gut was telling me there was something so very wrong with this whole situation right from the start. No wonder I hadn't been able to write about it on that notebook, sitting in Beerbelly. No wonder I'd taken no comfort from the private, draped space of Village Corner, or the vast, towering columns of Apollo's Temple. There was a reason why my emotions had been twisted and stunted beyond recognition and that reason was not a thoughtless new boyfriend who didn't understand or respect me . . . that reason was Demir.

Ömer took the last few corners before Demir's apartment block with a care that suggested to me he was curbing his anger as much as I was. As he pulled to a stop and put on the hand-brake, it took just one look at a particular vein twitching rapidly close to his David Beckham hairband to tell me I was right. I reached over and placed a hand gently on his arm. "You've been so helpful, Ömer. I'll go and speak to Gillie now. It's just round that corner, isn't it? I don't think it's a good idea if you come with me."

His chest ballooned with a huge, deep breath and he exhaled slowly through pursed lips. "Okay, Jess. You right. But you tell Mesut I round corner, okay? I here for lifts and what-ever you need."

"I will. Thank you so much." I gave him a small peck on the cheek and climbed out of the car, shutting the door gently behind me. I walked over to the dusty, cracked pavement that I knew led to Demir's apartment and concentrated on making sure my steps stayed firm, and that I wouldn't fall on the uneven ground that seriously needed İpeklikum Council's attention. I was so angry, it felt as though my wrath might wrap itself around my tendons and a twisted ankle seemed entirely possi-ble. And that was the last thing I needed on top of everything else.

As I got a few steps closer to the sandy-coloured apartment block, I heard voices. I looked beyond the lamppost that was obscuring my view with its hundreds of inexplicable wires stretching up and out like an intricate dreamcatcher and saw Gillie and Mesut sitting on the chipped, marble steps. The sight of Mesut sitting like that, knees drawn up and head tossed high and his silken, jet-black hair cascading down his back made my breath catch in my throat. He looked far more purposeful than he had beneath the majestic branches of the wishing tree. He had his hands outstretched towards Gillie, as if trying to make a very important point.

Gillie sat cross-legged, a rolled-up cigarette between her fingers, slowly dropping ash onto the step beneath her. The top half of her body was frozen, eyes fixed resolutely on Mesut, but her sandaled toes were tapping, twitching, just beneath her flared jean hems. She bit her lip and I thought I detected a tiny, repetitive flinch that occurred in between whatever words Mesut was saying to her.

I crept closer, keeping out of sight behind the web of wires across the street and listened for a clue about what was going on. It was Gillie's voice I heard first. "What do you mean he 'spiked' you? Do you even know what that word means, Mesut?"

"Yes Gillie. I knows it. I promise you. He putting pills in my drink. In Ömer's drink. He using the wine he brought. The special wine?"

"The special wine? But no – that was something he bought specially for you. I wanted to go with him to get it but he said it was better if I went to Kaz and Ömer's first. He was just being nice."

"Let me I ask you something, Gillie. Why you think he not let you going with him? To get the wine?"

"It was just so I wouldn't be bored at the supermarket. He knew how badly I wanted to see Jess."

"Really? You not noticing that he also not drink the wine himself all night?"

"Well, no, you're right – he didn't. But that doesn't mean anything. And anyway, why would you be telling me this now? Shouldn't you be telling Jess if this is what really happened? She's the one who's totally pissed off with you. Has Ömer put you up to this? I know how much he hates Demir." Gillie had a point. Why go to Gillie first and not me? I leaned forwards and felt a tingle stream down my spine. I couldn't work out whether it was pleasant or not.

"I telling you Gillie, because it more important."

"More important than my best friend in the world?" Gillie stubbed out her rollie and folded her arms across her chest. Her toes stopped tapping.

"This important Gillie, because Demir dangerous man. I know how much you means to Jess. I need you know all this so you can leave. As soon as possible. I not forgive myself if something happen to you too. Ömer and me? We handle it. He cannot hurt us. But he can hurt you, Gillie, and I not let that happen. Ever."

"And Jess?"

"And Jess . . . my Gulazer . . . this morning I am making wish and I am hoping, praying, that she will see truth. Then . . . is up to her. I not force her doing anything." He dropped his head and stared down at the ground, at the same time as bringing his fist to his chest and pounding it softly, as if he was trying to dislodge something deep inside.

"I don't know what I'm supposed to do with this information, Mesut. What am I supposed to do?" Gillie appealed towards him, eyes gleaming and full.

Mesut looked up at her and did his best to straighten up. "You needing get out, Gillie. You needing get out of that apartment. You can stay with me, or we find you hotel. I will help you with all your stuff. You not let him worry you."

Gillie stood up and smoothed down her jeans. She looked up towards the direction of Demir's apartment and I followed her gaze. There was a twitch of a net curtain, but nothing more. "I don't know. I just can't get my head round this. I'd fucking kill him. He knows that. Would he really do something so completely stupid?"

"He would." I said, throwing my cracked voice over to

where she was standing on the steps. I was moving forwards now, arms outstretched and heart leading the way. "He did. Gillie, he did."

I felt two sets of eyes widen as soon as they set themselves on me. Gillie jumped down the steps and met me on the pavement. She grabbed my hands and clutched them to her chest. "Fuck, Jess, did he really? How do you know about it? I can't believe the little bastard . . ."

"I know because Ömer told me. I've just found out. But he did it, Gillie. And Mesut is right. It's not safe to stay with him, if he's capable of doing shit like that. Let's get you out of there." I dropped one of her hands but kept hold of the other, and we made our way up the steps, towards the main door. I could feel Mesut's eyes on me the whole way but couldn't look at him yet. This was about Gillie first, and us second. He must have felt something similar because he met Gillie halfway down the steps and grabbed her other hand so that the three of us trooped up the steps together, an unstoppable force.

Before we could even pull the heavy, metal door open, Demir was there, glaring down at us all. His eyes were aflame with something dark and dangerous, as wide and scowling as a thunderous night. His legs stood stubbornly like squat tree trunks in a storm and he was clearly determined to block our path.

"You not believe him, Gillie. Whatever he say, whatever he blame me for – it all lies. You not trust him before you trust me. You not!"

"Demir." Gillie spoke calmly and with measure, which is more than I would have been capable of. "Please step to the side so I can go up to your apartment and get mine and Jess's stuff. I know what you did to Mesut and Ömer. It was really stupid and really dangerous and, if I'm honest, you're lucky they don't report you. Now please don't make this any harder than it needs to be."

"He deserved it." Demir sneered, a curl to his lip that made me wonder how Gillie could have ever been attracted to him. "Ömer deserved it too. You and Jess need to see what idiots they are. Kahrolası piçler! They fucking bastards! This should have showed you that!"

"No, Demir, it's just made me see what *you* really are. You've really shot yourself in the foot and thank the lord nobody got hurt in the process. Now, let. Me. Past." Gillie broke free from mine and Mesut's grasping hands and hurled herself towards the door, expecting him to jump aside to avoid her. But he didn't. His responses were as sharp as his scheming little mind and he grabbed her hard by the shoulders.

"You stay with me, Gillie, my love, you stay with me and lose them far behind you. I not care what Jess thinking of me but you Gillie, you are important to me!"

"If I was so important, you wouldn't have spiked my best friend's boyfriend! Can't you see, you complete and utter ball-bag? Never mess with your woman's best mate!" And with that, Gillie snapped her shoulders violently free from his grasp and belted past him into the corridor and up the stairs. Demir's eyes burst even wider than they had been before and stared down at his empty hands and the space where Gillie had been just milliseconds before. As soon as it registered that she was no longer there, his eyes landed on Mesut and flashed wildly, his jaw squared off with the density of a rock and a roar escaped his gritted teeth with all the fire and fury of an ego that has been smashed beyond all recognition. They say there's nothing like a woman scorned, but Demir was about to re-write history.

It wasn't until I saw his treacherous, black form lunge through the air that I knew I was going to stop him. His crooked, chunky fingers and awkward, writhing limbs sailed towards

Mesut with an alarming speed and my intuition kicked in before my logic could. Or maybe it was my gut.

The thud was sickening. His chest hit both of my fists in the most clumsy, ungainly of ways, but it didn't matter. It did the job. Demir catapulted backwards and even the shock that throbbed through my knuckles, my hands, my wrists, didn't distract me from the look of pure terror on his face as he fell backwards. Eyes wide, mouth agape, throat gurgling to make some semblance of noise. Good. Let him know what it felt like to be out of control.

When his head hit the sharp angle of his own doorway, I have to admit it did make me gasp. Because the silence that followed was unnerving. For a few seconds, all I could hear was Mesut breathing raggedly behind me and Gillie opening and slamming drawers upstairs. I flexed my fists open and closed, in an effort to tease out the vibrations that lingered there and stared down at Demir who was as still as a stone. "Fuck." I whispered to myself. "What have I done?"

"You teach him lesson, is all I think, Gulaz . . . Jess." Mesut moved swiftly in front of me and crouched down to inspect Demir. He felt Demir's forehead, inspected the back of his skull and dipped his ear down to listen for his breath. "Ah, is okay. He just knocked out for few minutes, he not properly hurt." Mesut stood and turned his body towards mine. I still couldn't see his eyes. He bowed his head forward and brought his fingers to his lips in prayer position. "You saved me Gul . . Jess. You saved me. I needing thank you."

"And how are you going to do that?" I said, a smile, I could feel it, tugging at the corners of my lips.

He took a step forwards and chanced a look up. My eyes were there, ready and waiting for his, and when they finally met in that instant, I lost all coherent thought. There was a discernible whoosh as everything around us fell away and we were cocooned, instead in an ever-flowing, soft and sumptuous energy that defied space and time. Gone were the steps beneath my feet. Gone was Demir lying in the doorway. Gone was İpeklikum and the streets and the cracked pavements and the winter cloud. Instead there was just us and a silent under-standing that the connection was still there, despite any earthly meddling that might have thrown it into doubt.

"How you wanting me thank you?" He asked, and the warm weaving of his fingers through mine pulled me back to the present moment. "What can I do for you?"

"My beautiful, darling man . . . you can get up those stairs and help Gillie grab all of our stuff. My case is the blue one. Gillie's is pink and bejazzled."

"Bejazzled?" he asked with a smirk that made me want to devour him then and there.

"Oh god, I'll explain that one another time." I laughed. "I'll stay here and watch over our patient. You just get the stuff as quick as you can." We both looked down at Demir. He was out for the count.

"I not wanting leave you with him. What if he wake and try hurting you?"

"Didn't you see me in action? I'll just use that very effective chest-slamming technique again and it'll be fine. Seriously though – I'll shout for you if he tries anything and anyway, Ömer is just parked around the corner and waiting to get us all out of here. Okay? Go and help Gillie. That's what you came here for anyway, isn't it?"

"It is." He looked at me as if seeing me for the first time, brushed a rogue hair away from my cheek and leaned inwards, stopping just millimeters away from my lips. "But I'm wonder-ing, can I help you too?"

"You can." I breathed. "But not yet . . ." I pushed him gently away and in the direction of the stairs. "Go."

———

Gillie stepped over me for the final time, hauling yet another bag of god-knows-what across the road to Ömer's car. The poor little sporty number had probably never had so much stuff squished into it, and the already low-to-the ground chassis was virtually kissing İpeklikum's many and varied potholes. "That's the last one Jess. Do you think he'll wake up soon? Do you think we should be worried?"

"Nah, it's only been five minutes or so. He'll come round in a minute and hopefully feel suitably ashamed of himself once he realises we've all deserted him." I hadn't told anyone, but Demir had been making tiny little snuffling noises and rolling his limbs back and forth for the last few minutes. He was already coming around.

"Jess! We ready and packed." Ömer shouted from across the road where he'd pulled up to help us out. "You coming?" Mesut was loading the last bags into the boot of the car and trying to shut the door. But he looked up to find out my response to Ömer's question, his brow raised and his eyes searching yet again for mine.

"Yeah, give me a minute!" I called, softly. "You just turn the car or something, I just need to do one thing." I looked down at a slightly stirring Demir. His eyelashes fluttered against cheeks that were yet to be plagued by his nasty grimace. His thick hair was tousled lightly by a breeze that didn't know how mean he could be.

"He looking almost like real person like that, isn't it?" Mesut had come over and crouched down next to me, inspecting Demir's twitching face as it danced on the edges of consciousness.

"He is a real person, Mesut. But yes, I know what you mean. He almost looks innocent."

"I thinking you mean 'masum' in Turkish. But he not masum. Jess. He not."

"No. not right now, he isn't. Can you give me a minute with him? I'll be ready soon, I promise."

Mesut looked at me with a confused smile, but helped to prop Demir up against the door frame anyway. Demir's chin started to bob and sway and he opened his eyes, looked at us both, blinking and bewildered. "Why you wanting time with him? Unless you wanting use your fists again?"

"No. No more fists." I snapped my fingers in front of Demir's face and he grimaced, showing his reactions were sensitive, yes, but absolutely fine.

"I not like leaving you with him. I just standing there, okay?" Mesut pointed towards the mass of electrical wires stretching from the lamppost where I'd been standing earlier. "Just if you needing me."

"I'll be fine." I smiled. "Just give me a sec."

With Mesut gone, I positioned myself in front of Demir's slowly awakening body, sat on my knees and fixed him with a purposeful look. He swung his head around, eyes flicking in all directions, body still too heavy and cumbersome to move. "Gillie?" He wailed.

"There." I pointed at Ömer's car, which was currently doing a three-point-turn to get out of the street. "She's coming with me now."

"No." He murmured. "She better with me."

"I think we've established, Demir, that Gillie is definitely not better with you. You made sure of that when you spiked those drinks the other night and then lied about it through your teeth."

"You . . . you not so perfect." He sneered, slowly reclaiming the Demir I recognised.

"No. I'm not. I'm human and I'm not perfect. Which is why

I fell for your very devious act of pretending you were the one with the moral high ground."

"Kaz? She knows?"

"Typical. Never mind Gillie. Never mind Ömer and Mesut, who you put in actual danger. You just want to know if Kaz has been clued in on what a shithead you really are. And if your several thousand pounds worth of investment is still going ahead."

"Well, is it?" He asked, that sharp, angular pull on his cheek transforming his face back into the torn and twisted arrangement that I knew so well.

"I very much doubt it, Demir. Note to self: Don't poison the nearest and dearest of your business investors if you want to see a single lira of their money come your way. But don't worry – I've just come into some money myself and I've been looking for a way to spend it."

He couldn't help himself. A tangible spark dashed across his previously slack-jawed features. "Money? You need to . . . spend it?"

"Yes I do. Here, let me help you up." I hooked my arms under his armpits and heaved him to his feet. He was just about able to stand up himself, so I let go and watched him steady himself by grabbing hold of the door frame. He rubbed the back of his head and tried smiling at me. It wasn't pretty. "I want to give you some money, Demir, but first I want to say something."

"I listening, Jess. Even though you hitting me, I listen to you."

"Yeah, well, sorry about knocking you out, but that was the door frame really, not me. And if you come fists flying at someone I love then I'm not going to take it kindly. Understood?"

"Understood." He nodded, becoming ever more pliant with the possibility of finance in the air.

"Before I give you anything, I just want to say that I understand you are human. I understand you are flawed. I understand that your life and your experiences have brought you to this point in time, and that there may even be lifetimes before this that have made you the way you are by means that you might never understand."

"What?" His eyes drooped fully and his mouth hung open like an empty sack. It didn't really matter whether he understood me or not.

"What I mean is, that I don't know what's made you this way, or if you'll ever change. You put Mesut in real danger just because your ego hurt and that's just not acceptable. You hurt me beyond measure . . . nearly made me lose something ridiculously meaningful and what's more, you then pretended to *help* me afterwards, which was a really shitty thing to do. And God knows, the ways in which you've hurt my Gillie. That's the hardest bit for me to get around."

"Get around?"

"Yes. I'm finding a way around it. Because, Demir, I want you to know that I forgive you . . ."

"Forgive?"

"Yes. You crushed me, you really did. But by doing that, by crushing my flower that was blooming so beautifully, all you've done is release the fragrance." I breathed in and smiled broadly. "Can you smell it? It's amazing."

He stared at me with questions plastered all over his face. "I thought you said you . . . what about . . . the investment?"

"Oh yeah. I nearly forgot." I reached into my jeans pocket and pulled out a couple of twenty lira notes. I held out my arm towards him and flicked my fingers, gesturing for him to give me his hand, which he did. A greedy habit of his, I guessed. "I want you to upgrade your offices." He nodded his head and I stuffed the notes into his hankering hand. "Buy some goddam flowers.

And every time you walk past them and sense their fragrance filling your lungs? Their scent lacing the air? Think. Of Me."

And with that I spun on my heels, skipped down the steps and over the road to Mesut. The night was starting to chase away the afternoon and it was getting cold, so he'd grabbed a purple hoodie out of my case and draped it around my shoulders as soon as I reached him. It was one of my favourites.

We jumped in the back of the car together, Gillie clawing for my hand as soon as we landed. She took it and kissed it several times over. "I hope you put him in his place you wonderful being. I'd do it myself but I'm far too mad right now."

"Oh, I think I did. But now it's time. Ömer? Let's get out of here." On my very word, Ömer revved the engine and the wheels of his very impressive car spun dramatically against the tarmac. We shot off into the waiting depths of İpkelikum, leaving Demir far behind us and I suddenly remembered, with a rapturous shiver, that it was New Year's Eve.

42

I AM MESUT

"Gillie will be alright, you think?" Mesut asked as we walked together, away from his house. I looked behind me and saw the velvety, maroon glow of the electric fire pulsing softly from the depleting square of the living room window.

"You gave her all the tea and all the biscuits and all the blankets humanly possible so yes, I think she's going to be fine." Once we'd got back to Mesut's house, and Ömer had sped off home to talk with Kaz, the three of us hadn't made any kind of plan at all. We'd just unloaded all of our stuff into a corner of Mesut's living room and gone round switching on lamps and heaters and the kettle. It felt like a switching on of awareness, of acceptance. And we all needed it.

Gillie had been surprisingly okay about Demir being a total fuckwit. She'd muttered into her packet of chocolate biscuits that she'd wished she'd stuck with Baileys and mince pies after all, but other than that she seemed pretty calm. "It's not like you didn't try to warn me." She'd said, as we'd brewed mugs of honeyed tea. "But I was far too horny to listen to anyone. Never mind. Totally his loss."

"Totally." I'd agreed.

I'd asked Gillie if she wanted to do something nice later, especially considering that we were about to kiss goodbye to 2006, but she respectfully declined. Okay, maybe not that respectfully. "Fuck no." She'd moaned, from a cocoon of blankets set up opposite the flickering TV that looked like it might hold out for a few ancient episodes of Countdown. "I want to see how they do Turkish subtitles for the ten letter round. But you two please go off and do something romantic and wonderful. It would be a crime if you didn't, after everything."

I looked at Mesut and he grinned back, reaching out his arm and opening his palm. "You want to walk?"

The ghost of a memory tickled my mind as he said those words, because I knew he'd said them to me before. Outside Beerbelly. Three months ago. When we'd finally given in to whatever strange forces had flung us together. And this time, my answer was exactly the same.

"Yes."

We'd spent a good twenty minutes without really talking, traipsing through the spindly, wintery weeds that blighted the fields between Mesut's house and the beach. It was as if we were holding out for the open magnificence of the shore. As if it would somehow endow us with the knowledge of what each of us needed to hear and say.

Now we were finally here, I focused on several things: the soft shushing of our bare feet in the sand, the gush of waves breaking into soft and delicate ripples the closer they got to the shore, and the slow dipping of the sun as it fought against that early evening mist so that everything was treated with a rough and striking sparkle.

"I'm so glad you okay." Mesut said as his fingers brushed mine, but didn't quite catch them. "I'm glad you finding out the truth about what is happen."

"And I'm so pleased that Ömer told me. I know he had his

reasons to keep it quiet, but he wanted me to know that you weren't in the wrong. He was doing it for you. He's a good friend, you know."

"I knows it."

I stopped in my tracks and looked out to sea. The water was slowly surrendering to the dusty darkness of the sky and Bodrum's pendulous hills were disappearing piece by piece. I imagined myself sitting on Kaz's balcony earlier that day, transferring money into Sandra's account. So much had happened since then.

"I had some news." I turned to Mesut and took a breath. Slow. Deep. He watched me intently, his eyes still and focused. They were an entirely different pair of eyes to the wildly vibrating ones I'd tried to look into after Demir had spiked his drink. These ones were mine. "I found out that Trev died. Of his addiction. Sandra called to tell me."

"Oh. That is bad. And so very sad I think."

"Yes, so very sad."

"And how is this making you feeling? Is must be strange for you? And you find out after you thinking I taking pills. Oh Gula . . . Jess. I wishing I there for you. Really I wishing I there." He stretched out his arms and I was in them in less than a second. He held me tight and every one of his muscles that bent around my own emitted a firm sense of tenderness. There was no room for anything else.

"I wish you were there too, but some things we just have to get through on our own, don't we? I don't know. It made me feel very weird. I cried and cried after I found out. And I can't honestly say all those tears were for him . . . I didn't even know Trev in my adult life, did I?" I shifted my head on his chest so that I could look up at him. I saw the dark speckle of stubble across the cocoa swish of his jaw. His eyes were shut tight as he listened to me, his lashes skirting the mounds of his cheeks.

"But is okay you cry. He there at very start, when you just little girl. He crushing you, Jess. And people who crush us, they mean something to us also. Even if that meaning not nice."

"You're so right. Do you know what I did though? To balance things out?"

"Tell me."

"Well, I might have been a rich woman right now, if it hadn't been for what I did next."

"I not understand. You rich woman?"

"No. Not anymore." I chuckled and wriggled from his arms ever so slightly – just enough to lead him over to a nice little alcove I'd seen tucked up in a corner of the beach. There'd be a bit more shelter there, and a pretty awesome view of the mist as it burned out along with the setting sun. We sat down on a rock and faced each other. "I found out that I sold all my paintings in that café, Epic, which was awesome."

"Yes. Awesome."

"But not long after that, I found out about Trev and once I'd really thought about it," I smiled as I remembered the words I'd read on the stone at Apollo's Temple, "I knew that the only thing I could do to help and show my forgiveness, was to send some money for the funeral."

"You sending money? To who?"

"I sent it to Sandra, because I know she'll make sure it gets spent wisely. And she'll give any leftovers to a rehab centre that will help more people like Trev. So sorry Mesut – I was a rich woman for a grand total of about twenty four hours but now I'm back to square one. Which is crap because I guess I could have used that money for us to see each other more regularly."

He leaned forwards from his spot on a rock opposite mine and beckoned for me to meet him halfway. He spoke so that the breath from his words brushed my lips with something that might have been love. "I not caring about money. We will always find a way my Gulaz . . ." He duck his head down and those lips were momentarily lost. "Jess."

"Yeah, about that." I smiled, lifting his chin back up with my fingers, stroking that strong and beautiful curve of his jaw. "I'm sorry I said I didn't want you calling me Gulazer. I was just being a huffy little cow because I thought you'd been an arsehole. I do want it. I love that name. So you can keep calling me it, if you like."

"Really? You still my Gulazer?"

"Of course I am. I even tried to get hold of some yellow roses to bring to you – just to show you I forgave you. But apparently they're really hard to get this time of year. I put Gillie on the case and even with her shopping super powers, she couldn't make it happen."

"Wait. Forgive me?"

"Yes, but that was before I knew what had happened with Demir. I thought there was some real forgiving to do and I was going to come and find you and give you a huge bunch of yellow roses, offer to always be friends and be on my way. Oh god Mesut, now it's you that needs to forgive me. I'm so sorry that I just assumed you'd taken those pills. I was feeling unbelievably fragile because I'd spent forever looking through Kaz's photos and was totally freaked out because so many of them were similar to mine."

"Freaked out?"

"Yes. Upset. Because it suddenly felt like what he have together, this . . ." I gestured at the rocks surrounding us, the rising moon, the short but definite distance between our hearts, "it felt like this might not be that special after all. That it was nothing different to what any single white tourist and enigmatic barman might have, given a couple of weeks and a few sunrises to watch."

"Is different." He said, firmly.

"I know. I do know. I just had a wobble. And then seeing you well, like that, after the pills, I just assumed the obvious and didn't stop for a second to consider it might not have been your choice. I just went off past experience and what Jack used to do to me. To us."

"Jack. He not me. I not him." Mesut gazed across the space at me and our eyes locked in the way that they often do. I was so glad to be in that moment, but aware, also, of the intensity of it, so that it prickled the skin on my neck and gatecrashed the depths of my heart.

"I not him. I am not Jack." He was a slim, dark shape, adorning the rock like a stubborn shadow, refusing to die along with the sinking winter sun. Because night was approaching and he was still here.

"I am Mesut."

"I know that." I croaked, my voice dry and quiet.

"Do you?" He asked just once, leaning his body a fraction of an inch closer. I knew what he was saying with these few words, the tilt of his body and the ferocious plea in his eyes. I knew what he was saying because it wasn't just him speaking, it was me too.

He is not Jack. He is not Trev. He is not any of them. He will not be able to hurt you in those ways because he wouldn't even know how. He is new and he is ancient. He is familiar and he is different. You have found him because your souls were never going to escape each other anyway. He won't hurt you with intention. You won't hurt him with intention. But you might hurt each other for any number of other reasons . . . reasons that are human and fallible . . . for you are not yet as wise as your souls know you can be.

"I am Mesut." His hands were on me now, cupping my face. His voice had transformed into something strong, resolute. His eyes challenged me to say otherwise but that deepest compassion flickered between us and we both understood why he had to say these words. It was for us. Not just me. Us.

A sudden gust of wind whipped through the alcove we were sitting in and the dry surface sand was snatched up from the ground so that it danced wildly in whirls at our ankles, then up, up, above our heads. I felt the rasp of it against my skin and the blasts of it through my hair and I saw how the moon had finally landed in Mesut's eyes, giving him the inescapable look of an angel of the darkest kind.

"I am Mesut." He said again, softly now, he buckled forwards to his knees and his hands slid and found the flesh under my clothes with the merest whisper of a movement. "I need you to know." And I suddenly remembered the meaning of his name: *very deep happiness*.

"I do." I said, and all of my bones softened at once under his hands. "I do know."

He pulled me in and gathered me up so it didn't matter if my bones turned to butter. We moved, in that strange vortex of whirling sand and bitter moonlight, towards the depths of the alcove, where the stones were more ancient, more enlightened than we were. And more coveting too.

In the shadows he kissed me strong and hard with a seductive smile hidden inside. His fingertips pressed my ribs and all of my organs smiled too. The very roots of me were begging, tremoring to be touched by him, and judging by the way his breath had sharpened, the hardening of every muscle under taut yet flexing skin, he wanted me too.

We nodded silently and watched each other as we each removed our clothes. Jumpers, T-shirts, jeans, socks and underwear fell like teardrops all around us and formed a circle less like a ceremonial arrangement, and more like chaotic relics of lust. In the inky depths of this tiny cave, I could just make out the soft, dark curl of hair against his billowing chest and traced its inexorable journey downwards, to where my hands flew now, wanting, needing to smooth pleasure into his very soul, starting with what was hard and ready.

His hands had a very similar idea. One of them moved without hesitation between my legs and the other grabbed my lower back, helping me to pulse instinctively against his hold. Gasping wouldn't even cover what happened to my breath. All I know is that every time he curled his fingers in a certain way, then rocked them steadily inside me, my breath cracked wide open, like a piece of fruit falling on a stone.

Then we both struck stone. Without even a word, he'd flipped me round so that my hands were left empty but warm and sizzling, and I was laid out flat and open, my heels scraping off sand-coated rock and my buttocks thrilled by the rugged cold. My spine momentarily objected to the hard and unforgiving surface beneath me but then arched in twisted pleasure as his mouth sank downwards and his tongue moved with relish inexplicably deep inside me. I knotted lengths of his hair in my hands and pulled him further in, his nose bumping into exactly the right spot and sending jolts of euphoria as far up as my scalp. I never knew until that moment that sex could reach your head as well as your heart.

I couldn't stand it any longer, we had to be as close as humanly possible. Because being human was all we had to work with.

I dragged my knotted knuckles upwards so that his head had to surface from my thighs, and he followed less than willingly. Nevertheless, he used his drenched tongue to work his way upwards, making a moan that was as long and sonorous as the waves crashing only metres away. His tongue traced over my belly button, my waist, the underside of my breasts and the pink flare of my nipples. He found the dip of my collarbone, the curve of my neck and his mouth finally found mine in an explosion of salty sweetness. It was as effortless as the way he then slid inside me, quenching a succulent hunger that was surely older than the both of us, surely sweeter than the dying mist that beaded on the surface of our skin.

Thousands of tiny particles erupted across my groin in hot and desperate waves. They struck out further and further across the soft bulges and ripples of my body and I realised perhaps for the first time, and in the dull and diminishing light of the alcove, that sex was never meant to be anything to do with the way it looked . . . but everything to do with the way that it felt.

Mesut whispered warm and wondrous words to me in a growl meant for my ears, but that I felt all the way down to my toes. They were all in Turkish and I had no idea what he was saying, but they had the desired effect.

"Benimle olsan bile seni istiyor ve özlüyorum. Sonsuza kadar ruhunun ruhuma sahip olmasını isityorum."

I tipped and rocked my hips with every rough and hardened consonant, with every oiled and silken vowel, and his whole body shifted upwards so that his chest aligned with my shoulders and I took the weight of him as gladly as I'd taken him inside me.

This was the beginning of the end, I just knew it. I knew it from the exultant thrum deep between my legs, from the jarring croak both of our voices had been reduced to, from the dawning shiver that claimed our limbs and from the completely ravishing blackness that threw itself, finally over my soaring consciousness.

———

I woke with the welcome sensation of heat licking my face in soft, kindly waves. Even before I opened my eyes, I knew there was fire nearby because my eyelids were shielding a tender, orange glow and a crackling sound grabbed at my ears. I shifted against the flat rock I'd somehow fell asleep on. Apparently my whole left side was lost to pins and needles.

"Ah, you awake, Gulazer? I not knowing if waking you is good idea." Mesut was crouching at the mouth of the alcove, now fully dressed apart from his shirt which he'd laid over me, along with all of my own clothes as a kind of patchwork blanket. He had built a fire. Small but blazing and it was throwing a ruby warmth against the surface of all the surrounding rocks.

"It's a good idea." I gave my left arm a tentative stretch and it yelled back at me in a million tiny protests, whilst the garments on top of me slid almost completely off. "How long was I asleep for? Shit. I'd better get dressed."

"Not long. Just about twenty moments. You too comfy in my arms and I not want move you but even when I getting up, you keep going with the sleeping."

"I do love a good nana nap." I confessed, pulling on my cold and sandy underwear. What happened twenty minutes ago felt like another time, another place, but I knew in my bones it was raw and recent. The interesting patterns driven onto the sand-coated rock proved that.

Once I'd pulled on my purple hoodie, savouring its cosy, familiar fabric, Mesut smiled up at me, patting a patch of sand just next to him. "Come. Sit with me. I want ask you something."

"Of course." I gave him his shirt to put on and nestled in close to him, willing the numbness in my legs to be revived by the closeness of the flames. "Wow – you certainly know how to build a fire. This is so lush." He circled his arms around me and I noticed that he smelled even more delicious with the charred fragrance of burnt wood clinging to him. "What did you want to ask me?"

"Is important question." He sighed and I hoped whatever it

was, wasn't too soul-stirring. After today, I doubted my soul could take much more. "I need to know, Gulazer . . . what is 'nana nap'?"

A smile broke across my face. "Well, it's a key principal in the daily living of anybody with a full and healthy lifestyle."

"Efendim? I mean, pardon? You lose me, Gulazer."

I lifted my head and looked into those eyes, those beautiful pools of dark chocolate brown. They had sparks of gold flying through them as quick and energetic as the fire could make them. Just when I thought I couldn't find him any more hand-some too. "A 'nana nap' is just a short sleep, Mesut. A snooze. Like a sleep you might have in the middle of the day to give you more energy. It's something an old lady might do."

"I get it. Nana nap. Okay. You old lady then, yes?"

I felt those fingers of his brush across my cheeks in a way that felt startlingly familiar – maybe even not of our time, and replied. "Yes I'm an old lady. Ancient, in fact. And you will come to learn that nothing comes between me and a nana nap."

"I will remember." He chuckled and picked up a stick to poke at the fire. After he rearranged the burning driftwood a little, so that more air could get through and improve the way it was burning, he settled the stick down on a nearby rock. This sent me into sudden fits of giggles.

"Oh god." I managed, catching my breath and grabbing Mesut's arm to stop myself from falling back. "You just reminded me of 'The Tears of His Sword'."

"Efendim? The tears of his what?"

"'The Tears of His Sword'. It was a book lying around in Beerbelly and Gillie gave it to me to read after, well, you know, everything . . . and I tried to read it to cheer myself up but there was this scene in it . . . a love scene in an actual cave with ample thighs and leather sheaths and most definitely a heaving bosom or two. And, oh god, there was a huge, shaggy horse called

Eleazar and if only I'd known we'd find our own little love cave, oh, maybe I could have enjoyed it a bit more."

"Love cave." He repeated to himself. "I liking this idea. Love cave."

"I like it too." And we kissed long and slow, in a way that punctuated the whole concept of a love cave so that it would never, ever escape our memory. "Except now it's not just an idea. It's reality."

"You my reality, Gulazer. I liking that too."

We nestled for a little while longer, the moon now shining down on us definitively, but its white snare beamed back by the cheery blaze of our little fire. I felt so reassured by our reunion and the way things had played out over the last twenty four hours, that there was a kind of solidness spreading through me . . . and it was nudging me, ever so gently, into asking Mesut something that might sound wrong at first, but I knew was completely right. At least, for me.

"Mesut. It's my turn to ask you something now."

"Tabi. Of course, Gulazer." He turned to face me, drawing his knees up so that his elbows rested on the top, wrists and fingers swinging low so I could grab them and stroke them as I spoke.

"You know this year has been exceptional for me, yes?"

"Yes. I knows it."

"You know that so much has happened and my life has changed in ways I could have never predicted – it's been hard and it's been scary but I feel I'm in the right place. For now."

"Is good."

"It's so good. In fact, sitting here now, next to this gorgeous fire you've built and – to be honest – pretty much basking in the glow of the incredible time we had in there . . ." I motioned over to the depths of the alcove and then brought my eyes immediately back to him to check if it caused a smile. It did. "I feel so, so right being here and, well, I'm wondering if you would do me a huge kindness."

"Anything, Gulazer. You knows."

"Would you, well, can you . . . leave me alone?"

I looked intently at him to see what happened to his eyes when those words registered with him and I saw that a certain light of recognition joined the golden sparks reflected by the fire. Then a beam, which started as a shimmering, slip of a thing, spread warmly across his lips and I knew he understood. "I will leave you, Gulazer. You needing time on your own, isn't it? Time with your own soul."

"Exactly. It feels like the right thing to do. It feels like the only thing to do."

"Yes. Is okay. I leave you now. And there is lots more wood down other end of beach for when your fire needing it, okay? You needing anything else? Food? Drink? You cosy enough?"

"Oh my God, I couldn't be cosier." I said. "Don't worry about me. I have everything I need. Just give me a bit of time. But promise you'll meet me at midnight? With these hands?" I pulled them to my waist. "With these eyes?" I looked straight into them. "And with these lips?" I kissed them time and time again until he gently peeled me off him, laughing now.

"Yes, Gulazer, I bringing everything, don't worry. Where you want meet? Here?"

"Hmmm, I might have a little walk in a bit, so let's meet on the far end of the beach, near the harbour?"

"Yes. I knows it. But before I go I wanting do one thing." He arched an eyebrow and gave me a playful grin.

"Seriously Mesut? I've only just put all my clothes back on."

"No. Is not that." He laughed. "Here. Come close." He pulled me in towards him and flipped open his phone. He positioned us so that the flames lapped enthusiastically behind us and the beach stretched out further beyond. "We taking picture of us now. Happy one. Smile, okay?"

"Okay." I smiled, which really wasn't hard all things considered, and he took several snapshots of us. "Why did you want a photo now? To remember our love cave?"

"I always will remember love cave." He sighed, grinning. "But no, I take photo to give to Kaz and Ömer."

"Kaz and Ömer. Why?"

"I need to give to Kaz's photo basket – yes? It no good she only have old photos. This one, with you and me, much more important, isn't it?"

"It is." How I loved this man.

"I go there now, while you sit with your soul."

"But where will you get a photo printed from your phone this time on New Year's Eve?"

Mesut laughed and pulled me in for a final cuddle, before jumping to his feet and brushing the sand off his jeans. "Gulazer, you not know by now? This İpeklikum. If you knows right people you can getting anything."

"I couldn't get you any yellow roses."

"Yet." He laughed, a rich, deep rumble that matched the darkness falling all around him. "You not get yellow roses yet."

"I don't know, Mesut. You might have to put up with just me." I smiled up at him as he backed away, becoming every second more enveloped by darkness.

"That would be okay too. Enjoy your time, my Gulazer. I see you in 2007."

"Just at the cusp of it." I reminded him. "Just at the cusp." And suddenly, with my words trailing behind him, he was gone.

43

COUNTDOWN

Lindy slammed her hands down on the table in mock rage. "I don't believe you, Jess."

"What?" Jess was smiling and her face was flushed with the overspill of emotion. "What's wrong?"

"You're telling me I spent half the night in yours and Mesut's flipping love cave? I knew that place had a vibe going on. I bloody knew it."

"A vibe? Hah. You could be right. But don't worry – you and I were sat far away from the love cave bit – we did all our chatting on neutral ground, I promise."

Lindy fanned her face because, for the last ten minutes, she'd really felt the heat of those tealights burning above them. "Phew. I mean, I'm not even into all that hetero stuff but even I need a cold shower after hearing all of that." She checked her watch and glanced up at Jess, who was smirking. And rightly so. "Not long til you have to meet him though. I wonder what will happen to Demir. Will Gillie go back to good old Oliver? When will you be coming back to Turkey? How will you afford it? Are you and Mesut going to have beautiful little babies? How are you going to do that living so far apart? Bloody hell, how is this all going to work?"

"Woah! Take a chill pill!"

"At least you know where you can get me one." Lindy winked.

"Funny. Honestly though, I've no bloody clue. I'm still letting everything settle. And can you see now, Lindy? Can you? That you coming to join me at my fire tonight was the best thing I could have wished for? This whole thing was worked both ways, you know."

"Anyone would think we'd been thrown together or something." Lindy agreed. "That it's magic. You know, if we didn't know better."

"Yes. If we didn't know better." Jess raised her almost-empty wine glass and Lindy met it gladly with hers. There was a soft and cheery chink that quickly got lost in the busy soundscape of the restaurant, but not before it summoned a smile from both women.

"I can't believe it." Lindy said, after downing the last drop of her wine. "It's really over. It's the end of your story."

"Well, not really. Or at least, I hope it's not." Jess emptied her wine glass too and set it down on the table, arranging it next to Lindy's and their empty dessert plates. "I think I'm still sitting here with you. I don't reckon I'm going to disappear into thin air." Jess started prodding herself and giggling. "There's a bit of life in me yet, even though we've managed to get through two whole bottles of wine tonight."

"Three." Lindy corrected her. "We had one on the beach too."

"So we did. Oh well, looks like I'll be writing my book with a hangover."

"You're going to be writing tomorrow?"

"Every day, baby. Every day." Then Jess asked a waiter for the bill in Turkish. "It's okay with you, isn't it? I'll need to make tracks in a minute if I'm going to go and find my man."

"Of course. No worries. Hey. Wasn't that your phone beeping?" Lindy felt sure she'd heard it, under the jovial sound of mingled voices, where there was a rising tone of excitement as the clock neared midnight. Jess moved some paper napkins around and found it, flashing festively. She flipped the screen open.

"Oh yeah. It's from Gillie. It says . . . *Guess what? I tracked down the yellow roses after all. Where are you? I'll send them over now.* And she's put a winking emoji. Weird."

"Weird and impressive. Will she know where this place is? How on earth did she manage to get them just a few minutes to midnight on New Year's bloody Eve? You said she was a natural shopper, but this is just above and beyond."

"It is. But Gillie never lets anything get in the way of her and a shopping expedition. Anyway, I'm asking her how she's done it. And sending her our location. I wonder if she'll bring them herself? Oooh, I'd love to introduce the two of you." Jess finished typing out her message and looked up at Lindy, her head tilted to one side and her eyes searched for something. "What about you though, Lindy? You'll be okay when I go in a few minutes?"

Being left alone on New Year's Eve? Midnight imminent and no way of knowing what kind of shit the universe had in store for her in the coming year? "Fuck yes." She grinned. "Have you taught me nothing? I'm more than okay. I'm fucking amazing and the universe is obsessed with me – what more could I want?"

"Yey!" Jess celebrated with a little shimmy on her floor cushion. "If I had any wine left I would be toasting the hell out of that." Then a little wooden treasure chest was placed on the table by the waiter and Jess looked at it casually. "It's the bill. For some reason they always bring it in a treasure chest. It's a thing here." She chucked a couple of notes inside and tutted like a proper local when Lindy tried to get her purse out. "This one's on me, Lindy, honestly. You can get it next time." The remark sounded so flippant and normal that Lindy almost didn't notice the strangeness of it. Because she might never see Jess again.

"Okay. If you're sure. And thank you. Not just for the meal, but for all of it."

"Uh, uh, uh. Nope. No thanks. You're grateful, I'm grateful. Let's just both agree we're level, okay? Ooh – there's my phone again. It'll be Gillie."

"What does she say?"

"She says . . . *Kaz and Ömer helped me get the roses – they knew someone. Look outside. You'll see.*"

"Cryptic." Lindy gasped. "Come on then, let's go find your roses. Time's nearly up."

"On it." Jess replied, and the two of them hoisted themselves out of their perfect little bolt-hole of cushions, tealights, wine glasses and treasure chests and moved through the warm mass of the restaurant, out into the pin-pricked black of the night.

———

The promenade itself was virtually empty but the restaurants and bars stretching along it were bright and pulsing. Vivid and blinking oranges, greens and pinks were splashing out onto the dark walk-way, beats and rhythms of pop music colliding softly together and sudden peals of laughter ringing out of every propped-open doorway.

Lindy took off her shoes and enjoyed the cool hardness of the red brick underfoot. She'd never seen the main strip look so bare and she enjoyed the sight of it stretched out ahead of them, disappearing into the darkness ahead like a secret tunnel. The walkway was so still, so peaceful, only enhanced by the roar of the waves nearby and the crammed-in energy of the adjoining restaurants. Jess paused to sit on a bench and removed her shoes too, sighing as she looked all around her.

"Well, I can't see anyone with a bunch of roses, can you?"

Lindy turned her body towards the beach and took a full, deep breath of sea air before turning back around and surveying the scene for Jess. "Nope. There's nobody. Oh, hang on – there's somebody kind of loitering in that doorway over there. Where the souvenir shop is."

"Where?" Lindy pointed the doorway out. Sure enough, there was a dark figure hunched over something. A basket? A box? The shop was shut up for the night so there wasn't much light to see who it was or what they were doing. "I see. Let's get closer."

The women held their shoes in one hand and, without discussion, used their spare hands to hold onto each other. They edged forwards and squinted to make out who this mysterious figure was, so that they could a.) make a run for it if it was someone dodgy or b.) welcome whoever it was into their very strange yet enjoyable New Year's Eve night.

The bulky, billowing shadow started to include depth and lines and folds and swishes of fabric and it was Jess who gasped first, the light of recognition leaping into her eyes so that Lindy had to work hard to figure out what on earth was going on here. "It's Fatma." Jess whispered. "It's Fatma Hanım."

"I'm sorry, who?"

"Lindy . . . it's the rose lady."

Lindy felt a cold draught where Jess had suddenly left her side to rush into the doorway. She delved back into her mind where Jess's story was still suspended and it wasn't long before she found what she was looking for in a burst of easy joy. Of course! The rose lady who Mesut bought all those flowers from. If anybody could get yellow roses, it would be her.

Lindy joined them in the doorway and saw within an instant why the rose lady had been hunched over, unable to leave this spot and come out onto the promenade to find them. She was guarding the biggest mountain of flowers Lindy had ever seen. Every single one of them yellow. Every single one of them a rose. And every single one of them fresh and frivolous and blooming brightly. They were a far cry indeed from the wilting bunches in Mesut's kitchen sink that Jess had previously described.

"Oh wow, oh wow, oh wow!" Jess was exclaiming over and over again as the old lady, Fatma, fussed around her, spouting her own stream of Turkish words in a voice that was coarse and scratchy but laced with pure fondness. Lindy caught the words 'güzel' and 'canım' which she'd heard people use before and was sure they were endearments of some sort. And the name 'Mesut Bey' chanted like a sparkling spell as Fatma walked around Jess, looking her up and down and prodding her with a smile, nodding as if she approved of her on every level.

"Tanrı seni korusun. Oğlum Mesut'a iyi davranacağını. Onu kollayacağını biliyorum."

"What is she saying, Jess?" Lindy asked.

"I've no flipping clue! Something about treating Mesut right I think. I feel like this is a bit of a caution before she bestows some of those incredible flowers on me. God, Lindy – how much do you think I should offer her? They're so funny about taking money over here."

"It depends how many you're having. Because you can't possibly carry all of those to the beach and, well, time's ticking on you know."

"I know. I've got to bloody well get on with this. Right." Jess reached into her pocket and dug out some notes of Turkish Lira – quite a lot as far as Lindy could tell – and tried to push them into Fatma's hands, but she snapped her hands away as if Jess had been serving up the plague.

"Hayır! No monies. Please."

So she did speak some English after all. "Yes Fatma Hanım . . . please take something. You've brought me so many beautiful roses!" Jess was trying her best but the old lady had already turned in her many, layered skirts and stooped low to scoop up some roses. She turned back to face Jess and pulled one out of the arrangement in her arms, running the tip of her finger along the stem.

"Bak . . . hiç diken yok." Jess and Lindy both looked closely at the green length of the stalk and realised what she was saying. No thorns.

Lindy sucked in a breath and whispered to Jess. "You do realise that means she's spent the best part of her night ripping out thorns, don't you? All for you and Mesut."

Jess nodded and gave a peal of spontaneous laughter. "She's flipping amazing! Fatma Hanım, you are amazing!"

"Shit! Watch out – I think she's going to attack you with them." Lindy took a leap backwards because the old woman had surged forwards with an athletic grace nobody could have thought her capable of, brandishing her armful of roses that she was now placing all over Jess's body with impressive skill. Jess squealed but stood still and let Fatma do her work, not daring to interrupt the bizarreness of the moment.

Lindy watched as Fatma rapidly wove stems together so they'd stay in Jess's hair. She twisted and turned the stems so the bloom of yellow roses adorned her neckline, her hood, her cuffs, her waistband and her pockets. Wreaths of flowers were wound around her upper arms and thighs, smaller flowers wrapped around her ankles and – just to top everything off – Fatma reached into her almost empty rose basket and pulled out a pre-made crown of roses that fit perfectly on Jess's head. The finished result was an outlandish but beautiful spectacle – Jess was a vision of sunshine yellow and looked fit to head a flower fairy parade at a carnival.

"Fuck, mate. I don't know what to say." Lindy laughed. "You truly live up to your nickname."

"Right?" Jess was smiling wider than Lindy had seen so far that night. And there had been a lot of smiles. "What the hell though? I feel like a flower fairy! Mesut's going to think I've gone mental."

"He'll love you for it."

The old lady was standing back and brushing the odd rogue leaf from Jess's body, all the while shaking her head and smiling with silent tears tracking over her soft and rounded cheeks. "Tanrı seni korusun. Çok güzelsin Gulazer, seni daima sevecek."

"Wow, he must mean a lot to her, your man."

"I guess so." Jess sighed as she figured out how to move in her new paraphernalia. She took Fatma's hands in her own and fixed her with a kind and grateful look. "Fatma Hanim. Çok teşekkür ederim. Thank you so very much. Really."

But Fatma was having none of it. She placed Jess's hands back down by her sides, kissed her gently on the rose-adorned forehead and did her trademark swish back to her basket. She picked it up and moved off into the shadows, not a penny lining her pockets, not a word more of her troubles, and not a backwards glance.

"That's that then." Lindy observed.

"Yeah. That was weird. But hey! What a way to see out 2006. Can't complain."

"Definitely not. And you're finally doing what the words said on the stone at Apollo's Temple aren't you? Sharing your fragrance or something? You smell incredible."

"Okay, rather than calling it an old dear attacking me with hordes of roses, yeah, let's call it that. Sharing my fragrance."

Suddenly there was an unmistakable change in the atmosphere out there on the street. Lindy and Jess moved to the centre of the bare, open promenade and soaked it up. "Sounds like this is it." Jess said, nodding towards the merry clamour of the nightlife surrounding them. "They've started the countdown."

It was true. The lively jumble of songs that had clashed in their ears earlier had come to a hush now and there was a phenomenal, booming chant of numbers pounding through İpeklikum. The two languages collided in elevated excitement.

On, dokuz, sekiz . . .

Ten, nine, eight . . .

Lindy was suddenly gripped by the need to tell Jess how much this whole night had meant to her. To somehow put into words how much had stirred in her since finding her by her fire in the alcove and how this night would never, ever leave her. "Jess . . . I . . . Oh shit. It's been fucking fantastic meeting you."

Jess took Lindy's hand and rolled a delicate band of tiny, golden roses from her wrist, transferring it straight to Lindy's.

Yedi, altı, beş . . .

Seven, six, five . . .

"Well I hope you know it's been fucking fantastic meeting you too . . . and I'm going now . . . he's waiting."

"Yes, of course he bloody is!" Tears slipped through their laughter like perfume on a breeze. "And go write those bloody novels, okay?"

"I will." The two women hugged as best they could without harming the roses. They squeezed yet more laughs out of each other and their lips came to rest right next to each other's ears so they could hear each other's breath as real and present as if listening to a sea shell.

Dört, üç, iki . . .

Four, three, two . . .

"And Lindy, this life you've got . . . ?" Jess said it in the sweetest of whispers but the firmest of pleas.

"Yes?"

"It's yours."

Bir.

One.

Jess let go in an instant, as if she might disappear on that fated stroke of midnight. But she didn't. Instead she turned in her blazing, yellow glory and jumped down from the promenade onto the soft surface of the beach with a joyous yelp.

Lindy stood and watched her, vaguely aware of the hordes of happy people spilling out onto the walkway behind her and music kicking back in, the mood of the night carrying on with an entirely new pace, a new energy. She noticed how Jess's figure quickly turned from a vivid, tangible person with texture and movement and feelings and breath, into a fleeting, shadowy shape becoming less reachable with each step she took across the dark sand.

And it wasn't long before Lindy could see another shape in the distance. Tall and slim, graceful and sleek, almost like a wild cat the way it darted purposefully towards the shape that was Jess. It was only seconds until the two forms had locked together in one solid silhouette, their edges blurred against the rushing of waves rolling endlessly behind them.

Lindy turned back towards the promenade, stretching up over the hill that led back to her apartment. With a deep breath that took in a blast of sea salt, midnight sky, spilled cocktails, aromatic spices, clashing perfumes, clammy skin and everything else the moment had to offer, she stepped forwards. She had a smile on her lips and a lightness in her soul. And so, she kept on walking.

EPILOGUE

"Gulazer, how you do it? How you getting all these yellow roses and why you wearing them?" He breathes the questions into my hair and I move my hands from around his neck to straighten my crown of yellow roses. Even though there aren't any thorns, I still feel the scratch of the stem on my temples.

"Can't you guess?"

"I never guessing with you." I can barely hear him above the crashing brawl of the waves who are seemingly celebrating the New Year too.

"It was Fatma Hanım. Your rose lady."

"Tabi. Of course it was!" And he smiles good and proper, surveying my brand new body ornaments. "I impressed. You did it."

"Gillie did it." I have to correct him. "And Kaz and Ömer."

"See?" He laughs. "If you knows right people, you get anything you want in İpeklikum."

"Well, I certainly got what I wanted." I kiss him hard and full, wanting to pour the magic of the night right into him so he'll understand what an incredible time I've had since I last saw him. "Did you get your photo printed?"

He shrugs as if the answer is obvious. "Yes. Tabi. I giving to Kaz and Ömer and they very happy with it. Is best part of their collection they says. And what about you? You have time sitting with your soul on beach? You enjoy your New Year's Eve?"

"God, I don't know where to start, Mesut. But yes, it was amazing. I met someone . . ." I look over my shoulder back at the main strip of clubs and restaurants, thinking Lindy might still be up there. Maybe the last threads of my story have kept her there, the strong links of the connection we made still hovering. But no. There's a blank space. She's gone.

"Someone?" He pulls my chin back around with a single finger, then pinches my cheek. "But what about time with your soul?"

I laugh. Even though I love this man with parts of me that are potentially deeper and older than the skin I'm standing in, I wonder if he could ever really understand the connection two women can make with words, with tears, with honesty. "Don't worry. I got that time with my soul. And then some."

"Is good."

"Is good."

"You want to walk?"

"I really do." But just before he grabs my hand I find a rose nestled just next to my heart, where the rose lady swirled a garland over my shoulder. I pick it out and hold it to his nose. He breathes in deeply and I might be wrong but I swear a sparkle leaps to his eyes that has nothing to do with the pearly moon above us or the stars shimmering high. "Nice?" I ask.

"Is beautiful."

I take the rose and prop it behind his ear, the black sheen of his hair making the petals burn all the more brightly. "Yes it is." I agree, and then I take the warm bulk of his hand and hold it in mine. "Now shall we walk?"

"Yes, but Gulazer, you dropping something on the ground.

Look." He points down at the sand as black and formless as the sky now and I see what look like golden tears scattered all around us. It's the petals from the roses starting to fall and reminds me in one beautiful swerve of memory, of our clothes pooled around us in the cave earlier tonight.

"It's okay." I move us gently out of the circle of petals and we start to follow the silvery line of the shore. "Let them fall."

And so, we keep on walking.

THE END

MORE BY ABIGAIL YARDIMCI

Life Is Yours (Book 1)

Destiny Is Yours (Book 2)

Everything Is Yours (Book 3)

My Little Ramadan - Coming soon

Lockdown Love Letters - Coming soon

ACKNOWLEDGEMENTS

Getting to the end of this trilogy and even contemplating how I'm going to thank everyone is a big and scary thing. I've thanked a lot of very important people in the first two books, so this imminent onslaught of names is very much 'finale-related'. And who doesn't love a good finale?

For starters, massive, bottom-of-my-heart-type thanks to one of my oldest and bestest (yes, I'm going with 'bestest') friends, Louize Cattermole. You are the Queen of WhatsApp crisis chats and without your very well-read brain cells, I could not have made this book so crisp and satisfying. You. Totally. Rock.

Jenny Rutter, what would I do without our late-night, wine-fuelled chats? Thank you for letting me gatecrash one of those precious nights with my fold-out plotting poster and helping me see where the story had gone wrong. It all finally clicked, thanks to you.

Thank you, also, to the people who helped me ensure Trev's voice was authentic and true-to-life: John Lane, Cheryl Grant, Jackie Passmore, Steven Cook and Tracy Brown. Trev wasn't the monster Jess thought he was and you saw to that.

Tony and Maria Wright at Change U. You might not know

it, but you had a massive impact on me when you trained me as an NLP practitioner back in 2014. Without you, Sandra wouldn't be as cool as she evidently is and Jess wouldn't have had such an awesome experience at the past life party.

I want to express special gratitude to Hayley McLean who not only gave me the beautiful endorsement for the book cover, but who also beat out the path towards Body Positivity for me. You are one of the most inspiring and authentic people I know and I'm so grateful that we know know each other.

Translations were delicately crafted by my beautiful international friends (aka adopted family), Teresa Plana Casado (for the French) and Kamuran Aydın (for the Turkish). Thanks to you, when readers reach for Google Translate they won't get a whole load of unintelligible gibberish.

I am increasingly realising that other authors - especially those of the Indie variety - are ridiculously generous with their time and support. So gargantuan thanks go to: Evie Alexander, for encouraging me even when she didn't know me from Adam; Margaret Amatt, for ensuring the book was not bereft of commas and giving up her precious writing time to do so; Anita Faulkner, for always being in my corner and helping me shout about my books to the world; Chrissie Parker, for helping me see this trilogy has earned its right to be on people's bookshelves; Isabella May, for her endless self-publishing wisdom; Gary Heads, for years of cheering me on and making sure I didn't give up; and Sandy Barker, for reading this book when you were literally still reeling from the shock of an earthquake. I can't ask any more than that.

To Team Yardımcı . . . you never fail to amaze me with how dedicated you are to reading and checking the early drafts of my books. I can't believe you chose my books to do that with. Thank you a million times, thank you.

Bailey McGinn - your cover designs send shivers up my

spine and I'm completely delighted to have collaborated with you yet again on this book. Let's do more!

I have some incredible super-fans who really go the extra mile to spread the word about my books. Extra special thanks to Sue Baker and Fiona Jenkins - I hope you know how much I appreciate your time and support. And yey for Thursday Night Lives!

Dad - It's been years since you left me on my own with my writer's ambition. I can't believe I did it without you. Or maybe I didn't. ;)

Mam - I know my books aren't your cup of tea but I'm grateful for all of the help and steadfast advice anyway. You have no idea how much your own achievements got me to this place.

Matty - As above. I know my books really aren't your thing, but your influence is in here anyway. It's tip-toeing through the humorous bits, sliding through the suspenseful parts. Let's keep that stealthy action going.

Baran and Azad - Thank you for the squeezes and the snuggles and for putting up with extra hours on the PlayStation when I was obsessing over tricky chapters. I know how much of a hardship that was. ;)

Mustafa - Let's just take it as read that there would be no trilogy without you. Thank you for not being big-headed about it and giving me endless inspiration for Mesut. Still though, he's not a patch on you. x

ABOUT THE AUTHOR

ABIGAIL YARDIMCI is an author, painter and mindfulness practitioner. She is a Geordie girl living by the sea in South Devon with her Turkish husband and two terrifying kids. She loves to blog and gets her kicks through mindful parenting styles, creative living and chocolate.

Abigail's writing inspiration comes from scratching the surface of everyday life to find the underlying magic that connects us all. The fire beneath the frustration, the creativity beneath the boredom, the stillness beneath the chaos.

The Life Is Yours Trilogy is published by Soft Rebel Publishing and there are more books by Abigail on the way.

Abigail LOVES connecting with her readers so check her out on social media and sign up to her mailing list now to get a FREE poetry e-book called 'What About Now?'

———

www.abigailyardimci.com

 facebook.com/AbigailYardimci

twitter.com/abigailyardimci

instagram.com/abigailyardimciauthor

Printed in Great Britain
by Amazon

77100061R00210